RUNNING WITH THE WOLVES

Abandoning all but the briefcase, they ran off into the darkness, hoping against hope they hadn't been seen. Searchlights flew after them, making them weave as they fled. The thunder of engines gained on them, a low building took shape ahead, a last refuge. Engines drummed nearer, voices warned them to stop. Shots rang out, he lost his footing, she stooped to help him – 'You're hurt!' she cried, and together they staggered on . . .

Also by Jonathan Kebbe
available in
Mandarin Paperback

The Armalite Maiden

JONATHAN KEBBE

Running
With the Wolves

A Mandarin Paperback

RUNNING WITH THE WOLVES

First published in Great Britain 1992
by William Heinemann/Mandarin Paperbacks
an imprint of Reed Consumer Books Ltd
Michelin House, 81 Fulham Road, London SW3 6RB
and Auckland, Melbourne, Singapore and Toronto

Reprinted 1994

Copyright © Jonathan Kebbe 1992
The author has asserted his moral rights

A CIP catalogue record for this title
is available from the British Library

ISBN 0 7493 1252 1

Printed and bound in Great Britain
by HarperCollins Manufacturing, Glasgow

To Vivienne

with gratitude and love

Acknowledgements

For specialist information I am greatly indebted to
E.B., Clive English, Shane Enright, François Fromm
and Anne Fromm, Carey Harrison, Shanthi Jacob,
Nick Kafkarkou, Charles Kebbe, George McLaren,
Philip O'Loughlin, Moussa Saker, Martha Teichner,
John Wall and Harry Webster.

For their valuable assistance I am most grateful to
Bob Albertson, l'Embassade Française en Irlande
(Service Culturel), Michelle Boury, the Gardaí
(Swords), Simon Gerrard, Greenpeace (Eire), Elayne
Greensted, Francis Harvey, Jeff and Jane, Timothy
Kebbe, Vivienne Lafferty, M. et Mme. R. Maes,
Rajie Muttukumar, Pascalle Purcell, Victor Ross,
Christianne Schirrmann, Fabrice Sellem, Maria
Sofroniskou and Monsignor Alex Stenson.

I would also like to thank Francis Morrin and Alex
Barnicoat for providing the perfect retreat; Imogen
Parker for her kindness and professional expertise;
Laura Longrigg for her excellent editing; Lisa Glass
for all her invaluable help; and John Hamilton and all
the Heinemann team for their graft and enthusiasm.

Special thanks are reserved for Vivienne who so
loved the Bordeaux Brigade; Carey – inspiring writer
and champion goat-keeper; Pascalle and Shanthi for
whom no trouble was too much; and above all
Christine Simpson for her unflagging support and
indispensable work on each draft of the manuscript.

• • • 1 • • •

PARIS, 20 DECEMBER: He did not avail himself of his chauffeur and bodyguard to visit Madame Mazarin's establishment that rain-lashed Friday night. He drove himself, and wore dark glasses when he handed over his keys to the doormen, who greeted him with a discreet *Bonsoir, monsieur*, as if they didn't know that he was Security Minister Claude Lusardi, hard man of the government.

Lusardi's presence at 46 rue des Maquignons should have been an in-house secret, but someone with dangerous sympathies – a chambermaid, one of the girls, a doorman? – must have leaked the information, well in advance. For shortly after the minister entered the building beneath a doorman's broad umbrella, and while his car was being moved to the clients' carpark at the rear of the building, one of the most wanted men in France arrived in the narrow street by taxi.

Clean-shaven and wearing tinted glasses and an elegant suit, the man bore scant resemblance to the portrait of Jean-Jacques Revallier glowering from a thousand wanted posters across the city. Presenting himself at the door, he was admitted just in time to catch sight of the broad frame of Claude Lusardi, mounting the low-lit stairs with the Vietnamese girl who had for some time been meeting his peculiar requirements.

Tearing his eyes from Lusardi's receding grey head, Revallier surrendered his coat and parted with several thousand francs for a glass of Perrier, a charge which covered all the delights of the evening. As he took his drink to a secluded corner, Madame Mazarin detached herself from the company of an elderly gentleman who could have been a judge, and came over to him, a wide-hipped glittering woman with sluggish gait and clear appraising eyes in a face frozen in make-up.

He rose with a little bow at her approach.

'Back so soon, monsieur?' she greeted him, evidently not displeased to see him again, appreciative perhaps of his dark good looks and courtesy, 'I trust this means you were well satisfied?'

Revallier's smile indicated, in all humility, that he was.

'Remind me by whom, monsieur?'

'Mirabelle, madame.'

'Ah . . .' she sighed, always pleased when her matchmaking instincts succeeded. 'And for tonight?'

'I requested the same, if that's still convenient, madame?'

She gave him her most gracious half-smile so as not to disturb the carefully made-up illusion of her face, and on cue the young lady herself appeared, leggy and bright-eyed, sucked into a brief sequinned dress, with page-boy hair and a single tumbling earring, and the rather intense glow of one who lacks confidence and seeks encouragement. Two nights on and he'd almost forgotten what she looked like, her awkwardly pretty face, with its overlong nose and eager little mouth, her touchingly shapeless foal-like walk.

'You look lovely, mademoiselle,' he said.

She smiled and glanced away. Madame reached quickly to lift Mirabelle's chin with a corrective finger. Then blessing them both with a benign look, she moved away in her slow territorial swagger to address another client.

Mirabelle took a breath, shy, anxious to please, a provincial girl too vulnerable for this trade, he thought.

'Shall we?' he nodded towards the red-carpeted stairs.

She took his arm a little too tightly and they fell into step.

2

'I'm so pleased you came back,' she confessed, 'to me, I mean.'

'I was thinking you'd say: no! please, anyone but him.'

'Naturally that's exactly what I said, but . . .' lowering her voice, 'Madame threatened to shoot me!' They laughed, at ease with each other.

At the top of the stairs they proceeded arm in arm down a gallery hung with erotic prints on panelled walls and with silk stockings on the doorknobs of occupied rooms. Sounds of muffled laughter and human intimacy accompanied them to the end of the passage. So did Mirabelle's breathless chatter, which Revallier scarcely heard, his mind distracted, listening hopefully for the bass tones and belly laugh of his quarry.

With almost any other politician, his task would have been relatively straightforward, but Claude Lusardi was built like a wardrobe and enjoyed an unusual reputation for resorting on occasions to physical violence. It could be very messy.

She opened a door and showed him in. 'With you, monsieur, it's different,' she was saying, bending down to peel off one vermilion stocking and tie it to the outer doorknob before closing the door. In bending down, she implicitly invited him to savour a bountiful view up her tight dress, before turning to him half-coyly, half-brazenly to seal the invitation.

Despite the need to keep his mind focused on uglier business, he found himself strongly aroused, and recalled the other night, after she'd practised her fledgling art on him, how he had made her lie back and peppered her spicy body first with little kisses and then with voracious explorations of the tongue.

A carafe of dark wine waited on a low round table. She gave him what she took to be a long cool look and knelt on a cushion to pour two glasses. Loosening his tie, he glanced at her regretfully. The room, with its heavy drapes which made him want to check that no one was hiding behind, and its deep-set scarlet lampshades which cast dim pools of private light, had not been properly aired; despite the overkill of perfume spray, he could smell the lingering odours of human exertions, reminding him that Mirabelle could have had several clients this evening already. She came to him now, her one bare leg glowing, her hips wiggling in an unconscious parody of sexual allure, and handed him his wine. They clinked glasses, drank deeply.

'Would you like me to undress now?'

'In a minute,' he said and, taking her by the hand, led her to the window, parted the drapes and peered out through the shutters at a rainswept street. He checked his watch. No time to lose.

'Anything wrong?' she asked.

'Come.'

He brought her to the bed and laid her down on her back.

'Won't you take off your glasses for me this time?'

He removed his false glasses. She reached up with both hands and touched his face, a slim long face which pleased her greatly. 'You have beautiful eyes, monsieur. What is your real name?'

He hesitated. 'Jean-Jacques.'

She smiled approvingly.

'And yours, mademoiselle?'

'Amélie.'

'I'm going to tie you up, Amélie.'

Her smile wavered, her eyes lighting on the cotton scarves in his hands. A quick laugh, 'You're going to tease me.'

He bound her to the bed-head by the wrists and then produced the gag.

'Tell me,' he said, 'where's the minister?'

Her face went blank.

'The big politician,' he insisted, 'with the Vietnamese girl?'

'I don't know.'

He knew she was lying. 'Okay,' he said, parting her mouth with the gag and fastening it behind her neck. Her eyes filled with fear. So this was the real monsieur, the dark side he'd kept hidden. She wanted to cry out, Please don't hurt me, but the gag stretched her mouth too tightly to utter a word, the pressure making her cheeks bulge, draining them of blood.

'It shouldn't be for long,' he said and turned to leave.

He meant to go without a backward glance, but at the door he looked around and met her crucified gaze. He returned, lifted her head and loosened the gag a fraction. Now, instead of choking her, it caught in her mouth, making her strain compulsively to repel it with her tongue and teeth. He slackened it further, until finally it lay loose on her chin.

'Promise you won't call out.'

'I promise.'

As he looked searchingly at her, she murmured, 'The VIP floor above.'

'What?'

'He's in one of the rooms upstairs.'

He bent and kissed her damp forehead.

Out in the gallery he listened for a moment, then took the stairs to the next floor, located the firedoor at the back of the building and thrust it open to admit Janine Vallence, the woman who featured with him on so many wanted posters.

'Everything okay?' she hissed.

'*Parfait*!' he grinned, 'only I don't know what room he's in.'

'Terrific!' she said, still high from the operation they'd carried out earlier in the evening.

'He's on this floor,' he whispered.

5

Leaving her umbrella by the door, she started down one side of the corridor, Revallier down the other. She wore lavish make-up and a clinging mini-dress which exaggerated her hips and scant bosom. Only the flat heels of her knee-length boots comprised the erotic uniform for the sake of mobility.

Moving from one stockinged door to the next, listening for Claude Lusardi, they heard from one room the crack of a whip, a hushed conversation from another, and then around the corner an elderly chambermaid appeared laden with linen. Recovering from the surprise, Vallence seized Revallier's arm, he clapped a hand on her bottom and, laughing together, they swayed along the gallery until the old woman had gone.

'Ah!' exclaimed Vallence, her ear to another door.

Revallier came over and flattened himself against the wall. Vallence glanced at him, he nodded, she knocked and entered. In an instance she saw her mistake – not the minister, but an anonymous pot-bellied male and his full-bodied consort cavorting on all fours, chasing each other's bare buttocks round and round in circles. Vallence hastily apologised and withdrew.

Losing patience, she threw open the next door . . . to find a withered old man in the arms of a young woman, bald head nestled in her breasts. In the next a fully dressed individual was seated in an armchair smoking abstractedly, while a young lady pleasured herself on a divan.

'*Ça y est!*' Revallier beckoned, listening at a door across the landing. Vallence knocked, looked in and froze involuntarily at the sight of *him*: Claude Lusardi in the bare flesh, bestriding the Vietnamese girl on a double bed; driving into her from behind with such force that he scarcely heard the intrusion.

'*Excusez-moi, monsieur,*' Vallence repeated calmly, 'they're at the street door, asking questions.'

'What? what do you want?'

6

'The press, monsieur –'

'The press!'

His thighs shook, and fell still. So great was the length and girth of his sagging body that the Vietnamese girl was barely visible, an insect hiding under a rock.

'*France-Soir*, *monsieur* . . . at the street door.'

'Ach . . .' he groaned and lifting his bulk from the girl, he sat dazed for a moment on the edge of the bed, his flushed and shrinking member hanging its head. His breathing was bad, so were his teeth, and Janine Vallence felt pity for the girl who was covering herself with a sheet.

'Do they know I'm here?' he growled.

'Madame is telling them you're not, so if we're quick,' she held out his pants and trousers, 'you can slip out the back way and they'll never know, and you can return whenever –'

'*Salopes*!' he swore, but he rose unhurriedly, not unduly worried. France was too sophisticated to be shocked by the sexual exploits of its leaders. Still, it was an infernal nuisance and he began to dress hastily.

'Quick as you can, monsieur,' Vallence urged, revulsion hidden behind a mask of concern, while the girl, peering over the top of the crumpled sheet, looked curiously at the woman she'd never seen before.

The minister zipped himself up and defiantly flexed his shoulders as Janine Vallence helped him on with his jacket. How was he to know that the woman now handing him his tie was a leader of Les Gardiens de la Planète – The Guardians of the Planet, the ecologist guerrilla group he thought he'd all but smashed.

'Hurry, before they discover your car.'

'They'll discover it all right when I run them over.'

She handed him his coat and he followed her to the door, where she restrained him to check the corridor. For a moment he was troubled by the firmness of her grip, but before he could unravel any suspicious threads of thought,

7

she said 'All clear, monsieur,' and ushered him away, hoisting an umbrella when they reached the firedoor.

'Leave it,' he snapped and, motioning her to go ahead, he gripped the iron rail and followed her down the fire escape through torrential rain to the carpark. He did not see the lurking figure of Jean-Jacques Revallier, or hear him splashing up behind to deliver a flat-fisted clout to the back of his head, a quick blow which pitched him forward on to his knees like a man suddenly moved to prostrate himself in the wet.

Hands seized him, hauled him to his feet. He struggled, Revallier hit him again and with Vallence's help dragged him to a stolen car reversing into the carpark, driven by Tahar Ben Amar, a third member of the group. A final flurry of blows from Revallier, and Claude Lusardi was captured.

Hearing his cries, the doormen came running, only to be scattered by a warning burst of gunfire from the speeding car.

Ten forty-five p. m., and across the city, in a roomy apartment at the top of a venerable building overlooking the eighth *arrondissement*, a number of people were leaving a party.

Being fellow residents of the building, they hadn't far to go.

'Thank you for coming, *mesdames et messieurs*, and safe journey!' Kasha jested, closing the door.

Her guests tittered politely as they filed down the passage to the lift. Kasha had invited them all for a pre-Christmas drink – four floors, two sprawling apartments per floor, sixteen residents, many of whom had accepted, and almost all of those had showed up. Kasha's motives were mixed. A relative newcomer herself, she quite liked the idea of meeting her neighbours. She knew only Nathalie and Robert, who lived next to her. But there

8

was a more compelling reason. Duke Edouard de Montfort, top executive in France's atomic energy industry, lived – rather surprisingly – one floor below. In spite of his years, he still cut a dashing and controversial figure in European society, and Kasha was keen to interview him. Only he hadn't arrived yet.

'*Dieu merci*!' sighed Nathalie, kicking off her shoes, 'thank God they've gone.'

'*Chérie*!' her husband Robert chided her.

'God, what pompous bores.'

'*Vraiment tu exagères*, they weren't *that* bad.'

'They were unspeakable! weren't they, Kasha?'

Kasha flopped and took up her wine. 'We should think ourselves lucky. Madame Beauregard could have recommended *every* new restaurant in town, and Monsieur Leval might have given us his company's results for last year as well.'

Nathalie lay back on the couch laughing helplessly.

'What do you expect?' argued Robert, 'they're not used to such naked exposure to neighbours . . . not to mention meeting Kasha.'

'What's that supposed to mean?' objected Nathalie.

'*Que tu es naïve*!' Robert grinned, draining his glass and looking to the only other male present for support, 'Isn't it obvious, Alain? Kasha made them nervous.'

Alain, a tall lumbering genial man in his early forties and separated, with two daughters he saw regularly, had been going out with Kasha for some time. He took a pull on his cigarette before replying. 'You mean because she's Asian?'

'They're completely thrown,' said Robert, beginning to slur his words, 'meeting an *Indian* woman – Third World! non-European! non-*white*! who's stunningly beautiful, cultured, self-assured *and* in her own home. Need I go on?'

'Nonsense!' cried Nathalie, 'you talk such stupefying crap when you've had a couple of glasses. She's a cut above them, that's their problem.'

'But that's what I'm saying!' Now turning to Kasha, 'Am I right? They were petrified of you.'

Kasha shrugged merrily, 'Maybe the real problem is that I'm British and work for a British newspaper.'

'*Voilà*! there you have it,' Robert delighted, 'Asian and English, what a galling cocktail for our elevated bourgeois neighbours to swallow.'

Nathalie began slapping his leg hard. Robert cried to Alain for help, then struck back by wrestling Nathalie into a position where he could kiss and bite her neck to the accompaniment of lustful growls.

'No! *Robert*!' she shook him off, 'molesting your wife in public, it's disgusting.'

'Anyway, we're all wrong,' declared Robert, 'we French are supposed to hate the British, the blacks and the Arabs. It's not true. We hate everybody.'

While the others laughed, Alain smiled and got up and refilled everyone's glass. He was older than the rest by at least ten years, and tonight, the age gap felt like a gulf. He wasn't quite himself. Kasha was leaving first thing in the morning for two weeks in India. He had harboured some hope that she would have invited him. After all, they'd been seeing each other for the past twelve months. She hadn't mentioned it, and suddenly Christmas with his parents in Val-les-Bains in Ardèche, and the long haul through New Year in Paris without Kasha seemed desperately bleak. While he was up, he put on one of his slow moody jazz records, lit another cigarette and looked at the rain.

When he turned around, he found Kasha looking at him, smiling. His heart sank. She winked. He winked.

'Kasha deserves a medal is all I can say,' concluded Nathalie, 'for inviting that lot.'

At that, an ironic chuckle from Alain.

'Don't you dare!' said Kasha pointing a finger in mock warning.

Alain clapped a hand over his mouth, 'My lips are sealed.'

'What are you up to?' Robert leaned forward, peering conspiratorially at Kasha.

Kasha's wide smile said, wouldn't you like to know?

'Your motives, I begin to suspect, were less than pure.'

'It's none of your business,' said Nathalie.

'You two are in cahoots, *c'est sûr*. Let me see . . . ah! something to do with the de Montforts?'

'Warm,' conceded Kasha.

'Got it! you wanted to lure the duke to do a piece on him, observe him at close quarters and then carve him up.'

Kasha joined her hands contritely, 'I confess everything.'

'*Et pourquoi pas?*' defended Nathalie, 'the great man exposed to Kasha's skills.'

'He doesn't give interviews!' Robert reminded them.

'If anyone can persuade him,' Alain observed dryly, 'it's Kasha.'

'That may be,' said Robert, pointedly consulting his watch, 'but he's not coming, is he?'

'He said he and his family would be late,' said Kasha, 'separate functions to attend.' Robert was beginning to get on her nerves.

'Bah! now who's being naïve.' He tore off his tie and reached for the wine, 'these people move in the clouds, we don't exist.'

Topping up everyone's glass, he raised his own to propose a toast, 'To the humble, the hopeless and the desperate!'

They drank to that, and then Kasha got up to add oil to the miniature ceramic burner effusing the apartment with sandalwood, a sign of her confidence that the de Montforts would come, or perhaps a little magic to entice them.

'Nothing ventured,' she declared in English, 'nothing gained.'

'What's that?' said Robert.

'It means you're a crashing bore!' supplied Nathalie.

While Robert and Nathalie squabbled playfully, Alain followed Kasha with his eyes. She wore a simple silk *salwar kameez*, a kind of pyjama tunic in shell-pink, setting off her glowing skin. She wore her burden of thick black curling hair loose over her shoulders, shot with fine sprays of jewellery like fireworks in a night sky. When she wore her hair up, she could almost look her age, but tonight she looked eighteen. Watching her, he wondered, not for the first time, what she saw in him.

He was far from young, he was too heavy, smoked ardently and could do nothing with his lanky hair. He knew he had charm, and possessed, when required, the smart suits and social graces expected of a professional man. But deep in himself he was a dreamy bohemian, adrift in the modern world, disporting himself, as now, in slacks and a baggy jumper. She said she liked him the way he was, unkempt and unruly, that it suited him. And he loved her for not wanting him to be more like Robert, who always looked crisp and cool, even now, half drunk and at the end of a gruelling year at the office.

'*Hé!*' he said, 'look what I forgot.'

A short full-bodied Christmas tree stood dressed and lighted on a low table, a little hoard of presents beneath its branches. Alain went over, collected three shoe-box-sized gaudily wrapped gifts, and distributed them with grand gestures and a *joyeux Noël* for each. To their cries of expectation he warned, '*Calmez-vous, mes enfants*, don't get excited, they're only sillinesses.'

Kasha had already discovered the other present from Alain under the tree, gift-wrapped from an expensive jeweller, breaking their agreement not to buy each other anything.

'*Ho-là-là!*' exclaimed Robert, rummaging in coloured tissue to fish out a bold tie-pin depicting Santa Claus riding a laden sleigh. Digging in his pockets, he pulled out his tie and stuck the pin through, 'Why didn't I have this sooner? I could have worn it to the office.'

Throwing up clouds of tissue, Kasha and Nathalie jumped up together and jostled laughing in front of the mirror to try on their festive earrings – Nathalie a pair of polystyrene snowmen, Kasha a pair of antlered reindeer in full flight.

The doorbell rang; everyone froze. Robert hopped up to rearrange himself, Alain lowered the jazz and tidied away tissue and empty bottles, Nathalie hunted for one of her shoes.

'Best behaviour, children,' said Kasha, starting to remove her new earrings as she headed for the front door.

'Don't,' said Alain, 'leave them on.'

She hesitated a moment, then with a careless laugh replaced the reindeer she'd unclipped, went into the hall and opened the door.

There he stood, Duke Edouard de Montfort, white-haired and stern of eye, bearing himself with a faintly mocking air of authority, a fine figure of a man in his late sixties, something between a statesman and an ageing filmstar, the kind of man who improves, like wine. He had a dozen red roses in one hand, a bottle of cognac in its elegant box in the other. His smile broadened at the sight of Kasha's earrings.

'*Dis donc*, if I'd known, I'd have come as Father Christmas.'

'I'm thrilled you could come at all, sir.'

She accepted his gifts coolly.

'I'm delighted to make your acquaintance at last, mademoiselle, after so many tantalising glimpses.'

'I was also looking forward to meeting *madame la duchesse*,' she said quickly.

'She's gone ahead, we have a small villa in Sardinia where we're spending Christmas with friends. But my son and daughter-in-law have arrived, I hope?'

'No, not yet.' She helped him with his coat and led him through.

'They must be delayed,' he apologised, 'I hope we're not keeping you up?'

Kasha introduced him first to Nathalie.

'So nice to meet you once more, madame,' he took her hand tenderly in his. 'How well I remember your enchanting children. If I recall correctly, you're a doctor?'

'You're quite right, sir,' Nathalie blushed happily, 'about my profession anyway, I'm not so sure about the enchanting children.'

De Montfort laughed, 'And tell me, where do you work?'

'The intensive care unit at Hôpital de la Pitié, in the thirteenth . . .'

Looking on, Kasha felt a surge of pride, almost as if Nathalie were her sister, or lover. With her bobbed hair and pretty pointed face, Kasha found her beautiful and very French, and rather wonderful for a working mother.

Edouard de Montfort shook hands gravely with Robert, a gravity that mocked gently, thought Kasha.

'A solicitor, if I recall?'

'An architect, *monsieur le duc*.'

'*Ah, excusez-moi, monsieur!*'

'Actually I've been admiring your new headquarters, I've a clear view of it from my office.'

'Many people are scandalised by it, my wife considers it an abomination!'

'That's why I like it, it challenges. We forget how people once decried the Eiffel Tower, now universally admired as the symbol of Paris. People are afraid of change . . .'

Robert was in full flow, and Nathalie glanced at Kasha for help.

' . . . disturb their familiar surroundings and they panic, they want everything to blend, but why should –'

'Excuse me for interrupting,' said Kasha, 'but what will you drink?'

'Whatever you're all having, mademoiselle. A little wine would be very nice.'

Nathalie presented him with a selection of Florentines and frosted petits fours.

'*Non merci bien, madame*, some of us' whispering confidentially as he patted his ribcage, 'have to watch our weight.'

'I shouldn't have thought that was a problem for you, sir,' she said blushingly.

'Most kind, madame, but I assure you I can assume elephantine proportions without the slightest effort.'

Alain had found a vase for the roses and set it down on the coffee table. 'We haven't met, sir,' he said, transferring his cigarette to shake hands.

Kasha introduced them, observed their brisk handshake, de Montfort's reserved friendliness, Alain's air of polite indifference. He was even a little defiant this evening, she thought, and could guess why, and felt bad about it. There would be time to talk later.

'Don't tell me,' said de Montfort, 'another journalist!'

'Another doctor.'

'*Pardonnez-moi.* My tactlessness is legendary.'

'Monsieur Guillancourt is an eye surgeon,' explained Nathalie helpfully.

'Hence the glasses,' said Alain, tipping his spectacles, 'the blind treating the blind.'

'Imagine mistaking a surgeon for a *journalist*!' quipped Kasha, happily denigrating her profession. 'Please . . .' she motioned everyone to sit down as she handed the duke a glass of wine. He smiled into her eyes, a deep searching smile which sent a ripple of tension down her legs. She sat down in the nearest available place and raised her glass.

'To our honoured guest, and to you all, wherever you will be, a very pleasant Christmas.'

'And to you, Kasha.'

'Yes, and to you, mademoiselle,' said de Montfort, finding her eyes again.

They all drank, sighed, averted their eyes.

'I thought you were having everyone in, mademoiselle?'

'They've been and gone.'

'You missed absolutely nothing, I can assure you, sir.'

'Robert!' Nathalie scolded, and appealed to de Montfort, 'what is one to do with such a husband?'

'Please don't tempt me to answer, madame!'

He sat back, legs crossed and sipped his wine. 'I must say, this is very pleasant,' he said looking round approvingly at the simple décor, the luscious pot plants, the sense of space extended by the cream-coloured walls, and the magnificent Indian tapestry, 'and so charmingly decorated.'

'Little to do with me, I'm afraid,' said Kasha, 'apart from the tapestry. I'm borrowing the apartment from a friend, which leads me,' she said quickly, 'to be so bold as to ask an indiscreet question . . . if I may?'

Her friends held their breath. Kasha had a gift for the unexpected faux pas.

'But of course,' said de Montfort, 'ask anything you like.'

For all his bonhomie, Kasha sensed something about him which did not encourage intimacy. She smiled gratefully, 'I was wondering why a man of your means and status chooses to live, when in town, in such a comparatively modest apartment block in this less than fashionable *quartier*?'

'With people like us!' added Nathalie.

Edouard de Montfort laughed heartily, 'To escape from my friends across the river!' he exclaimed, and reached over to pat Nathalie's hand. 'You do yourselves a great injustice. It's so much nicer living – or trying to live – normally, among people who don't flaunt themselves, and anyway,' he waved an expressive hand, 'I enjoy far too much luxury as it is.'

'I've heard, *monsieur le duc*,' Kasha came in quickly, 'that you're really quite ruthless . . .' the room held its breath, 'with yourself . . . and that your frugality has its roots in your wartime exploits?'

'I don't take a cold shower *every* morning, mademoiselle, if that's what you mean, but yes, the occupation and the war left their mark, I'm still wary of the sapping influence of material comfort, I try to keep things in proportion. But you, mademoiselle Sharma,' he brightened, 'I'm far more interested in you.'

The tables were turned, de Montfort obliging Kasha to talk about her experiences as a foreign correspondent, in revolutionary Nicaragua and famine-stricken Somalia in her early twenties, to more recent postings in Belfast and Beirut, and to get her to discuss her strategy of focusing on the way events affect the lives of women, which had become her trademark. Alain noted, with relief, that she didn't mention the one experience which had nearly broken her, worse even than the slaughter she witnessed in the Chatila refugee camp in 1985, and which she only ever spoke about with him.

Finally, when Kasha and de Montfort were both reluctant to talk further about themselves, an unspoken truce was called. Robert uncorked more wine, de Montfort lit up a cigar and everyone but Kasha breathed more easily. As they talked and laughed, their tongues loosened by wine and by the slightly frivolous mood which seemed to have infected everyone, Kasha observed how at ease Edouard de Montfort appeared to be. He was known to be on first name terms with the President, and to entertain at his country château notables from around the world. He seemed to be one of those rare aristocrats who moves easily in any circle, and is sometimes happier out of his milieu. Watching him arguing good humouredly with Robert, Kasha had an image of him high on a hay wagon, helping his peasants while the sun shone, pitchfork in hand and stripped to the waist, perspiration streaming down his chest.

As he talked, waving his cigar to illustrate a point, she wondered how on earth she was going to broach the subject of an interview. The mighty nuclear energy industries of Europe were under attack from all sides, and Edouard de Montfort was supposed to be working on plans to revive their fortunes, in conjunction with his son Maurice, whose public relations company, M de M, had been given the task of rescuing the industry's tarnished image. It was Edouard on whom Kasha wanted to concentrate, not so much the charismatic industrialist and former resistance hero, which was all well documented, but the *man*, his philosophy, his motivation, his attitude to women . . .

She could tell that he was almost ready to leave. She offered him more wine and he awarded her another lingering smile but declined. His cigar was burning low. Now was the moment, it had to be now.

'*Monsieur le duc . . .*' she stole a brief pause in the hubbub, 'I was wondering how you would feel – '

The doorbell rang, a drawn-out peal.

Kasha broke de Montfort's gaze, excused herself and went to open the door.

'*Bonsoir, mademoiselle*, I'm sorry we're so late, these infernal functions.'

'I'm so pleased you could both come.'

'Delighted to meet you at last, mademoiselle. Is my father here? *Très bien*. This is my wife, the Countess von Hammelburg . . .'

Kasha smiled at Maurice de Montfort's German bride, who in return inclined her head guardedly.

'Is it still wild out there? You look frozen, *madame la comtesse*, come into the warm.'

Kasha's sympathy coaxed a faint smile from the young woman.

'Forgive us, mademoiselle,' said Maurice, reluctant to surrender his coat, 'but something has come up and I don't think we'll be staying once my father hears.'

'Can't it wait until morning?' said the countess unexpectedly.

'I don't think so, *chérie*.'

Her face closed, not unlike a disappointed child, thought Kasha, warming to her.

'I'm sure you've time for one drink, monsieur,' said Kasha.

'All right, all right,' he laughed indulgently, 'I can see I'm outnumbered.'

Kasha caught the countess's eye, and as she helped her off with her coat she saw she was pregnant, as much as six months. She was also startlingly young, tall and pale, swanlike in her bearing, her head and torso barely moving as she walked through to the salon, as if invisible hands were keeping the custody of her face.

Kasha invited Maurice to go ahead.

Suave and debonair, Maurice was more conventionally handsome than his father, but Kasha found his charm a little too insistent, too imposing.

While Kasha made cheery introductions, Edouard de Montfort rose and kissed his daughter-in-law's dry brow, enquiring tenderly after her wellbeing, drawing a soft glow from her.

Alain produced two glasses of wine.

'*Non merci, monsieur*,' said the countess, 'perhaps you have a mineral water?'

Everyone sat down, but Maurice didn't sit back like his father. He remained on the edge, waiting his moment to announce something. 'May I?' he produced a cigarette case.

'I wish you would,' said Alain, pouring the countess's water, 'these killjoys give me a hard time.'

Yes, thought Kasha, there was a hard edge to Alain's

humour tonight, a reaction no doubt to her leaving in the morning, and perhaps also to the de Montforts, their compelling maleness, their way of breezing in and taking over, their smooth confident manners and classy cashmere suits. What Kasha couldn't or didn't want to see was that Alain had picked up the instant rapport, or whatever it was, between her and Edouard de Montfort, the sensuousness of the smiles he reserved for her.

'I'm sorry to introduce an alarmist note to the evening . . .' Maurice de Montfort was saying.

The company hushed. Edouard de Montfort levelled a weary look at his son.

' . . . but I understand something occurred tonight which I should mention right away to my father.'

'Well, Maurice?'

'Les Gardiens de la Planète have kidnapped Claude Lusardi.'

Edouard's expression matched the scepticism in his voice. 'Where did you hear this?'

'My driver – '

'Your driver!'

'Got it from the radio. Apparently the GP have also attacked the aerodrome at Bretigny.'

'In the same evening? In their current state of decline?'

Maurice shrugged, as much as to say, as he lit his cigarette and sucked with relish, that he was merely reporting what he'd heard. Edouard gazed hard at him and sat up, 'If you'll excuse me, *mesdames et messieurs*, it's getting late and I think I'd better see what all this is about.'

'You can listen here,' Kasha suggested, and went over and removed an embroidered Indian cover from a TV set, angling it to face the company, and flicked to a news station. There was no bulletin scheduled for this hour, so the news pictures which formed on the screen confirmed that something had happened, was happening: a rain-soaked reporter standing at the gates of an aerodrome, pointing through high wire and paramilitary police towards the floodlit outline of a distant hangar.

The phone was ringing. Kasha answered it and without taking her eyes from the screen listened intently, scribbling notes. 'I'll see you there,' she told her colleague and hung up.

'It looks as if they *have* got the minister.'

Edouard de Montfort glanced at her without expression and returned to the news.

'*It is believed . . .*' the reporter was shouting over the clatter of unseen helicopters, '*that Revallier and the man known as his Arabian Shadow broke in under cover of darkness around 6 p. m., and dressed in Dassault Rafale Company uniforms and armed with official passes gained entry to the hangar housing the Éclat 229 strategic nuclear bomber, which was due to be unveiled before a host of dignitaries next month. Telephone warnings that several devices have been planted came through minutes ago, that the plane will – I quote – TAKE OFF IN UNEXPECTED FASHION AT MIDNIGHT.*'

He consulted his watch; everyone in Kasha's apartment did the same. '*Nine minutes to go,*' he shouted, '*and as we've come to expect from the GP, the warnings are last-minute and precise, leaving insufficient time for the devices to be located and made safe . . .*'

The news presenter cut in to tell the reporter he'd be back to him in a minute, '*but first . . .*' swivelling to face the camera, '*we return briefly to Yvette Herriot in rue des Maquignons . . .*'

A reporter stood beneath an umbrella in a narrow street, her face intermittently lit, along with shiny cobbles and police capes, by revolving blue lights. '*It's from this luxurious maison de passe close to the river in the seventh arrondissement that a client was abducted half an hour ago by a man posing as another client and by a woman posing as an in-house prostitute, and using an Arab getaway driver. The patronne of this select bordello and most of her tight-lipped*' *staff refuse to confirm or deny the identity of the kidnap victim, but we can be fairly certain that he was indeed Claude Lusardi, the Security Minister, and that his abductors were Jean-Jacques Revallier and Janine Vallence. If this proves to be the case, then the GP have struck twice at the heart of the establishment in a single night . . .'*

Edouard de Montfort was on his feet, 'If you'll excuse us, mademoiselle, I must be going.'

'I hope this doesn't affect you personally, sir?' Kasha probed gently.

'Not the business at the aerodrome, but Claude Lusardi, while not a personal friend, is someone with whom I'm obliged to work closely.'

The de Montforts said their good nights, and as Kasha handed over their coats and showed them out, she ventured one more question, 'Would I be correct in guessing, *Monsieur le duc*, that Security Minister Lusardi possesses knowledge of a sensitive nature regarding your plans for the nuclear industry . . . which you wouldn't wish to fall into the wrong hands?'

Edouard turned in the corridor, his gaze intent and searching. A moment's hesitation, then 'I would prefer if you did not report that, mademoiselle.'

'Then I won't.'

'And I would also appreciate . . .' holding her gaze, 'if you would let me know anything you hear or discover which you feel could be of interest to me.'

Her turn to hesitate. 'Of course.'

He seemed touched. 'I'm most grateful,' he smiled, 'and thank you once again for this evening. I hope it won't be the last we see of you.'

The request was on her tongue, the word 'interview' bursting to get out. But something told her that tonight he would have to say no. She returned his smile.

Closing the door she took off her earrings and hurried to get out of the apartment. Robert had moved closer to the

TV, Nathalie perched on the arm of his chair, Alain standing behind, all glued to the set. The news was back at the aerodrome, the drenched reporter speculating on how Revallier and his Shadow had succeeded in obtaining passes and uniforms, and noting in the stirring tone of a sports commentator that there were only five minutes remaining to midnight . . .

Alain smoked distractedly, thinking of Kasha going out into the dark and the rain, which beat against the french windows with frightening force. He'd foolishly allowed himself to count on having Kasha to himself at the end of the night, to anticipate, with that unfailing anguish of longing, making love with her, and talking and laughing softly under the duvet into the early hours. They weren't going to see each other for two weeks, but she was going out into the night. God knew when she'd be back, and any minute now she'd pause to look at him on her way out, invite him to stay, promising to wake him.

The relationship was out of balance, he needed her too much. It wasn't that she was indifferent to him, she was tender and affectionate, but either there was little passion in her by nature or he hadn't ignited it. She'd said something strange once: 'it's almost easier to make love with a man you don't love,' then qualified it with, 'who makes no demands.' Confused, he tried to change. For a time, between his work, the children and one or two friends, he tried seeing her less and making no demands. But they crept back in, pressing against his heart. She did say she wanted children one day. Was it mad to dream?

'Take care,' Nathalie embraced Kasha. 'Since Alain's working in the morning, I'll drive you to the airport.'

'Can you take the time?'

'Of course, so long as there's no emergency. Knock for me at eight.'

As Kasha turned to leave, she looked at Alain and stopped to incline her head and smile apologetically, as if to say, Another spoiled night, I'm sorry. 'Why don't you sleep here? I'll jump up and down on you when I get in.'

He made no move towards her, but smiled, 'Good luck tonight.'

She blew him a kiss and was gone.

'*Viens vite*, said Robert, 'two minutes!'

Kasha ran down the corridor to the lift. In the lobby she waved a greeting to the security men and ran into the rainswept courtyard where her embarrassingly scratched, dented and dated car stood impervious among the gleaming up-to-the-minute models of her neighbours. As she shook off her shoes and started the engine, she was grateful to Alain for installing a heavy-duty battery, ending her run of false starts. Otherwise, given that she could only claim for petrol and not the car, her Renault 16 was ideally suited to the cut and thrust of Paris.

The engine revved noisily, she manoeuvred the car carefully out of the courtyard into rue de Liège, tuning the radio back and forth until – '*and I now make it precisely midnight, troops stand tensely along the perimeter fence, the wind and rain unrelenting . . . firecrews stand by on the inside, and if Jean-Jacques Revallier is as good as his warning, then the enormous hangar lit up across the airfield –*'

The explosion, thirty-five kilometres south of the city, made Kasha duck instinctively as she swung the car through the lights at the end of the street.

Across the city, in a rundown canal-side district, Claude Lusardi was being manhandled into an icy cellar, where a fourth member of the GP brigade was guarding another captive. The fourth member was twenty-two-year-old Ricardo Cruciano, a slim smooth-faced Italian with blond flowing hair; the captive was the much older Brazilian ambassador, Gurtuilo dos Santos, who sat quietly on his own with a glass of wine, obliged to wear wraparound dark glasses through which he could see nothing. Lit by a bare electric bulb and heated by a one-bar fire, the cellar was low, wide and flanked by forbidding alcoves stacked with stores. The walls wept with freezing rain.

Revallier and the Algerian, Tahar Ben Amar, hauled Lusardi across the cellar and flung him into an old stuffed armchair, where he sat up scowling and gasping for breath.

'Just in time!' exclaimed Ricardo.

They followed his gaze to a black-and-white television perched on a flaking oildrum. The hangar at Bretigny aerodrome was ablaze, the *Éclat 229* engulfed in the inferno. Revallier and Janine Vallence linked arms and danced a little jig.

'You should have heard the bangs!' said Ricardo, 'one after another in perfect sequence like an arpeggio.'

Ricardo glanced at the new prisoner. They'd snatched all manner of industrialists who refused to clean up their act, as well as ambassadors of almost every leading industrialised nation from the US and UK to Japan and Poland, but never a government minister. Normally they issued communiqués condemning the respective company or country's dire ecological record, frequently they demanded sweeping environmental measures. This time it was more personal.

Señor dos Santos, nursing his glass of wine, had heard the violent arrival of the new hostage. He'd grown accustomed to milder treatment after two months at a secret location in the country, confined but otherwise treated as an honoured guest, once even permitted a dead-of-night call from a public booth to his wife.

Janine was gazing at the TV screen, where fire tenders were vainly lobbing arcs of water into the unquenchable flames. 'My heart goes out to our splendid armaments industry.'

'*Vous êtes fous*,' Lusardi burst out, 'completely insane!' Blood dripping from his nose found his lips, and he licked at them with bitter satisfaction. Wiping his mouth brusquely with the back of his hand, he reached in his jacket for his cigarettes and lighter. 'The sheer bloody-minded futility of it, the work . . .' he broke off abruptly to turn his head and spit on the floor, ' – of degenerates!'

Janine Vallence laughed, 'Listen to him!'

Revallier stood back, still clean-cut in his tailored suit, keeping his feelings in check, fingering the revolver in his pocket as he stared at the man he'd loathed from a distance for a long time. Lusardi had secured special measures for combating the GP, masterminding the programme of raids and mass arrests which had led to the destruction of six out of seven brigades and had brought the GP to the edge of extinction, with only Revallier's command brigade still operational. Eight members shot dead, twice that number incarcerated, along with hundreds of active supporters. To thousands Lusardi was a hero rescuing France from the dark Green menace. To Revallier, he was a thug, a murderous traitor to the true traditions of France.

'They'll soon rebuild it,' Lusardi scorned, 'it'll have its day and fly, and what will you have achieved by this senseless desecration?'

'Desecration?' mimicked Janine. Still reeking of scent and sheathed in the sleazy bosom-enhancing dress worn to Madame Mazarin's, she stood hand on hip, jauntily holding a cigarette, 'That's rich from you – *monsieur le ministre* –' she jeered, 'a man who wears his vulgar brutality with pride, and enthusiastically sponsors state terrorism . . .'

Lusardi's smile broadened with amusement and pity.

'And pray tell me, monsieur,' Janine took a casual drag on her cigarette and stepped closer, 'if this – ' waving at the television, 'is mindless desecration, what do you call the nuclear hellstorm the *Éclat* is designed to deliver? *Our* targets are solid inanimate industrial plant and occasionally military hardware, *yours* are demonstrators, saboteurs like us, or entire civilian populations singled out by that plane – *human beings*!'

'Spare me the rhetoric, mademoiselle, save your facile dung-brained dogma for your breathless supporters . . .' Sucking hard on his cigarette, Lusardi smiled contemptuously in Janine Vallence's face, 'and savour your little triumph while you can. The cheap trick you pulled on me tonight: I'll have you all yet behind bars, or . . .' his eyes shone, 'despatched like the rest of those queers and Bolsheviks you called comrades.'

The room had fallen very still, save for the passage of Lusardi's cigarette hand and the whistling of his breath; nervous glances darted to Revallier. Revallier stared at the minister, finally drawing his gaze, causing even Lusardi to be still. He looked into Revallier's eyes and slowly looked away, taking in the swept floor, the shoes of his captors, the crumpled suit of the man sitting across the cellar. He lifted his eyes and blinked at the man.

'You haven't met,' said Janine, 'Security Minister Claude Lusardi . . . Señor Gurtuilo dos Santos.'

'So! it's you, ambassador . . .' Lusardi seemed inclined for a moment to go over and shake his hand, but thought better of it, opting for the relative safety of his sagging armchair, 'we've been most concerned about you, monsieur, we've searched rigorously, you've no idea . . .'

'I'm most grateful, *monsieur le ministre.*'

Both men lost for words.

'How are they treating you?' Lusardi enquired at last in a low voice, as if they were alone together.

'Well, thank you.'

Lusardi nodded, weighing the ambassador's comment.

'But it's appalling, dragged away in the night, imprisoned against your will . . .'

The ambassador's turn to nod. Lusardi rounded on Revallier, '*Putain de bon Dieu*, what do you want with this man? he's not responsible for the destruction of rainforests

27

or the fate of primitive tribes, he holds no sway with his government. You've no right to use innocent men as pawns in your game and to put innocent families through hell – '

Revallier moved, walking slowly, ominously slowly and erect in a bee-line for the politician. Gripping the arms of his chair, Lusardi raised his head and saw his fate reflected in the GP leader's eyes.

'Jacques . . .' breathed Janine, but she was too late.

Reaching Lusardi, Revallier plucked the cigarette from his bruised lips, tossed it away and pulled out a gun. It wasn't Lusardi who closed his eyes in anticipation but Revallier as he seized Lusardi by his ash-grey hair, jerked his head back, pressed the muzzle to a throbbing temple and spoke in a lethally quiet voice through clenched teeth, *'Gabrielle Rouquet . . . Marc Solowig . . . Jean-Pierre Juppé . . .'* pausing to jerk Lusardi's head a notch higher, *Bruno Ultsch . . . Gilles Darron . . . Kyoto Yamashita . . .'*

Revallier's comrades tried reasoning with him, but he was deaf to them. Teeth bared, eyes blazing, he cocked the revolver; a round echoed in the chamber. Lusardi stared crookedly at the cracked ceiling.

'Joseph Guiraud . . . Marie-Ange Lecoeur . . . recognise any of these names, minister? Real people, flesh and blood and members of families, gunned down with no opportunity to surrender.' He pressed the muzzle deeper into bone and sinew, 'What of their liberty? their lives?'

'They forfeited their lives –' croaked Lusardi.

Reacting as if something had snapped in him, Revallier pocketed the gun, seized Lusardi by the throat and in one violent move lifted his colossal bulk half out of the chair, and still fastened to him, thrust him down again, toppling the man, the chair and himself over on to the floor, where Lusardi came to life, trying desperately to free himself, to prise the killing fingers from his windpipe. Succeeding in dislodging them for an instant, he gulped and tried to rise, only to be rocked back by the impact of Revallier's fist in the jaw, and to feel the hands at his throat again, digging deeper, squeezing the breath out of him to the point of drowning.

'Jacques!'

Tahar and Ricardo fell upon Revallier from behind and tried to drag him off; Janine pounced and tried to break the grip of his hands, but in his maddened state he was invincible . . . until a hand slashed across his face, stunning him because it was Janine's hand. 'You stupid bastard, get control of yourself.'

He let go. The grotesque scrum disentangled itself, and Lusardi fell back frothing at the mouth. Revallier walked out without a word, up the narrow stone steps, through the workshop where the cars were parked and up to the simply furnished apartment where Tahar and Ricardo lived. He lit a cigarette and stood at the window looking out at the rain, the rain whipping up and down the canal, blurring the ugly tenement blocks across the water and turning the street below, the lamp-posts, parked cars and cobbles into streaming fluid like itself. Sirens wailed across the night.

Something had truly snapped in him, he'd wanted to kill Lusardi, he'd wanted to squeeze the breath out of him, to see his eyes start from their sockets and glaze over, wanted him to pay for all the blood spilled, for all the blinding lies fed to the public, wanted him to pay for dragging France deeper into a police state. It was too late to repress what he'd felt in the cellar, to deny that urge, that *decision* to take Lusardi's life, as if he were taking back a stolen possession, to stop it like an electric current, as though he, Revallier, had a God-given right to flick the switch.

Gazing out over the canal, he had the feeling that he'd just taken a fateful step across a dark divide from which his comrades would never be able to recall him.

He heard Janine come in, heard her pause and look at

him, her silence eloquent, her disappointment reaching him in waves. He wondered if he and Janine would make love tonight, and if they did whether she would hold herself back or fuck with renewed intensity. She said nothing. After five years together she didn't need to. She went to the bathroom, peeled off her dress, dragged off her wig and started to remove her make-up. She was twenty-nine, but saw in the mirror a woman of forty. When Revallier first met her she was a student with fresh cheeks and long straight hair. Now her hair was cropped brutally short so she could switch wigs like hats, and her long expressive face had grown thin. Her eyes, once described by Revallier as beautiful, were deep-lined and sagging.

Brusquely she wiped off the vulgar make-up and washed her face. She was livid. Revallier had come within a gasp of killing a man. That Lusardi was a senior government minister, albeit a brutally repressive one, did not make it any better. The GP's record was unmatched worldwide. One death in five years, the Bordeaux Brigade killing a cop a few months ago during a police raid in which all their members died. More police had been wounded, some seriously, in shoot-outs, but the GP operated a strict code, and tonight Revallier had broken it. Whatever the provocation there was no excuse for such a drastic lapse in discipline. She was disappointed in him, but she was also envious: amazed by the abandon of his rage, the freedom to kill which he'd suddenly taken unto himself.

She emerged in jeans, sweater and long raincoat. Revallier had a well-oiled submachine-gun waiting on the table. He was on the phone, listening, saying nothing, transcribing information to a Paris roadmap. '*Merci, Toto*,' he said and hung up.

Janine was at his side, studying his thick red pen marks on the map, denoting the night's police response to the abduction: sealed railway stations, convoys, road-blocks.

Normally as they selected a safe crosstown route, they'd be cracking jokes, outdoing each other in acid humour. But as Janine hooked the submachine-gun under her coat, Revallier said nothing, and Janine's sharp departing sigh said everything.

'Janine . . .' he called after her.

She turned and met his gaze. He was never good at getting his tongue around an apology, or admitting he'd made a mistake. Now his voice was full of emotion. 'We nearly had a corpse on our hands.'

'Yes,' she said.

'That could have been a little inconvenient.'

'A little. If you're trying to tell me something – '

'Yes. I'm sorry.' A ghost of a smile. 'I'm sorry I didn't kill him.'

They burst into laughter together.

Ricardo was waiting in the old Citroën with the ambassador in the back when Janine went down. The garage doors were open and she checked outside. Rain beat down, making the cobbles dance and the gutters roar and boil over. A saturated man was walking unsteadily towards the rundown workmen's hotel a few doors away, a car crossed the bridge spraying water like a boat, sirens rose and fell like keening at a distant funeral. Keep coming, Janine told the rain, welcoming the extra layer of darkness it provided.

Turning away, she climbed in beside Ricardo and spread the map. The Citroën, which started at a touch, dated from 1938. Restored and revamped by Tahar and Ricardo, the harmless-looking saloon harboured beneath its snappy bonnet an engine capable of doubling its original 70 kmh, and its elegant curved bodywork was fortified to withstand a modest hail of bullets. With barely a whisper it crept out of the garage, swished along the canal and headed west across the north face of the city. Monitoring the route and clutching the submachine-gun under her armpit, Janine asked, 'How's the old fascist?'

'Lusardi?' replied Ricardo with a laugh, 'I left him sitting back gazing at the TV – stunned.'

'By what he was seeing on TV, or by Jacques' assault?'

'Neither! He just can't believe he's been left in the custody of an Arab. When Tahar handed him a cognac, he was so stunned he took it.'

Señor dos Santos sat quietly in the back, imprisoned by his dark glasses. His hair was freshly washed and he wore a clean white shirt, compliments of Revallier. It was on just such a night as this that he had been grabbed two months before on the steps of his residence. Now he sat very still, hands folded in his lap, as though afraid the slightest movement might provoke fate to cancel his freedom.

'Let's hope the police don't detain you for too long, monsieur,' said Janine, eyes darting for danger, 'so you can be with your family.'

'Yes indeed, madame.'

He respectfully addressed her as madame although everyone knew that she and Revallier were not married.

'Have you any plans in mind, monsieur?'

'I don't know,' he replied, afraid of tempting fate, 'maybe to return with my family to Brazil for a while.'

'You won't forget to send us a postcard?' said Ricardo.

The ambassador smiled, 'I don't think I have your address, monsieur.'

'What! he goes on holiday without knowing where he went.'

Approaching Pigalle, Janine directed Ricardo to turn off the boulevard and pull up in a side street.

'That's it,' she said, and turned to Señor dos Santos, 'I'm sorry we had to keep you for so long, monsieur.'

'I'm sorry my government has been so inflexible.'

'Please give this letter to the police.'

He reached blindly and received a sealed envelope containing a demand for a parliamentary enquiry into the deaths of eight GP members in twelve months, and warning that Lusardi's freedom would be dependent on the state's returning at least ten members of the GP. Revallier and Janine knew full well there was no possibility of ten being released, but four would do to form a new brigade.

'*Au revoir, monsieur.*'

'*Au revoir, madame.*' His voice trembled, his eyes brimming over. He'd maintained a dignified calm throughout his ordeal and suddenly it was over; he was returning to his wife and children, to their illuminated faces.

Janine watched Ricardo take the ambassador by the arm and lead him off hunched beneath an umbrella, until at the end of the street the rain drew a veil over them. At the head of boulevard Rochechouart, Señor dos Santos would find a taxi rank.

She switched on the radio, '*. . . and while the hunt intensifies across the city and beyond, news of the airfield bombing and particularly of Claude Lusardi's abduction are already sending shockwaves through France and round the world to Bonn, London and Washington where the Security Minister is well respected . . .*'

Trailing rainwater, Kasha returned to the apartment around 1.45 a. m. The living room was in darkness, dimly shadowed by street light through the uncurtained french windows, so that it wasn't until she was halfway across the room, sodden shoes in hand, that she realised there was someone curled up on the couch, wrapped in a blanket, breathing evenly.

She hung her saturated coat in the bathroom and emerged towelling her hair. Carefully depositing her heavy shoulderbag on the draining board in the kitchen, she paused to examine her feelings, her disappointment that she wasn't eager to wake him as promised. The truth was she wished she had the place to herself, so that she could sit down quietly to transcribe the report she'd taped in rue des Maquignons and in the car driving back. She loved company, music and noise, the place overflowing with friends, but she also loved the silence of her borrowed apartment late at night, going from room to room alone with her work and her thoughts.

While the kettle boiled, she wrapped her head in the towel and looked down at the deserted middle-of-the-night street, awash with rain. Perhaps I'm just over-tired, she thought, turning away to root among her selection of teas. She loved Alain, she was sure she loved him, she'd never known a kinder, more considerate man. He was funny and intelligent, they laughed a lot and talked about everything. Everything but their relationship. Stop it, she told herself, leave it now. Her eye strayed to the unwashed wine glasses ranged beside the sink, and she thought of Edouard de Montfort with a quivering sensation in her belly which she couldn't have named, and almost unwillingly recalled his smile, the obscurely suggestive glint in his stern mocking eyes.

She made a pot of camomile and went quietly through the living room to her office to set to work. Only no sooner had she sat down at her word-processor than it struck her that the sleeper in the next room was strangely quiet for Alain. Perhaps due to his smoking he tended to snore, sometimes tamely, often – she'd tease him – like a tormented rhino. She took a sip of tea, got up and returned to the living room. Too small beneath the blanket to be Alain, the sleeper's breathing was almost soundless, like the lapping of a distant shore. As she got nearer, a board creaked under her bare foot, the sleeper stirred, turned her head.

'It's you!' said Kasha, moving Nathalie's feet a little so she could sit down, 'what are you doing here?'

Nathalie smiled dreamily, not sure where she was.

'Not another row with Robert?'

'I tried to wait up for you,' Nathalie said, starting to sit up.

'Don't get up,' Kasha touched Nathalie's head and lightly stroked her hair, as she would a child. At the same time she glanced towards the bedroom where she expected Alain to be sleeping.

'Alain went home. I didn't want you to return to an empty apartment.'

'I'm used to returning to an empty apartment, silly.'

'*Nom de Dieu*, your hand's cold!' Nathalie sat up clutching Kasha's hand and demanded the other one too, and rubbed them both and held them in hers. 'You're shivering, you're going to catch cold.'

The heating was off for the night, and a chill lay on the apartment. Kasha sat still, her hands in the hands of a friend she hardly knew, a woman with whom she'd clicked from the start. It felt strange, her hands in Nathalie's, almost too intimate, and she wished Nathalie would let go, and was pleased when she didn't.

'Alain went home . . .' Kasha said, concerned.

'I'm to remind you to open his present.'

'*Merde*! I never gave him his. What time did he go? Maybe I'll call him.'

'Now? he'll be asleep. He left with Robert, I don't know, around one. *Tiens*! It's just coming back to me, I was dreaming they went off and got drunk together.'

'Alain and Robert?' said Kasha doubtfully.

The dream was returning to Nathalie: 'They came back with two strange women and Robert was smoking an enormous pipe! God! what's that mean? But never mind them!' she patted Kasha's hands excitedly and let them go, 'why don't *we* have a drink?'

'Good idea, what will you have?'

Kasha got up and plugged in the Christmas tree, illuminating a corner of the room so she could see the assortment of drink standing on the sideboard.

'You know what I'd like?' said Nathalie daringly, 'a whisky!'

'Whisky? I don't think we have any. Wait . . . ah! what have we here?' Picking up a bottle, she read out in English, 'By appointment to the late Queen Victoria and Edward the Eighth half a bottle of Ballantine's *very old* Scotch Whisky.'

'*Comme c'est romantique*! You must join me.'

'*Ho-là-là*! that's some report I'm going to type up tonight! Which reminds me, we'll have to fax it to London on the way to the airport.'

'The bombs, the brothel!' Nathalie remembered, 'how did you get on?'

'Ice? Water?'

'No, neat! How did you get on? Bring the bottle over so we don't have to keep jumping up. Did you see anyone?'

Kasha screwed up her face in disappointment. 'I *saw* all kinds of people, but could I get near anyone?' She deposited the bottle on the floor, handed Nathalie her drink and fetched her own. Then she sat down again beside Nathalie and they dashed glasses together.

'*À la tienne*!'

'*À la tienne*!' Kasha replied, and they drank lustily, laughing and spluttering at the ferocity of the whisky.

'Here, come and get warm,' invited Nathalie, pulling back the blanket. Kasha hesitated. 'Make yourself comfortable that end.'

Kasha sat herself at the opposite end of the couch and stretched her legs to mingle with Nathalie's, and they spread the blanket between them and grinned at each other. 'God, they're freezing!' complained Nathalie, taking Kasha's feet one at a time and rubbing them vigorously, then gently, soothingly, and finally taking both together and nestling them between her thighs. 'There, how's that?'

'*Merveilleux*!' Kasha sighed.

They drank, Nathalie reached for the bottle and took Kasha's glass and sloshed in another liberal measure. They crashed tumblers again, took a mouthful of the fiery stuff and winced.

'You saw *no* one? no famous backsides whirling down the street?'

'Everyone was leaving as I arrived – doormen, chambermaids, a white-coated butler and a thin line of startled young ladies displaying a variety of surprising costumes, and finally *madame la patronne* carrying herself with regal disdain – all whisked away in a fleet of cars for questioning. I've never seen anything like it.'

'What a shame, imagine the secrets you'd have teased out of them.'

'I'll tell you what I did learn.'

'What?'

'The minister was caught *in the act*.'

'*Non*! how did they do it?'

A regretful shrug, 'No one was saying a thing . . .' Nathalie clucked her tongue in disappointment. 'But rumours were rife,' said Kasha encouragingly, 'I heard that Jean-Jacques Revallier tied up and terrified one of the girls and that Claude Lusardi was plucked from the arms of a pair of lovelies and lowered naked from a window.'

Nathalie fell back laughing, and was still laughing as she reached behind her head to pull a wrapped gift from under the tree. She handed it straightfaced to Kasha, who opened the tag thinking it was from Alain.

'Nathalie!' Kasha rebuked, 'you shouldn't have,' and looked at her friend with large disapproving eyes.

'*C'est rien*,' Nathalie insisted, 'a token.'

Kasha smiled helplessly and began to pick at the knotted ribbon with her nails.

'Rip it off, *chérie*!'

'*Mais non*, it's too beautifully wrapped.'

'Not by me.'

Kasha wouldn't be hurried. Carefully peeling away the expensive paper and tissue, she gasped, 'They're beautiful.'

'I've never known anyone else wear them like you do in the middle of winter. You've no idea the fun I had trying to find them.'

Kasha retrieved her feet and tried on the sandals, ankle-tie evening sandals, silver-coated. She sighed with pleasure and then frowned at the famous label, knowing how much Nathalie must have spent. 'Token indeed!' Another reproving look, met with a happy mischievous grin from Nathalie.

'Nathalie,' said Kasha casually, pointing, 'can you reach me that one?'

Guessing it must be Alain's gift Kasha had decided to open, Nathalie stretched behind her to reach a present tucked under the tree and handed it to Kasha, who handed it back.

'For you.'

Nathalie dropped her jaw and glowered, hiding her surprise and pleasure. 'Bitch!' she said, and started tearing at the wrapping . . . and stopped herself. Imitating Kasha, she assumed an exaggerated air of decorum and opened the present with fussy delicate fingers. Kasha smiled as the paper fell away, and Nathalie held up a curious pair of padded slacks, brightly and beautifully patterned. She looked intrigued and puzzled, as much as to say, They're gorgeous, but what *are* they?

'For your holiday!'

'Ah! ski pants!'

'I'm sorry it's such a practical present.'

'Practical!' Nathalie laughed, 'they're incredible, I'll cause accidents.'

'At least you'll look good when you fall.'

'Robert will refuse to ski with me. *Tant mieux*, some handsome stranger will come to my aid.' Reaching forward she kissed Kasha. 'Talking of handsome strangers, what did you think of Edouard de Montfort?'

'He seemed very charming.'

'As a *man*.'

'You mean – ?'

'You know what I mean!'

Kasha, cornered, took off her sandals and joined her long legs again with Nathalie's under the blanket. Nathalie regarded her gravely, holding the rim of her whisky glass in her teeth, 'Well?'

'Something attracts me, something repels me.'

From Nathalie a sharp intake of breath, 'Attraction and aversion, fatal combination!' They laughed together. 'I tell you something . . .' said Nathalie. Kasha looked at her, not sure she wanted to hear. 'He certainly took a big shine to you.'

'You think so?'

'It couldn't have been more obvious.'

Kasha shrugged with apparent indifference.

'At the same time,' said Nathalie, 'I don't think he knew what to make of you.'

Kasha said nothing, then gave a wry smile, 'He asked me to let him know if I heard anything.'

'There, you've a perfect excuse to knock on his door.'

'His associate Claude Lusardi lowered naked from a window, I can't imagine he'd want to hear that.'

'I'm sure he'd be only too glad to see *you*.'

Kasha returned a nervous little laugh and fell silent, and they both lay back with their thoughts, Kasha thinking of Alain alone in his apartment, wishing she could comfort him. She knew he'd wanted to come to India, and she would have been happy if they could have travelled together and met her family and relations without its meaning anything. She sighed miserably to herself, guilty for not telling him how she felt. She was afraid even to talk about their relationship, for fear of attributing too much importance to it.

Nathalie dangled an arm to the floor and set down her glass. Her head was spinning, she felt seasick. 'Kasha?'

'Yes?'

'Are you going to marry Alain?'

'Marry?' Kasha laughed, as if the idea had never occurred to her.

'Come on, you can't say *he* hasn't thought of it, it's written all over him.'

'If it happened, I wouldn't want it to be anything we drifted into.'

'You're afraid of marriage, aren't you?'

'I'm afraid of being enclosed. In a small space.'

After a time she heard Nathalie's whispered breathing, and she thought of fetching another blanket for Nathalie and going to her own bed. But she felt too heavy and weary to move. She pulled another cushion under her head and lay listening to the rain pelting the windows and roaring in the guttering.

· · · **2** · · ·

MONTMARTRE CEMETERY, 11 JANUARY, 6 A. M: Never having met a living soul among the graves at this hour, Georges Bolivar was surprised, on his second circuit, to catch sight of footprints in the snow. Wild cats inhabited the walk-in tombs, but these were human prints, several sets.

He stood panting in the stillness, scanning the bleak tombscape. Not a sound, not a breath of movement, snow-dusted avenues deserted, headstones shrouded in fog.

His occupation required sharpness of mind and body, and this was his favourite time and place to train. In the pre-dawn quiet of these winter mornings, with few people abroad and the cemetery closed, he would hoist himself over the parapet of the road which passed overhead and drop like a cat among the graves, landing with remarkable spring for such a big man.

For a few more moments all was quiet. Then he heard a faint pulse beating through the cemetery, the muted percussion of feet. Spinning around, he glimpsed them, all in white tracksuits, bunched and bobbing as one, treading fog towards him . . . and vanishing.

Silence again. Only his breath pumping in the thin air. His experience should have warned him to be wary, but he was too irritated by the thought of other joggers trespassing on his territory to do anything but curse, resolving to speak to them sharply if he ran into them. He never considered who they might be, simply assuming it was safe to run on. A rare mistake.

The first tomb-lined avenue he turned down was clear one moment, alive with hooded figures the next, materialising from nowhere to fall upon him. In the seconds left to defend himself it occurred to Georges Bolivar, as they beat him senseless, that these were no routine hoodlums, and he no ordinary victim.

Dragged into a dank vault, he was bound and gagged and arranged on the altar steps in the broken light of a stained-glass window. Relieving him of his keys, they closed the rusting door and left him to sleep awhile among the celebrated residents of the cemetery: Emile Zola, Degas, Offenbach . . .

Two of them then drove to his apartment in Pigalle, fitted a small but powerful device to the underside of the limousine he was to have driven that morning, set it for seven-thirty, and prepared to deliver it to its destination.

While his chauffeur-cum-bodyguard lay entombed in Montmartre Cemetery, Duke Edouard de Montfort looked out of his study window, unaccountably troubled by the stillness of the morning, fog masking parked cars and occasional pedestrians in the street below. He checked his watch: 7.10, his car was due shortly for a prompt 7.30 departure.

He returned to his desk, which was laid for a working breakfast – hot croissants wrapped in a *serviette*, selections of jam, fruit and cheese, arranged on a fresh white table-cloth – and was pouring himself another coffee when Clotilde, the elderly maid, called from the end of the passage, *'Venez-vite, monsieur.'*

He took a sip of coffee and walked briskly to the salon, where Clotilde had the TV on, showing Claude Lusardi holding a press conference late the previous night, declaring emphatically that he hadn't uttered a word to his interrogators throughout his captivity.

'Poor man,' said Clotilde with feeling, 'thank God he's all right.'

De Montfort chuckled. 'Lusardi's indestructible. One feels sorry for Revallier and friends having to endure him for three whole weeks.'

Greying and stooped, barely a year older than de Mont-fort but lacking his youth and vigour, Clotilde didn't trouble herself to rise to his wicked humour. She'd worked for his parents since before the war, she'd ironed his shirts and changed his linen for nearly half a century, she'd slept with him on numerous occasions during the war years and after, even though he had a fiancée in Paris and a lover in the country, and despite the fact that she'd never been anything to look at, while he had been witheringly attrac-tive. He'd been rough with her, he'd mocked and teased, but never unkindly, and treated her between the sheets not as a socially inferior domestic but as a woman. No one among his friends or colleagues, among the multitudes who'd worked for him, least of all, she suspected, his wife, knew him as well as she did, and no one was more devoted.

'And how did they treat you, Monsieur le Ministre?'

'No better than a dog, but then what can one expect of these people . . .?'

'It's appalling,' lamented Clotilde, 'look how he's lost weight, they must have starved him.'

Edouard laughed again, 'They clearly haven't managed to curb his spirit.'

Crumpled and unshaven, Lusardi beat the table with his fist and harangued a journalist, *'Are you mad! Chained like a dog in a darkened room and I'm to be grateful for my release?'*

Beside Lusardi sat an impeccably dressed detective with a strikingly chiselled Latin face, detached and silent, Commissaire Philippe Goujon, the man leading the hunt for The Guardians of the Planet.

'While expressing dismay at your ordeal, minister,' began an off-camera female correspondent, *'and relief at your deliverance, I can't help recalling how you've been telling us for the last few months that the GP were a spent force.'*

De Montfort scarcely heard the end of the question, so sure was he that the voice belonged to Kasha Sharma, whom he hadn't seen since the night Lusardi was snatched. It wouldn't be true to say he hadn't thought of her since, but he'd been too engrossed in work for more than a passing fantasy. Now, hearing her voice again, he experienced a powerful urge to ravish her.

Disconcerted by the question, Lusardi quickly recovered, *'Firstly, my ordeal is of no importance and secondly, no one can deny that we've reduced the GP to a shadow of their former selves. However, it would be madness to discount their wider influence, when daily we hear of copy-cat terrorist cells popping up like poisonous fungi in Belgium, Holland, Germany – Switzerland! where will it end? To combat this creeping menace, it's vital . . .'*

Edouard looked at the time: 7.19, his car would arrive any minute.

Questions were now being fired at Commissaire Goujon. Why, with such vast resources at his disposal was he incapable of catching Revallier?

'*Because he's slippery,*' replied the unruffled detective.

The minister had effectively been traded for scores of GP supporters; wasn't that surrendering to terrorist blackmail?

'*Not one terrorist, guerrilla, saboteur, has been released,*' he stated impassively.

The GP often struck again immediately after releasing a hostage. Who or what did the commissaire expect to be the next target?

'*Whether a bombing or a kidnapping, it will be the act of an increasingly desperate band of outlaws, whose time is rapidly running out.*'

'Enough!' said Edouard, and returned in haste to his study, where he took a sip of coffee and then extracted from the open wall safe a heavy armour-plated briefcase complete with a pair of handcuffs looped in the handle. Closing the safe and replacing the framed print of huntsmen galloping in the Bois de Vincennes which concealed it, he carried the case to his desk, closed the thick dossier he had been working on, and squeezed it into the briefcase. Locking the case, he set its inbuilt alarm and went over once more to the window. A thin sheet of snow lay on the pavements, the road, the roofs of cars, and dense fog still covered everything.

He glanced at the time, 7.20, and smiled. Fog, terrorists, the media, the prospect of death, nothing could ever seriously unsettle him. He had nerves, if not quite of steel then of some comparable substance.

Clotilde knocked and entered with a tray.

'You haven't touched your breakfast,' she complained.

'Just leave me the coffee. I need to be light of mind and foot today!'

'Another vital meeting, I suppose?' she poked fun at him, loading up the tray, 'what would France do without you?' The mocking, mildly vengeful tone failed to disguise her unflagging admiration.

'Never mind France,' he turned from the window, 'what would Europe do without me?'

'Only Europe, monsieur?' she said folding the table-cloth and withdrawing with arthritic slowness, 'you're too modest.'

The phone went, and he lifted the receiver.

'*Bonjour, papa*! did you sleep well?' The sweet tones of Cornelia, his daughter-in-law, from the adjoining apartment, 'won't you have your coffee with us before you go? Maurice insists you haven't time.'

'I'm afraid he's right, my dear . . .' he heard a car and looked out to see his Mercedes pull up with its police escort, 'we're leaving right away. Be good and don't strain yourself, you're carrying the hopes of the family!'

Laughing at her light-hearted reply, he opened a drawer and removed his old service revolver, and hung up.

The smile left his face.

Draining his coffee, he dabbed his lips and glanced at the time: 7.23.

On his way down the hall, Edouard de Montfort paused before the long mirror. As ever, he cut an impressive figure for a man in his late sixties, robust, straight-shouldered, with a full head of white hair, white brows and an aura of distinction befitting a secretary-general of the CEEA, La Confédération Européenne à l'Énergie Atomique, Europe's Paris-based nuclear energy authority.

More than any other man, Edouard, by his efforts and vision, had been instrumental in making France world leader in nuclear power. While other nations sheepishly closed nuclear plants, France vigorously expanded, beating off the protests of conservationists and ecologists like so many irritating wasps.

A final glance at his reflection and he proceeded down the hall with the air of one who knows his own importance. Clotilde was at her post to help him on with his coat.

'*Bonne journée, monsieur*,' she murmured, opening the door for him.

As he stepped out, his son Maurice arrived along the corridor from his own apartment. He handed him the armoured briefcase and handcuffed the handle to Maurice's left wrist. Then they fell into step along the corridor.

'All right, Maurice?' Edouard enquired sharply, while they waited for the lift.

'Yes, of course.'

One thing Edouard couldn't abide in a son of his was nerves, especially on such a momentous morning.

Emerging in the lobby at 7.27, they received their separate mail from Madame Klonowska, the concierge.

'Dreadful weather, *messieurs*.'

Leaning back to avoid the odour of her rotting gums, they thanked her, crossed the courtyard and strode into the morning.

The Mercedes stood double-parked in the road, driver mechanically polishing its flawless bodywork. As Edouard stepped between parked cars, the driver turned to meet him with neither the face nor frame of Georges Bolivar.

'*Bonjour, monsieur*!' heels together, slight bow, 'I'm afraid Monsieur Bolivar's had an accident.'

'Nothing serious, I trust?'

Holding the rear door open, 'No monsieur, but sufficient to –'

'Good. Let's be off.'

Edouard ducked into the back, closely followed by Maurice.

The driver closed the door, checked his watch – 7.29, and rapidly surveyed the street: two concierges chatting, out of range . . . a postman working his way through the gloom . . . the café on the corner about to open. Knocking on the rear window of the car, he called something about having to use the facilities across the street.

Maurice looked at his watch. For a moment he thought the second hand had stopped, stuck halfway between 7.29 and 7.30. Then he saw it was moving . . .

Across the street, the driver, instead of entering the café, turned the corner and vanished. Rigid in the ticking car, Maurice, deathly pale, exchanged looks with his father.

'OUT!' barked Edouard.

With his cooler, drier hands, Edouard was the first to open his door. Bursting from the car, he ran clear, shouting at passersby and the secret service escort to take cover.

But Maurice, seizing his door handle, discovered to his horror that he was shaking too much to grip. Encumbered by the briefcase and sweaty hands, he made the car rock in his desperate struggle to escape. While his unseen second hand galloped home and the minute hand flicked on to 7.30, he abandoned his door and dived for the other side, spilling into the road, setting off a piercing alarm as the briefcase hit the cobbles. Finding his feet, he propelled himself towards the open arms of the building, bawling a warning at the bewildered Madame Klonowska in the doorway.

Colliding with her, Maurice waltzed the concierge roughly into the entrance, narrowly missing someone else on her way out. He tried to find the voice to stop her, but Nathalie Sainte-Claire was already . . .

The morning exploded, the street disappeared. One moment Nathalie was stepping out on her way to work, the next she was being scooped up by invisible hands and tossed away like a doll, her slight figure flung through the air and striking the pavement.

Kasha was asleep when the blast shattered her dreams and made her spring up, instinctively protecting her head. With shock waves still resonating, she grabbed a dressing gown and ran to the living room, switching on lights.

Her top-floor windows had survived, but she could see nothing but smoke through them. Bursting open the french windows, she leaned over the balcony and saw fires burning in the blacked-out street, figures groping in the eerie darkness.

Pulling on the first clothes that came to hand she ran along the corridor, passing Robert, who was standing dazed in his doorway in pyjamas.

'What's happened?'

'A bomb.'

Only on her way down the stairs did she remember that Nathalie frequently worked early shifts and realised that Robert had been standing there in mortal terror for her life.

Taking two stairs at a time, she arrived in the lobby just as Madame Klonowska was being helped to a chair by one of the security guards. Kasha ran on through the courtyard into the street. At first she could see little in the hellish darkness. Then through swirling smoke she approached a huddle of figures crouched and coughing over a body. She knew who it would be, but kept her hopes alive until, sinking to her knees beside Edouard de Montfort, she saw Nathalie lying twisted and very still on the pavement. Pillowed by someone's jacket, her face was ghastly but unscathed, and what Kasha took at first to be the shiny lining of Nathalie's coat became a swelling pool of blood beneath her.

Those few seconds coughing and kneeling over Nathalie seemed an eternity, and all the time in the back of her mind was Robert, where was he? would she be the one to have to tell him? was he about to appear at any mo—

A commotion in the doorway made her look round to see through the smoke someone in his dressing gown being restrained by one and then by both of the secret service men. Kasha jumped up and made her way over. Shouting and struggling, Robert fell still, gaping in hope at the sight of Kasha coming through the smoke. Then he read her face, the unbearable confirmation. Kasha's hands went out to him automatically, as if he were a hurt child, but he shrank from her, from everything except an all-consuming need to break free and reach his wife. Screaming hysterically, he fought with all his strength, and still they held him.

'Let him come,' Kasha pleaded.

They looked at her as if she were mad.

'Leave him!' she ordered with authority, and one hand at a time, half-heartedly, they released him. He staggered forward, Kasha caught him by the arm and led him to the waiting huddle, which made way for him fearfully, as though he carried something contagious. Supported on one side by Kasha, on the other by Edouard de Montfort, he fell on his knees and howled, filling the morning with his agony.

When the ambulance rushed her away, Nathalie was alive. Robert, heavily sedated, and Madame Klonowska were also driven away in shock. In the revolving blue dawn of police lights, Kasha tried to persuade an ashen-faced Maurice de Montfort to go too, offering to drive him herself. Rallying bravely, he declined, but allowed himself to be led indoors, where the young German countess, forbidden by her father-in-law from going outside, was waiting to thank Kasha and receive her husband.

Edouard was talking to detectives in the courtyard when Kasha touched his arm. 'I'm sorry to interrupt, monsieur le duc, but are you all right?'

'*Ma chère Mademoiselle Sharma,*' turning to her with a grateful smile, 'they'll need to do better than that.'

He was very pale and tight-jawed, clearly making a tremendous effort.

'Who did it, do we know?' she demanded.

'According to these gentlemen, the GP.'

'Jean-Jacques Revallier just claimed it,' put in one of the detectives.

Television crews and reporters were arriving, shepherded by security men. De Montfort swore, Kasha murmured her excuses and fled. 'We'll need to speak to you, mademoiselle,' a detective called.

Waiting for the lift, she heard Edouard reacting impatiently to the press. 'How should I know? They can't get me by fair means so they resort in their panic to foul. But rest assured . . .' Kasha looked around to see his rallying defiant face, the shaking fist, the de Gaulle posture, 'we shall not be diverted one iota from our resolve to continue striving for the greater prosperity of France and Europe . . .'

On her way up in the lift, Kasha told herself to stay calm, put her emotions on hold. She'd make a strong cup of tea, sit down at her computer and dash off a report to London. In her shocked state, she couldn't believe it was *really* Nathalie. But as soon as she entered the sanctuary of her apartment she began to have trouble breathing. At first she thought it was the effects of smoke, but quickly realised that the bomb, the stench, the sight of Nathalie on the pavement had awakened horrific memories of Bhopal, the world's worst industrial disaster, which she'd covered just over a year before.

Calm and clear-headed in the heat of the crisis, she was shaking as she ran to the bathroom to throw up.

· · · 3 · · ·

Eleven p. m., a dismal district of the city, a café leaning between darkened buildings, throwing its shabby light across a silent stretch of canal.

In the smoky interior, the owner is visibly distracted, his collection of regulars a blur. All he can think about are the desperadoes dining in the back room. Keeping the door ajar, he watches them, three men and a woman, the four most wanted people in France.

Pouring himself another drink, he glances feverishly at the newspaper outspread on the counter: *In the wake of the rue de Liège bomb, Interior Minister Gaston Batisse has offered unprecedented rewards for information leading to the capture of surviving members of Les Gardiens de la Planète . . .*

Louis Bonnait's hand was shaking. No one, save himself, had any clue where they were tonight. His was one of the few establishments they dared frequent. Incredible! he marvelled, watching them clinking glasses and cracking jokes. Only this morning they plant a heinous bomb, and tonight they dine in my brasserie as though immortal. He laughed under his breath and caught the eye of an old customer.

'Business not so hot tonight, eh Louis?'

Bonnait shrugged resignedly, and as they bitched about life, he was smiling to himself: *If you only knew who I have in the back room, the gang who've led the cops such a merry dance these last five years, terrorising the industrial community, kidnapping diplomats, raising hell from Cannes to Calais . . .*

'But money's not everything, eh!' declared the old man, 'there's dignity and honour,' he coughed, 'and health!'

'To honour and dignity!' echoed Bonnait, his bloodshot eyes roaming the newspaper, seizing on the choking sums – one million francs on the heads of remaining members of the GP, double for leaders Jean-Jacques Revallier and Janine Vallence. In the rear of his second-rate restaurant sat six million francs, enough to retire and drink himself to death.

Just then Bonnait was distracted by a sudden movement in the back room, Jean-Jacques Revallier rising to his feet. Bonnait trembled. The force of Revallier's love was said to be eclipsed only by the savageness of his hate. But there was no discernible anger on his face, he was merely raising a glass to his deputy, Janine Vallence. The other two were rising to complete the toast, a young man with blond flowing locks, and the one they called Revallier's Arabian Shadow. Who these two were no one knew. Even here they wore tinted glasses. As Bonnait watched, the lights suddenly blacked out in the back room. Before Bonnait could wonder what had happened, the darkness was relieved by Revallier bearing a lighted cake and placing it with exaggerated ceremony before Janine Vallence, who emitted an embarrassed *'Oh merde!'*, clapping a hand over her mouth. The draught from her arm ruffled the little flames, which took a moment to settle into a tremulous glow. Admonishing her foolish comrades, she lit a cigarette, frowned and relented, gracing them with a slow sardonic smile. Strangely lit, the three men stood around her in silence.

'A wish . . .' someone murmured.

Janine laughed lightly, her darkly shadowed eyes shining, one gypsy earring catching the candlelight. The blond man began singing 'Happy Birthday' softly in English, the other two following suit in thick accents. Lowering her eyes, Janine gazed mysteriously into the flames, her complement of thirty candles rapidly melting. A smile brushed her face, a wish taking shape. Looking up she caught Revallier's eye and they both broke into laughter. Ricardo disapproved, 'A wish must be taken seriously.'

'But I am!' protested Janine, wet-eyed with laughter.

The Algerian, Tahar Ben Amar, smiled easily, hiding his anxiety. Tonight Janine glowed, oozing life from every pore; tomorrow she could be dead. They all could. In the last twelve months the police had rooted out every other GP brigade in France. Everyone was after their blood, and now, after yesterday's cruel bomb, vital support would melt away, doors which had always been open would be shut in their faces.

Revallier turned to the door to attract Bonnait's attention. The proprietor perked up and presented himself, all discretion and dependability: '*Monsieur?*'

'A round of Armagnac before we go.'

A devoted little bow and Bonnait withdrew to root breathlessly behind the bar, returning in time to see Janine Vallence poised to blow out her candles.

Revallier stood at Janine's side, hand on her shoulder. '*Un, deux, trois . . .*' Janine took a breath and blew. Flames reeled and expired, plunging the room into fleeting darkness . . . only for a few diehard candles to rekindle, raising a laugh.

Janine hesitated, smiling benignly on her little band of survivors. She looked lovely. The life she'd chosen had marked her face, but she still radiated sensuality, life! For this evening she'd discarded leathers and jeans for a clinging dress and crimson lips, her whisky-blonde wig tumbling in curls about her eyes. They were all a little in love with her again tonight.

She inhaled, and blew – darkness! '*Bravo!*'

Lights on, Louis Bonnait came forward to pour their drinks, and Ricardo, dropping to one knee, launched into a tender rendering of a Puccini love song, while Janine, cheek in the palm of her hand, returned his mock-adoring gaze with bleary feline pleasure.

Tahar had to smile, his reckless comrades like children, rocked into lightheadedness by the recent fate of sister brigades and by the damning fall-out of the rue de Liège bomb. But someone had to stay awake, and from time to time Tahar wandered out of the back door and round to the front to check the murky street, the silent canal. Returning, he lit up a coarse Safi cigarette, took up his drink and fell in with the company, all the time listening to the night and surreptitiously watching Louis Bonnait – the clumsy way he cleared the table, the sweat on his puffy face, the furtive twitching eyes of a drunk or someone very nervous. Leaning back on his chair, Tahar observed what Bonnait couldn't see: Revallier rising, reaching inside his jacket and moving up behind him.

Bonnait started at the shoulder tap. Paling, he turned to meet Revallier's gaze.

'Please,' said Revallier, 'how much do we owe you?'

'Oh, monsieur . . .' a look of wounded pride.

Revallier insisted; Bonnait wouldn't hear of it.

'Trop gentil, monsieur,' said Revallier replacing his wallet.

Tahar smiled over the rim of his glass, observing the familiar ritual. Revallier's offer, the proprietor's refusal, all because of events long ago, when Bonnait's daughter Léonie lost a case against the employer she'd accused of a brutal sexual assault. The judge's decision to spare the defendant on grounds of the girl's provocation spurred Bonnait to take the law into his own hands. Discovering the scoundrel's address, he waited one night with a pickaxe handle, beating the judge to within an inch of his life as he stepped from his car. Charge: attempted murder. Since the violated judge was grimly influential, there was no leaping of lawyers to Bonnait's defence. His only hope lay in a young champion of the underdog, Jean-Jacques Revallier. So calm and tenacious was Revallier's defence of his client that he saved Bonnait from an interminable gaol term. Since Bonnait was then penniless, Revallier waived payment. *One day I may require a favour*, he predicted.

Mumbling something about 'enjoy the rest of your evening,' Bonnait withdrew balancing a laden tray, and shut the door behind him.

Tahar felt the chill of the closed door, and was on the point of going to investigate when the company fell silent, and he found everyone looking at him, looking at one another, the same question on every face.

'Keep singing,' said Revallier, rising.

Crossing the room, he gently opened the door and saw at once the bar deserted, the laden tray abandoned on the counter, the room drab with late-night drinkers and no Bonnait.

Covering her head in a hood, Janine slipped past Revallier and picked her way between tables to the street door. Outside the night was quiet, a couple receding along the canal, a car rumbling over cobbles, no sign of Bonnait. Returning indoors, she caught Revallier's eye. He was already behind the bar, slipping through the door to the proprietor's quarters.

The hall was dim; from the top of a flight of stairs came Bonnait's fearful whisper, ' . . . *all four of them, the two I told you and –* ' Revallier was already in full flight up the stairs, '*the Arab and one other, but hurry!*' Bonnait's scuffed shoes, flannels and bulging waist came into view . . . he looked around, paled, words quenched, his expression dissolving into cow-eyed terror. Revallier was upon him, prising the receiver from his fist and cradling it, breathing hard, saying nothing, only shaking his head sadly like a disappointed parent. He reached inside his jacket and Bonnait gulped at the sight of the knife, his eyes glazing over as it flashed before him, his torso folding like a puppet, joining the threadbare carpet in a heap.

Footsteps up the stairs.

'Jacques,' Janine appalled, 'what happened?'

'I was too late,' said Revallier hauling Bonnait to his knees and propelling him into an armchair. Bonnait opened wide his eyes and focused on the severed telephone cord. Close enough to catch Bonnait's drink-sodden breath, Revallier whispered hoarsely, 'One last favour, monsieur.'

'Anything!'

'No descriptions of my men.'

'I'll make something up.'

'Or I'll return for you.'

'Believe me!'

'As you did for the judge.'

'I swear!'

'For God's sake!' cried Janine, seizing Revallier's arm.

They took to the night.

Shrouded in mist off the canal, they walked rapidly to the Citroën waiting in the alley. As they scrambled into the car, far-off sirens rent the night. The car started at a touch, ghosted down the alley and swept on to the waterfront. Picking up speed, it rushed like a graceful illusion along the canal.

While Tahar scoured ahead and watched his mirrors, the others were busy shedding clothes for an array of costumes sealed in a suitcase, Revallier a modish suit and Janine a black satin dress and cascading red wig. Even slimmer than Janine, Ricardo in the front seat slithered into a red velour dress. Given his natural mop of curls, he had no need of a wig, only a hand mirror and passing lights to concentrate on his make-up. A final touch of mascara, a lascivious glance in the mirror. 'Terrorist to tart,' he declared, 'in four minutes!'

'CRS,' whispered Tahar.

The warning sent a shiver through the car, a pair of darkened coaches crossing their path, CRS paramilitary police spilling into the streets. Sharply dropping the wheel, Tahar swept the saloon into a side street and raced between badly parked cars and late-night bars towards . . . the arms of an inevitable road-block!

'*Daniya-el-Ghaddara*,' he cursed softly, turning into another narrow street, swinging and swerving to avoid cars and milling people.

'Here,' said Janine.

Tahar brought the car to a smooth halt.

'Reverse, quick!'

Without pause, he thrust the car back across a cramped junction into the path of an oncoming taxi. The cabbie howled, Revallier clapped Tahar and Ricardo on the shoulder, 'Dump the car, meet back at base when things have died down.'

Revallier and Janine piled out of the Citroën and into the taxi.

While sirens multiplied down gloomy boulevards, Tahar spirited the car through side streets and into a back lane, pulling up behind a truck, cutting lights and engine. From the boot he lifted a slim awkward contraption into the road, and then a strip of canvas which he unrolled with Ricardo over the entire car, securing it with rubber clasps round the bumpers.

A brief fierce embrace and Ricardo was away over the cobbles on high clicking heels, a pretty blonde tripping along in fishnet tights, with a flimsy coat and shoulder-bag. At the corner, Ricardo turned, winked and was gone.

The contraption at Tahar's feet unfolded into a bicycle. A last glance at the invisible Citroën, and he pedalled off over the cobbles, concentrating on the safest route to the relative sanctuary of the Arab quarter.

A few streets away a cab driver was throwing up his hands: another road-block, choking traffic, CRS police demanding papers, 'You know who they're after, that Revallier gang.'

Revallier from the back, 'You think so?'

'It's their own fault, they've had it this time.'

'Let's hope so,' said Janine.

'*Putain*! Will you look at this!' Armed CRS peering into every vehicle. Janine and Revallier exchanged glances and started getting out.

'Hey! where are you going?'

Revallier thrust a banknote into the driver's fist, 'We're a bit pressed for time.'

They turned the first corner and strolled arm in arm towards the nearest night-club. When they reached it, the street was thronged with cabs, pricey cars and couples hurrying in from the cold. Before going in, Janine drew Revallier into the shadows to straighten his tie. She stood back and laughed. Despite the stylish trenchcoat, jazzy shirt and fashionable fake glasses, he was still – with his ferocious stubble and dark wavy hair – the handsome rogue gazing from a thousand wanted posters.

Even as Janine exchanged her earrings for a more conventional pair and lifted the collar of her fake fur, Revallier prayed her disguise was good enough.

Once inside, they realised they were in Gangsters, the voguish, scrupulously respectable club for budding high-fliers. Plush and select, the only undesirables to be found were in the vivid murals, life-sized portraits with epitaphs such as 'Shot dead by Ange Faota in the Dead Rat, Pigalle, 25 December, 1934', or 'Mathieu Costa, boss of the Corsicans, mortally wounded in his café, 9 July 1949 by Jeannot Fredericci'.

The club was high, wide and suffused in perpetual dusk. A gloomily romantic effect was created by luminous pulses projected on the underside of mock bridges. Slow searchlights feeling out the clientèle added a quasi-sense of menace. Songs of the thirties and forties, and the occasional burst of nostalgic police sirens, clinched the illusion, enabling patrons to stretch out their weekend sipping cocktails in some dreamy underworld version of old Paris.

Avoiding the slow sweep of searchlights, Revallier and Janine surrendered their coats, ordered a table and separated.

The black-and-pink tiled ladies' room was occupied by one other woman, about twenty-five thought Janine, a tall hipless blandly beautiful creature coolly appraising herself in the mirror. The two women paraded before the sweep of mirrors attending to details with the concentration of athletes, a trace of lipstick, sprays of perfume, subtle adjustments to clothing and, as they angled their profiles, their eyes met, and the young beauty, expecting a hasty evasion, wavered under the assault of Janine's gaze. Hastily putting away her make-up, she left.

Alone, Janine worked quickly to refit her wig, and then

to put in deep-blue contact lenses to match her eye colour in the photograph on her false papers. As she was finishing, she met her deeply lined reflection in the mirror and smiled wryly. How strangely her life had turned out, by instinct non-violent but immersed in an increasingly savage struggle; by nature sparkling and gregarious, yet long-estranged from friends and family, with only the gang to sustain her. Her life was a rope bridge swinging high over jagged reefs, no point in looking back, and nothing ahead. For a weak moment, as she stood returning her own gaze, she envied the young woman who had just left, trying to imagine herself about to rejoin friends for the aimless pleasures of an all-night party. Instead she found herself checking windows for potential escape routes, before going to find Revallier.

In the men's room Revallier completed a gruelling electric shave, and was gelling his hair tightly back over his scalp and tying it into a neat pony-tail, when two men, younger than he, came in and swaggered over to the urinals to piss ostentatiously. 'Enticing new prospect, eh?'

'Ripe for in-depth research!'

'Because with a solvency margin like mine . . .'

'Yours!'

'*D'accord*, maybe she could accommodate both our deposits.'

'Flexible investment strategy!'

'You pinch her holdings, I'll squeeze her assets!'

Squalls of laughter.

As they zipped themselves up and gravitated to the wash basins, Revallier put back on his false glasses, splashed cologne on his cheeks and replaced his toiletries in a leather clutch bag.

'Hope to fuck this one's willing,' said the one on his left, combing his hair.

'Long as she doesn't carry any unpleasant hidden charges,' replied the other to groans of revulsion.

'Men with a mission!' they cried, making for the exit.

A rapid search for possible escape routes and Revallier re-emerged with the cool detached air of the trend-setting fashion designer featured in his false papers.

Janine was already at the table, smoking hazily, mysteriously self-contained. As he sat down, a waiter stepped up to pour two glasses of champagne, wished them an enjoyable evening and withdrew. Revallier looked at the bottle in its bed of ice and frowned. She'd picked the most expensive in the house. How, he wondered, were they going to pay for it? When he looked up, she was grinning at him.

He raised his glass to meet hers.

'Happy Birthday.'

Ricardo didn't get far. While his taxi crawled towards a road-block, he discovered to his amazement that he was carrying Tahar's false papers and not his own.

He paid the driver and got out. Recovering a high heel he teetered with practised poise to the notorious rue St-Denis, where droves of furtive males sloped past steamy bars, sex-shops and peep shows, eyeing warily the silhouettes in doorways and alleys, women alone or in clusters for a chilling neon-wide kilometre, coldly aloof or peeling clients off the street to spirit them away for a brief two-hundred-franc coupling in some bleak half-imagined room.

Pausing in a doorway, Ricardo took out a compact and by the filmy red light of a bar, rouged the cold from his cheeks, repainted his lips and outlined his long-lashed Mediterranean eyes. Shivering in his scanty clothes, he swung his bag by its thin strap over his shoulder and proceeded with studied grace along one narrow pavement, evading the dagger looks of women on whose pitch he was trespassing, discouraging the attentions of hungry men with an absent air, all the time worrying about Tahar carrying the wrong papers.

Some men were not easily deflected. Ricardo's golden curls, boyish bullfighter shape and long fishnet legs caught the eye. A car drew alongside.

'*Chérie . . .?*' Ricardo paid no heed, '*chérie!*' the man insisted.

In the corner of Ricardo's eye a jet-black Jaguar slid closer, the driver reaching casually to stroke his thigh.

'It's a cold night, beautiful . . .' his tone smooth, reassuring and loveless, 'how much?'

Though only twenty-two and the baby of the gang, Ricardo wasn't easily alarmed. '*Non merci,*' he said lightly and strolled the other way, prompting the man to laugh hollowly and see him off with a stream of unsheathed obscenities.

Resuming his promenade and trying to take his mind off the plight of Tahar, Janine and Revallier, Ricardo found himself thinking of his family, his resplendent mother and fiery father, his galaxy of sisters, all baffled by his disinclination – the only son – to embrace the role of heir to the family jewellery business, perplexed by his quitting university – a brilliant physics student – to toil in a repair garage in Paris. Little did they guess, when they welcomed him home at Christmas, fussing over him, toasting him around the table in their Florentine villa, that many of the Gardiens de la Planète's most spectacular acts of industrial sabotage were the handiwork of their beloved Ricardo.

In an all-night café close to Cimetière de Belleville in the Arab quarter on the east side of the city, Tahar Ben Amar sat pensively over a bowl of *chorba*, listening to the ebb and flow of sirens across the night.

Now that he was safe, he saw his hand was shaking as he lit a cigarette. Another perilously close escape; it wasn't funny any more. His loyalty to Revallier was unswerving; like Louis Bonnait, Tahar was a former client, defended by Revallier years before against a charge of grievous bodily

61

harm to a slum landlord who'd been terrorising the community. Tahar's faith in the cause was also unshakeable, but the battle was lost. Revallier would have to face it; it was time to go home.

Home: he gazed into space, the voices around him faded, his thoughts drifted home to El Madheur, the heady air and prickly light of the mountains, the cool of the trees where once he ran with the other boys to pick mushrooms at first light. Then the day the myth of his childhood exploded, turning him overnight into a man and setting him on a crooked course to Revallier. Against his will, and sparked no doubt by the night's narrow escape, *that* day flashed before him, a market day in June 1959. Tahar's father and his partner, Gaga Ben Said, laughing over a sack which had spilled its beans on the floor and under the polished shoes of four strangers. The laughter ceased, his father seeming to know that these men were French security police and that a *kawad* had betrayed him, one who knew that his coffee shop was used by soldiers disloyal to the occupying French – Senegalese Muslims and Algerians of the Seventh Tirarieur – to smuggle arms and food to the guerrillas in the mountains. Hiding among the sacks, Tahar watched his proud handsome invincible father marched away to Firmet Lahmar, where they sat him on broken glass, pumped him with detergent, beat him with rubber hoses, and, when he applauded them for learning so well from the Nazis, applied electrodes to his toes and penis.

Just then the door burst open and in ran a frightened youth, a minor felon caught up in the wrong hunt. He stood gazing with pleading eyes at Hamou behind the bar. Everyone looked up: the panting fugitive and leathery old Hamou staring at each other. Shouts came from the street – a raid!

While Hamou cursed the boy and led him downstairs to hide, Tahar felt in his jacket for the reassurance of his expertly made false papers. But as sirens wailed nearer, Tahar's fingers found an unfamiliar shape, and when he took it out, he was holding Ricardo's wallet. He opened the wallet and found himself staring at a photograph of a dissolute Ricardo in drag, rejoicing in the name Carmen Tintoretto, registered prostitute.

The shock momentarily undid him. Then he slapped money on the table, seized his coat and got up to leave, but the moment he looked outside, he knew it was hopeless. CRS troops were sealing the street at both ends, barging into bars and clubs and bundling suspects and resisters into caged vans.

Tahar went back inside through a crowd of nervous customers and hurried down the stairs at the back. In a storeroom stacked to the ceiling with supplies, Hamou was burying the young fugitive in a mountain of grain sacks. 'Remember, I never saw you come down here,' he called to the boy.

'You never saw me either,' said Tahar.

The old man beheld his long-time customer and friend with dismay. As he looked at Tahar, it began to dawn on him who he was. Two days ago he might have been sympathetic. But the unspoken question was in his face: what in God's name are you doing mixed up in – ? Tahar started to explain, Hamou stared at him, Tahar's mouth ran dry, he looked in Hamou's eyes, Muslim to Muslim.

The old man brusquely motioned him to hide and hurried out pulling the rickety door shut.

Tahar stood a moment in the claustrophobic silence weighing his options. 'Keep quiet, I can hear you,' he told the unseen boy. Resolving not to join him under the sacks, he stretched to clear a space on the deep top shelf running crookedly around the room. Then he swung a broom head at the solitary dangling light bulb, plunging the room into darkness, drawing a stifled cry of alarm from the boy.

'Keep that up,' said Tahar feeling for the ladder, 'and we'll be sharing a dungeon together.'

He climbed to the top shelf, pulling the ladder up after him. Stretching out on his back, he was replacing alongside him as many glass jars as he could when he heard the drumming of boots above, the frightened and infuriated shouts of Hamou's customers and then boots thundering down the stairs.

Doors crashed open along the passage, the storeroom door was kicked in, and a powerful flashlight entered, darting madly as a trooper felt for the light switch. When he found it and it failed to work, he let his torchbeam roam.

Tahar closed his eyes tighter, his heart hammering against his chest wall as though trying to break out.

An exultant shout! Cries of pain from the boy, two or more men arriving to drag him away, leaving the first man demolishing stacks of canned oil, kicking over boxes of dried fruit, clearing shelves of bottled olives from the lowest upward, to the accompaniment of shattering glass, finally stretching and unhooking a machete from the wall to reach Tahar's darkened level, sweeping back and forth, dislodging his thin line of jars before blindly catching Tahar's belt and slashing him from buttock to knee.

The trooper ran out and up the stairs, boots and shouts faded, vehicles rumbled on and receded. Tahar lay still, a handkerchief clamped to his thigh. Then he clambered down and stepped over debris into the lighted passage. No sound above. They'd taken everyone. All, save Hamou and the boy, would probably be released.

Parting the incision in his trousers, he examined his leg. The wound was superficial, the pain sweetened by relief, soured by grief for Hamou. A nod of thanks in Allah's direction and he climbed weakly to the street.

Ricardo knew he should have waited longer, but he was cold in his thin dress and plastic mac and was tripping along the street in search of a taxi when a shivering woman in a doorway nudged her companion, 'Putain, les poulets!'

Ricardo turned and saw gun-toting CRS roaming through the crowds, scrutinising faces, selecting individuals for rapid frisking, the crowds rearranging themselves in their wake.

Ricardo walked on, trying to hurry without appearing to, imagining he could keep out of range of the danger, until he spotted the forage caps of CRS men coming in the opposite direction. He stopped, rooted, watching the black leather tide closing in from both sides, wondering what he would do if they demanded his papers, when a vaguely familiar voice sent a chill through him.

'I'm sorry about before . . .' the man at the wheel of the black Jaguar smiled, cigarette smoke curling from his lips, 'Come with me, no one but you will do.' Ricardo's eyes darted left and right, looking for the unexpected exit. But the CRS were wading closer and, apart from bars where he would feel trapped, there was no way out. 'Five hundred francs,' he said.

The man's easy shrug said, it's all the same to me what you charge, and as he reached over to open the door, Ricardo went round and got in. The man eased the wide-bodied car off the kerb, a CRS man flagged him down, checked his papers and stooped to get a look at his pretty passenger, absently painting her nails. Returning the papers, he waved the driver on. As they pressed through the congestion towards the nearest free-flowing boulevard, Ricardo took a quick look at his 'saviour', thirties, white suit, open shirt, brash rings on his fingers. At first glance the man looked like a flashy well-heeled operator, but a closer look showed his suit was shabby and his face scarred down one cheek. He'd been coldly charming beforehand, but now that his prey was captured he didn't speak, merely chain-smoked as he drove, his deadpan eyes fixed on the road.

'Where are we going?' Ricardo asked vaguely, making a mess of his nails.

Sitting back and steering one-handed, the man said nothing.

'Somewhere exciting?'

No reply. The night parted before the speeding Jaguar. Turning on to Pont de la Concorde, it surged across the Seine to the Left Bank. Paris reeled, tight turns, blinding lights, Ricardo guarding his nerves, saving his wits, watching closely as they closed remorselessly on some given point. Suddenly they were pulling over in a quiet street, engine running, wipers beating time. Deadpan lit up another cigarette as he waited.

Ricardo glanced at him and sensed an ideal moment to escape. But before he could act two figures with upturned collars materialised on the corner and Ricardo's silent companion flashed his lights, flung his cigarette out of the window and drove off again, drawing up sharply to allow the men to get in the back. Doors slamming, the Jaguar swept on.

Ricardo shuddered. The newcomers sat back without a word, men about the same age and same loveless mould. How would they react when they discovered he wasn't female? Outwardly docile, he hung his nails to dry on the dashboard, glancing about repeatedly, trying to follow directions and street names as they pressed into the prosperous seventh *arrondissement*, until from behind came a pair of perspiring hands and a cool silk scarf round his eyes, blinding him.

For a time he sat limp with apprehension, the city hurtling by unseen, his captors silent. Suddenly he sensed an opportunity, a half-chance, the sound of cars slowing towards a major junction. Obeying the red light, the Jaguar reined in, engine panting. Ricardo sat still, hand feeling furtively for the door handle, the captive woman in him trembling, the experienced young guerrilla concentrating, trying to imagine what Revallier would be counselling. Hearing cross-traffic slowing, sensing the lights about to change again, he held on a moment more and then, without warning, tore off his blindfold, seized the handle and flung himself at the door. Which would have burst open, pitching him into the road, had the man not quickly flicked a switch, locking all the doors with a gratifying *clunk*. With padded shoulder and powdered cheek, Ricardo struck the immovable door. As he retrieved himself, someone called him a stupid bitch, slapped his face and retied his blindfold even tighter.

Lights changed, the Jaguar surged into the night, scattering traffic in its path, leaving all in its wake. No one laughed or spoke, the foiled escape bid a formality, a trap springing shut on one more hapless creature. Ricardo straightened his dress, recrossing his legs as if nothing had happened. Pulse racing, he fumbled a cool hand through his silky locks and sighed.

Minutes later the car swung off the road, up a slight incline and over smooth tarmac into a hushed crescent. The men got out, someone opened Ricardo's door and pulled him out by the wrist. With sleet pelting his cheeks, he found his feet and felt himself gripped under his arms and marched up a flight of stairs and in through a broad entrance to an echoing lobby. Hurrying him into a lift, they removed his blindfold, the lift soared, Ricardo cringed from the cold heat of their eyes, praying that in the close confinement they wouldn't spot the masculine flaws in his features.

They escorted him quickly down a carpeted corridor to a door marked eighty-four, and manoeuvred him into a de luxe suite stale with tobacco fumes and the superficial luxury and tasteless fittings of a quick-let holiday apartment. As they directed him to a coffee-stained sofa, Ricardo observed the array of photographic and video equipment waiting to be brought into play.

Lighting cigarettes, they poured themselves drinks and turned their attention to Ricardo sitting primly on the sofa, handbag in his lap. They refilled glasses and, without taking their eyes off him, coolly contemplated this angle, that routine, a sordid fairytale of willing degradation. While one looked to his cameras, the other two stubbed out their cigarettes and approached the sofa with the detached air of executioners, only the grotesque swellings in their crotches betraying their morbid excitement. Ricardo lifted his long-lashed eyes. Deadpan was regarding him strangely, as if wondering why the little whore wasn't reacting to form – no tears, no spitting rage, merely sitting up, knees joined, demure even.

'Strip.'

Ricardo lowered his eyes, his face puckering as he sniffled and opened his handbag to take out a handkerchief. Yielding to form at last, they thought, a lip-biting terrified young woman lifting her handkerchief to her nose and dropping it to reveal – a gun!

A petite handbag pistol, effective up to twenty paces. Ricardo fired, three muffled bursts through a pocket silencer, three spumes of smoke, two punctured trouser legs and a hole in the cameraman's rump, gaping mouths, stunned eyes, bloodsoaked groping hands, three men reeling backwards, colliding in their panic for cover.

Reaching for the telephone, Ricardo plucked from his bag a list of taxi numbers and caught Deadpan's eye across the room, 'This address, *s'il vous plaît, monsieur*?' a winning smile, 'and what about my fee?'

Resisting the lure of alcoves, Revallier and Janine sat at an open table sipping ruinously expensive champagne. Caught from time to time in the slow sweep of simulated searchlights, they studied a sheaf of enlarged photographs. Taken in wintry pre-dawn gloom, they showed the de Montforts leaving their apartment block in rue de Liège.

'There!' Janine drew Revallier's attention to a shadowy band around Maurice de Montfort's wrist as he ducked into the back of the Mercedes, 'and here,' another photo taken immediately after, with something shining round the wrist catching the street light. 'I tell you, he's handcuffed to that bloody case.'

Revallier looked closer, and nodded solemnly. The handcuffed briefcase and police escort were proof enough that the de Montforts were spiriting schemes back and forth across Paris in the utmost secrecy, and Revallier and Janine were convinced that if they could capture the briefcase, they would be in possession of a carefully plotted text dedicated to ruthless promotion of the nuclear industry, and to the shameless undermining and discrediting of the Greens in general and the GP in particular.

She slid across a second set of photographs. Taken through the flawed glass of a café window, they showed Indian journalist Kasha Sharma leaving the same building. Dressed in bright colours and bangles, she lit the street like a bomb-site poppy.

'Be careful, Jacques.'

'Don't worry.'

'I mean *her*. Nice and exotic, just your type.'

Looking at the pictures of the tall poised Asian woman, he smiled, dismissing Janine's concern.

'I'm serious,' she said, knowing him only too well.

But his thoughts had turned to more immediate concerns. Refilling their glasses, he raised his to propose a toast.

'To Tahar and Ricardo, may they get through safely.'

They clinked glasses and drank and Janine looked away with a troubled look in her eyes.

'What is it?'

'Jacques . . .'

Her voice was heavy with resolve. He knew what was coming and he knew it had to come. Their eyes met. 'It's time,' she said, so softly he barely heard her. He didn't need to. They'd talked about it before, only he'd never expected the end to come so soon.

'We live day and night in the shadow of death,' she was saying, 'and as if that isn't enough, our reputation was blown to bits by that bomb this morning. Thousands, millions who openly or quietly sided with us curse us now. They can hunt us like vermin now. Even if that woman doesn't die, *nous sommes fichus*, we're fucked.'

He looked at his hand lying under hers on the table. Any day now they would be separated, he and Janine. They'd never planned to stay together. They'd been fiercely in love at first, erotically obsessed with each other, but operating together so closely was bound to take its toll, and while mutual respect survived their love had withered, or to be more accurate, they had agreed from the start that love was to be discouraged, deliberately and brutally. Bad enough to fear losing your closest comrade, but when that comrade was your lover, you learnt to dread love and keep a captive heart.

'I don't want to bury you,' she said, 'I don't want you to have to bury me. We'll see this job through, steal the bastard's secrets and then . . .' she took a sharp breath, and let it out slowly, 'go our separate ways.'

A shadow of a smile crossed Revallier's face, a tender look, giving no hint of the rage in his heart. Lowering his eyes, he became still, dangerously still, and she said nothing. Then he sat back and lit a cigarette and looked through the blur of smoke at the people at surrounding tables. The women were wonderfully well groomed, their faces artfully painted and all seeming – in the dreamy lines of their every gesture – to have attended the same school of authentic allure; the men were all pitching to form and striking the right pose and turned out in modish suits designed apparently by the same repressive tailor. Everybody was bleating and bragging and resolutely relaxed, their voices and bodies in one accord, 'we have money, we have style,' murmured Revallier, 'we die all day so we can live at night. Secure within our hard-earned disillusions, we've solved the problem of life.'

Tears ran down his face without troubling his calm expression. 'Don't they realise the party's over?' He angrily ground out his cigarette.

He felt Janine watching him, he looked at her, she was thinking, *Very soon we're going to part, and in all probability we will never –*

'All right then,' he smiled broadly, raising his glass, 'to one more dazzling operation!'

'To one more – ' the words caught in Janine's throat, her eyes, staring past him, clouded over. No need for Revallier to ask what was wrong, nor even to look around. Janine was still staring past him, calm with fear, monitoring the enemy's arrival. While she put away the photos, a loud quarrel was breaking out, management refusing to bring up the lights, a CRS officer threatening to take the place apart as he despatched his men through the club, generating with their black uniforms and thuggish swagger just the right aura of official menace and unofficial licence. It didn't matter that most of the club's clientèle were too young to have experienced the German occupation. The CRS – Les Compagnies Républicaines de Sécurité – with their forage caps and riding boots, inspired an unconscious memory of Nazi rule. A dozen men carried out the search, moving briskly from table to table demanding papers.

As they came nearer, Janine tried to attract Revallier's attention, but she'd lost him. He was turning to glower over his shoulder, one hand reaching into a pocket, prey to sudden madness. She kicked him under the table, he met her gaze, she seized his hands and held them, 'Now look into my eyes as you used to.'

A pair of leather boots arrived, the stock of a shouldered

submachine-gun brushed the tablecloth, a young trooper thrust out a gloved hand, '*Vos papiers!*'

'*Chéri* . . .' Janine coaxed Revallier, 'the gentleman's waiting.'

Like infatuated lovers they disentangled fingers and delved absently in pockets. Accustomed to snappier reaction, the trooper blinked at the couple's mesmeric response. Caught in their spell, he watched as Janine and Revallier, without taking their eyes from each other, lazily held up their ID cards. A sip of champagne and they rejoined hands as if alone together. While the trooper examined the IDs and glanced repeatedly at the two people they were supposed to represent, Janine held Revallier's gaze. 'We were toasting the future, *chéri* . . .' touching glasses, they drank, 'however brief it may be.'

Not trusting himself to speak, Revallier lifted Janine's fingers to his lips and kept them until the trooper snapped, '*Merci, monsieur, madame!*' and brusquely returned their papers.

The CRS withdrew, the club settled down, the search a faintly exciting distraction, echoes of another world.

Janine and Revallier sat back for a time in silence, Janine grinning over the rim of her glass.

'In '68 when France erupted,' said Revaillier, 'when the youth of the Western world caught fire, I believed things were changing. But look at them . . .' taking in everyone with a flick of the wrist, 'not a murmur of protest.'

'People are intimidated,' she defended them, 'the guts have been kicked out of them.'

He laughed scornfully. 'Let's go.'

As he started to rise, she waved a little slip of paper – the bill! Champagne, 475F. He rolled his eyes to heaven and sat down. In his wallet he counted 75F, enough for a taxi. 'And you?'

She smiled: none.

'*Formidable!*'

As they looked about speculatively, he spotted the two loud-mouthed studs he'd encountered in the men's room. The young woman sat with them, the dreamy blonde Janine had encountered in the ladies' room. As Revallier watched, he saw the men ostentatiously arguing over the right to foot the bill. Revallier rose, removed his jacket and rolled up his sleeves. 'See you at the pay desk.'

As he approached their table he saw the young woman, plainly not enthralled by her escorts, looking drearily about.

'I trust everything is to your satisfaction, *madame, messieurs?*' he intoned, hands behind his back.

'Splendid! we'd like a taxi right away.'

'Certainly.'

Thanking the gentlemen and inclining a polite smile in the direction of the lady, he picked up the bill and its accompanying crisp new notes and turned away.

Side-stepping searchlights, he made his way between tables to rejoin Janine near the exit. She helped him on with his jacket, and he presented the modest bill and cash for wine and snacks at the pay desk.

Collecting their coats, they strolled arm in arm into the night.

4

South-west of Paris, near the village of St-Sulpice-en-Maréchaux, a broad-faced stone house stood out in snow-covered countryside. Set back off a little used road and surrounded by orchards and outbuildings, it must have seemed to the occasional traveller a haven detached from the hurly-burly of the modern world. The buildings were old but sound, flowers poked through snow-smothered window boxes, goats wandered in and out of the goat-house, and two vehicles, an old jeep and a newish Toyota, stood in the shed which served as a garage.

Known as The Old Forge, this was the American's place.

He'd lived in France since the war, first in Normandy with his French bride, then here at La Vieille Forge. Though he spoke fluent French and ate, drank and dressed like a rustic Frenchman, Monsieur Luke Morrel was still known as the American, and Madame Isabelle Morrel, a university lecturer, as the American's wife.

At eleven o'clock on the morning after the Paris bomb, Isabelle was lying on in bed and Luke was busy in the kitchen. He'd milked the goats at first light, leaving out a frothing churn for the co-op to collect, saving the rest to make cheese and yogurt. He'd been to the village for provisions, and now, with family coming for lunch, was chopping and rinsing, engrossed inventing a new dish. Although he disregarded recipe books and cooked impulsively, Luke, unlike Isabelle, was an orderly man, and had the kitchen the way he wanted it: a mix of old and new, wood-burning range and stainless steel pans, old-fashioned walk-in larder, de luxe blenders and mixers, and everything in its place.

With the radio on, he didn't hear Isabelle come down until she was ferreting in the bread bin. She had nothing on but her dressing gown and ankle socks, and her eyes were smudged with eye-liner from last night's dinner party.

'You look like a panda,' he said.

'Don't you like pandas?' she slammed the bread bin and began to hunt. 'Don't tell me you didn't buy any brioche?'

'I probably did,' spreading himself in front of the groceries, 'but you're too late!'

She tried to push him aside. '*Cochon*! you've hidden them.'

'You'll spoil your lunch, have an apple.'

'Listen mister,' switching effortlessly between French and English, 'I work my ass off all week, and on Saturday morning I'm entitled to breakfast any hour I choose.'

'*Écoute, madame*, I can't fix lunch and fall over you at the same time.'

'I'll be in and out in two minutes.'

'*You* could wreck an entire civilisation in two minutes.'

They'd had this argument a thousand times and they never tired of it. When his back was turned, she started rooting in the shopping bags on the floor.

'Hey!' shooing her away, 'this is my kitchen and I don't take kindly to trespassers.'

It was physically difficult for a plucky but petite woman to argue with a broad-shouldered man of six-foot-three who remained unbowed by age or work.

She picked up a chair, dragged it over to the warmth of the range, stamped it down on the floor and sat down. '*Brute*! all I want is my brioche and coffee.'

He laughed, switched on the kettle and set out a fresh filter paper to make coffee.

'The pink dawn over the snow was something. You don't know what you missed. Now look at it.'

'God, you people are such a bore.'

The kettle boiled, she got up to make her coffee and grimaced as if in pain, 'Not that dirge at this unearthly hour,' she said and pulled out the radio plug.

'Who introduced me to Chopin, for Chrissake? *Merde*!' The rice was boiling over, 'Now look what you done!'

'Me!'

As Luke flicked the lid off the pan and reduced the heat, Isabelle casually reached between his legs and found his balls in the soft crutch of his old jeans.

'Hey!' he protested, stirring the rice.

But he didn't stop her, and as she fondled him her smile broadened, pleased she still had the power to bring him on hard as a horse.

Gently removing her hand, he returned it with a grave smile. 'Don't start, madame, or you know where it'll lead.'

A speculative downward glance and she met his eyes with a look of deep disdain, as much as to say, I doubt you're up to it, mister.

With a regretful smile which said, Okay, you've had it, he switched off the cooker and began to undo his apron.

A shocked intake of breath and Isabelle backed towards the door and fled with Luke in hot pursuit. Halfway down the hall he caught her. She made a frantic bid to escape, but he captured her in his arms, seized a heavy coat from the rack and wrapped her up. Over his shoulder she went, shrieking and laughing as he carried her across the freezing yard to the warm-smelling goathouse. For the goats, momentarily startled, this raucous behaviour wasn't new and they sensibly ignored it.

Grinning and howling, he buried her in warm straw. She pulled at his beard, spat gleefully in his eyes, fought like a cat while he dug in the straw to part her legs. Beneath all the hysterics, she was strongly aroused. The so-called menopause had failed to cool her. She found Luke at sixty-three more than ever an immensely appealing male, a modern man with the wild still in him. Willing but squeamish when first she'd given herself to him, she learned from him the savage beauty of sex, releasing instincts in her which were finally freer than his . . . enabling her to release in him the full tenderness and violence of his hunger.

For his part he still found her, close on sixty, highly attractive, a plump, fleshy, earthy woman, whose sexiness made her lack of recognised beauty unimportant. Not as pretty as girls he used to date in Tucson, she was always more mysteriously attractive, the only woman he ever knew who could bring him to those howling climaxes in which he utterly lost himself.

Out of fun and curiosity she'd strayed a few times in

nearly forty years together, but no man had seriously distracted her, particularly since Luke tolerated her flings with the wry grudging amusement of a man who knows he's number one.

She knew Luke too strayed from time to time. He was an innocent and denied nothing. He was smart enough to know when to and when not to and who with, and secure enough to keep his feelings in check. So if, when he took his goats to be serviced by Madame Delecourt's *bouc* in the next village, he completed the transaction, as everyone whispered, by paying the young widow his respects, Isabelle was more amused than offended.

But now, in the sweet-sour goathouse, as she wrapped her bare thighs around his head and rode his face with her sex, she had the awful feeling they were about to be disturbed. Laroche's dilapidated VW could be heard a mile away, and Luke, his face buried in Isabelle, couldn't fail to hear it either.

'Shit, piss and corruption!'

Rattling and roaring, the old VW crossed the yard and whined to a halt. A tinny door slammed, Laroche was heard making for the house. '*Holà . . .*'

Isabelle fell back laughing.

'Shhh . . .' he clapped a hand over her mouth.

'It's okay, finish,' she said, 'you've time.'

Luke shook his head. In these matters he could be shy as a doe and hurried to make himself respectable.

Enter the slight dark-eyed figure of Jean-Baptiste Laroche, a sixty-year-old builder who lived alone. Isabelle, in her ankle socks, was standing demurely holding her dressing gown together. Unaware of the straw in his salt-and-pepper beard, Luke smiled sheepishly.

'*Zut!*' Laroche's pinched unshaven face broke into an embarrassed grin. 'Forgive me, but I come on a matter of great urgency. Well . . .' he reconsidered, 'relatively speaking.'

*　*　*

It was a short drive through a quiet winter landscape to the village, where Laroche and Luke pulled up outside the bistro. As they kicked snow off their boots and went inside, a great shout went up from the corner. Nine men, three generations – from Etienne barely out of school to octogenarian Bruno Pissani, who lost a leg at Verdun – sat around a table, a pile of money in the middle.

'Bonjour, *monsieur!*' blushed *la patronne*, a big-boned handsome young woman laying tables for lunch.

Luke smiled into her eyes.

Her strapping husband, Félix Bajolet, was among the nine in the corner, watching Luke from under his black brows.

Accepting a seat and a glass of Ricard, Luke and Laroche touched glasses with everyone around the table. Even seated, Luke towered benignly, carrying himself with an air of roguish authority, and on this occasion with a faint whiff of the goathouse.

Seeing the exceptional heap of banknotes on the table, Luke cocked a speculative eye and surveyed the group.

'As I've often tried to remind you, gentlemen, I've been watching birds all my life . . . like you because they're beautiful, extraordinary, maybe because we wish we could be more like them . . . but I'm no expert.'

'Orrrh . . .' a chorus of polite contradiction greeted his modesty.

'It's true. One day I'm going to get it all wrong.'

'So, even experts make mistakes,' said Bajolet, 'let's get on with it.'

Removing his beret, Luke drew himself up, drained his glass and licked his moustache, '*Bon d'accord,* I'm ready.'

Félix Bajolet waited another moment for quiet. Then reaching inside his coat, he pulled out a feather and laid it carefully on the table, like a murder exhibit.

Luke leaned forward. Everyone leaned with him.

It was a speckled grey-brown feather, superficially unremarkable. Luke gave a little grunt and scratched his beard. Then he took out a battered spectacles case, removed his steel-rimmed glasses and put them on; holding it up to the light, he slowly twirled the feather by its barrel tip, like a jeweller examining a precious stone. The group fidgeted, watching his every move, the pride of amateur ornithologists at stake, not to mention considerable sums of money.

'Where was it found?'

'I found it, monsieur,' piped Etienne, a slender youth who bird-watched daily in spite of warnings not to go alone because of his epilepsy, 'I've a hide on the river near the ruins at Les Vaux de Louchard, just this side of the de Montfort estate. It floated down as they flew over.'

'Unfortunately,' supplied Bajolet, 'they're nesting *inside* the estate, so we've got problems identifying them.'

'But you saw them?' said Luke.

'Yes, monsieur,' replied Etienne, 'but I don't fancy going back, not after yesterday.'

'What happened yesterday?'

'They were nearly blown up in town . . .' Etienne's rising tone said, Didn't you know? 'by a bomb.'

Luke looked surprised. Evidently he was the only one present unaware that Duke Edouard de Montfort and his son, whose country residence was barely four kilometres from the village, had narrowly survived an assassination attempt in Paris the previous day.

'I try not to listen to the news. Who did it?'

'The GP,' snorted Bajolet, as if to say he could have predicted it.

'Who says they did it?' challenged Laroche.

'What do you mean who says they did it? Revallier claimed it!'

'*Bah*!' Laroche laughed contemptuously, 'any fool can call up a news agency and say, this is Jean-Jacques Revallier, fuck you, bang!'

'Pay no attention to him,' said Charron, the schoolmaster, 'he's winding you up.'

But Bajolet's blood was up, 'Revallier claimed it, everyone knows he claimed it, you may not like the fact, Laroche, but there it is!' He flexed his moustache triumphantly.

'Duke de Montfort may represent an industry some find repellent,' contended Charron sucking his pipe, 'but to try to kill him . . .'

'It's not like Revallier to set out to kill,' Laroche insisted.

'Fighting for the environment is all well and good,' said Bajolet, relenting a little, 'but car bombs? We should never have dropped the death penalty.'

'It's not his style!' Laroche exploded, 'he'd never do such a thing.'

While Bajolet threw up his hands in despair, and others waded in deriding Laroche's obstinacy, Luke looked at the little man who'd helped him settle in to The Old Forge, helped him renovate the house and convert the goathouse. He'd seen Jean-Baptiste in all kinds of humour, but never as impassioned as this.

'Because it's on TV and in the papers it's true? You're like a bunch of glass-eyed sheep. If the TV says, *This happened*! you believe it, *That happened*! you believe it, *The President shat a gold bar this morning*! you believe it!'

Bruno Pissani banged the floor with his crutch.

'The feather!'

The group shook itself and settled down. All eyes on Luke.

'Ducks,' he declared.

'Yes!' said Etienne.

'Outer tail feather . . .'

They watched him intently, trying to read his pale blue eyes, the lines in his weathered face, the verdict forming on his lips – trying to guess which way he'd jump, with old Pissani and those who'd plumped for Pochard, or with

Bajolet's gang who were betting on Garganey. As they watched him concentrate, reducing possibilities to a mental short-list, the whole room fell still, truckers and labourers and Madame Bajolet all leaning over to look. The rules of the game stated that in the unlikely event of everyone getting it wrong, then Luke, assuming he got it right, took the money.

The silence lengthened, the master was in trouble.

Luke looked up sharply at Etienne as if to say, You sure you found this here, boy? Etienne returned his gaze unflinchingly, and with a perplexed grunt Luke returned the feather to the table. Removing his glasses, he gazed into the distance.

'Marbled Teal.'

Silence.

They looked at him in astonishment. Then uproar: *Marbled Teal*! Had Monsieur Morrel taken leave of his senses? Did he realise what he was saying? Had he uttered dodo or pterodactyl there could hardly have been greater disbelief. Félix Bajolet hammered the table for quiet.

'Monsieur Morrel,' he intoned with pained respect, 'Marbled Teal don't winter in France.'

'This pair does.'

'Impossible, monsieur, they'd never come this far north.'

Luke spread his hands, smiled regretfully and pocketed his glasses in readiness to depart.

'They're rare enough as it is,' insisted Bajolet, mastering his feelings behind a mask of politeness, 'and they never set foot in France.'

'We'll see,' said Luke rising.

'What do you mean we'll see? How can we when we can't reach them?'

'We'll get permission.'

'Permission!' scoffed Bajolet, 'when have they ever given permission?'

'Try again, this could be special.'

'We phoned last night, the Duchess said "No, no, absolutely out of the question!" They wouldn't grant us a glimpse of the last bird on earth.'

'With respect, monsieur,' said old Pissani, 'what would Marbled Teal be doing here?'

Luke shrugged as he left: 'A couple in love, you never know.'

Laroche, strangely subdued, drove Luke home.

'You coming in with me?'

Laroche looked sideways at him. 'De Montfort's estate?'

'Early this evening, after dark.'

'You crazy!' Laroche enjoyed practising his English on Luke, 'five fucking kilometres of – how you say? *fil-de-fer barbelé . . .*'

'Barbed wire,' said Luke, smiling at Laroche's *fife fooking kilometres.*

Laroche abruptly turned up the volume of the car radio: *'and only quick thinking is believed to have saved their lives, but Madame Sainte-Claire is reported to be in a critical condition . . .'* Laroche glowered at the radio as though it had personally offended him, *'The hunt has been stepped up for GP leader, Jean-Jacques Revallier, who claimed responsibility minutes after the blast, dashing at a stroke his organisation's much vaunted reputation for guerrilla operations without bloodshed.'*

Laroche switched off the radio and, rolling a cigarette from the pouch in his lap, allowed the old VW to drift on the snowy road. As Luke reached to steady the wheel, he saw great tears welling up in the little builder's eyes.

'You okay?'

'I can't believe it,' he murmured.

'What, that the GP wouldn't – '

'It's against everything they stand for.'

'Don't get carried away. Terrorists, guerrillas, whatever you want to call them, they're not angels. Maybe they got desperate.'

'They don't put bombs under cars!' Laroche rounded on him, eyes blazing.

They completed the short journey in silence. Luke got out, ducking his head back in. 'Are you coming?'

'They shoot trespassers, *mon vieux*.'

Luke closed the door; Laroche rattled away.

Isabelle was laughing and chatting on the phone when Luke went inside. Waving to her, he ran up the stairs and climbed the ladder to his loft, a vast space creaking with shelves, spread with Navajo rugs and smelling mustily of wood, books and leather. On the solid table which served as a desk stood the vintage typewriter which had hammered out a score of novels. Never a big seller in America, his science fiction series, with their vision of a perilous, tense but optimistic future, had for years enjoyed a cult following in Europe, until he'd found himself devoting more thought and energy to involved correspondence with readers than to fresh material. Now, for once, he was attempting a straight novel. With age, he was beginning to look back instead of always ahead to humanity's prospects. Set in Paris in the torrid twenties, it was the story of an American returning to look for the girl he met at the end of the Great War.

Even with family coming for lunch, he would normally have flicked through the latest rough pages of the new manuscript, but now he went straight to the bookshelves. On his knees he found the volume he was looking for, carried it to a work table and swept a space for it. Under Marbled Teal he found a set of faithful artists' impressions, prompting a nod of recognition. Hearing a car slowing on the road and turning into the yard, he rapidly scanned the text, picking out telling snatches: *Already rare in their breeding grounds in Spain, mainly concentrated around the*

Marismas of the Guadalquivir . . . and further on: *FRANCE, last official sighting, Gironde, January, 1940.*

If he was right and proved it, his would be the first official sighting in France for nearly half a century.

He was about to go down to his grandchildren when he heard their whispers on the ladder, and saw Valerie, five, peeking into the loft. Luke put away his glasses and, with that deep slow conspiratorial smile reserved for her, went quietly over and lifted her through the trap-door into his arms. They beamed at each other, rubbed noses. Then he put her down and scooped up the smaller package, Kiki, two, and exchanged a loud lip-smacking kiss with him.

To free Luke to be with the children, and to have some time to herself with Sylvia, Isabelle took over the lunch. Splitting a bottle of wine, the two women talked and laughed as they worked, while out in the yard Luke and the children tried in vain to build a snowman. Isabelle's sister Camille arrived with her husband Daniel, and everyone sat down to a noisy meal.

In the afternoon the children all helped milk the goats and check for elusive signs of imminent labour. They were examining Simone when Luke noticed the time. It was getting dark.

Collecting his maps and equipment, he excused himself and made his farewells. Sylvia walked him to the garage.

'Don't get caught, papa,' she kissed him, 'they might not share your sense of humour.'

The road was clear and deserted for a time, but soon a car appeared, its solitary cock-eyed headlight and raucous din signalling the approach of a familiar VW, coming on with the best speed it could muster. Spotting Luke's jeep, Jean-Baptiste Laroche leapt to his brakes and staggered to a sliding halt. Executing an eccentric five-point turn, he finished up alongside the jeep practising his English. 'You know where you going?'

'Not exactly,' Luke chuckled, 'but you're going to show me.'

Shaking his head. 'I don't think you should go.'

'And pass up an opportunity like this? Imagine the faces of the ornithologists in Paris.'

'You really think – '

'Yes.'

Laroche blew a sigh. '*Écoute, mon vieux*, you don't know these people. After yesterday, if they catch you . . .'

'I feel bad trespassing on someone who nearly got blown up, but that isn't going to stop me. You coming or not?'

Laroche scratched his ear and re-lit a roll up.

'I'll show you, but I won't go in.'

With Luke following, Laroche drove through the village, and at the war memorial took the straight road through the valley, where a low moon rose over the wooded slopes and raced them as far as the ancient abbey ruins. Turning right at a lonely crossroads, Laroche took a winding road through silent countryside and turned without warning into a concealed lane. He knew exactly where he was going, yet pulled up with no estate or château in sight.

Dousing engines and lights, they stepped into the heavy silence. The moon drifted in and out of cloud, a fine mist gathered in the hedges.

'Where are we?' Luke's expression said, There's nothing here.

With a furtive grin, the old builder motioned him to follow, leading off with his slightly shambling gait, the result of efforts to rebuild him after a hit-and-run accident ten years earlier.

Shouldering his equipment, Luke followed him into the wood, intrigued that he knew the way. The trees closed ranks behind them and barred the way forward, but Laroche weaved purposefully, pausing now and then to get his bearings and re-light his cigarette. The wood grew darker, their steps crisper over snow-sprinkled ground and frozen leaves.

Then the wood thinned, pale light ahead, trees petering

85

out to reveal a high fence, stout paling crowned with coils of barbed wire. It wasn't going to be easy, Luke was thinking, but Laroche carried on along the fence. Shadowed by signs declaring *PROPRIÉTÉ PRIVÉE – DÉFENSE D'ENTRER*, Luke pursued the little man until he turned dramatically and pointed . . .

An old beech tree, felled by lightning or age, had collapsed across the fence, its cloven trunk offering a trespasser a convenient leg-up, its sprawling upper limbs subduing the barbed wire and drooping almost to the ground on the far side.

Luke gazed through the fence across the open expanse of the estate.

'This is as far as I go,' said Laroche, 'you too if you have any sense.'

'We can be in and out of here in no time.'

Laroche shook his head gravely, 'You don't play games with these people.'

Luke tried to read him in the darkness.

'Where are the ducks?'

'There's a bench in an exposed screen of alders by the river. They're on the far side, I think.' While he spoke he was tying the end of a ball of twine to the fence. Without another word he turned and walked away, unravelling as he went.

Luke waited for Laroche's steps to fade, then armed with this new silence, turned to the fallen beech. A sloping route, part burl, part convenient branch, took him up into the barbed wire. The estate fanned out before him, dimly illuminated by a thin cover of snow. A distant smear was the river, a dark smudge the lonely cluster of alders Laroche had mentioned. Away on the right, rising out of a belt of woodland, lay the château, dark and brooding.

Reaching for his wire-cutters . . .

· · · 5 · · ·

His sleep was deep and untroubled that night. When the alarm shook him at 5 a. m. he stretched quickly to silence it before Isabelle could wake.

As he put on warm clothes, he recalled his recce the previous evening, how he located the ducks on the near side of the alders, not the far side as Laroche thought. He was afraid he might have scared them off, but an hour's wait was rewarded by the sight of them returning low over the river. It was too dark to be sure, but their size, flight and outline conformed with Marbled Teal.

Going downstairs, he thought of the reaction at the Ornithological Society in Paris if he managed to record them. In the kitchen he packed himself some breakfast, pulled on his oil-skin jacket and went outside. All was still and dark.

He loaded up the jeep, and by 5.30 was following his headlights across the misty plain, whining down through the village, past the shuttered bistro and into the valley, picking up speed down the long straight road, the world to himself, the sound of the engine, the whistle of the air rushing in round the open sides of the jeep, burning his cheeks and clearing his head.

The abbey ruins materialised through the mist. He throttled down at the crossroads and followed the route Laroche had taken the previous evening, until his lights picked out the turning. He took the jeep quietly into the lane, crunching through pockets of thin ice. Stepping into the silence, he gathered his equipment and, tailed by a watchful moon, entered the wood. Picking up the trail of Laroche's twine, he threaded his way through the trees.

The wood grew darker, the silence deepened, making him set down his feet carefully, each step carrying before him, announcing his presence.

You don't play games with these people . . .

The wood thinned, he advanced under his equipment with something of the old combat tension beating in his breast, the rapture of a trained soldier dropped behind enemy lines, alive to every pulse and clue of danger.

He reached the fence, the broken beech tree, and climbed carefully, pausing at the top. The estate lay bare and wide, the moon-glow off the snow lending it an eerie light. Distant folds of mist marked the river, remote towers the darkened château. Lowering his equipment into the estate, he followed heavily. Picking himself up, he set off for the river using dead ground and hollows for cover, crouching now and again to scan the approaches through binoculars.

When he reached it, his whitewashed canvas hide was still intact in its bank of scrub, nothing disturbed, no tracks in the snow but his own. Lying flat he zeroed in on the nest site, too deep in sedge to see, but landmarked by the log bench and the elbow of alders sheltering it. For a time he couldn't tell whether the ducks were at home or not. Then as the moon lit the field a tufted head popped up, then another, the ducks shaking themselves and moving off in the direction of the river. He followed them through binoculars, but it was too dark to be sure what they were. Proceeding soundlessly, they slipped through bulrushes into the river and were quickly swallowed in mist.

Hoping they wouldn't return too soon, he quietly erected an umbrella-like reflector to draw in whatever sounds they made. Then, keeping low, he left his hide and covered the forty metres to the site. The ducks had fashioned themselves a well-concealed nest and trodden a loosely defined track to the river. Working rapidly, he mounted a camera with 200mm mirror lens overlooking the duck track, to be triggered by remote control from the hide, leaving him free to operate a second camera by hand. Hard by the track he secured a microphone to record the ducks as they returned. Trailing trigger cable back to the hide, he set up the second camera with 400 mm telephoto lens in the eye-slit of the canvas. Finally he checked all his switches, unpacked his telescope and settled down to wait.

Somewhere a missel-thrush called, pre-empting the dawn chorus. The cold gnawed at him, he took a swig of brandy and picked out a buzzard circling over the distant château. Feeling the dawn creeping up, he looked at his watch, and then over his shoulder in time to see the hazy red rim of the sun pushing up through a blurred skyline. Turning around again, his attention was suddenly drawn to the river, two dark smudges forming in the mist.

He reached for his telescope, extended the draw-tubes, lifted it to his eye. Training the lens, he homed in on two small ducks winnowing close together . . . about forty centimetres in length, tall necks, long narrow bills, shaggy heads, arched nape feathers on the drake. The only remaining doubt was the colouring, and it was too misty to be sure.

As dawn crept along the river, he watched the ducks evolve, dipping and dabbling: camera shy, the drake circling his mate, stretching and jerking his head and emitting his weak passionate love song.

Here they come, parting the water towards the bank . . . hand sliding over snow, he felt for the controls of the tape recorder. Stretching a little further he triggered the microphone and camera hidden alongside the duck track.

The female was turning for home, bedding in her bill, the drake hard on her heels, and as they clambered out of the water, he saw through the telescope the pale-spotted grey-brown plumage and dark distinctive eye-shading of

Marbled Teal. His heart beat faster. What were they doing here, and in January?

Kneeling up behind his long-range camera, he flicked his switches, and was on the point of starting to take pictures when there came a glint of light from the wood ahead, the sun striking something in the trees.

To his left the ducks were pausing to preen themselves. Once more he took aim, and again a flash from the wood, nearer this time. On the wood's edge a lapwing leapt in fright and flapped away screeching.

And he saw it.

A white car, coming slowly through the wood from the direction of the château, nosing into the open about 150 metres away.

Dawn on a Sunday morning? No road in sight? Straight through a wood and advancing slowly across the meadow towards him. Amazement stilled him. In the corner of his eye he saw the ducks waddling down their track between himself and the approaching automobile. As it whispered closer, they stopped, made periscopes of their necks and craned towards the sound.

Snapping out of his paralysis, Luke sank slowly and lifted his binoculars. The car kept coming at a crawl, noiselessly flattening the sedge. The ducks remained stiff as statues, the car coming on regardless, smoothly, as though on a track beneath the snow, until a bump in the meadow briefly lifted it, sufficient to frighten the teal. Eeping in panic, they stumbled back down the track all the way to the river. For a moment they were lost in mist. Then with a splashing of wings they left the water and flew off along the river.

Luke's heart hammered the ground, the white car came nearer and nearer until, twenty metres short of the nest site, it rolled to a halt close to the sheltered bench, engine humming, exhaust fumes drifting towards Luke's hide. He pressed flatter still, peering between frozen tufts of grass, wondering could the driver see his camouflaged position, or was he sun-blinded anyway?

As the car basked in the sun, the tremor in its bonnet ceased. Then both its front doors opened and two men got out, the passenger gesticulating, and started towards Luke.

His fist closed around the telescope. *Relax, gentlemen*, he prepared to tell them, *I'm an ornithologist, not a terrorist.*

The men came as far as the bench and faced each other, their voices carrying over the river. Luke gazed in awe. They hadn't seen him, didn't know he was there. He lifted the binoculars. The passenger, a man dressed for the country, was pointing accusingly. The other man, who was shorter and leaner, wore sunglasses and a suit under his coat. Unperturbed by his accuser, the driver suddenly reached inside his coat and drew forth something which flashed in the sun.

Luke flinched, poised to witness murder, a blade driven into flesh, blood in the snow.

Instead the driver sheltered a flame and lit a cigarette, trailing wisps of smoke and the odour of Gauloises towards the hide.

The other continued to remonstrate, then abruptly turned away, lit a cigarette of his own and appeared to gaze across the river. His relief illusory, he drew angrily on his cigarette, turned and pointed accusingly again. As though to antagonise him, the driver brushed snow from the log bench, made himself comfortable and smoked leisurely, replying to questioning with a patronising calm.

Finally they seemed to arrive at a truce, their voices dropping to murmurs as they returned to the car. The white Volvo started up, whined through a reverse turn and, following its own tracks, recrossed the meadow and melted into the wood. A final glint and it was gone.

The piston in his chest began to slacken. Rising to his knees, he concentrated on the point where the car had re-entered the wood. He shook his head and smiled. He could almost have imagined it, but the tracks were clearly visible. He left his hide and began to follow them across the meadow.

When he reached the melting point in the wood, he found a broad passage cut through the trees, a route to the river.

He returned to his hide and gathered all his equipment. Before setting off he peered into the haze, wondering would the teal ever return. If not, had his automatic camera and tape recorder done their job? Retracing his steps, he laboured across the wilderness, scaled the fence and followed Laroche's twine through the wood, rewinding as he went, reflecting on the enigmatic teal and the quarrel he'd witnessed. Lost in thought, it was only when he was emerging from the wood that he heard voices.

His jeep was surrounded by a crowd of men. Luke stood stock-still in the shadow of the wood. The men were olive-skinned, North African labourers, in their Sunday best, milling around, hands in pockets, discussing the jeep, toe-poking its wheels. They weren't doing it any harm, it was simply an odd vehicle to come across in the lane, a 1940s' US Army jeep. Long ago resprayed red, now faded to earthenware, it looked more of a joke than a military option.

Luke stepped boldly into the lane. The men fell silent. One of them, an elder with thin lined face and Charlie Chaplin moustache spoke up. 'This yours, monsieur?'

Luke didn't deny it.

'American?'

'That's right.'

A chorus of nods from those who'd got it right. They seemed to be of all ages, from teens to Chaplin, who looked a weathered fifty or sixty, and was probably a lot less.

'You American, monsieur?'

Luke met the man's coal-black eyes and nodded.

Glancing about he saw it in all their eyes, his American-ness, not accusing looks, more like incomprehension. They divided their blank gazes between Luke and his assorted cameras and trappings. No one spoke.

'It's probably older than most of you,' Luke nodded at the jeep. As he did so, he caught the eye of a youth, a slender youth with shiny black hair and bold beseeching eyes. He wore a cheap suit with faded white shirt showing over a jumper. Luke would have looked away again, only something in the boy's face attracted him.

'You like it?'

The boy glanced at the jeep and blushed.

'Get in, go on!'

The youth smiled, embarrassed.

'Do you drive?'

'Yes, sir.'

Luke tossed him the keys. 'Give your friends a ride along the lane.'

One moment all was quiet, the next they were piling into the jeep, five or six young men, with the youth who reminded Luke of his own son as he used to be, struggling with the gears, grating them and looking round apologetically.

'It's okay,' said Luke, 'it's tough, it can take anything!'

Finding his confidence, the youth took the jeep gingerly down the lane, leaving Luke with a memory of teaching Serge to drive, Serge who ironically now lived with an American woman in Philadelphia.

Luke talked with Charlie Chaplin and his crowd of muted followers, polite talk, the snow, the peace and quiet, lapsing finally into silence. The jeep returned, the grinning youths alighted, helped Luke load up, and waved as he drove away.

He drove fast, wondering how much his tape machine and cameras had captured, picturing Félix Bajolet's face when he saw the evidence, and already hearing the restrained but hearty congratulations of the ornithologists of Paris.

• • • 6 • • •

PARIS, MONDAY, 7.15 A. M.: It was a dark cold murky morning, the city already groaning with traffic, cafés doing brisk business, pedestrians hurrying by behind raised collars, when Jean-Jacques Revallier turned the corner into quieter rue de Liège, formally dressed in a dark grey suit and trenchcoat, attaché case under his arm, walking slowly, one ringing step at a time, a man too early for an appointment.

His hair was a little long; he would have looked like an entrepreneur with a rebellious streak but for the wide false glasses which restored an air of conformity as he looked up at the building across the street. The de Montforts' floor was lit up behind heavy drapes and, above the de Montforts, Kasha Sharma's attic apartment spilt light from open curtains. How, he wondered, would she react to what he had in store for her? He felt a brief stab of guilt, and quickly suppressed it. This wasn't the moment for doubt.

Halfway down the street he approached the café, which wasn't quite open yet. Feeling exposed, he unfolded a copy of the suitably respectable *Le Figaro*: *REVALLIER DENIES CAR BOMB . . . Interior Minister Gaston Batisse last night poured scorn on a call to a news agency from GP leader Jean-Jacques Revallier denying all knowledge of the rue de Liège bomb. 'On Friday he claims it,' pronounced the angry minister, 'on Sunday he repents, the Greens at last are showing us their true colours.'*

Revallier smiled, then lifted his eyes and froze the street with a look, visualising it as it must have looked on Friday at about this time, quiet one moment, shaken to its foundations the next. He saw the blue Mercedes leap into the air and crash disembowelled to the cobbles, heard the whoosh of smoke and the rage of flames and then he saw Madame Sainte-Claire from apartment seven, swept off her feet and hurled to the pavement.

Now everything was nearly back to normal, a few windows still boarded up, a parking meter missing, a deep scar in the wall opposite. Just then the imposing door opened and out stepped the stooping figure of Madame Klonowska, like a crab from a stone. While she leaned on her broom and raked the street with her dark little eyes, Revallier walked on, trusting she hadn't seen him. As he reached the café, the cobbles drummed with the approach of a car, the blazing headlights of a Mercedes and its police escort.

'Bonjour, monsieur!' the sing-song greeting came from behind, the café opening.

'Bonjour, madame,' he smiled, seeing himself in her eyes, a well-heeled new customer, something between rakish and respectable. The café had caught the tail end of the bomb. He took a seat by a brand-new windowpane, just as the equally new replacement Mercedes swished to a halt across the street. Out of the car climbed Georges Bolivar – lately recovered from a spell in Montmartre Cemetery – glowering at the street.

On cue, white-haired Edouard de Montfort appeared, Maurice on his heels, armoured briefcase covered by his overcoat. Revallier stiffened with wonder and loathing, trying to get a brief clear fix on Edouard's face before Bolivar ushered father and son into the back of the car and climbed behind the wheel. A spinning of tyres on damp cobbles and the Mercedes sped away, pursued by its escort. In twenty minutes, traffic willing, Bolivar would deliver his masters to the European atomic energy headquarters south of the river.

Madame Klonowska appeared once more, looked up and down the street and, absently giving the front step a couple of flicks with her broom, withdrew, closing the door.

Revallier ordered coffee, checked his watch and opened his paper to find himself gazing at his own likeness, artists' latest impressions of himself and also of Janine, Tahar and Ricardo, drawn undoubtedly from Claude Lusardi's descriptions. Crude sketches they might be, but they were growing strikingly true-to-life, and Revallier knew it was becoming too hazardous to operate. He smiled inwardly. Having long schooled himself to thrive on danger, he still enjoyed the unequal contest.

In a prominent article carrying over from the front page Claude Lusardi's appalling captivity was documented in meticulously inaccurate detail. He'd never been denied food, no one – after Revallier's initial murderous assault – ever laid a hand on him, interrogation had been gruelling but well short of torture, and on no occasion had he overheard his captors bragging and joking about the car bomb. I should have killed him, mused Revallier.

Seven forty-five, dawn working slow changes in the street, a desultory sleet falling, the kind of morning that can turn depression into suicide, only Revallier was taut with dread and excited with anticipation as he looked up again at Kasha Sharma's windows and saw the lights still on. She worked mostly from home, but on Mondays usually took the Métro to a press office in town. According to Ricardo's research, she was born in India, lived most of her life in London, had British nationality and was well respected as a spirited, uncompromising journalist.

'Ça va, monsieur?' the *patronne* enquired.

Her extravagantly bandaged arm, certainly the result of flying glass, invited comment, but he kept his eyes in his paper and absently agreed to more coffee.

He was skimming a report headlined *BOMB VICTIM*

STILL CRITICAL, when he glanced up and saw Kasha Sharma's lights were out. She was on her way down. He found his wallet and waited, fingering the razor-sharp blade in his pocket.

The door across the street was opening. He looked and there she was, tall and composed, her high Aztec brow catching the street light, her nose twitching, testing the morning. Sombrely dressed beneath a pale dufflecoat, she wore her hair up, dragged tightly back to lay bare her full face, arched brows and earrings. Revallier gazed. Ricardo had said she was extraordinary. Opening a broken umbrella, poking it into shape, she set off . . . a few steps, no further, and stopped to look at her feet.

For a moment, as Revallier left money on the table and rose, he thought she was having second thoughts about her silver sandals. Then, watching from the doorway, he realised from the way she stood, head inclined, lost in thought, sleet catching her bare ankles, that she was gazing at the spot where Doctor Sainte-Claire must have lain, reliving events of seventy-two hours earlier. They shared the same corridor, perhaps they'd got to know each other.

She walked on. On lightly-clicking heels she reached rue d'Amsterdam, a one-way torrent of steel jostling for the city centre. From a newsstand on the corner she bought a selection of morning papers, dropping them into her deep shoulderbag. Then turning downhill she joined the flow and counterflow of humanity on its way to work, walking so leisurely she might have been strolling through a bazaar. Now and again she lingered at a shop window, drawing harmless pleasure. Then rejoined the tide, umbrella bobbing, unaware that the face on the front of some of her newspapers was closing on her from behind.

At the junction with Gare St Lazare, she waited to cross. Tucking in behind her, Revallier caught the mélange of aromas off her jet-black hair. She crossed the road and descended into sleazy rue de Budapest, a short cut to her Métro station. A few early prostitutes made a brave display. Freezing in scanty clothing, they let Kasha go by, reserving what heat they could muster for Revallier. He saw none of them, his eyes alert for what was about to happen, one hand tightening the grip on the blade in his pocket.

As Kasha reached the sombre archway at the foot of the street, a quick olive-skinned man broke from the shadows and grabbed her bag, tearing it from her shoulder. The force of his pull twisted her round, but she was strong and quick to react, and instead of letting go, kept her feet and clung to the strap. Passersby froze in horror or looked on impassively – an Asian woman, an Arab man, nothing to do with them. The mugger gave a violent wrench and Kasha fell. Surprised to find himself pulling her along the ground, he raised an arm to strike her, only for Revallier to step in and seize his wrist.

Smothered by Revallier, the assailant fought back. A brief ferocious struggle and he broke free and fled through the archway into rue St Lazare.

People came forward to lift Kasha to her feet and brush her down.

'Call *les flics*!' someone cried.

'I *am* the police,' said Revallier, taking Kasha by the arm. But before he could usher her away, a pair of legitimate *flics* came running.

Revallier, flashing false police ID said, 'Quick!' and pointed through the arch, 'a mugger in a woollen hat.'

'*Un sale raton*!' a bloody Arab, someone reminded him.

'Left down rue St Lazare,' Revallier urged.

'No, right!' another contradicted.

'You blind? he went left.'

The cops bounded away, radioing for assistance. Revallier took Kasha's arm once more. 'Give the lady room.'

The lump of human curiosity barely budged. Someone

retrieved his portfolio, another returned the broken umbrella, Kasha murmured her thanks and allowed herself to be led gently back towards rue d'Amsterdam.

'Are you hurt, madame?'

'No . . .' she was limping slightly and clearly in pain. Pausing, she turned to him. 'Where are we going, monsieur?' Her voice was airy with shock, her French fluent.

'Anywhere. I'm no cop, just don't like fuss.'

'I thought you waved a police badge?'

'They didn't look too closely,' he lied.

At the traffic lights, as they waited to cross, her dark eyes rested on him, appraising her rescuer. It was also his first close sight of her, her frank eyes, her sleet-moistened skin. She wasn't the slight and slender creature he imagined most Indian women to be. As well as tall and sturdy, she had a full, wide-boned face and bold, almost exaggerated features.

'Are *you* hurt, monsieur?' she guessed. 'You're very pale.'

'So are you, madame.'

Pain, sharper than expected, flickered in his eyes.

'What happened?' she insisted, motioning to his stiff arm, the hand thrust out of sight in his coat pocket.

'Let's get across first, madame.'

Lights changed, they crossed to the west side of rue d'Amsterdam and drew closer into the doorway of a shop not yet open. He produced his hand and opened it.

'*Wow*' she murmured in English.

The blade had gone deeper than intended, a clean split, flesh from flesh. Oozing blood, dark and rich, filled his palm. Enveloping his hand in both of hers, she closed his fist. 'You should go to hospital, monsieur.'

Shaking his head, 'I've an appointment at ten. If they'd patch me up right away it'd be okay, but I could be there all morning.'

She took a handkerchief from her pocket, and with her

99

long brown fingers gently prised open his fist, pressed the handkerchief to the wound and closed it again. 'You need stitches.'

'It'll have to wait.'

'Unwise, monsieur.'

'Was it wise clinging to your bag like that, madame?'

She gave him a slightly startled look. 'Was it wise of you, monsieur, to rush to the aid of a complete stranger?'

He smiled in acknowledgement of the mild rebuke.

'You're shivering,' he said. 'Where were you going?'

'To work. It's not important . . .' her voice tailed off, as though she might have said the wrong thing.

'Let me get you a taxi,' he said, 'you're probably in shock.'

'And you, monsieur, you're white as a sheet.'

She took his hand once more and had another look at the wound.

'Unexpectedly dyed,' he observed as she replaced her blood-soaked handkerchief, 'I hope you like red.'

'Come,' she said decidedly, 'I live a few minutes away. We'll patch you up and put you in a taxi.'

He hesitated, covering his triumph.

'It'll only take a few minutes, you can't go round like that.'

With a smile of mock surrender, he motioned her to lead the way. A moment's awkwardness as they turned to go, her battered umbrella too feeble to accommodate two divided people. He offered his arm and she linked him so lightly he could scarcely feel her as they started up rue d'Amsterdam. They didn't hurry. After a few clumsy moments they fell into step and proceeded in thoughtful silence, sleet peppering their faces beneath the umbrella, her smell faintly reaching him, perfume and oils, nothing too strong, but sufficiently intimate to distract him from his wound.

At last she said, 'What line of business are you in, monsieur?'

'I design clothes, fashions.'

He spoke flatly, without conviction. She glanced at him.

'And you?' he said quickly.

'Journalist. How's the pain?'

'What pain?' he quipped, catching her eye.

She smiled and looked quickly away.

Be careful, Jacques – he remembered Janine's warning.

They turned left into rue de Liège. 'Just down here,' she said.

Along the street, the concierge looked up from polishing the step, eyes narrowing at their approach.

'Don't mind Madame Klonowska, monsieur. She's wondering what Mademoiselle Sharma is doing on the arm of a strange man at this hour of the morning.'

'Quite right.'

'She imagines every strange man is a terrorist.'

'You never know.'

'I regularly invite worse.'

'Really?'

'Journalists.'

'God forbid.'

'Since Friday's bomb, Madame Klonowska is extremely nervous.'

'Of course!' Sudden dawning. 'It happened round here somewhere.'

'Right here.' She stopped short of the entrance.

'You mean . . . you share the same block?'

'The de Montforts have the entire floor below mine and Nathalie Sainte-Claire lives along my corridor.'

'The woman who . . . how is she doing?'

'I rang again this morning: no change, deep coma. The car was there . . .' pointing, 'double-parked. As they got in, the driver vanished. Only the duke's quick thinking saved them.'

'Quick thinking?' A note of scepticism slipped out.

It was lost on her. 'Nathalie left earlier than usual and walked – ' Her voice breaking, Kasha swallowed her words and turned away abruptly. 'Come, monsieur,' she said and, trying her best to close her umbrella, stepped into the entrance. Revallier donned his false glasses and followed.

'Back so soon, mademoiselle?' said Madame Klonowska from the door of her private *loge*, her shifting eyes taking in Kasha's soiled coat and her tears. Behind the respectful smile, she spoke to Kasha as though to a wayward teenager.

'Yes,' said Kasha breezily, 'I slipped in the street. Luckily a friend of mine was on hand to pick me up,' she added quickly, hoping to escape interrogation.

But the concierge shuffled forward, eyes fixed on Revallier, demanding introductions. Kasha obliged.

'This is Madame Klonowska, our superlative concierge, and this is Monsieur –' turning to Revallier, she blanked.

'Michel Kerlesquin,' Revallier put in helpfully, '*Bonjour madame!*' Touching Kasha's arm, he gave a little bow and ushered her on, leaving Madame Klonowska stranded.

As they crossed an inner courtyard, its air of bygone Paris strained by parked cars, Revallier tensed at the sight of two figures stepping from the shadows, muscular men wearing crisp suits and uncompromising expressions.

'Me again, messieurs!' Kasha greeted them.

They nodded cordially, but concentrated on her male companion.

'They'll want to see your papers,' said Kasha, 'these gentlemen protect certain illustrious residents.'

Casually keeping one bleeding hand in his trouser pocket, Revallier produced papers identifying him as Michel Kerlesquin, businessman from Rennes. While one mustachioed security man ran an electronic detector over Revallier's person, the other perused his papers. Counting on the protective influence of his apparent friendship with Mademoiselle Sharma, he calmly returned the bruiser's gaze. Tension thickened, the guards' masculine credentials obscurely called into question by Mademoiselle Sharma's escort.

'I'll take a look, monsieur.'

'Is that really necessary?' said Kasha.

'Purely routine, mademoiselle.'

Revallier surrendered his portfolio. The previous night it had contained photographs of the de Montforts and Kasha Sharma. Now the guard found brochures, business letters and enlarged photos of male and female models displaying the latest fashions. Briskly replacing everything, he zipped up the portfolio and returned it with a politely contemptuous 'Merci, monsieur.'

In the close proximity of the lift, Kasha apologised, 'I forgot about them.'

'No problem.'

'They're a nuisance, but harmless.'

'I'm sure,' agreed Revallier, reflecting on the reputation of the elite S37 counter-insurgency unit.

Under the stark lights of the lift, Kasha looked drained, her bold features slackened by shock.

As they stepped from the lift and proceeded along the top-floor corridor, Revallier removed his glasses and took rapid mental photographs of the lay-out, expecting it to be duplicated on the de Montforts floor below.

'Nathalie Sainte-Claire's apartment,' murmured Kasha, indicating a door halfway down the corridor. 'I wish Monsieur Revallier and his friends could see her husband haunting the hospital like a ghost.'

'You haven't any doubts that they did it?'

Throwing him a curious look. 'Have you?'

'I suppose not.'

Unlocking a door marked eight, she admitted him to a spacious apartment and turned up soft lights. A blur of city sounds and daylight filtered through lace curtains, sprawling house plants shone. Fitted with floor cushions, and cane furniture, the apartment smelled sweet and invited the visitor to spread out and relax.

'Shall I take your coat?'

He dragged his coat over his clenched fist and handed it over, catching her eye with a polite smile.

'May I use the phone?'

'Please do.'

Limping slightly, she went into the kitchen, switched on a kettle and washed her hands. He moved to the window, parted the lace curtain an inch and was disappointed not to see a familiar figure in the café across the street. More than disappointed, he began to worry.

'Coffee?' she offered.

'Please.' He went over to the fireplace. 'Do you mind?' he called, indicating his interest in a run of framed photos on the mantelpiece.

'No,' she smiled from the kitchen, 'I don't mind.'

The first frame he picked up led the viewer through a terraced garden awash with fruit and flowers, a middle-aged woman – Kasha's mother – posing in a blue sari on the rim of a fountain. Behind her, over a whitewashed wall, rose a timeless landscape of scorched rock. In another picture a tall handsome Indian in a Western suit stood holding the reins of a favourite mount. Kasha's father – Jivat Sharma – was, according to Ricardo, a celebrated racehorse owner. The most intimate pictures were unframed shots of a woman with young children – Kasha's elder sister? – and snaps of Kasha playing with the children.

A smell of coffee reached him, he checked his watch and returned to the window. Looking out, he was relieved to see Tahar sitting in the window of the café. Rid of his overalls and cap, he sat in a smart suit and overcoat reading a paper, for all the world a dapper North African Businessman.

Revallier went over to the phone and dialled a number. While it rang he made a mental note of Kasha's number. When his call was answered, he asked for a

Monsieur Hafid and carried the phone to the window in time to see Tahar leave his seat and move out of sight to take the call.

'Monsieur Hafid? Michel Kerlesquin, I'm going to be a little late.'

Tahar replied with coded reassurances.

'All's well,' continued Revallier, as Kasha came through with the coffee, 'except that we may be in a little deeper than intended . . . about ten-thirty then?' he concluded and hung up, wiping blood from the receiver.

'Help yourself,' invited Kasha, setting down the tray on the coffee table. 'First aid coming up!' she said, leaving the room.

'You're limping,' he called after her.

'I'll live!'

He sat down on the couch, and through the glass tabletop met his own face staring at him from a stack of newspapers. THE BOMBER! shrieked the paper as he turned it over.

'*Quelle pagaille!*' a cheerful cry from the bathroom, 'Look at the state of me!'

He heard her lock the door. If she was going to clean herself up, he might just have time . . .

Rising quickly, he went to the door of a wide sloping room fitted out with computer, filing cabinets and wall-charts, a white room greened by plants, an office belonging to someone busy and ordered, pens in mugs and papers in neat piles. A precautionary glance over his shoulder and he drifted in and picked up the latest printed sheets from the word-processor: *EUROPE TO LINK UP WITH BRITAIN AT LAST!* – the title of a piece in English about the proposed undersea rail tunnel between England and France. On the walls were charts and diagrams of the tunnel, and satellite photographs of Kent and the Pas-de-Calais.

SHOTGUN WEDDING UNDER THE SEA ran another

headline, Kasha apparently curious as to the rush to complete the improbable union. Revallier, even with his limited English, nodded approvingly, though there were things he could tell her about the motives behind the tunnel.

In the bathroom Kasha washed her grazed knee and calf, and caught herself in the mirror, not the composed woman and professional journalist she had presented to Michel Kerlesquin, but the Kasha she inhabited, frequently tormented by self-doubt, and still traumatised by Bhopal. Paris was to have been a relatively tranquil posting, a chance to regain her nerve. She never imagined a bomb going off in the street, maiming, maybe killing her friend, or that three days later she'd be attacked by a mugger.

She threw cold water over her face and calmed herself down. It didn't help that she felt strangely unsettled by Monsieur Kerlesquin. It wasn't to do with his looks; it was more that she felt he wasn't quite what he seemed, something false in his smoothness.

Unpinning her hair, she let it fall and began to brush it out with a shaking hand.

He was on his feet looking at the tapestry on the far wall when she emerged. The change brought about by her fallen hair was so marked that for a moment he gazed at her as though she were someone else.

'It's beautiful,' he said.

As she set down ointments, bandages and a bowl of hot water on the coffee table, she followed his gaze to the tapestry, with its panorama of jewelled elephants, turbaned peasants, queenly women bearing pitchers, a majestic castle clinging to a scorched hillside, tigers lazing in jungles, an eagle wheeling in a powder-blue sky.

'Is India really that exotic?'

'That's just Rajasthan.'

'Such variety in one region?'

'A region the size of France, and it's only the Western eye that sees it as exotic.'

Another mild rebuke, he observed, sitting down and pouring two coffees.

'The way people refer to India,' she smiled lightly, 'you'd think it was some charming backwater, its people hothouse curiosities . . .' Sitting on the arm of the couch, she reached for his wounded hand, 'People forget that India was civilised when the French and English were still peasants, and the United States undreamed of . . .'

As she unfastened his cufflink and folded back his bloody sleeve, her hair fell forward, thick and black and shiny, and touched his face, smelling sweet and dark. Whatever mysterious fragrance she used, its compelling odour would stay with her every lover for ever.

'Rajasthan,' he said idly, 'wasn't that where the Indian government exploded its first atomic bomb?'

'Yes.'

'Developed from its civil atomic energy programme.'

'That's right.'

'You don't approve?'

'Approve?' Her voice rang with disdain; she opened his fist, removed the blood-soaked handkerchief and examined the wound.

'Everyone else was testing bombs,' he said.

From Kasha a contemptuous grunt, 'I suppose that makes it all right?'

'What's more,' he seemed to recall, 'wasn't public opinion behind Mrs Gandhi's decision?'

'Oh yes,' she agreed, 'a nation's ego boosted by a grotesque display of nuclear prowess. How come you know so much about Indian nuclear politics?'

Shrugging innocently, he reached left-handed to take a sip of coffee.

'You know what coded message they sent Mrs Gandhi

from the test site confirming the successful explosion?' The telephone interrupted her, she reached but let it ring, '– *The Buddha smiles!*' she quoted with a flash of anger, 'To anyone acquainted with the teachings of Gautama Buddha . . .'

She lifted the receiver, '*Salut, Alain!*' her expression responding to someone she felt at ease with. 'I *did* leave for work, but got jumped in the street, someone tried to snatch my bag . . . ah no, a bruise or two . . . no, I still have it . . . nothing of any importance, you know my bag! I just don't like being pushed – or rather pulled around . . .' She was laughing now, and he fell to wondering about the man she was talking to. 'What happened to him? I beat him up of course . . .'

Her eyes met Revallier's, 'Actually, a very kind gentleman came to my rescue . . .'

He held her gaze, his clear steady eyes fathoming hers.

' . . . and received a knife wound in the hand for his pains. I'm putting a bandage on him since he refuses to go to hospital. No,' she laughed, 'not even I could bully him. Yes of course I'm all right, see you this evening, *adieu*.'

Replacing the receiver, she resumed her perch on the arm of the couch and took his hand again, cradling it like a wounded bird: a fine hand, she noted, slim and strong, running in black hairs and defaced by a number of small but marked scars. Gently prising open his fist, she began to clean the wound.

'Apart from fashions, does my saviour have any other occupation?'

'I follow – I nearly said *exotic* women – '

'Just as well for you you didn't!'

'in case they get mugged.'

'In the hope of being invited back for coffee?'

'Exactly,' Their eyes met and veered away. 'And you, mademoiselle, apart from journalist?'

'Nurse!'

'Of course.'

His hands were also tanned, she observed, not with the sunburst of a package holiday, but the slow bronzing of the outdoors. A fashion designer with scarred and weathered hands?

As she cleansed the wound she felt tremors of his pain, but he sat quietly, trustingly, his hand in hers. She glanced at him. Mid- to late-thirties? No wedding ring. A man who knew himself, knew his power. One who travelled lightly, weapons out of sight.

He watched the concentration on her damson lips, the going-to-work lipstick faded, leaving them moist and defenceless. He thought of Janine, how rough she would have been – and frequently was – compared with this refined creature. He experienced a tingling in the scalp from being handled so tenderly. Blood oozed, she dabbed carefully around the edges of the cut, her hair falling forward down one side, leaving her neck unprotected. She dipped blood-soaked cotton wool into the stained water making it darker still.

'She even turns water into wine.'

With a reproving glance, she laid his hand palm up on her knee and began cutting plaster into sutures. Then she drew the edges of his flesh together and set down the strips of plaster like railway sleepers. She had broad strong hands, and her fingers worked quickly and carefully, as though fluting a delicate piece of pottery. She bound the hand flimsily in muslin, then securely with bandage, tying it under the wrist and leaving the fingers free.

'*Voilà!*' she said. Returning his hand, she caught him frowning at his restricted movement.

'Are you questioning my handiwork, monsieur?'

'Too thick, too tight.'

'You should have asked Madame Klonowska to do it.'

He laughed. 'Shall we take a look at your leg now?'

'Thank you, no. More coffee . . . before you go?'

The hint was blunt. He let it pass.

'You're not easily panicked, are you?' he said. 'Most women freeze when attacked.'

'You mean men don't?'

Submitting to yet another rebuke, he went on, 'You reacted instantly. You've had lessons?'

A begrudging smile. 'My father made it a condition, a long time ago, of my living and working in Europe.'

'Self defence?' sounding merely curious. 'What kind?'

'I don't remember exactly.'

'Were you good?'

'You trying to gauge your chances?'

A short laugh. 'What else!' He rose to leave.

'Shall I call a taxi?'

'Thanks, but I'll stroll to the corner.'

As he led the way into the hall, she had a feeling he was working up to the time-honoured question. His style, she predicted, would be direct: what are you doing tomorrow night? For the sake of her pride she wanted him to ask, but she'd thank him warmly and decline. She had her hands full, what with Nathalie and Robert, the dinner party to cancel, the Channel Tunnel report which she had to finish before the signing ceremony in Lille on Monday next.

She helped him on with his coat, the bandage sticking in the sleeve.

'Told you it was too thick, mademoiselle!'

'Next time, monsieur, I'll let you bleed to death.'

There was an easiness between them – and an edge. She opened the door and stood back to let him out. In the corridor he turned.

Here it comes, she thought.

'Thank you, monsieur,' she got in first, 'I won't forget what you did. I hope you won't forget to visit a hospital and have your hand seen to properly.'

'Thank *you*, mademoiselle,' he replied, '*Au revoir*!'

He was gone.

LA VIEILLE FORGE: While wet snow was falling, trying
to gather in the stony yard, Luke was in the warm
goathouse unable to concentrate properly on milking his
thirteen horned and hardy *Alpines Chamoisées*, mischievous, engaging copper-coloured creatures with a black
stripe down their backs. What made today different from
other mornings was the cassette in his back pocket.
Isabelle was still in bed when he got back the previous day
from the de Montfort's estate. He wanted to wake her, tell
her about the teal, the men in the Volvo, the Arab boy who
reminded him of Serge. But at 8.30 on a Sunday morning
he would have got an oblivious response, if not a stream of
colourful abuse.

Then friends arrived from Paris for lunch and stayed for
dinner and didn't leave until nearly midnight. He could
have told them all about the tape, could have played it and
almost did, but something stopped him. After they'd gone,
hooting and waving into the night, he turned to Isabelle,
'Honey, you know those ducks I recorded this morning . . .'

'Later, please *chéri*,' she said, all afluster, hurrying to her
desk to try to sort herself out for the morning. So he hadn't
told her what he was carrying in his pocket, and still
wasn't sure what it meant.

Resisting the urge to hurry the work, he settled into a
rhythm, taking them as they came to him, each goat
knowing her place in the herd's order, from surly Madeleine to prankish South Dakota, who liked to chew his

collar and nibble his ear while he milked her, and looked amazed when he told her to cut it out. When he finished, he left the churn by the side of the road and stored the rest in the fridge.

'*Merde*, I'm going to be late!' cried Isabelle stamping down the stairs and gathering up her files and books and running round for her cigarettes, keys, receipts for the dry cleaners.

'Take it easy, you wouldn't want to shock your students by arriving on time.'

She wore scuffed boots and blue leggings and a turquoise jacket which clashed horribly with her dyed red hair, gathered in a pile on top of her head. She stood out conspicuously in the English and American Literature Department at the Sorbonne and had once been taken for a cleaner. At the door she grabbed her coat from him, apologised for leaving him with all last night's dinner things and blew him a kiss.

'*Chérie*?' he detained her.

'What!'

'Get this developed for me, will you, at the university?' He held up a roll of film between thumb and forefinger, 'It's important,' and dropped it into a little self-sealing plastic bag which he handed over.

'The ducks? Don't worry.' She took the bag in her teeth and ran.

He watched her get into the car and drive away. Then he went inside for his tape recorder, and, closing the front door behind him, crossed the yard and the road and took the track leading up to the derelict cottage, a graceless stone dwelling he was renovating for Sylvia and the kids, for friends and visiting relatives from the States.

Turning the rusty key, he pushed his way in.

The walls were stripped to bare stone, dust and wood-shavings carpeted the floor, gutted windows shone taut with polythene. The spacious ground floor was really two former rooms knocked almost into one. The dividing wall, stone by rugged stone, was all but gone, and without it the upper floor stood suspended in time, held up by three horizontal planks wedged beneath the ceiling by three pairs of extended poles. A maddened bull, loosed indoors, could have brought the house down in a trice. A mighty girder lay diagonally across the floor, waiting to be hoisted into place.

Sweeping out the grate, he built a fire and put a match to it. He lit the stove and filled the kettle. Finally he swept a space for the tape machine and sat down heavily on a cement sack against a wall; his back gave him trouble which he couldn't shake off as he used to. He rewound the tape, waited for it to click off and was about to press PLAY when he heard the drone and kick of a familiar car.

Seeing the smoke from the chimney, Jean-Baptiste Laroche came rattling up the track. The engine petered out like a dying propeller, a car door slammed, light steps bounded up, and in burst Laroche swinging a plucked chicken, 'Salut! Ca boume? You're alive! Nobody caught you – here!' lobbing the bird, fresh from his own flock, into Luke's arms. 'And this!' flourishing an unlabelled wine bottle.

'Ah!' said Luke, guessing it was his favourite Calvados, 'what's all this about?'

'Affection, esteem . . . shame.'

'Shame?' Luke hauling himself painfully to his feet.

'Abandoning you to the devil the other night.'

Luke went over and gave the little man a back-slap. But when he tried to take the bottle, Laroche wagged a finger at him, 'How do I know there's anything to celebrate?'

Luke pointed dramatically at the tape machine.

Incredulous, 'You mean . . .?'

Luke grinned.

'Merde! You recorded them? When?'

'Dawn yesterday. And took pictures.' With a wave he

invited his friend to take a seat on the girder. Laroche chuckled, sat down and began to roll a cigarette with calloused tobacco-stained fingers.

'In the next days,' he stumbled merrily into English, 'we put up this *poutre* – how you say?'

'Girder.'

'Before the fucking house fall on your head.' He sealed a perfect cigarette with his tongue, caught it between his lips and lit up with a sigh. He looked tired, his eyes bloodshot, his hollow cheeks charred with several days' growth of beard. Luke returned to his sack, pressed PLAY and upped the volume.

The spools turned . . . and suddenly, distantly, the bare walls rang with the shrill love song of the drake . . . the little noises of the ducks leaving the water and waddling along their track to the nest. Then a hush, a long silence while the ducks stood rooted, riveted by the sight or sound of the car . . . cries of panic taking them back to the river . . . finally the sound of their flight into the haze . . .

For a moment longer Luke sat still, eyes shut, a deep smile of satisfaction on his face. But when he opened his eyes, anticipating Laroche's delight, he saw he was barely listening, lost in his own thoughts.

The sound of car doors opening and shutting roused Laroche with a jolt, a startled look as he thought a car had pulled up outside. Then soft footfalls were heard approaching, and Laroche realised it was all coming from the tape.

'*Vous avez fait du joli, une sacrée chienlit!*' – you've made a bloody mess of things.

'*How many times must I tell you, it was Crozier's operation.*'

'*Crozier laughs in my face. Il s'en fout!*' – he doesn't give a damn.

'What the fuck was that?' asked Laroche.

Luke pressed PAUSE, 'Two men in a car disturbed me while I was recording.'

114

'I thought you weren't caught?'

'They didn't see me.'

Releasing PAUSE: *'Damn the fog! why didn't it occur to him?'*

'For what time should he have arranged it? Does everyone leave home early when it's foggy?'

'He assured us –' the breeze snatches away the first man's words and disrupts the other man's reply.

' . . . in dreams, monsieur. In the real world innocents are caught in the crossfire. It's a tragedy . . . for those concerned,' his voice fades as he is heard to stroll away, *'but in the wider scheme of things –'*

'Quelle putasserie!' – what a fuck-up, *'it couldn't be worse.'*

'On the contrary, it couldn't be better, particularly if she dies.'

Luke paused the tape, met Laroche's eye, both men looking at each other to confirm what they had just heard: *surtout si elle meurt* – especially if she dies.

'You didn't want to know,' murmured Laroche.

'Didn't want to know what?'

'Putain . . .' Laroche whispered in awe, getting to his feet in a dreamy kind of slow motion, taking a few dazed steps in the direction of the door. He stopped, staring.

'What did they look like?'

Luke had the scene in his memory, the river, the car, the surrounding woods and the tips of the château. But when he tried to recall the men, they were like indistinct figures seen through a steamed-up window.

'The one who's upset was quite tall, thirty-five, forty, wore wellingtons and a good overcoat.'

'Recognise him from anywhere?'

'Should I have?'

'What about the other man?'

'About the same age, shorter, leaner, not unlike you!' Laroche didn't smile. 'Also wore a heavy overcoat and drove the car . . . a white Volvo.'

Laroche frowned, a white Volvo. 'Registration?'

'Never occurred to me.'

'Never occurred to you?' Laroche whirled round, 'two men involved in some dark conspiracy and quarrelling over it at dawn on a Sunday morning and you don't think of taking down the number?'

This was an entirely new Laroche, and Luke didn't much care for him. 'I couldn't make out what they were saying,' he replied evenly, 'I had no reason to think there might be anything . . .' he faltered. 'If the pictures come out, you never know. Who's Crozier?'

Laroche looked away, as though unwilling to reply.

'They mentioned a Crozier,' persisted Luke, 'as if to suggest he was behind . . . whatever it is we're hearing.'

Laroche turned and fixed him with a long sad look, like a friend delivering bad news. Still fixed on Luke he re-lit his neglected cigarette and took a deep pull.

'Raymond Crozier is Head of the DST, the internal secret service.'

'Counter-espionage? anti-terrorism, right?'

'*Bravo.*'

They regarded each other in silence, then, 'Is there more?' asked Laroche, nodding at the machine. Luke released the button, and the quarrel resumed, the first man, the passenger, calling the driver *un salaud sans merci* – a heartless bastard.

'*May I remind you, monsieur,*' the driver caring nothing for the other man's opinion of him, '*that we all agreed to the plan.*'

'*Batisse,*' the other cuts in, '*what's he say?*'

'*Batisse?*' the driver laughs, '*he isn't losing any sleep.*'

Luke glanced at Laroche and abruptly stopped the tape. 'Who's Batisse?'

Laroche looked at him, his face a blank, as though reluctant to tell him.

'Well?' pressed Luke, 'anyone we know?'

'The name means nothing to you?' marvelled Laroche, his amusement a smile of sympathy for one who still doesn't realise the deep shit he's in.

'Somebody in the government?' thought Luke.

'*Batisse? Peuh!*' swotting the name like a fly, 'Gaston Batisse, a nobody, nothing to worry about . . .' a studied pause, 'only Minister of the Interior.'

'Aha!' Luke smiled gratefully, and dropped his eyes out of the firing line of Laroche's gaze.

At length Luke reached and released the tape.

'*What about Lusardi?*' continues the passenger.

'*Nothing would disturb Lusardi's sleep.*'

Luke reached with a wry smile and stopped the tape again. 'OK, who's Lusardi? Another nobody?'

'Precisely, another nobody, a flea in a Paris *pissoir*, Claude Lusardi, Minister for Security.'

'Ah yes,' Luke vaguely recalled, 'the fellow the GP let go the other day.'

'*Isn't he worried that it could get out?*'

'*It's only you who's panicking.*'

'*There mustn't be any more devices.*'

'*That's not for you to decide, but I doubt any more will be necessary. Relax, monsieur, you're still in shock.*'

'*Nonsense, I'm fine. We'd better get back, it's getting late.*'

'*Ne vous tracassez-pas,*' says the driver, louder now as he leaves the bench, '*our little package has already more than achieved its purpose.*'

Luke stared at the tape machine, but whatever else they say is lost as the two men are heard moving away. Doors clunk open and close, an engine starts, a car reverses and moves off, receding into silence. Luke pressed REWIND, abruptly stopped the tape and pressed PLAY: '*Don't worry, our little package has already more than achieved its purpose.*'

He rose heavily and, avoiding Laroche's eye, stepped over the girder and fed the fire from a stack of rotten boards. Gazing into the flames seizing and devouring the wood, he said,

'How is the woman, the bomb victim?'

'It's ironic, *n'est-ce pas*? off to work in the intensive care unit of one hospital and ending up in coma in the intensive care unit of another.'

'What are her chances?'

'How would I know?'

Luke stared unseeing into the fire. 'And you think this tape says they didn't do it, the GP?'

From Laroche a sardonic laugh, 'What do you think?'

'And that there might be other devices.'

'No longer needed, now that Friday's "little package" has so brilliantly achieved its purpose.'

'Which was?'

'What do you think!'

'There could be some other explanation.'

'Such as?'

Luke bowed his head.

'This calls for a drink!' cried Laroche, conjuring two tumblers from his coat, 'a celebration.'

Luke turned, 'What are we celebrating?'

'The teal, or the truth about the bomb – take your pick!' Uncapping the bottle he poured two reckless measures and handed one to Luke. They clashed glasses and took swigs of golden Calvados which tasted like nectar to Laroche and ashes to Luke. Laroche held his gaze.

'I want the tape.'

Luke regarded him evenly. 'What?'

'You'll have it back, I promise.'

'What the hell do you want with it?'

'I have friends . . .'

'*Friends*?'

'who will make good use of it. I'll make a copy and return it to you . . . in time for a glorious unveiling at the Ornithological Society – tonight! isn't it?'

'What friends?'

'Don't worry about that.'

'What do you mean, don't worry about that? You want me to hand over my tape to some nameless, faceless friends of yours?'

'Trust me, I know what I'm doing.'

Luke laughed, a snort of disbelief. 'There's only one thing I can decently do – '

'Don't even think of it.'

'What else can I do? You stumble on a crime, you – '

'The police are dangerous, *mon vieux*.'

'This is explosive stuff – '

'Yes! and we don't want to waste it.'

'That's why I have to report it.'

'You stumble on a crime and automatically run to the police,' pacing now, waving his arms, 'without even considering options? That's not intelligent, that's not the Monsieur Morrel I thought I knew. Keep away from the police, they're unpredictable, they may not believe you. Worse – ' he stopped, pointed at Luke, 'they *may* believe you!'

'I'll be solving a crime for them, for God's sake.'

'What makes you think they want to solve it?'

'What makes me think *you* want to? You seem to have other ideas.'

'I want those bastards exposed,' said Laroche with venom, 'whoever they are.'

The two men stared at each other. Then breathing heavily, wheezing from the depths of his chest, Laroche turned and gazed lovingly at the tape recorder.

'Do you realise what you have there, *mon ami* . . .?'

Laroche's reverential tone hovered in the musty air. Luke experienced a wave of nausea. That tape which so excited Laroche filled him with horror. What was Isabelle going to say?

He focused sternly on Laroche. 'Those friends of yours – '

'Don't!'

'Don't what?'

'Don't ask. It's best for you, for them, believe me.' He smiled and shook his head, 'What a stroke of fortune, young Etienne spotting the ducks, you identifying the feather, climbing in to prove it and taping and maybe photographing the men behind Friday's bomb. Do you realise you have them by the balls?' he cried, coming forward with clenched fist and squeezing any number of imaginary testicles under Luke's nose.

'But they are many and powerful,' warned Laroche looking up into Luke's eyes, 'and you are one innocent foreigner living with your wife in vulnerable isolation in the country. Let me take the worry from your shoulders, allow me to do you this service. Forget about the tape and for pity's sake don't breathe a word of it to anyone, not even your good wife, or you never know . . .' composing a comradely smile, 'you could end up swimming in the French President's soup!'

Luke had to smile at the image.

'The tape,' whispered Laroche, 'you will let me have it?'

Avoiding Laroche's beseeching eyes, Luke inhaled deeply and tried to think. He wanted to say yes, if only to be rid of the damned tape, but his reason and gut feelings held him back. He studied his boots, and seemed to see them from a great distance, alien footwear, no longer the innocent old friends of yesterday. Everything, he had a terrible feeling, would be different from now on.

'I need to piss, I'll be right back.'

He needed to breathe, to think. He went out the back door and stood in the ragged white wilderness of the garden. If that woman died, he reflected, he could well have the men who did it. Then he cursed himself: what the hell were you trying to prove when you scaled that fence?

Lost in thought, he didn't hear Laroche leaving the cottage by the front. He lingered, breathing the cold air, watching a lone crow wheeling against the sky, until he was roused from reverie by the caterwauling of Laroche's VW trying to start – making a run for it?

Luke bolted, galloping through the garden and round the house in time to hear the engine finally catch, and to see Laroche urging the jalopy in fits and starts through a demented three-point-turn in his rush to escape. Charging across the ice to cut him off, Luke watched the VW complete its manoeuvre and lurch forward like a cow from a kick, Laroche bulging over the wheel, waving him out of the way, veering left and right as Luke moved to block him, throwing his bulk into Laroche's path.

A screech of bad brakes, the car beating itself to a staggered standstill, Luke's hands slapping the bonnet, the rust-eaten bumper jarring his shins.

Laroche sprang from the car tapping his head: *'T'es frappé, non*! – crazy!' he bawled, 'you can have your copy tonight if you want!'

Drawing himself up, Luke held out his hand, 'Give!'

'It doesn't belong to you any more, it belongs to France!'

'It belongs to me!' He clicked his fingers, 'Give!'

White with rage, Laroche reached inside his coat.

Luke caught the cassette.

Laroche barged back inside his car. He slammed the door, and one valiant hinge finally expired, dropping the door like a guillotine on the ice. Without waiting for it to fall over, he plunged into gear. From the gaping car as it lurched away he bellowed, 'Don't say I didn't warn you!'

· · · 8 · · ·

24 RUE DES MAQUIGNONS, 3 P.M.: In a room on the VIP floor of Madame Mazarin's select establishment, France's most favoured detective was paying his weekly visit.

Philippe Goujon preferred this quiet hour, when the place rustled with serenity, when every footstep was carefully considered and even the loudest of men spoke in whispers to their escorts. Furthermore, there was less chance of bumping into someone he knew and having to make small talk.

Not that he knew many people in Paris. He was a stranger here, an outsider, his accommodation a hotel suite within walking distance of his office. He had risen from humble Corsican origins to become a celebrated detective in Marseille, where he had been based for twelve years and lived contentedly as a bachelor. When the top police in Paris, under intense pressure from their political bosses, failed to defeat The Guardians of the Planet, Philippe Goujon was summoned to the capital, granted exceptional powers and given twelve months to crush the GP and hunt down its leaders. The twelve months were nearly up, and though the job was incomplete no one was complaining, since six out of seven brigades had been eradicated and Goujon had assured his masters that he was confident of catching Revallier and company. But Goujon was a fastidious, orderly man, and he preferred to take the twelve-month assignment literally. It was now 13 January, his appointment had begun on 23 January the previous year and, while it was unlikely that anyone else had noticed, he was conscious that ten days remained in which to accomplish a perfect conclusion.

This afternoon he was being received as usual by Jocelyne, whom Madame Mazarin considered her most refined girl, and who now sat with the commissaire on the low burgundy divan reading to him from Jean-Louis Pesquin's stylish biography of Napoleon Bonaparte, with Handel's 'Royal Fireworks' Suite playing softly in the background. As always, she had her hair in ringlets and wore a hired frock, purportedly of the Napoleonic period, white silk gloves to the elbow and a cameo mounted on a black velvet band around her neck. Much as he would have liked to have arrived in the narrow street by clip-clopping carriage and to be decked out in resplendent Napoleonic uniform, he was resigned to modern dress, impeccably turned out, as always, in an elegant close-fitting, powder-grey suit, soft silvery-grey Italian shoes and a whiff of expensive cologne, quite simply the best-dressed detective in France.

A tough, undersized scrawny youth, Philippe had needed all his blind remorseless determination to be accepted into the police force in his home town of Ajaccio, also the birthplace of Napoleon Bonaparte. Even then he worshipped the great man, and still now, in his forties, he was stirred to hear Jocelyne reading about Bonaparte's rise to power. In the low-lit room with the pretty young woman reading to him, all it would have needed to complete the illusion was the sound of horses in the street.

Instead he heard the grind of modern traffic, and from time to time he got up – gesturing to Jocelyne to keep going – and looked out between the curtains to scan the street. He was only too aware of what had befallen Claude Lusardi, and even when he returned to the divan he kept his gun close at hand. As Jocelyne read, he sipped his wine and smoked dreamily, turning now and again to dwell on Jocelyne's pale pretty face and to glance at her rising bosom. After a time he thanked her, and she put down the book, removed her slippers and spread herself tastefully on the divan.

He put out his cigarette, unlaced his shoes and stretched himself out beside her. She waited, and after a moment he touched her bare arm. She bore his tentative attentions patiently. He was not a pretty man, with his beakish nose and taciturn mouth, but he possessed a certain icy charm. As he traced a tremulous finger over the peach-smooth eminence of her bosom and along the tight tantalising cleft between, he asked, 'Have you been to the opera or the theatre this week?'

'No, monsieur, I'm afraid I couldn't find the time.'

'Pity. The new production of *Tartuffe* is wonderful, *exceptionnelle*.'

His hand made the halting journey down the ripples of her dress to her covered knee. Jocelyne reached slowly and carefully to draw up her dress and uncover a plethora of underskirts; she lifted the veils of silk and lace one at a time to reveal her long girlish legs trapped by bloomers.

Now the difficult bit: every move had to be performed by both parties with the utmost seemliness. The slightest indelicate movement on the part of the young lady, the merest hint of haste or immodesty in the bending of a knee or the baring of a breast and he was lost, his member shrivelling like a snail into its shell. Intuitively understanding his requirements, Jocelyne played the chaste bride, surrendering with a look of mild wonder and submitting to pleasure of the most restrained and civilised kind, culminating in a soft simulated climax, accompanied by a little shortness of breath and blushes to match his own. They they would adjust their clothing, enjoy the remainder of the wine, interspersed with pleasantries, and he would bend his lips to her hand and leave.

But this afternoon he got no further than pressing his lips to the warm outer regions of Jocelyne's thighs when the phone went – his portable phone bleeping on the coffee table. He offered his apologies and, with Handel still playing softly, rose and carried the phone to the window and took the call looking out. Knowing not to disturb him at this number, the caller apologised profusely; knowing his man Bloque wouldn't call unless it was urgent, Goujon accepted the apology and listened.

'What's his name?' said Goujon at length.

'A Monsieur Luke Morrel, an American writer, living here since the war.'

'*Bon d'accord*, hang on to him, I may be a bit late.'

He hung up, lowered the aerial and came back to the divan, where Jocelyne lay exactly as he had left her, awaiting his pleasure. But as he stood there looking at her, the Handel tape clicked off and someone roared with laughter in a neighbouring room. He knew it was no good, the illusion was shattered.

Luke waited to be seen. He sat in a high-ceilinged hall oblivious to the comings and goings of police officers and detectives. Now and then he got up and wandered out into the courtyard for air.

Steer clear of the police. Laroche's words returned to him – *they may not believe you* – worse, *they may believe you.*

He'd had a late lunch with Isabelle. He thought she'd forget or be too busy, but she arrived with two identical sets of photographs which had come out well given that they were taken by the automatic camera. There were eighteen prints of identifiable Marbled Teal. The rest of the film was mostly wasted on frosted sedge and glimpses of river. But then into the remaining frames came a dramatic intrusion, the front portion of a white car drawing up in the sun, its number plate just decipherable. In the final frames a blurred figure was seen emerging from the passenger side.

'Who could they be?' asked Isabelle, intrigued.

'Who knows?' he'd laughed, 'drug dealers, gun runners.'
She'd looked startled.

'*Je rigole* – I'm kidding!' Why worry her? She'd be anxious enough if the time came for him to testify.

'You're sure they were discussing a crime?'

'Laroche thinks so.'

'*C'est incroyable.*'

'I'm just going to hand the stuff over. It's not my problem.'

But who to hand it to? He'd been making calls all

morning, explaining what evidence he had and that he wanted an appointment with the Chief of Police. He could almost hear their sniggers: what class of idiot have we got here? But he persisted and eventually he was told to present himself at Police Judiciaire headquarters at 36 quai des Orfèvres.

To get there he drove the jeep through the Latin Quarter and over Pont Neuf to Île de la Cité, one of two great islands on the river, their seventeenth- and eighteenth-century turrets and towers rising majestically into a leaden sky. Turning down quai des Orfèvres, he'd grabbed a parking space close to the semi-palatial buildings accommodating the city's celebrated detectives.

They interviewed him, took a statement, but when they demanded to see his evidence, he shook his head, 'It's for the Chief of Police, or the man investigating Friday's bomb,' he glanced at a scrap of paper in his hand, 'Commissaire Principal Philippe Goujon.'

He was told to wait. Two hours later he was still waiting. Dressed, on Isabelle's insistence, in his old suit and tie, he was sitting forward lost in thought, when a man walked crisply up to him.

'Monsieur Morrel?'

Luke looked up and met the impassive gaze of a tall, slim, balding cop in a smart three-piece suit.

'Commissaire Christian Bloque,' he introduced himself flatly, 'would you care to follow me?'

Without waiting for a reply, the lanky detective walked off. Luke gathered his coat and went after him.

'Where are we going, commissaire?' he questioned him in the lift.

'You wanted to see Commissaire Goujon, monsieur?' replied the detective tartly, implicitly doubting whether Luke was worthy of the honour.

From the lift they proceeded in silence down a wide busy corridor which became quieter the further they went.

Doors of polished wood gave into offices hushed with restrained activity. Towards the end of the corridor they came to an unmarked door. Luke was ushered in, the door closed behind him.

He stood just inside a high-ceilinged office hung with oil paintings of Revolutionary Paris and furnished with the kind of solid antique pieces he would have expected to find in a stately château. By contrast, one corner was devoted to a bank of up-to-the-minute computers.

The room was still but for a graceful human hand behind an imposing desk, carrying a cigarette thoughtfully to and from a pair of thin lips. Commissaire Goujon was sitting half-turned to a window, profiled by the lights of the river, absorbed in a typed report. Luke was still wondering whether the detective was aware of his presence when he turned his head slowly and looked directly at him.

'The bird-watcher, I presume.' Impeccable English, spiced with French and a pinch of mockery.

From Luke a nod of assent.

The detective stubbed out his cigarette and resumed in French. 'You possess, I understand, evidence relating to the rue de Liège bomb. Show me, monsieur.'

Luke approached and handed over an envelope. Motioning him to a seat, Commissaire Goujon opened the envelope and spread the photos like a deck of cards across the bare desk top.

Luke lowered himself into a museum-piece chair, crossed his legs and observed the detective. About forty or forty-five, he was precisely dressed in a pale elegant suit. His hands and face were naturally tanned, a man of warmer climes. His features were sharp and dominated by a crag of a nose, a character actor's face, ugly but compelling. Drawing leisurely on a fresh cigarette, he picked up certain prints in turn for closer inspection.

'So this is Duke de Montfort's estate?' he observed without looking up.

'That's right.'

'Freely accessible?'

'No.'

'You had permission?'

'No.'

You were in effect trespassing.'

'Correct.'

'You make a habit of this, monsieur?'

'We sought permission – '

'We?'

'A small bird-watching group in my village, a few kilometres from the estate . . . and were refused.'

'Evidently you weren't inhibited.'

'You're looking at the first Marbled Teal to be recorded in France since 1940.'

Flicking over another photo, the detective raised a smile, 'They're not what you'd call spectacular specimens.'

'All that's rare isn't beautiful.'

'That concerns you, monsieur?'

'What, that they're rare?'

'The fate of the animal kingdom preoccupies you?'

'Some species of plant or animal become extinct just about every day. It's quite a thought, wouldn't you say?'

Commissaire Goujon crushed out his cigarette in an overloaded ashtray, sat back in his chair and said, 'The whole story, monsieur, from the beginning.'

It began, as Luke recalled, with Laroche interrupting him and Isabelle having sex in the goathouse, but he took the mystery feather as his starting point, how he was called on to identify it in the village bistro . . . his two incursions into the estate . . . the appearance of two men in a Volvo, and finally his encounter with the estate's Arab workforce around his jeep in the lane. Some protective instinct made him take care not to mention Laroche's role.

An impassive Commissaire Goujon listened in silence. When Luke finished, the detective remained silent for some moments more before putting out his hand.

'The tape, monsieur.'

Reaching into his pocket, Luke left his seat and placed in Commissaire Goujon's open palm the original cassette. Goujon extracted the tape from its case and crossed to the console of computers and tape decks. He slotted it home. He moved leisurely, not a man to be hurried, one whose forceful presence compensated for his lack of stature. Returning to his desk, he lit another cigarette and swivelled halfway to the window. Lifting his slim shoes on to the window sill, he sat back and closed his eyes as though anticipating a symphony.

The tape murmured, introducing the Marbled Teal into the room, their love calls rippling along dainty cornices, their cries of panic taking Luke back to yesterday's dawn and the astonishing moment when the automobile crept out of the wood towards him.

After the teal had fled, there followed a few moments of meadow hush, then the slamming of car doors, a quarrel filling the room, one man righteous and aggressive, the other slow and sly.

'You've made a bloody mess of things.'

'How often must I tell you, it was Crozier's operation.'

'Crozier laughs in my face, he couldn't care less . . . Damn the fog! Why didn't it occur to him?'

'For what time should he have arranged it? Does everyone leave home early when it's foggy?'

'He assured us – '

' . . . in dreams, monsieur. In the real world innocents are caught in the crossfire. It's a tragedy for those concerned, but in the wider scheme of things – '

'What a fuck-up, it couldn't be worse.'

'On the contrary, it couldn't be better, especially if she dies.'

'You heartless bastard . . .'

Luke sat forward, waiting for the detective's response to what sounded like a post-mortem of a crime which he was investigating. But as the wrangle ebbed and flowed, the commissaire continued to listen expressionlessly.

Hearing it again, Luke felt a tremor of horror, but as he watched Commissaire Goujon he saw no sign of disquiet . . . until the Interior Minister's name came up. He thought that he then detected a flicker of interest, if only in the way the detective paused in his rhythmic smoking, the name Batisse arresting his fingers for an instant, lips poised to receive the burning cigarette. Goujon resumed without further interruption, even at the mention of Secret Service Chief Lusardi. Even the chilling concluding line from the driver: 'Don't worry, our little package has already more than achieved its purpose,' drew no reaction.

The quarrel abated, fading altogether as the two men turned away and reboarded the car. The Volvo started up, revved softly and whispered away over snow.

Meadow stillness filled the room.

Commissaire Goujon gazed out over the river. The silence was oppressive, so was the heat. Luke loosened his tie and waited. At last Goujon swivelled round and broke the spell.

'Do you realise what you've brought me?'

'I think so.'

Doubtful, 'Do you?' Rising with an air of purpose, the detective crossed to the console to retrieve the tape. Cassette in hand, juggling it as if it were hot, he came and sat on the edge of the desk facing his visitor.

'Your tape and prints are worthless . . .' Lighting up a fresh cigarette, he inhaled sharply.

'What do you mean, worthless?'

'Until tests prove otherwise.'

'You mean I could have faked them?'

'These people,' pointing over Luke's head, 'are capable of anything.'

Looking around, Luke met the steely gazes of Jean-Jacques Revallier and Janine Vallence in life-sized artists' impressions on the back wall.

'You think I'm in cahoots with that lot?'

'Perhaps. These people are ingenious,' said Goujon, 'they make a bad mistake with the rue de Liège bomb, try to cover their tracks, switch the blame. They're full of tricks, monsieur.'

Luke held the detective's gaze. Did he really believe this was trickery, or was he asserting the principle that nothing can be taken for granted?

'I don't suppose,' ventured Luke, 'this is the most welcome information you've ever received?'

'No,' conceded Goujon, leaning back to contemplate the ceiling.

'Is that Volvo traceable?' pressed Luke.

'Of course.'

'Who do you think these men could be, on Duke de Montfort's estate at dawn on a Sunday morning?'

From Goujon a fastidious shrug. 'At this point I wouldn't care to guess. However . . .' easing himself off the edge of the desk, he withdrew to the window and looked out across the darkening city, 'I suggest you speak to no one about this, because . . .' a slow thoughtful drag on his cigarette, 'the minute I begin enquiries, your life expectancy declines.'

'What are you saying?'

'You don't strike me as a naïve man, Monsieur Morrel,' still addressing the city lights, 'you haven't brought me some titillating snapshots of a minister's indiscretions with a callgirl. If you and your gadgets are telling the truth, I shall be obliged to move against some of the most powerful men in France. In the meantime . . .' flourishing the cassette, he turned to face Luke, 'if word escapes about the existence of these,' he waved at the photographs, 'if the people under investigation discover that all that stands between them and arrest, disgrace and a long gaol term is an American bird-watcher living in some remote village with his wife . . . need I say more, monsieur?'

'You mean these gentlemen could knock me off?'

Goujon left the prospect ominously in the air.

'What about protection?'

'I would see to that.'

Stretching out his long legs and joining hands behind his head, Luke contemplated his situation. After a time, he sat forward and caught the detective's eye, 'If you don't mind my asking, commissaire . . .' feeling for a way of putting it, 'are you in a position to move against these kind of people?'

Returning to his seat behind his desk, Goujon fixed his dark Latin eyes on his questioner.

'Do you know who I am?'

Luke rode his gaze.

'Rest assured, monsieur,' said Goujon softly, 'no one in France is beyond my reach.'

'Ministers, secret service chiefs?'

Stubbing out his cigarette, Goujon's voice fell to a conspiratorial whisper. 'No one.'

Luke gave a satisfied grunt and sat for a time stroking his lush moustache.

'*Bon!*' said Goujon decisively, 'I will have your tape and prints analysed this afternoon, and all being well, you and I will re-enact your little trespass in the morning.'

Luke raised an eyebrow.

'I will collect you before dawn, monsieur, to make the replay as accurate as possible.'

'What, climb into the estate?'

Goujon smiled, 'I'm sure that won't be necessary. I expect the de Montforts will be co-operative. Tell me, monsieur, how many people know about your escapade?'

The question took Luke unawares. 'Only . . .' he faltered, 'my wife.'

'I trust we can rely on her not to . . .'

'Naturally.'

'And between . . .' consulting a typed statement, '8.30 a. m. yesterday and now, you've shared your experience with no one else?'

'That's right.'

'You saw no one, received no visitors?'

'My builder dropped by.'

'And you weren't tempted.'

'Sure I was tempted, he's another bird-watcher.'

'His name?'

'Laroche,' Luke still anxious to protect his friend, 'Jean-Baptiste Laroche. He's attending a meeting with me tonight. I only played him the duck bit.'

'Only the ducks?'

Luke nodded, surprised at how easily the lies were coming.

'What meeting tonight?'

'Ornithological Society at the Sorbonne. We meet four times a year.'

'So you've quite a coup to unveil tonight?'

'That's right.'

'You will naturally want to play the tape, show your pictures.'

'Yes.'

'So you've made copies.'

Luke wavered under Goujon's gaze. 'No.' Another measured lie. 'I was hoping to hang on to the originals for tonight.'

'Come now, monsieur . . .' lighting a fresh cigarette and inhaling deeply, 'let's be serious. You bring me evidence to sink a government and want to waltz off with it. I'll make copies of the prints and a copy of the duck tape, you will have them in the morning. For tonight . . .' a regretful smile, 'you'll have to make do with a sensational announcement . . . so!' Rising, he advanced around the

133

desk, indicating with an open hand that the audience was over.

'I will be at your house at six tomorrow morning.'

At the door Goujon turned and extended a hand. Towering over him, Luke shook his hand. Goujon's grip matched his resolute gaze.

'You're a lone witness, monsieur. Keep a low profile.'

Goujon withdrew and Luke found himself in the long high corridor with the faded red carpet. From an adjacent door Commissaire Bloque appeared, motioning Luke to accompany him. Luke expected Bloque to say something civil on the way to the lift, but the detective kept his silence all the way to the ground floor, where he dismissed Luke with a faintly scornful, *'Au revoir, monsieur.'*

Out on the waterfront Luke paused to breathe cold air into his lungs. Leaning against the parapet, he looked across at the lights strung along the river. It was the hour when offices close and Left Bank bars fill with people meeting for a drink on their way home or before the theatre. Through the rumble of traffic he heard music and laughter coming over the water, and his heart beat against the parapet.

He turned up his collar and walked along the quay to where his jeep was parked. Vaulting aboard like a young man, he started the engine, switched on lights and radio and wheeled into the traffic. Since it never occurred to him to give his mirrors more than a cursory glance, he didn't notice the unmarked car sliding out of its space and into his wake.

He crossed the first bridge over to the Left Bank and began searching for somewhere to park. He was reversing into a tight space when the news headlines reported the intensified hunt for Les Gardiens de la Planète, and mentioned in the same breath their victim, Doctor Nathalie Sainte-Claire, four days into her coma. He switched off the transistor and returned it to its hiding place under the seat. She was still alive, that was all he needed to know.

A few minutes later he paused on the fringes of Place de la Sorbonne, a small cobbled square at the feet of the university which always pleased him, an urban clearing holding back thunderous boulevard St Michel. Crossing the square, he entered one of the teeming cafés where students gathered after lectures to drink beer and – he liked to think – to argue philosophy, poetry and revolution.

Pressing into the heat of the café, he called home. Isabelle wasn't back yet. He left an apologetic message on the answering machine saying the meeting with the police had gone well, and reminding her he wouldn't be back to milk the goats. Then he squeezed into a corner of the bar, ordered a drink, took off his coat and scarf and looked out for Laroche. Laroche would still be mad at him, but he was ready for that.

Time passed, 7.20. He ordered another whisky, exchanged smiles with a pretty student and watched the time . . . 7.35, the meeting started at eight.

He made another call, this time to Laroche, hoping he wouldn't answer. If he was still at home, he wasn't coming.

'*Qui?*' Gruff and gravelly, Laroche the worse for drink or surfacing from sleep.

'I'm in town, where are you? you know I don't like drinking alone.' Pause. Smoker's cough from Laroche. 'You still angry?'

Laroche disentangling the phone to roll a cigarette.

'Angry? Why should I be angry? If you're stupid enough to go to the police, that's your look-out. Don't tell me you've been?'

'Yes, I – '

'You went!'

'The man I spoke to was convinced. They're going to investigate.'

Groans. 'Who? Who did you see?'

'I forget his name.' Another intuitive lie. 'But he was a topnotch – '

Laroche cursed under his breath. It wasn't a good line, people were pressed in around Luke and he tried to shield himself over the phone, barking in whispers, 'The guy's not the kind to be intimidated, he's prepared to move against *anyone* . . .' lowering his voice further, 'starting with the de Montforts first thing tomorrow . . .'

'Don't tell me you handed over the tape and film?'

'I had to.'

Silence from Laroche.

'Look, I'm sorry – '

'You've no copies?' Laroche broke in wearily.

'Sure I have.'

'What?' Laroche couldn't hear.

'Isabelle had the film processed and copies made of the prints, and I've made a copy of the tape.'

'Anything of the car or the men?'

'Yes.'

'Good, good.'

'I'll tell you when you arrive.'

The line went quiet. Luke wondered whether to tell him that Isabelle had the copies. There was nothing to show at the meeting.

'You are coming?'

'What? now?'

'Get the train, I'll drive you home.'

'In that go-cart of yours!' Mock derision, the old Laroche.

'Get down here, I'm going to need you.'

'Fuck you!' lapsing happily into English, 'I see you in the meeting, *ciao*!'

Click.

· · · 9 · · ·

At the end of a long afternoon in a stuffy office, Kasha came home surprised by the state of her nerves, edgy on the Métro and in the narrow passage where the mugger had attacked her that morning, shakily turning into rue de Liège and approaching the spot where Friday's bomb had thrown up memories of Belfast and Beirut, only this time taking for its victim someone she knew and loved.

Back in the tranquillity of her apartment she saw the time, 7.15, and began to hurry. Preparing to take a shower, she played back the messages on her answering machine: voices of concerned friends, some wondering was Wednesday's dinner party still on . . . an appeal from her editor in London to call . . . a few terse words from Robert returning her call . . . and then a voice which arrested her half-naked in the bathroom doorway: *'Mademoiselle Sharma . . . Michel Kerlesquin, forgive the liberty of calling, but is there any chance of seeing you before I leave Paris . . . say for dinner tomorrow night? Au revoir.'*

Alain arrived early to collect her to visit Nathalie; he had no sense of time. She opened the door dripping. He was standing with a bouquet of flowers and a sympathetic expression which said, Can you believe it!

'I'm fine,' she said firmly, taking the flowers, 'they make 'em tough where I come from!'

She found him a glass of wine and he was happy to wait while she got ready. He was double-parked in the street below, his doctor's sign enabling him to do so with relish and impunity all over Paris.

She'd spent much of the weekend with him, walking in the Bois de Boulogne and mooching in cafés, talking out her feelings, her horror and disbelief at the memory of Nathalie on the pavement. She had cried quietly in his arms last night. He was touched and concerned by her refusal or inability to grow a foreign correspondent's extra layer of skin.

Alain sat on the couch and picked up a newspaper. Jean-Jacques Revallier stared back at him under a headline *LES GARDIENS DE LA PLANÈTE DENY RESPONSI-BILITY* . . . a claim scorned by Interior Minister Gaston Batisse: '*The Greens have shown us their true colours . . .*'

Alain pushed the paper away and carried his wine over to the stereo unit to put on some jazz. He'd been so glad to welcome her home from India in the new year, she'd been in such good form, gay and full of life and affectionate. Now this.

He'd met Kasha in Bhopal. As an eye specialist, he'd been rushed out with the relief organisation, Médecins Sans Frontières. A hell-hole of a place to meet a woman! he told friends, the leaking chemical plant turning homes into gas chambers and littering the streets with the sandals of the fleeing. India's Hiroshima, they called it, thousands dying mercifully quickly, thousands more still dying today. Appalling memories were branded in Alain's mind, sightless retching mothers comforting sightless retching babies, children groping for their parents, and all over the town the unutterable stench of death. And then there was Kasha, calmly leading droves of blinded women to his makeshift clinic.

On the drive to the hospital she was very quiet.

'Kasha,' he said, as they crossed the river and headed into the fifteenth *arrondissement*, 'I think a holiday would do you good, do us both good,' he added tentatively.

She said nothing.

'How about a week in Tunisia or Morocco, somewhere

magical like the Atlas Mountains . . . ' he tailed off, stopping himself saying too much.

'That would be lovely,' she said vaguely, resting a hand on his shoulder. She was dreading seeing Robert almost as much as seeing Nathalie.

The modern St Michel Hospital was tucked away in the back streets on the south-west side of the city. Since she wasn't closely related, there was doubt about Kasha seeing the patient. In the intensive-care unit they kitted her out from head to toe in clear blue plastic. A tired young doctor showed her to the room, 'Try and speak to her. I'm nearby if you need me.'

The room was hushed, a body lay on a massive mobile bed, scrunched up on her back as though trying to be born again, a flimsy sheet concealing her worst injuries. Kasha sat down. Nathalie's face was bruised and swollen beneath the bandages. Patches of hair had been shaved to permit treatment of scalp wounds. Kasha was encouraged that Nathalie had already received plastic surgery, it seemed optimistic. But despite the electrodes taped to her skull and the wires and tubes sprouting from her like tentacles, she showed no sign of being alive.

Was this really Nathalie? Wouldn't she wake now like she did that night before Christmas, when Kasha found her curled up on the couch, waking with the bleary where-am-I look of a child. *I tried to wait up for you*, she'd said. *I didn't want you to return to an empty apartment*. The tears rushed Kasha's eyes and spilled over. She remembered how Nathalie had warmed her hands and thawed her feet between her thighs, and how it had felt almost unbearably intimate. How she longed for that closeness now, not this deathly, voiceless body. If only she would wake, how easy it would be to take Nathalie in her arms and believe in everything.

Kasha held her limp hand, leaned close to her ear and whispered and sang to her for half an hour. Now and then she moved her chair to the other side and tried the other ear. Nurses and technicians came and went checking machinery and taking readings. She held her head in her hands.

Afraid that Nathalie might throw up images of Bhopal and trigger a panic attack, Kasha was relieved to emerge resolutely calm. Stripped of her protective clothing, she found the doctor in his cluttered office, smoking a cigarette, jaded, cheerful.

'Well?' he looked up.

She smiled and shook her head. He put down his work and offered her a seat.

'How's her husband?' she asked.

His frown told her he was taking it badly.

'Is there no sign of recovery?'

The doctor hesitated, took a puff, and shook his head.

'She's going to die, isn't she?'

'Ah!' wagging his finger reproachfully. 'She's still there, she's tough.'

'What are her chances?'

Shrugging. 'Half of all patients in coma more than six hours die irrespective of treatment. She's been hanging in there . . .' consulting his watch, 'for eighty-five hours.'

Kasha gently, 'That doesn't tell me much.'

'All right. There's a slim chance she'll give death the slip. If she does, there's a real possibility of brain damage, altered personality. In short, paralysed, entirely dependent, a complete stranger to her husband.'

Remembering Nathalie and Robert fooling on the couch – *Arrête, Robert!* fighting him off, *molesting your wife in public, it's disgusting*! Kasha had to make a huge effort to stop herself crying in front of the doctor. He got up to show her out. She found Alain in a secluded room sitting with various members of Nathalie's and Robert's families.

Robert was standing hands in pockets looking out of a window. Kasha had phoned him daily at his parents, inviting him to come out at least for coffee with her and Alain. His responses were clipped and controlled. She felt his resentment, but of what? That she, a journalist more accustomed to danger, wasn't in a coma instead of Nathalie? She felt hurt by his coldness. Why could they not share their pain?

She took a deep breath and entered. Heads turned, looked blankly at her. Alain smiled, raising a questioning eyebrow. She shook her head sadly. Robert remained at the window, his back to her. She looked around, smiling weakly at people, until she met the gaze of Madame Gravier, Nathalie's mother, deathly pale herself, but still a lovely bright-eyed woman maintaining a gracious armchair patience. Kasha moved instinctively towards her, only to find herself lost for words. Madame Gravier reached for Kasha's hand and held it.

'She was terribly fond of you. She spoke of you often.'

Was terribly fond, Kasha winced. If her mother's given up hope, then . . . Kasha bit her lip, helplessly returning Madame Gravier's failing smile. 'I'm deeply fond of her, madame.'

Robert turned. Kasha hadn't seen him since the morning of the bomb, reeling in the street in his pyjamas. She started towards him, and thought for a moment that he would drop his defences and come to her. But he merely raised a hand in greeting, composed an all-purpose smile – gratitude, sorrow, resentment – and turned to the window again.

In the car, Alain announced he was taking her to dinner. She squeezed his arm and declined. She had work to finish and wanted an early night.

'You've been through hell the last few days, you need to switch off.'

'I will, but not tonight.'

Undeterred. 'Tomorrow then?'

'Monsieur Kerlesquin, the man who – '

'Your *saviour*.'

'left a message asking me to have dinner with him.'

A moment's reflection, 'Good. You'll accept of course?'

'I don't know.'

Eleven p. m., the sky clear and starry over the city, the air bitterly cold, catching in the back of the mouth as Luke strolled the side streets to find his jeep, hands deep in pockets, collar up, beret snug on his head, chuckling to himself, recalling the looks on their faces, the wave of incredulity which greeted his modest announcement.

Marbled Teal in mid-winter in Ile de France, just south of Paris? Wishful thinking, monsieur; even downright deceit, according to some of the looks aimed at him. With Commissaire Goujon retaining the originals, and Isabelle the copies, he had nothing tangible to offer. A smile and a shrug and he explained he was waiting for the film to be processed and the tape copied. He kept expecting Laroche to breeze in and cry: but it's true, oh ye of little faith! But he never showed his face, and Luke was closely questioned. Some, like Giles Blémant, who ran an antiquarian bookshop round the corner, and Doctor Rose Simon, who was an ardent fan of Luke's novels, treated him like a reliable witness. Others frankly cross-examined him, and he wondered had he answered too casually, concluding with a humorous shrug which said, It's okay, I don't expect you to believe me. But they couldn't quite resist him. Unwilling to wait three months for the next scheduled meeting, they voted for one the following Monday, when Monsieur Morrel promised to unveil his evidence.

Giles took him for a celebratory drink, then they parted and Luke came away in good spirits, keeping the *other business* at the back of his mind. He'd told the meeting about his trespass, but never mentioned the Volvo, the two conspirators. Now as he turned into the quiet back street where the jeep was parked, their shadows pressed in on him, he heard their voices, the angry pleading passenger: *Quelle putasserie, it couldn't be worse!* And the nonchalant jeering reply: *On the contrary, it couldn't be better, especially if she dies.*

If she dies.

As he approached the jeep, thinking about Laroche not turning up, thinking about the woman lying somewhere in a coma and of trying to find a news bulletin on the long drive home, he scarcely heard soft footfalls behind him, or the murmur of an anonymous van. Even someone's light touch on his shoulder didn't surprise him, some down-and-out bumming the price of a coffee . . .

A hollow voice. 'This way, monsieur.'

'*Pardon?*' Hands seized him. 'Hey!'

He tried to turn, but they were quick and uncompromising. Before he could focus, his arms were lashed behind his back. With two or three more seconds to react he could have unleashed his considerable strength, but these were professionals and they had him like a bear in a straitjacket, propelling him between parked cars and bundling him into the rear of a van. Even as he hit the floor the van was in motion, accelerating away before the doors slammed shut, hammering a relentless tattoo on slippery roads as it raced across the city.

No one spoke. They sat on him and he lay cheek-to-vibrating-floor, riding his terror like a steer on the slaughterhouse concrete waiting for the bullet. The strain on his pinioned arms and twisted neck grew with every jolt of the van. He was afraid they'd snap.

'We're going to free your arms,' someone said.

Even as they unshackled him, someone was lifting his head and slipping some soft material over his eyes: a blindfold. The van slowed for a moment, they lifted him off the floor and manoeuvred him firmly to a seat. Straightbacked and outwardly composed, he swallowed hard and gazed into oblivion. What were they going to do to him? What threats, deals, physical abuse? They can't do this, I'm a goddam American citizen!

Be careful, my friend – Laroche's words blew back in his face – *you don't finish up in the President's soup.*

The van rattled along a cobbled street, came suddenly to a decisive halt and reverse-turned into the echoing interior of a building. Back doors flew open, hands reclaimed him, urged him to his feet, pressed his head down and man-handled him into the void. He landed on solid ground, somewhere reeking of grease and engine oil, and they steered him around one wide obstacle after another and up a narrow flight of stairs into a warm thinly carpeted space . . . and sat him on a chair.

He sat in darkness. People could be heard moving quietly, purposefully. Fingers went to the back of his head, removing the blindfold, one hand resting on his shoulder, communicating authority.

His eyes smarted, adjusting to a long room, a simply furnished living room lit only by an open fire at the far end. A figure in dark glasses, silhouetted by the glow of the fire, was leaning on a mantelpiece smoking a cigarette and looking down the room at him. As he gazed, he realised the glow came from the simulated coals of an electric fire, and that the figure was a woman.

What was it Laroche had said? *I have friends who could make good use of your tape.*

The hand remained on his shoulder, comradely and threatening. He had a feeling he knew who it belonged to.

A door opened to his right, a young man in dark glasses appeared from a lighted kitchen, quickly back-heeling the door to shut out the light. Bearing a tray, he came towards Luke, toe-pushed an upturned crate closer to Luke's chair and set down the tray. Luke looked from the young man to the tray – a pot of steaming coffee and a bottle . . .

Of Calvados! the bastard! he thought, bloody Laroche!

'Please help yourself, monsieur,' said Ricardo in fluent

English with a trace of Italian. Luke looked up at the deceptively tender youth and fixed him with an incredulous gaze.

'Here!' said Ricardo, pouring a coffee.

Just then a movement to his right caught Luke's attention: another man in dark glasses, older and darker skinned, probably North African, a still, watchful presence.

Removing his restraining hand, the man at Luke's shoulder went to take up a position by the farthest window. Parting the curtain an inch, he lowered his glasses a fraction to look out at the street, and at the approach roads on the far side a glimmer of still water. In spite of the dim light, Luke knew, with a rush of nerves, who this man was.

It was the woman who spoke first. Stubbing out her cigarette, she eased herself off the far wall and came down the room towards Luke like someone at a party vaguely in search of distraction. As Luke watched, he saw that her hairstyle and colour didn't fit her photographs, and though she also failed to live up to the ruthless image they portrayed, he knew exactly who she was too. Hands in the pockets of a short leather jacket, she pulled up a chair and sat down.

'You must excuse the way we brought you here, monsieur.'

He looked at her blankly.

'We do occasionally lift people from the streets, but not ordinary citizens. We apologise.' Her quick smile said, What more can I say!

He remained speechless, and still shaking.

'We would have offered to meet you . . .'

'Why didn't you?'

'So you could betray us?'

'Why would I do that?'

'You preferred to take your tape and pictures to the police.'

145

With a sigh, Luke poured himself a Calvados, 'I stumbled on a crime . . .' tossed half of it back and smacked his lips, 'I took the only sensible course.'

'You took the soft option, monsieur.'

'The soft option would have been to throw the tape and pictures in the river.'

Janine Vallence frowned, glanced at Revallier.

'You expect me to hand over stuff like that to people like you?'

'And why not?'

'Because,' picking his words, 'I don't know you.'

'You know the police?'

'I know their job is to investigate crime, and they've assured me they're going to do just that.'

'Is that right?'

Luke stiffened at the implied ridicule, but her face and tone carried none. She merely watched him, undoing him with her gaze.

'You know why you're here, monsieur?'

'I was in the wrong place at the wrong time.'

Mock surprise, a twinge of disappointment, 'No, monsieur, you were in the right place at precisely the right time . . .' They stared at each other, 'if not for our sake . . . if not even for the sake of the truth . . . then at least for Doctor Sainte-Claire. You have heard of . . .?'

'Yes,' he said firmly, discomfited by the ease with which she had wrong-footed him. He would have expected different tactics. Now he drained his glass and looked about him. The long-haired youth had gone, the watchful African hadn't budged and Revallier leaned against the wall between the windows, arms folded, ominously silent.

'All those illustrious gentlemen,' resumed Janine, 'would have got away with that bungled bombing, deceiving the world and branding us monsters . . . but for you.'

Luke met her eye, the certainty of her gaze. Spreading his hands in resignation. 'What can I do? It's out of my hands now.'

Janine cocked an eyebrow.

'Commissaire Goujon has the tape and film,' said Luke reasonably.

'And you have the copies,' she replied reasonably.

Luke, almost imperceptibly, flinched. Laroche again!

'You've no right to hold me,' he said quietly. No one replied, his words drifted. 'I'm free to walk out, what you going to do, shoot me?'

Janine smiled, shrugged. Revallier moved suddenly off the wall and stood facing Luke and Luke involuntarily shuddered. The famed GP leader wasn't hugely broad or tall, but there was an air of certainty about him, of understated power, a light in those eyes like the light in Vallence's eyes, only more intense, a sensual sinewy man, intractable, ruthless and absolutely convinced that he was right and the world was wrong.

'You're free to go,' he said. Luke returned his cold, forgiving stare. 'You know we didn't plant that car bomb, your evidence could prove who did and why. Everyone everywhere believes we did it, only you know the truth. A lonely knowledge, n'est-ce pas? But if you can live with it, then go back to your goats and your novels. You could always *write* the other version, the one where the hero does the right thing.'

'What would you do with the copies?'

'Clear our name.'

'And get your revenge?'

Revallier smiled, the patience of one who doesn't expect another to understand. 'To expose them, monsieur, to point the spotlight at our politicians and police chiefs.'

'Goujon will have to do that for you.'

From Revallier a scornful smile.

'Given their resources,' said Luke, 'I think the police might just do a better job than you.'

'You're a writer of *fiction*, monsieur, a goatherd, a bird-watcher and, like most of your compatriots, politically naïve. It is not in the interests of the police to undermine the state they represent.'

Luke smiled, 'Maybe you people just can't stand the idea that the police, not you, might nail those bastards.'

Revallier breathed a heavy sigh, a crack in his composure.

'If you people didn't mess with explosives, they couldn't have set you up.' Luke held Revallier's gaze, who said nothing, only continued looking at him with a mixture of amusement and contempt.

'You people think yourselves so pure, a cut above the rest, but you're still terrorists. So far you've been lucky with your bombs – '

'Meticulous, monsieur,' Janine cut in.

'but your brigades have shot down police officers – '

'In shoot-outs when attacked, what should they have done, caught the bullets in their teeth?'

'and innocents have been caught in your crossfire. Okay, you've a good record so far with explosives, but one of these days . . .' Luke shook his head, witnessing some appalling outrage.

Revallier spoke low.

'We don't have time to fuck around with you, monsieur. We don't care what you think of us, your opinions are irrelevant; all that matters is that you happen to possess vital material which will clear us and put the blame where it belongs. Any fool can go to the police. Think about it.'

'I'll think about it if the police fail to act. In the meantime,' drawing himself up and pointing a warning finger, 'get off my back!'

'Get him out of here.'

He was led blindfolded down the stairs and into the rear

of a van which he recognised by its odour of rust and rags. Sitting rigid, he swayed with the vehicle, down muted back streets in the hands of a driver well acquainted with the dark side of the city.

He could have torn off his blindfold, but despite his anger he chose to keep it on. They didn't want him capable of giving away the location of their hideout, but he'd already picked up clues – the smell of machine oil below stairs, a glimpse of still water – and he was trying hard to forget them.

They drove in silence, the night wheeling by to the rumble of cobbles, the dry rattle of the van, the melancholic squealing of a distant siren. At one point the driver upped the volume on the radio for Luke's benefit, a middle-of-the-night bulletin from St Michel Hospital: Nathalie Sainte-Claire still in coma, no change. The bulletin passed through Luke's mind without trace. It was Goujon's problem now.

After a time, his blindfold was removed by hands so light and gentle they might have belonged to a tender girl, instead of the young fanatic he discovered beside him. Adjusting his eyes, he saw the African at the wheel, and, observing the way he drove, watching his mirrors for danger, Luke felt some of his anger subside, the sheer nerve of this beleagured band.

The van pulled up. Luke squinted past the driver's shoulder and recognised the street in the shadow of the Sorbonne.

'Should you feel moved to contact us,' said Tahar without looking round, 'make your way to the church of Notre-Dame-des-Près, boulevard du Montparnasse, and tell the priest you want to speak to the highest authority, because your need is great.'

Luke absorbed this curious directive and climbed out into the road.

'Don't be too hard on us, sir,' said Ricardo in English, 'we mean well!'

149

Luke returned his smile. 'Don't try to scare me next time, there was no need for this, we could have had Calvados at my place.'

'Too dangerous for us. They're watching you already.'

'What do you mean?'

'When you arrived at the Sorbonne, you were being tailed. See you soon again, I hope.'

'I doubt it.'

As he walked to his jeep he passed Tahar leaning out of his window. 'Monsieur?'

'What?' said Luke.

'Repeat what I just told you, about the church in Montparnasse, and you'd be putting lives in danger.'

'Don't worry, I doubt I'll even remember it.'

Reaching the jeep, he juggled his keys and turned around. The driver was checking his mirrors before setting off, the young man was climbing in beside him. Luke walked back.

'I'm not unsympathetic to your ideals, I probably share them, I just don't like the way you do it, kidnappings, blowing up installations, it's madness. There are other ways, they may be slower, less dramatic, but they don't . . .' groping for words which wouldn't sound hollow, 'fly in the face of decency and risk innocent lives.'

Tahar smiled patiently.

'It's our belief we've reached the point where all other preoccupations in the world, capitalism-communism, left-right, black-white, Jew-Arab, even the appalling suffering of millions of poor and starving, have been eclipsed by the issue of whether or not we will soon have a world at all. There's little time left and it's too late for polite persuasion. Good night, monsieur.'

The van pulled away. Luke watched it go, then looked at the quiet street, the parked cars and darkened buildings. It was after midnight, he had a long drive to reach home, and Commissaire Goujon was picking him up at six.

Luke woke suddenly, his head deceptively clear, a new day waiting to be filled with his manuscript, the cottage, the goats. Then he looked at the luminous time, 5.50, and remembered. Some inner clock had woken him.

He put on a light and got up. He'd slept in the loft so as not to disturb Isabelle. It was so dark and still, it was hard to believe the commissaire was going to show up at this hour. There would probably be time to milk the herd. But as he washed his face and put on his old suit again and a fresh shirt, he stopped and listened. The sound grew. He opened a skylight in the roof, felt a rush of cold air and peered out.

A helicopter, lights winking, was hovering beyond the cottage, searchlight probing the ground. All was white across the darkness, the yard, the roofs, the road and surrounding fields, covered by a light fall of overnight snow.

On his way down, he looked in on Isabelle to leave a note, hoping the din had woken her so he could tell her everything, relieved to find her asleep so he wouldn't have to. She must have been up in the night, checking that he was in. Her light was on, a tisane by her bed, and the latest Marguerite Duras novel had fallen from her hand on to the floor. As he picked it up he imagined trying to tell her about last night's encounter with Les Gardiens de la Planète, and could picture her face, wondering whether her old man was finally going off the rails.

As soon as Luke stepped into the yard he saw a figure

crossing the road. Outlined against the snow and pin-pointed by the glow of his cigarette, the detective strolled into the yard.

'Good morning, Mr Morrel!' Commissaire Goujon's heavily accented English wasn't as good as he imagined.

'Good morning to you, sir.'

The lightweight detective's handshake was vicelike, but tucked behind his collar and diminished by the sprawling yard he seemed less daunting than the immaculate detective Luke had met in town.

'You found me all right.'

'Ah yes! Personally I don't comprehend the technology, but I understand these machines can find a grub in a dunghill. What I don't understand is how a civilised man like you, monsieur, chooses to live in this wilderness.'

Luke laughed, 'Me civilised? you kidding! I was going to heat up some coffee, if you'd care – '

'*Non merci, monsieur*, we've no time to waste.'

The change in tone surprised Luke, the charm switched off like a light.

'We'll take the same route you took on Sunday, same vehicle.'

'Fine. I'll get my coat.'

The jeep was plainly not to the commissaire's taste. As they followed its headlights through a boundless winter landscape, icy air blew in round the windscreen and froze him to his seat. Luke glanced at him, sitting low and hunched over the parapet of his coat collar.

They whined down through the village, past the bistro which Luke hadn't set foot in since identifying the feather and on to the valley road, where mist rushed them, breaking in waves over the jeep. After the abbey ruins, Luke slowed towards a lonely crossroads.

'The precise route you took Sunday.'

'That's what I'm doing.'

Minutes later they turned into a narrow lane, snapping

pools of thin ice, headlights feeling the way, wipers batting stray snowflakes. Luke pulled up, cut his engine and lights. They stepped into the heavy silence, mist creeping over the fields, the dark sky beginning to break up, unravelling pockets of cold stars.

'This is where I left the jeep, and found the men when I returned.'

'The estate's Tunisian workforce. I made enquiries.'

'What do they do?'

'Work most of the year on the estate,' Goujon replied distractedly, his narrow gaze on the wood, 'and send their wages home to their womenfolk.'

'Anxious, commissaire?'

Cupping his hands, Goujon lit a cigarette and sucked hard on it before replying with barely disguised impatience. 'What do you think? Any of the men on your tape has the power to destroy me.'

'I thought no one was beyond your reach?'

'In principle.'

Shocked. 'In *principle*?'

'My power,' Goujon smiled wryly, 'is invested in me by the Interior Minister.'

Their eyes met. 'Batisse' murmured Luke. 'So the man who may have sanctioned the bomb is your boss?'

Goujon motioned him to proceed. Luke led the way into the wood, playing a flashlight over roots, dead leaves, patches of snow, trying to find his way without the benefit of Laroche's ball of twine. Walking in silence they reached the fence, and along the fence they came to the broken tree.

'This is where I climbed over.' The beam probed high into overhanging spools of barbed wire. 'You can see where I cut.'

Goujon nodded satisfied.

'The de Montforts are expecting us?' said Luke as they turned back.

'Yes,' replied Goujon, tagging along behind.

'What did you tell them?'

'To oblige me with an interview at this exceptional hour concerning a serious crime in which they may have been inadvertently implicated.'

'They didn't object to the hour?'

'They have to be in Paris early for a press conference.'

'How did they react?'

'I spoke to the duke. He didn't seem to mind.'

Their words carried through the frozen wood.

'What do you know about the duke, commissaire? Why would anyone want to blow him up?'

'Some sort of resistance hero, and now a heavyweight in the nuclear power industry, a man with a lot of enemies.'

Luke fell silent, pensive, almost too surprised by his sudden involvement in this business to think straight.

They reached the lane, and Luke turned to the detective.

'Could the de Montforts have been warned about the bomb at the last minute, an incoming call, say, on the car phone, giving them just enough time to get out?'

Goujon looked up at the stars, 'It's possible . . . anything's possible. However . . .' lighting himself a cigarette and blowing smoke across the lane into the hedges, 'I suggest you leave the investigations to me.'

They re-boarded the jeep and drove on.

'I'm not sure where we are,' said Luke.

Goujon's nod of the head said, Carry on.

The lane ended at a main road, Goujon indicated right, Luke followed Goujon's hunch and moments later a sign appeared for Château-de-Claireau. As they approached a concealed entrance, unseen floodlights blazed a cordon over the area. Luke swung the jeep through the glare and pulled up before the soaring gold-tipped gates. With no sign of life in the gate lodge, Luke was about to get out and investigate when his eye was drawn to movement high on the twin turrets supporting the gates, two sets of cameras peering down like gargoyles. He looked at Goujon, who was staring abstractedly ahead. As though his dark Latin eyes possessed some strange power, the gates parted.

Luke drove through on a straight ribbon of virgin road, the jeep's lights reaching in search of a skyline. As he drove, the moon followed, illuminating row upon row of leafless vineyards. Over the rise the château appeared against the first flush of dawn, its solid mass breaking up into rustic buildings clustered round a grand house, and all enclosed by high walls.

The road ran beneath the walls and turned through an arch into a courtyard lit with lanterns. Luke pulled up before the steps of the house, cut his engine and lights and climbed out. Silence. He looked about at the snow-dusted walls and bastions and felt for a moment like a traveller stumbling on the past.

A door opened at the top of the steps, framing a tall athletic figure in a dark suit.

'*Bonjour, commissaire.*' Georges Bolivar nodded respectfully to Goujon, courteously to Luke, '*monsieur.*'

Luke followed Goujon up the steps. Standing aside, Bolivar invited them to enter a chandeliered hall, and to pass through an arch presided over by a pair of knights in full-plate armour. Goujon went ahead, then Luke passed between the knights without noticing anything odd until a high-pitched bleeping told him that someone – he! – had set off an alarm. Bolivar stepped up smartly to switch off the noise and rounded on Luke.

'Empty your pockets please, monsieur.'

Luke fished in his pockets and came up with a rusty trowel. He smiled at it, as if rediscovering a favourite toy.

Bolivar wasn't smiling. 'I'll take that, monsieur.'

'I hardly think that will be necessary,' said Goujon, motioning Bolivar to hurry and lead on.

At the end of a stone passage, Bolivar knocked on a gilded rococo door. '*Entrez!*' rang from within.

They were shown into a wood-panelled study adorned

with Persian rugs, fine paintings and gold-inlaid antiques. Above the fireplace hung a range of hunting guns, old and new.

Maurice de Montfort, dressed for the city, was sitting behind an imposing desk smoking a cigarette. The duke, still in his dressing gown, sat in an armchair sipping a tisane. Father and son rose to meet the visitors. Maurice held back, Edouard – not in the least embarrassed by his state of undress – came forward.

'So, we get to meet the great Goujon!' they shook hands, 'the man nobody would want as his hunter.' Edouard all smiles, Goujon dignified in his restraint.

Luke wasn't introduced. He felt like a bear waiting to be called on to perform. Who did they think he was, Goujon's deputy?

Both de Montforts were fully alert, Maurice thriving in his role of image-booster for political parties, oil companies, the atomic energy industry; while the duke, once the atomic industry's rising star, now its white-haired elder statesman, looked relaxed, vigorous and in the peak of health.

'Coffee, gentlemen?' said Edouard, acknowledging Luke with an open smile.

'Thank you,' replied Goujon, 'but there isn't time.'

'Then don't keep us in suspense, commissaire!' he beamed, 'we're intrigued to know what this is about.'

Luke watched Goujon hesitate ... just long enough to light himself a cigarette and fix his gaze on Edouard de Montfort.

'Last Sunday morning, an ornithologist watching rare ducks overheard a conversation between two unidentified men, alluding to high-level government involvement in the rue de Liège bomb.' Goujon spoke with routine authority, calm to the point of tedium.

Edouard de Montfort looked at him blankly, the idea almost too outlandish to raise a smile. 'Why would *they* want to blow us up?'

'I would have thought, sir, that the answer to that was obvious.'

'Really? I must be even slower this morning than usual.'

Goujon continued, 'The conversation allegedly took place in the grounds of your estate at approximately this time.'

'In the grounds of the estate,' echoed Maurice, 'on a Sunday morning,' consulting his watch, 'around seven.'

Goujon nodded soberly. Father and son continued to regard him with wonder, as if expecting the great detective to break out at any moment into a helpless smile. But Goujon remained wooden, betraying no sign of finding the proposition absurd or otherwise.

Suppressing a snort of derision, Maurice intoned, 'May we know precisely where this *conversation* took place?'

'By the river,' replied Goujon, 'an improvised log bench in a screen of alders.'

'Really!' Maurice scarcely hiding his amusement, 'two mystery men sitting in the dark by the river, debating a government-inspired plot to blow up myself and my father?'

Goujon, pulling on his cigarette, did not trouble himself to reply.

'And who might this sharp-eared bird-watcher be?' wondered the duke, pouring himself more tea.

'This gentleman,' replied Goujon with a modest theatrical gesture, 'is Monsieur Morrel, who found time to take the first pictures of –' looking to Luke for confirmation, 'Marbled Teal in France for nearly half a century.'

Edouard de Montfort put down his cup, levelled his gaze at Luke and brought his hands together in a congratulatory clap.

'Forgive me, monsieur, if I haven't heard of *Marbled* Teal. I confess I've shot nearly every other kind.'

'That's all right, monsieur le duc, no one's heard of them.'

Something in the calm intensity of Duke de Montfort's gaze made Luke shudder, reminding him of the way Jean-Jacques Revallier had looked at him the previous night.

'What, may I ask,' said Maurice, 'were you doing on my father's estate, monsieur?'

Luke turned to reply, but Maurice overrode him.

'You had permission?'

'You refused.'

'I did no such thing.'

'Forgive me, *madame la duchesse* said no.'

'So how did you come –'

'I climbed in.'

'A trespasser!' chimed Edouard delightedly.

'Self-confessed,' added Maurice.

With a quick birdlike movement, Goujon stubbed out his cigarette in the nearest ashtray. 'With your permission, *monsieur le duc*, I should like to see where the alleged conversation took place. Perhaps one of you gentlemen would care to accompany us?'

'Come now, commissaire,' chuckled the duke, 'you're not taking any of this seriously?'

'I take everything seriously.'

'Well . . .' a helpless shrug, 'I'm sure you'll forgive me, in my present state of undress . . .'

'Very well,' said Maurice, consulting his watch, 'let's not waste any more time.'

'Amuse yourselves, gentlemen,' said Edouard following them from the study.

When they went outside into the sharp half-light of dawn, Georges Bolivar had the Range Rover ready. Luke had other ideas.

'That isn't what they used on Sunday,' he objected, his eye straying to the modern garage doors built into former stables.

Maurice looked blankly at Goujon.

'Apparently,' explained Goujon, 'the mystery men travelled in a white Volvo. Shall we take a look?'

With a sardonic smile, Maurice signalled to Bolivar, who produced a pocket control unit and aimed it across the yard. The double-doors of the garage lifted. Luke and Goujon walked over and counted seven cars, from Maurice's silver Porsche to the Duchess's Daimler. No Volvo, white or any other colour.

'Satisfied, gentlemen?' called Maurice, indicating a return to the Range Rover.

'No,' said Luke, who wanted to show that an ordinary car could reach the river, 'we'll take that one,' pointing to a sleek black CX Citroën.

Maurice laughed indulgently, 'As you wish, monsieur!'

Striding across to the garage, he climbed behind the wheel of the Citroën and reversed it into the open. Goujon got in front, Luke behind. The car swept through the arch and turned down an avenue of blue cedars. They drove in silence, Maurice apparently relaxed, Goujon detached, Luke catching de Montfort's eye now and again in the mirror.

The avenue petered out, the road rambled through a hamlet of dilapidated outbuildings, where the Tunisian workers, wearing gloves and threadbare anoraks, were boarding a tractor and trailer. As the Citroën went by, Luke spotted the ageing leader with the Chaplin moustache and the youth who'd reminded him of Serge. Then a great swathe of orchard filled the horizon, the road, now a dirt track, carving through it. The track, deceptively levelled by snow, was rutted, and furrowed by tractors, giving the low-slung Citroën and its occupants a punishing ride. When a belt of woodland brought the formal lines of fruit trees to an end, the track divided left and right, as though to parcel up the orchard. Ahead, through the trees, the river glimmered in the low light. As on Sunday, mist rolled off the water like breath.

159

'*Bon, voilà!*' exclaimed de Montfort pulling up, 'what now?'

'Through the wood,' said Luke.

Maurice chortled, 'Use your eyes, monsieur, the trees are packed, ground-cover thick, it can't be done.'

'It was done on Sunday; it can be done again.'

'Shall we try, monsieur?' said Goujon, as though mediating over a picnic location.

Shaking his head in disbelief, Maurice bumped the car along the edge of the wood, driving with his window down, pointing out the impossibly dense vegetation.

'Keep going,' said Luke.

Gradually the wood receded towards its narrowest point and a passage appeared, parting the trees.

'There!' said Luke quietly, exultantly.

If Maurice was discomfited, he didn't show it as he smiled and eased the car off the track and into the wood, where it belly-crawled through the trees, flattening fern, brushing snow from low branches, pushing towards the sharp light ahead. As it reached the last trees and nosed into the open, a ray of sun struck the windscreen. Squinting past Maurice's shoulder, Luke knew they were emerging at the point where the Volvo had materialised, and that in the piercing light his hide would have been invisible with or without its camouflage.

'Over there,' he ordered.

With a wry smile Maurice steered the car across the meadow. At any moment, Luke half expected the Marbled Teal to take to the air in fright, but the car crawled on towards the nest site and nothing stirred.

'Right here.'

Maurice obligingly brought the car to a stop. Luke got out and quietly approached the nest, pausing now and again to listen and to scour the river. Little by little he came closer to the nest until with one final stride he stood over it – and found it gone. A pillow of snow was all that remained.

For a moment he doubted his senses, but the path beaten by the ducks from the nest to the river was, to the keen eye, still discernible beneath its thin cover of snow. And looking up and shielding his eyes, he recognised the close formation of scrub forty metres away where his hide had been.

'Is this the place, monsieur?' Goujon at his shoulder.

'The nest was here . . .' toe-poking the ground, 'the duck-track there, and over there the hide.'

A doubtful silence, Goujon unconvinced. Luke met his impartial gaze.

'It's been removed,' said Luke.

'Something wrong, monsieur?' wondered Maurice, sauntering over puffing a cigarette.

'What happened to the nest?'

'Perhaps we're in the wrong place?' suggested Maurice tolerantly.

'Show him the photos, commissaire,' said Luke dropping to one knee to run his fingers through the snow.

Goujon passed an envelope to de Montfort, who took out a set of prints and flicked through them. 'Very nice, monsieur, but they could have been taken anywhere.'

'Get down there behind an imaginary camera, commissaire,' said Luke, indicating the precise location.

Goujon took back the photos. 'My men will arrive shortly to carry out tests.'

With a little grunt of triumph Luke scooped up and brushed off a handful of lumps resembling frozen soil, 'Droppings, gentlemen!'

A sympathetic smile from Goujon, 'It merely proves ducks were present, not men.'

'Perhaps,' suggested Maurice cheerfully, 'Monsieur Morrel rejoices in an overactive imagination. No nest, no bench. Commissaire, I'm a very busy man.'

No bench?

Luke spun round. The elbow of alders sheltering the

bench was there as before, but the log bench on which the driver had sat smoking, and which even now his mind could clearly envisage, was gone. Amazed, he stared. Then he walked over to where he thought it had been, and looked and found no trace, no tracks, no sign it had ever been there. Turning around, he found Maurice de Montfort standing apart, coat undone, one hand in trouser pocket, the other twirling his cigarette, on his face a considerate, almost benign expression.

'Maybe you're right, monsieur,' smiled Luke, 'maybe I dreamt the whole thing.'

Maurice returned Luke's grin with the gracious smile of one willing to forgive and forget. Then brisk and businesslike, 'Now if you'll excuse me, gentlemen . . .'

'Just a moment,' said Luke.

Turning away, he walked towards where his hide had been, willing himself to stay calm. *As soon as I begin my enquiries, your life expectancy declines . . .*

Reaching the location of his hide and finding the flattened spot where he had lain, he felt fleetingly a birdwatcher's lonely sense of contentment and instinctively looked towards the river in the hope of seeing the ducks reappear. But the river was silent and deserted under its cover of mist. To gain time and disguise his nerves, he stooped to examine the ground, as if looking for proof that he'd been there two mornings earlier. As he squatted in the snow with his back turned, he became conscious of heated words exchanged between de Montfort and Goujon forty metres away, de Montfort apparently incensed, Goujon dismissive. They were speaking too low for Luke to follow, but the intimate tone of the quarrel was strangely familiar, as was Maurice de Montfort's imperious tenor and the rasping nasal wit . . . of the Volvo driver.

Still on one knee, Luke slowly turned and found himself gazing at a scene which was as good as a replay of Sunday morning. It was as if by returning here, he – or Goujon –

had turned back the clock. There was Maurice de Montfort venting his rage, and there was *the other man*, his image slipping lightly as a shadow from Luke's memory and attaching itself to Commissaire Goujon.

The other man had worn dark glasses and perhaps a different coat, but he was Goujon's fit in every way, and even as Luke tried to resist the conclusion, Goujon was drawing forth from his coat something which caught the sun like a blade. As on Sunday Luke flinched, and as before Goujon merely lifted a lighter to his cigarette. A thin trail of smoke drifted the wrong way this time, but Luke's memory supplied the smell of Gauloises. His mouth went dry, he gazed in awe.

De Montfort and Goujon had ceased arguing, they were standing apart, watching Luke. For a foolish moment he thought of making a run for it. Then laughed at himself and strolled back hands in pockets, calmly looking both men in the eyes, half-expecting one of them to say, So, now you know! But all de Montfort said was, 'We've wasted enough time,' and turned towards the car; and Goujon at close range looked less like the Volvo driver, more the impeccable professional he'd met yesterday.

Re-boarding the sleek black Citroën, they drove back over the meadow, through the wood to reach the orchards. No one spoke. Luke tried to concentrate in the loaded silence. Could Goujon really be the Volvo driver? If he was, then Luke had reported a crime to a man who already knew all about it, and this morning's exercise was but a cruel charade. And if Maurice de Montfort was the Volvo passenger, it meant that he'd got into a car in rue de Liège knowing there was a bomb under it.

Impossible!

Luke began to sweat, confused by his own senses. Then he felt the fear trickling up the back of his neck, a sensation he hadn't known since parachuting into occupied France in forty-four.

'The Tunisians,' he said, 'I want to talk to them.'

'*Merde, vous exagérez, monsieur,*' Maurice losing his temper, 'you go too far.'

'I want to put a few questions to them, does that worry you?'

'You think I have nothing better to do than cater to your whims?'

'Where would they be now?' asked Goujon.

Maurice threw him a disbelieving glance.

'It shouldn't take long,' Goujon consoled him.

Maurice consulted his watch and cursed, but put up no further resistance. Composing himself, he reduced speed and drove with his arm on the sill of his open window, scanning the orchards on both sides of the track. Trees fanned out in all directions, fierce shapes against the dawn. Suddenly he pulled down on the wheel and glided the car off the track into the trees.

Luke tensed, his hand feeling for the door handle. In the driving mirror he could see dark intent on Maurice's face. As the car whispered over snow, weaving among the trees, a ray of sun flashed on the windscreen, betraying it, and at once the orchard came alive with running figures. Maurice thumped the accelerator, the car surged into a clearing and he leapt out.

'FREEZE!'

A score of olive-skinned men froze, the sun stood still, Maurice marched into the open, halted by a crackling fire and surveyed the spellbound scene. A priceless coup! It was rare to catch these hard-working men idle. The sun hitting the car had given some of them enough warning to scramble into the trees, but many were stranded, secateurs and pruning sticks in hand.

Luke recognised the men. Neatly dressed and garrulous on Sunday, now they looked mute and shabby in torn anoraks and caps. Save for the crackling of the fire, not a sound disturbed the clearing, until Maurice spotted the man he was after. 'Manou!'

'Monsieur?'

A wiry man with Chaplin moustache came forward, eyes lowered. Luke got out of the car, followed by Goujon. Maurice waited until the man stood repentant before him.

'Is this how your men work?'

'No, monsieur.'

'What do you mean no? I've just caught you warming your backsides at my expense. Can't you control them?'

'Yes, sir.'

'Because I can soon replace you, Manou.'

The humbling of Manou was the humbling of them all. Thankfully their women and children couldn't witness it.

'Do your men want to be sent home?'

'No, sir.'

'Tell them to work an extra hour after dark this week.' Turning to Goujon. 'All yours, commissaire.'

Goujon and Luke stepped forward.

'You know this man?'

Manou looked at Luke. 'No, commissaire.'

'Monsieur Morrel says he met you in the lane on Sunday.'

'No, commissaire.'

Luke spoke up encouragingly, 'No one is accusing you of anything. I'm trying to establish that *I* was there.' No reply. 'The American jeep, remember?'

Manou gazed past Luke's shoulder. Luke sought another face, the boy with Serge's eyes. Walking a little further he looked about and finally saw him standing under a tree. He went over. 'Remember the other morning, the jeep?' The boy contemplated the snow. Luke reached and touched his arm. The boy lifted his eyes. 'You took your friends for a spin . . .'

He held the boy's gaze. The boy bit his lip, and Luke thought he read a plea for forgiveness in his eyes.

Before leaving, Goujon hoisted the aerial of his portable

phone and spoke to the pilot parked a few kilometres away in Luke's field. The timing, Luke had to admit, was sweet. As they reached the château, Goujon's machine was arriving over the vineyards and landing out of sight.

In the courtyard Georges Bolivar was waiting by the Range Rover to ferry the de Montforts to their helicopter for the flight to Paris.

'I hope I've been of some service, commissaire,' said a relaxed Maurice de Montfort, bending to wipe his shoes with a handkerchief.

'Most definitely.'

'By all means carry out tests while we're away.'

'Your co-operation is appreciated.'

'*Bon!*' Maurice briskly shook hands with Goujon and turned to Luke. 'I trust we won't need to trouble each other again. *Au revoir, monsieur.*'

His face was smiling, his eyes were cold.

Edouard de Montfort appeared, coming down the steps dressed for the city, and moving with ease and purpose. '*Alors, messieurs*, what did you discover?'

His question hung in the air, no one ready to reply. From Edouard a perplexed smile, 'Explosives, an arms cache, a body?'

'Nothing,' said Luke.

'Nothing? What a letdown. You got me going for nothing!'

He shook hands with Goujon and turned to Luke with a glint in the eye, 'Let me have one of those precious photographs – signed! so I can frame it, and I'll overlook the little matter of your trespass.'

'My pleasure, sir.'

They shook hands, Luke feeling the measured strength of the man, and once again the cool intensity of his gaze.

Father and son boarded the Range Rover and were whisked away in a shower of frozen pebbles. Luke and Goujon stood in the open forecourt in silence.

Someone who knew I was coming here this morning, thought Luke, acted swiftly to have the nest and bench removed, and the Tunisians frightened into silence.

'Don't be disheartened,' said Goujon, putting on his gloves.

'Then you still believe me?'

'I'm taking your allegations very seriously.'

Luke looked him in the eye. Goujon gazed blankly back.

'I'll run you to your helicopter.'

'Thank you, I prefer to walk.' He made no move to go. 'Haven't you forgotten something?' Reaching in his coat he handed over two envelopes, the ducks-only copies of the tape and photos, and finally offered his hand. 'Lie low, monsieur, speak to no one, you'll be hearing from me.'

Turning up his collar he walked off. Under the arch he paused to light a cigarette, and to give Luke a final ambiguous look over his shoulder, before turning the corner out of sight.

Luke remained fastened on the space vacated by Goujon in the archway. Who are you, commissaire? a brave detective who just happens to resemble the Volvo driver? Or *are* you the driver, stringing me along, pretending to follow up my evidence? I have to know. I have to turn detective on you.

• • • 11 • • •

Putting the final touches to her article on the Channel Tunnel, Kasha noticed the time, nearly 7 p. m. Michel Kerlesquin – 'your saviour', as Alain called him – was calling for her in half an hour.

She was happy, light-headed and singing to herself as she tidied away her work and went through to undress.

Nathalie was recovering, she'd called the hospital and for the first time they sounded hopeful. She spoke to Robert, who was almost too excited to speak. Instead of slipping deeper into oblivion, he said, she seemed to be moving into lighter coma. 'Kasha, if Nathalie pulls through, let's all take a trip together!'

After a quick shower, she tried to decide what to wear. She wanted to look nice, but not so nice as to invite misunderstanding or so modest as to convey indifference. With minutes to spare she sat down in the living room to apply a little make-up and flicked on the TV to catch the news headlines: Aden on the brink of civil war; a call from Gorbachev for nuclear weapons to be phased out by the year 2000; US space shuttle Challenger postponed again. No mention of Nathalie, Friday's bomb or the hunt for the GP.

The intercom made her start. Michel Kerlesquin greeted her coolly, said he'd wait downstairs in the taxi. She said she'd be right down, and replaced the receiver. Her heart beat faster, a sudden foreboding. Was it really only from politeness and gratitude that she had accepted his dinner invitation?

No sooner had Revallier returned to the double-parked taxi than a familiar Mercedes drew up behind with its police escort. As he sat well back and watched the de Montforts enter the building, carrying the inevitable brief-case, he felt sure that the secret plans it contained would be in his hands by the end of the evening.

Down on the river, on the Île de la Cité, Luke patrolled quai des Orfèvres, watching the entrance to number thirty-six, waiting to see if Commissaire Goujon would appear at the wheel of a white Volvo. He had to know if Goujon was the Volvo driver and intended to haunt the quays until he found out.

All afternoon he'd watched and waited, collar upturned,

hands deep in pockets, the air freezing the breath in his mouth, too cold even for snow. Back and forth he paced, his eye on every car that came in or out of the arched entrance. In quiet moments he studied the lighted windows of the imposing building, trying to work out where Goujon's office was situated.

He looked at his watch: 7.30. Isabelle would be starting her picture-restoration class in St Germain. Over lunch he had tried telling her the full story, but they didn't have long, she was preoccupied with her new term and he ended up sparing her the worst. As they parted, she said, '*Chéri*, this business about the crime you overheard, it's all finished now, huh?'

When he hesitated, she looked troubled.

'Just about,' he reassured her, 'I need to see the police once more, that's all.'

At about 7.45, as Luke was losing hope of seeing Goujon, a man emerged, unnoticed by him at first because he was on foot. It was only when the police at the security barrier respectfully saluted him that Luke began to take interest in the slight figure hunched behind his upturned collar, walking briskly down the opposite pavement. The distinctive profile, with the dark brows and prominent nose, was unmistakable.

Since Goujon must spot him at any moment, Luke cast about for a ready excuse to signal, cross the road and address the detective . . . about what? protection?

The moment passed, Goujon went by without seeing him, past the official carpark and down a row of closed shops until he came to the restaurants at the end of the quay and went inside one of them. Still on the opposite pavement, Luke followed until he came level with the restaurant. Through softly lit windows he could see diners at table and waiters moving about, but no Goujon. He crossed the road and peered quickly in at a window, picking out Goujon at a secluded table exchanging pleasantries with the proprietor.

As he turned away and took up a new position on the far side of the street, he had a feeling it was going to be a long night.

Sitting back in the taxi, Kasha and the man she thought was Michel Kerlesquin found little to say to each other. The incident which had brought them together the previous morning no longer worked its charm. The charged and ready banter was missing tonight; they were strangers, barriers up.

As the taxi drove through Pigalle and began its steep ascent towards the heights of Monmartre, it slithered on frozen snow, drawing relieved laughter from the back, encouraging Revallier to have the driver stop short of the restaurant, so they could walk a little way like tourists.

It was icy underfoot, Revallier took Kasha's arm and they fell into step, walking in silence up the narrow winding streets until, emerging near the top, he drew her to the edge of a parapet with a view of the city shrouded in mist and darkness.

'Paris at our feet,' he breathed.

'Spread like a jewelled mantle,' she said, her voice echoing the slightly strained tone of his.

They walked on and crossed a square. Teeming in summer with artists and tourists, it was now low-lit and glazed with snow. On the far side a restaurant spilled its light into the street.

Inside was quiet, a few intimate couples, light laughter, the chink of wine glasses, a bow-tied waiter popping open a bottle and firing the cork into the street. A waiter descended on Kasha and Revallier, took their coats and showed them in hushed tones to their table, where they stood and faced each other for a moment like duellists. In that moment he seemed to see her again for the first time. She wore a cotton dress over silky, pyjama-like trousers tucked into boots. What made the simple cream-coloured outfit striking was the addition of the long matching scarf or shawl which she wore round her head like a soft hood, and down to her knees like a frivolous cloak.

But as before, what struck him most was the challenge of her clear dark eyes.

They took their seats, eyes averted. A waiter flipped their wine glasses and lit the candle. The flame caught Kasha's earrings, her skin. Revallier's eyes wandered, familiarising himself with the lay-out, as researched by Ricardo. Five years a hunted man, it was second nature to seek exits everywhere, and to check the faces of fellow diners.

'Wine?' he invited.

'Yes!' she said brightly, reaching for the list. Nathalie was coming back to life! she'd finished her article on the Channel Tunnel, tonight she was going to enjoy herself.

Revallier returned her smile. Normally at ease with women, he felt strangely naked with this one.

'Mind if I ask what you're wearing?'

She smiled at his tactful tone.

'Well you did pull me up yesterday,' he reminded her.

'Did I?'

'I'm trying not to treat you like some exotic plant!'

She cocked a warning eyebrow. 'It's a *voile kurta*, a stylised Punjabi suit.'

It was a modest outfit. While he could see her strong brown arms through the airy sleeves, there was little hint of Kasha's breasts behind the chain-stitch embroidery.

'And the shawl?'

'A *duppatta*,' she replied, unravelling the loose folds from her head, 'made of heavier cotton *khadi*.'

Her head fell bare, revealing her shiny black hair dragged smoothly back over her scalp, exposing her full face and forehead.

'A *duppatta*,' he repeated, relishing the word. Yes, he thought regretfully, I like you. I like you a lot.

The wine came. As he sampled it, she was observing him. He wore a loose double-breasted suit, olive green with silk tie to match. His hair, not unlike hers, was pulled hard back off his forehead and drawn into a discreet thong at the back.

Revallier raised his glass. 'Your health!'

Glasses touching, 'And yours!'

They drank, she shivered, the rich dark wine warming her. It was hard to say why she liked this man, why she was pleased to be in his company. There was something magnetic about him, but there was also an unnatural stillness which made her nervous. The deep lines around his eyes spoke of a life lived too well or too stressfully. He gave off an aura of certainty and strength, but there was tension in his lower face, a tightening of the jaw betraying nerves. His lips smiled easily, but his eyes were deep and watchful. She had the feeling that this open man was really closed, that he was by nature detached and private and very hard to reach. She recalled having the same feeling about Edouard de Montfort.

The waiter came to take their order.

Revallier, who could never eat before an operation, donned his false glasses and ordered a light hors d'oeuvres and fillet of sole. When Kasha began negotiating a selection of side dishes, Revallier was at first puzzled. Then he saw that one vital element was absent from everything she picked.

'You're not . . .?'

'Yes,' she confessed with a relaxed smile.

The waiter caught on, '*Ah bon! mademoiselle est végétarienne?*'

'I'm afraid so.'

'No need to apologise,' said Revallier, privately cursing Ricardo – the only vegetarian in the brigade – for falling down on this one.

'It's hard for people to understand,' said Kasha, 'meat is

as basic in France. . .' a moment's reflection, 'as wine and sex! Wouldn't you agree?' she surprised the waiter.

'Well, yes, mademoiselle, certainly in my case!'

He smiled and withdrew.

Revallier, disconcerted, 'You should have said something, we could have gone elsewhere.'

'Never occurred to me.' She took up her wine and laughed at him, a dazzling, girlish, unexpected laugh, and he laughed with her, grateful this wasn't the kind of romantic evening he once indulged in. Tonight the objective was to get at the de Montforts. Kasha Sharma was merely his unwitting dupe, his means of reaching them. No weakness of any kind, he reminded himself, must inhibit him from making full use of her. 'Have you heard any news of your neighbour?' he asked.

'I found everyone in buoyant spirits at the hospital this morning; first signs of improvement, reduction in fever, breathing a little easier, heart action less frantic – I'm so happy! I'll sit with her again tomorrow morning and whisper in her ears.'

'You think she'll pull through?'

Encouraged by his sympathy, 'She's still in the third level of coma, the fourth is brain-death. She seems to be progressing to level two, which wouldn't be as critical. Talking of hospitals . . .' draining her glass with a rustle of bracelets, 'I hope you had your hand properly seen to?'

'Of course,' he lied, refilling her glass and his own. Tahar had stitched him up, dubiously assisted by Ricardo, with Janine looking on mockingly: *You were meant to graze yourself, Jacques; God, you must have fancied her!*

'May I see?'

He frowned.

'Please,' she insisted.

Her lips glistened with wine, he surrendered his hand across the table. She unravelled the bandage, and with

173

fingers still chilled from the outdoors, turned the hand palm-up and held it firmly to examine the wound.

'You were very brave, monsieur, tackling that man.'

'Call me Michel, please.'

'Give me your other hand, *Michel*!' she exaggerated.

Trying to guess her intentions, he obediently complied. She took both his hands palms-up in hers and studied them at length. Nodding to herself, 'Psychic hands . . .'

Since she volunteered nothing more, he said, 'As opposed to what?'

'Square, spatulate or philosophical. Yours are strong but delicate for a man, shapely and sensitive – psychic hands.'

The feel of her fingertips made his palms arch with pleasure and sent frissons down his back.

Her silence invited further curiosity. 'Meaning what?'

'By nature you are loving, spiritual, idealistic. There's nothing practical about you. You'd make a poor administrator, accountant or lawyer.'

At *lawyer* he repressed a smile, yet she looked up, ready for him.

'Don't you get idealistic lawyers?' he said.

'Yes, but theirs is a stormy road, rocked by controversy. More often artists and actors have psychic hands, psychologists and nurses, models even and yes – fashion designers.'

'And terrorists?'

She considered. 'Possibly.'

'Aren't they idealists too?'

'Only by conviction. Their cold-blooded methods are the antithesis of idealism, don't you agree?'

She held his gaze, and fell to wondering again about his tanned, scarred hands, hardly the hands of a fashion designer.

'Maybe they don't have a lot of options,' he said.

'Terrorists? Balls!' she said with passion. But without venom. For the moment she'd forgotten about Nathalie.

The wine was deep and dark, her mood light and careless. She took his hands once more, her own hands warm now with the heat of his.

'Your well-developed Lower Mars suggests a man of stamina and aggression, the kind who never gives up!'

He said nothing, nor did she feel obliged to look up for confirmation.

'Your Mount of Venus . . .' feeling and squeezing the pillowy flesh at the base of his thumb, 'reveals a warm generous nature, but oh dear!' bending his thumb, 'lack of flexibility could be your downfall . . . and these mounds,' testing the base of his fingers, 'betray reckless ambition and a flamboyant streak of lawlessness!'

As she began to re-bandage his hand, she anticipated some reward for her efforts, if only a look of grudging admiration. But his faintly mocking gaze yielded nothing.

'How's my life line?'

Covering her hesitation she said vaguely, 'You've such a scramble of lines . . .'

'There are clear breaks,' he insisted.

Ricardo had read all their hands; Tahar's was bad, Janine's worse, and Revallier should have been dead several times over.

'Yes,' she conceded, 'you've inherited in your left hand a tendency to live dangerously, and your right hand shows no urgency to check that tendency. If anything – ' she stopped herself and met his knowing smile. 'That doesn't mean,' she assured him, 'that you're going to die prematurely, merely that you're more inclined than others to take risks.'

'And you?'

'Me?'

'Your hands . . .'

'Ah no!'

Before she could escape, he captured her hands. Their eyes met, vied, her hands hot in his. Softening his grip, he gently prised hers open with his thumbs. 'Tell me,' he whispered.

'This is piracy, monsieur,' she said straightfaced, 'you should be ashamed.'

'I am. Tell me.'

She twitched her nose, a niggling itch. He released one hand, she scratched and surrendered it again.

'I've square hands, as you can see . . .'

With involuntary tenderness he spread her palms wider. She shivered.

'They show I'm much more sensible than you, level-headed, organised, boring! I take risks, but unlike you, they're calculated. I'd make a splendid accountant!'

Together they gazed at her palms, he holding on longer than was strictly necessary, she letting him. Then gently she removed her hands, took up her wine and sighed with pleasure.

'You take this seriously?' he said.

Shrugging, 'A little.'

'What *do* you take seriously?'

'My work, my integrity . . .' the waiter arrived with the hors d'oeuvres, 'my appetite.'

Revallier glanced at his watch. He was running late.

The wine went happily to Kasha's head. Without quite realising it, she longed to loosen up for an evening, but with Michel Kerlesquin she couldn't really relax. Even while he paid her close attention, nodding gravely or smiling with amusement at her anecdotes, he wasn't altogether there. Discouraged, she'd break-off in mid-flow with – ah well! and he'd immediately confound her with – and then?

'The snake bracelet,' he mused, 'doesn't suit your character.'

The jewelled cobra coiled around her wrist winked in the candlelight.

'What do you know of my character?' peering at him over her wine glass.

A speculative smile, 'I see in you grace and strength – a tigress, not a snake.'

'Another Western prejudice, Michel. The snake is shy, nervous and sleepy, quite like me really!'

She was beginning to relax and enjoy herself, even to feel a certain relief that he didn't live in Paris, because a man like this could seriously disrupt a woman's life. Now and again, when their eyes met and briefly lingered, she fell to wondering what he had in mind for later.

Despite her efforts to pay for the meal in gratitude for his chivalry the day before, he insisted on paying, 'I asked you out.' She thanked him, trusting he understood that yielding to him here did not imply favours later on.

In the taxi he maintained a discreet distance, and mentioned catching a late train, the 11.55 to Rennes. Surprised, she glanced at her watch: 10.35; should she invite him up for coffee? They'd have about forty-five minutes together. Not to would seem rude. To do so was tempting fate.

As they turned into rue de Liège, Revallier could only guess what might be going on in Kasha's mind. He usually knew when a woman liked him, but this woman he couldn't read at all. All he needed was to be asked in for coffee, taking him smoothly past the security guards in her company, and therefore legitimately out again later on with the de Montforts' secret plans.

The taxi pulled up outside the building. It should have been simple for Kasha to thank him and get out, but the thought of not seeing him again struck a bleak chord. The driver waited, moments piled up, finally she said,

'It was a lovely evening, thank you,' and reached for the door.

'Kasha,' she looked over her shoulder, 'I want to see you again.'

'Call me.'

Again she went to get out.

'One more thing . . .' he was holding a gold cufflink in his open palm, 'I've lost its twin, I can only think in your apartment . . .'

'When I was fixing your hand?'

'Forgive me, but they came from my mother,' that bit was true, 'would you mind –?'

'You want to come up and look?'

'If I may.'

She consented with a smile, and while she insisted on paying the driver, he got out and looked up to make sure the de Montfort lights were on. The taxi pulled away, Kasha went to open the street door and felt Revallier's hand on her arm.

Her heart stopped.

But all he said was, 'Do you suppose they'll search me again?'

'I doubt it, they know you now.'

'What if they're not the same ones?'

'True, they work shifts.'

'Would you mind taking this for me?' With a rakish smile he proffered a man's leather handbag, 'it contains a mildly incriminating substance.'

She said okay with a casual little laugh.

'You better slip your bag inside,' he suggested.

She hesitated, he reached, she yielded up her tiny bag. It fitted inside his, he zipped his up and handed it back. She took it and tucked it under her arm as if smuggling illegal substances for virtual strangers was something she did all the time.

Remembering to put on his glasses and hide his injured hand, he followed her inside the door, past Madame Klo-nowska's *loge*, from where a TV screen flickered, and across the open courtyard, where two men in smart suits material-ised from the shadows, same world-weary swagger as the last pair, different faces.

'*Bonsoir, messieurs!*' Kasha greeted them, 'You're back again.'

'Can't keep away, mademoiselle.'

They knew her; they didn't know her companion.

'And you are, monsieur . . .?'

'Monsieur Kerlesquin,' replied Kasha, her tone implying they ought to know.

One of them briefly frisked him, thanked them and motioned them to proceed. In the lift Kasha leaned against the mirrored wall and smiled, 'You were sweating.'

'Did it show?'

'I could tell.'

Under the lift's harsh lights she looked jaded, her aura worn away. She was still badly shaken, reflected Revallier, and against his will he felt a tremor of conscience.

They passed the third floor, where the de Montforts lived, and emerged on the fourth. Along the corridor they passed Nathalie's silent door without a word. Once inside her own apartment, Kasha extracted her bag from inside his, and, with a look of mock suspicion, laid his curiously heavy bag on the hall table. Then she hung up their coats and followed Revallier into the living room.

The apartment felt strangely unfamiliar. He'd only seen it in daylight. Now, under the influence of soft lamps, it seemed smaller, more intimate. When she came through he was gazing at the wall tapestry, transported to the heat and light of Rajasthan. It was a deceptive faraway look, screening his thoughts: how to play the next thirty minutes; what to do if the guards downstairs compared notes and considered what he might look like in a boiler suit, beard and beret . . .

'Make yourself at home,' Kasha said on her way to the kitchen.

She was in two minds, to slip into the bathroom and touch up her face, or to let him see her as she was, tired and lacklustre and shaken to the core.

He watched her in the mirror over the fireplace, filling a kettle, reaching for coffee filters from a high cupboard, showing her firm brown ankles as she stretched. Despite the grim itinerary of the evening, which should have held his full attention, his thoughts ran wild.

She made tisane for herself, coffee for him, and brought the tray through without looking at him. The wine, the candlelight, the need to escape from Friday's bomb and yesterday's mugging had all inclined her to relax with him. But the more she thought about it, the more reasons she found not to. Like anyone he was entitled to his inconsistencies and quirks, but he had too many, such as his outdoor complexion and the slightly soiled fingernails which no amount of scrubbing could quite clean. In fact nothing in his manner or conversation suggested someone given to fashion design. Once or twice, in the intimacy of the restaurant, he'd seemed to be on the point of spilling his secrets, of offering some explanation for behaviour which others might have thought unexceptional, but which she found suspect. Then that faraway look would come into his eyes.

Setting down the tray she looked across to where he was standing with his hands behind his back, and met his eyes, compelling eyes, the kind that sweep a woman up and dash her on the rocks. Her heart jolted, something more about those eyes disturbed her. It was as if they were inadvertently alerting her to something which should have been obvious.

As she sat down and poured his coffee, her eye was drawn to the blank TV screen which over the weekend had been filled with the face of Jean-Jacques Revallier, and immediately a wild thought occurred to her. The thought was absurd, but even as she dismissed it, she was glancing down through the glass-topped coffee table, seeking the mustachioed face of the GP leader on the front page of *Le Matin*, but the papers had been rearranged and she wasn't going to look with him watching.

'Sit down, please.'

While he came and sat down on the couch, careful not to sit too close, she couldn't shake the wild idea from her head.

'You know who you remind me of?'

'Who?'

She let out a nervous laugh and tried to tell him, but could only shake her head, too choked with laughter to speak. He laughed with her, fearing the worst. With effort she stopped, swallowed and changed the subject.

'Did you find it?'

Find it? 'The cufflink,' he said hastily, 'I think you may be sitting on it.'

She rose a little too quickly, he moved across, paused a moment, speculating on where it might have gone, then delved with his good hand beneath the cushions. He frowned, he wasn't having any luck. Then 'Ah!' he exclaimed, surfacing with something in his fist. Opening his hand he revealed his find.

'*Bravo*! You must be relieved,' she poured her tea, 'I'm only surprised you didn't mention it on the phone.'

Suddenly she was staring at him, everything falling into place. He met her gaze head on.

'How's your Channel Tunnel project going?'

'Fine.'

His tone had become mechanical, hers sharp and cold.

'There may be more to it than meets the eye,' he said.

'Oh?'

'Why go to such lengths to rush through a rail link between two countries who can't stand each other?'

She found a curious smile, 'For a man in such a . . . in such an urbane profession,' she faltered, heart beating hard. 'Tell me, why work in a business that doesn't interest you?' Her back was straight, her eyes clear and direct.

'Most people do.'

'You don't strike me as that kind of man.'

'You don't know me.'

'How do you go about creating, say, a new line in dresses?'

'Dresses? Same as anything else: I think, meditate, study the market.'

'Really? and then?'

Ricardo had supplied him with superficial information on trends and styles, but as he began to prattle about inspiration in nature and transferring it to the drawing board, he stopped short, repelled by his own lies. He looked away, 'You're right.'

She waited, breathless.

'I'm not really interested in fashion.'

She laughed coldly, 'I don't think you know much about it either.' She rose abruptly and stood with one hand on hip, mouth taut, eyes resolute. 'Tell me something, monsieur . . .' the regression to *monsieur* was ominous, 'why do you put on reading glasses each time you enter the building? Could it be something to do with getting past the security men?'

'My glasses,' he confessed, 'I should be wearing all the time.'

'You're a poor liar, monsieur.'

'I'm a good liar as it happens, only I find it difficult to lie to you.'

She left the room.

'Where are you going?'

She didn't reply and he knew exactly where she was going.

He was on his feet, but she was already in the hall and out of sight . . . the night's grim business in the balance, months of patient planning. He moved quickly, and was halfway to the door when she reappeared, his bag in her grip, zip open, hand inside.

She'd found it.

He stopped. She was gazing at him. He could have

reached her in a burst, seized the bag, knocked her out if he'd wanted. But he watched her draw forth the gun and hold it away like something putrid. While she continued to hold it so, the trigger undiscovered by her rigid fingers, he could still have stopped her.

'Who are you – Monsieur Kerlesquin?'

'Why do you ask,' he held her gaze, 'when you know already?'

As she dropped the bag on the floor and lifted the gun in a careful arc and aimed it at his body, he felt the heat of her terror coming at him in waves. Such was the tremble in her hand, the dance of the gun's muzzle, that a hail of bullets could have taken him anywhere or missed him altogether.

Her lips moved in an effort to speak, but she was too appalled.

'Mademoiselle . . .'

'Bastard!' she blurted in English, 'you fucking bastard . . .' the words spilled like tears, 'if Nathalie dies . . .'

'Believe me . . .'

'Don't' she cried, 'don't lie any more, or I swear to God . . .'

He froze, she was going to do it.

'No more lies,' he promised, and, moving very slowly, he turned his back and went over to the window.

Shaking uncontrollably, she stared at the back of his head. His promise amounted to such a simple confession that it silenced her. She had in her apartment the most wanted man in France. She could have yelled, but no one would have heard, and anyway, it wasn't her style. You're the one in control, she told herself.

'Battalions of armed police and detectives failed to find me . . .' he muttered to himself as he gazed out of the window, and here he was at the mercy of a journalist.

Hearing her lift the telephone, he turned around. He saw the change in her, her posture, her air of command, the gun no longer waved at him, but held confidently by her side. Eyes fixed on him, she stood like an army officer preparing to shoot a deserter, but with just sufficient humility in her bearing to offer a glimmer of hope.

'Call the police by all means, but hear me first.'

Her eyes said No.

Casting about for a saving line, he could think of nothing better than, 'Give me two minutes, for God's sake.'

She laid the receiver on the table, freeing her hand to tap out a number.

'We've never endangered lives, what kind of insane departure would this be?'

'You tell me.'

'I don't want the de Montforts dead, I want them alive to answer–'

'What's this then?' shaking the gun at him, 'if it isn't to do the job you botched on Friday?'

'It's not them we're after, it's the briefcase, the one Maurice de Montfort chains to his wrist . . .' she regarded him blankly. 'Have you ever seen him wearing a coat? It's always covering his wrist. It's the plans inside I want –'

'The bomb, monsieur, Friday's bomb.'

Sadly shaking his head, 'Not us, mademoiselle.'

'You claimed it.'

'A voice claimed it,' he said quietly.

'Who else would do it, for Christ's sake?'

'Use your head. We're damned now, *they're* laughing . . .' pointing down through the floor. 'With one outrage they've destroyed us.'

'With only one brigade left you were beaten anyway.'

She clapped a hand suddenly over her mouth, unable to believe she was talking to the man responsible for Nathalie's injuries. She ached to shoot him, to see a bullet cut him down.

'But not disgraced. We enjoyed massive support, we had a pure record–'

'Pure?'

'Clean. Kasha . . .' he appealed to her, 'can't you see we've been set up?'

'Like you set me up?' she said, recoiling from his stab at intimacy and nodding bitterly as the facts rearranged themselves into an ugly new picture. 'The mugging, your wounded hand – my God! even the cufflink, you arranged the whole thing – bastard! all to gain access to *them*!' her turn to point through the floor.

'Yes,' spreading his hands in surrender, 'I admit all that, but not the bomb.'

She stared at him, desperate to believe him. With doubts and horror jostling in her face, she took a deep breath and replaced the receiver. 'Give me proof.'

He thought for a few moments. 'I can't.'

His simple admission frightened and reassured her. Either this man was a consummate actor, or conceivably . . . pointing the gun, she gestured him to sit down in the armchair. He obeyed and spoke up.

'But there is proof,' he sat back, hands on thighs, 'On Sunday at dawn, two men drove to a lonely spot in the grounds of Château-de-Claireau, the de Montfort's country residence, confident that the time and place would ensure they weren't seen or heard. They weren't to know a local man, an American called Morrel, was crawling round after wild ducks. He tape recorded the ducks *and* the two men, implicating them, along with Interior Minister Batisse, Security Minister Lusardi and Secret Service Chief Crozier in Friday's bomb.'

Kasha returned his gaze steadily.

Revallier went on, 'One of the two men was furious that an innocent woman had been injured . . .' Kasha blinked. 'The other man apparently co-ordinated the operation, including our heroes' timely escape from the car and my phone call. A brilliantly executed plan, except for your neighbour leaving early because of the fog. Why waste tears over her? he is heard to say, so much the better if she dies.'

'Why?' an anguished cry, 'why!'

'Why?' Revallier flared, 'in one stroke we're cut down, our support undermined, our cause defiled, legends one minute, butchers the next.'

Kasha unmoved. 'You have the tape?'

'He surrendered it to the police.'

She regarded him steadily, but felt like screaming.

'You see my position, monsieur? Beneath my feet,' pointing the pistol at the floor, 'the men who accuse you; sitting before me the man who accuses them. And their version, you must admit . . .'

'Go see the American, in the village of St-Sulpice-en-Maréchaux in the Vallée de Chevreuse.'

He looked at his watch and rose.

She tensed, pointed the gun at him.

'I'm sorry,' he said, 'I'm ashamed, I'm guilty of everything you say – but not the bomb.'

She met his penetrating gaze, reassured, sceptical.

He started to leave.

'Where do you think you're going!'

'I'm going,' he said firmly.

'I want your story.'

'What?'

'A taped interview,' she said in a low, grave, determined voice.

A contemptuous laugh, 'A journalistic coup! The woman who tracked down Jean-Jacques Revallier!'

'– when battalions of armed police and detectives couldn't,' she reminded him. 'An *innocent* man would welcome the chance to clear his name.'

He took a few more steps towards the door and stopped. The thought of an interview repelled him, but tonight, tomorrow, any day could be his last.

She faced him, eyes animated, 'Not my version, not theirs, your voice, your story.'

'Call me.'

Scornful, 'How can I?'

'I will let you into a dark secret . . .' he hesitated for a moment, scrutinising her. 'To reach me, go to the church of Notre-Dame-des-Près on boulevard Montparnasse and tell the priest your need is great, you have to speak to the highest authority.'

He regarded her gravely, as if entrusting a child with her first errand. His voice fell to a whisper, 'You realise what I've just given you?'

'Yes.'

He stepped closer, holding out his hand for the gun.

Shaking her head firmly, 'No.'

They stood looking at each other.

'If you're lying,' her voice fell to a whisper, 'if Nathalie dies . . .'

Taking his coat and bag, he let himself out, leaving her standing with her empty threat.

<h2 style="text-align:center">• • • 12 • • •</h2>

Down on the river, Luke looked up at the clear cold stars and wondered how much longer he would have to wait.

Inside the restaurant Commissaire Goujon was rounding off his meal with a cognac and a *café corretto*, thinking about Jean-Jacques Revallier, wondering in what dark corner of the city he might be hiding tonight. He'd missed him and his gang by minutes the other night, the candles barely dry on a birthday cake in a canal-side bistro.

In the twelve months since being summoned from Marseille to take over the hunt for the GP, his success had become legendary, his name synonymous with swift, clinical killings, one hideout after another located and eliminated. Only Revallier's gang had eluded him; once they were accounted for, he could leave Paris in triumph and return south to a champion's reception, a thought which evoked visions of flag-waving crowds thronging the streets to welcome Bonaparte home from the wars. He settled the bill, put on his coat, drained his coffee and left.

Over his shoulder Luke saw Goujon emerge, lift his collar and set off in the direction of Pont Neuf, where he turned right and started to cross the bridge. Keeping his distance, Luke followed, wondering where Goujon was going on foot. Perhaps he didn't have a car, didn't drive at all, let alone a white Volvo. Maybe he'd hidden it, or dumped it.

At the foot of the bridge Goujon waited for lights to change, crossed beneath the Samaritaine department store and turned a corner out of sight. Afraid of losing him, Luke broke into a run and then carefully followed him into a network of quiet streets, turning another corner in time to see the detective mount the steps of an hotel and disappear. Crossing to the shadows of the church opposite, Luke took in the small dignified hotel squeezed between old buildings and wondered what Goujon was doing in there.

At length he looked at his watch, it was getting late and he was thinking he ought to contact Isabelle when a police car turned the corner at speed. Gazing guiltily into its headlights, Luke turned and strolled on. The police car pulled up sharply, his heart hammered. When no one got out, he looked around. Goujon was coming down the hotel steps; a blue beacon came to life on the police car's roof, Goujon ducked into the back and the car sped away.

At the risk of being seen, Luke hurried after it. At the end of the street the police car's siren erupted as it swung into the traffic. Luke reached the open thoroughfare and looked left and right for a cab. Cars rushed towards him, one, two, three taxis went by occupied . . . and Goujon's demented blue lamp melted into the night.

Panting from his exertions, he walked rapidly back across the river, found his jeep and drove away, watching his mirrors in case he was being shadowed, anxious to get home and play Isabelle the tape.

As he battled through the traffic in the Latin Quarter, the eleven o'clock news came on the radio. Thinking about Goujon, he wasn't paying any attention until the name Doctor Nathalie Sainte-Claire registered: '*a finalement succombé à ses blessures . . .*' – has finally succumbed to her injuries, – '*et la mort a été confirmée à huit heures ce soir . . .*'

The words 'and was confirmed dead at eight o'clock this evening' reverberated in his head. He tried resisting it, to fight it off, but he felt it going in like a knife, tearing his breath away. Even as he made himself drive on normally, telling himself it was nothing to do with him, he knew he was lying, it had everything to do with him. Driving south through the city, he became aware that he was getting close to the church he'd been trying to forget about, the one the guerrillas had told him to go to if he changed his mind. He knew Paris too well, his route cut through Montparnasse, it would scarcely be out of his way, and any minute now he would come to the junction at Port Royal and have to decide: straight on for home, sharp right for the church.

Pulling up at the crucial junction, he sat hunched over the wheel, staring through the windshield. Until Sunday, life had been simple. The goats could be a maddening chore, the writing a relentless taskmaster, and he and Isabelle sometimes nearly killed each other, but life was good, always had been, and now he was suddenly afraid of throwing it all away, because a woman with whom he had no connection had died. His pulse quickened, the seconds ticked away, the lights poised to change, he could feel the tension rising in the engines revving all around him, he rapped his knuckles on the steering wheel, willing the green lights to hurry, so he could ram down the accelerator and run for home before some soft matter in his head bent his judgement the wrong way. Straight on was the logical course, the direction from which a lighthouse would have been beckoning; to the right lay the unknown, perils hidden beneath the surface. Was that God pointing to the right? or the devil in disguise? You've no connection with that woman, he bellowed at himself. Then how come she's pulling? How come she's pulling so hard? The lights had changed, klaxons trumpeting behind him, he felt like leaping into the road and cracking a few Parisian skulls. Instead he thrust into gear and swung the jeep recklessly into the right-hand lane, provoking more furious protest, and raced off along the boulevard. A church loomed into view, a gothic-inspired edifice set back in a little park off the road. He drew up, switched off and sat back to let his heart settle.

Luke got out, looked quickly about and entered the grounds of the church. Prepared for it to be closed, he was surprised to see a glimmer of light in a stained-glass window. Piles of swept snow made a path to the front door. The door was locked; he walked round the side to a porch, where a candle burned in a glass jar. He tried the door, it opened and he went in.

Treading softly over a mosaic floor, he paused in the nave, where the vast cathedral-stillness of the place was suddenly disturbed by singing, neither harmonious nor choral, but the caterwauling of a drunk somewhere in the candlelit reaches of the church, and voices trying to restrain him. As Luke followed the singing deeper into the church, he thought he could feel, over the sea of chairs, a momentary draught of night air . . . or if not a draught, the sound of the city fleetingly introduced by someone's exit or entry. But a long look over his shoulder revealed nothing, and he went on until he reached a stone staircase. The rumpus came from below, he followed it down the stairs to a brightly lit kitchen. The singing had ceased, an argument taking its place on the far side of a partition. Looking about he saw he was in a crypt, converted into the spartan kitchen and whatever lay through a curtained doorway.

Peering through, he was met by an improvised dormitory: people old and young bedding down for the night on mattresses, and in the aisle a young priest remonstrating with a wretched wild-eyed man in a wheelchair clutching a bottle.

'They're turning me out!' the man appealed drunkenly to Luke.

'If he would just give me the bottle,' reasoned the priest.

'Can you beat it, monsieur, throwing me to the devil on a night like this!'

Disconcerted by Luke's gaze, the fellow allowed the priest to prise the bottle gently from his grip.

Luke withdrew and paced the kitchen until the young priest came through, drawing the curtain behind him.

'Bonsoir, monsieur, how can I help you?'

'I want to speak . . .' trying to summon the precise phrase, 'to the highest authority.'

The priest nodded, understood, as if he'd been expecting Luke.

'You have something, monsieur, for our mutual friends?'

'They're not friends of mine.'

'I see. But you want me to give it to them?'

'I don't have it on me.'

'I will get through to them soon as I can.'

'What's wrong with now?'

'It so happens I can't reach them until later tonight . . . if you'd care to wait?'

'No.' A moment's reflection as he moved towards the

stairs. 'What may I ask,' he went on in a lowered voice, 'is a priest doing mixed up in this business?'

The young man's smile suggested he often asked himself the same question.

'Part of your calling, is it?'

The sharp tone took Father Igor Boury by surprise. But he was used to attack and smiled again. He got it from all sides, upsetting the left because he provided an oasis of traditional liturgy, outraging the right by holding ecumenical prayer meetings and political seminars attended by Catholics, Moslems and Marxists. The authorities disapproved, but what could they say when his congregations held up so well in this increasingly godless country?

'Yes, monsieur, I do believe it's part of my calling.'

'Steeping yourself in politics?'

'The poor and hungry are politics, monsieur, so is the poisoning of God's earth.'

'No qualms about working with . . .with such violent people?'

Leading Luke further out of earshot, '*They*, monsieur, are you and I, only bolder.'

'Terrorists, bolder?'

Mild surprise, 'Terrorists?'

'Fanatics then.'

'If it's considered fanatical to devote yourself to the protection of the world, then perhaps it's a pity we're not all a little bit more fanatical.'

'You heard about Doctor Sainte-Claire, I take it?'

'They didn't do it.'

'*I* should know that, but indirectly, weren't they responsible? Aren't you?'

Father Boury lowered his eyes. Luke had hit a nerve.

'Why don't you light the fuses yourself?' Luke hissed, 'turn your crypt into a bomb factory, pay the poor pocket-money to assemble them?'

Silence from the priest.

Luke regarded him sternly and apologised, 'I'm sorry.'

'Thank you for being honest, monsieur. I do take responsibility, and it weighs on me, but if you believe in Christian theology, it follows we are tenants and caretakers of this world, each one with a responsibility to protect it.'

'Some would say in a democracy there are legitimate ways of doing that, like the ballot box and the shareholders' meeting, and when you reject that you've got anarchy.'

Father Boury drew Luke's gaze. 'Do you believe that?'

Luke didn't reply.

'Isn't anarchy what we have now?' said Igor Boury, 'uncontrolled industrialisation, poverty and pollution, all leading remorselessly towards environmental catastrophe. We possess the technological knowhow to water, feed, shelter and educate everyone on earth, instead we pursue a blind strategy of so-called economic growth, which leaves a minority gorged and bloated, the great seething majority wretched and desperate, and which is steadily poisoning the planet we depend on. This is anarchy of the worst kind, masquerading as normality, lulling us into a foolish sense of security, even as we unwittingly commit collective suicide.'

Luke said nothing, but looked severely, searchingly at the priest.

'The books you write, monsieur, are about what?'

'A world in which the inheritors of the future are trying not to repeat the same mistakes.'

'With ballot boxes and shares?'

Luke smiled, 'No. No governments either, and no nations, an advanced world, sophisticated in its simplicity.'

'Then I think perhaps you understand.'

'I like being consulted, not bullied. Your friends are getting into bad habits.'

'If you're willing to give them another chance,' a speculative smile, 'then I'm sure you'll be hearing from them.'

Father Boury made to show Luke upstairs.

'It's okay, I'll see myself out.'

He found his jeep and drove off, going over what the young priest had said, and pulling up at the first phone booth to call home. Isabelle sounded strange. 'You okay?'

'We've had visitors.'

'Who?'

'Whoever they were, they must have been pissed off, they've wrecked the place. Where are you?'

'Still in Paris.'

Her silence told him he should have been in touch.

'Is somebody with you?'

'Two policemen.'

'I'm on my way.'

In a country lane thirty-five kilometres south-west of the city, a large van marked Electricité de France was parked on the verge. During the afternoon, two men dressed as labourers worked in the ditch, apparently repairing cable. Now, with darkness encamped all around, they sat inside drinking coffee and waiting.

Soon after midnight, headlights approached, a police car.

'It's the Nose,' warned one of them, and they quickly tidied up.

The police car drew up, out stepped a slight dapper figure who was quickly admitted to the van. A young man removed his headphones and came to attention.

'All quiet, commissaire.'

With a flick of the wrist Goujon dismissed them, and they went out to resume work on the cable by arc lights. Removing his coat, Goujon took the young officer's place and slipped on a pair of headphones. Spools turned slowly before him, monitoring a conversation in a house across the fields. The notes in front of him told him he was eavesdropping on two gendarmes in the American's kitchen. They'd been there since 21.20 hours, accepting coffee and cognac at intervals.

Casting an eye over the other machines, Goujon wondered where Madame Morrel might be. Switching seats, he slipped on the corresponding pair of headphones, flicked a switch and listened in to the living room, where someone could be heard moving about.

Removing his headphones, he lit a cigarette, poured himself a coffee and sat back to wait.

Leaving behind the grim high-rise suburbs, Luke drove flat-out down the dual carriageway through the Bièvres Valley and into open countryside south-west of the city, approaching home towards 1 a.m.

The house was lit up, a police car stood in the yard. Taking a deep breath, he let himself into the house. Two gendarmes got to their feet in the kitchen, mumbling sympathetic greetings. Some attempt had been made to clear up, but he could see at a glance that his home had been taken apart.

He went through and found Isabelle reclining on the floor in front of the fire, halfway through a bottle of wine. A hoover stood by, a basin of dirty water, cleaning rags. She'd thrown herself into purging the house, but could do little for the moment about the ripped carpets and slashed upholstery.

Looking around he took in the items which, as he'd feared, were *not* missing: the TV and stereo unit. She looked up, twisting her mouth into a fateful smile.

'Welcome home! – *home*! the one place you're supposed to feel safe, the one place that's yours.'

'I got back as quick as I could.'

She drained her glass and cocked an eye at him, 'Are you having an affair?'

A short way across the night Commissaire Goujon roused himself as the nearest machine clicked on and the spools began to turn. He'd missed the first words which had activated the machine, but when he put on the headphones he heard Madame Morrel's light-hearted, '*Are you having an affair?*'

'*No, why?*' Morrel amused.

'*I found this in the grate . . . one of our dear burglars smokes Dunhill.*'

'*I'm not so sure they were burglars.*'

'*No,*' she seemed to agree, '*you had money lying around in the loft, which they didn't touch, but the room . . .*'

Her tone suggested havoc. Goujon clenched his teeth. Captain Nitze smoked Dunhill, God help him.

'*I did try telling you about it, you thought I was fantasising.*'

'*Can you blame me? Chéri, who did this?*'

'*I don't know.*'

'*Like hell!*'

A deep sigh, '*To placate Laroche, I told him about the copies.*'

Goujon tensed.

'*What's Laroche got to do with it?*'

'*He's with them, that's why I got snatched by them.*'

Them? Goujon enthralled. Was he hearing what he thought he was hearing?

'*You really were picked up by the GP? Chéri-*' dismay – '*I thought you were joking.*'

'*Bundled into a van, manacled, driven off into the night!*'

'*Be serious!*'

'*I am being serious.*'

Madame's shock allowed Goujon a rare moment of awe. Lighting a fresh cigarette from its predecessor, he waited with bated breath for the American to tell him what he really wanted to hear.

'*Did they mistreat you?*'

'*Not really.*'

'*Did they frighten you?*'

'*A bit.*'

'*I'm sorry . . .*' They fell to whispering, consoling and reassuring each other. Goujon rolled his eyes to heaven.

Still more irritating, the Morrels had a habit of drifting in and out of French and English.

'Where did they take you?'

Goujon froze, cigarette halfway to his lips.

'Some dingy little apartment above a canal or river. I was blindfolded.'

Press him, woman!

'God almighty! and now this – bastards!'

'It may not have been them.'

'They can't be up to much if they can't even fake a burglary.'

'Maybe they weren't trying too hard.'

Goujon nodded approvingly. Perhaps he'd underestimated the American.

'Chéri, I think you should ask for police protection – what's so funny?'

Morrel stopped laughing. Goujon knew what he was thinking.

'Sounds funny, that's all. You want to hear the tape?'

'Not really!' Madame's turn to chuckle, and Goujon's to permit himself a modest smile. Hadn't he known all along the American was lying?

'I think I'll go up first and take a peek at my room.'

'I'd leave it, you might have more stomach for it in the morning.'

Someone was poking the fire. 'You heard about –'

'Nathalie Sainte-Claire?' Madame reading Morrel's thoughts, 'Yes.' A damp log hissing and catching, 'Luke, we're getting rid of those damn goats!'

'What?'

'It's bad enough coming home to this without having those animals going mad. I had to leave everything and see to them again. It's not my job to milk your goats.'

'Our goats.'

'Your goats! And you've just lost one.' Pause. 'I found it dead, I tried to revive it.'

'A kid? Simone's?'

'How should I know?'

Was that Morrel leaving the room?

'They've been in there too . . .' Madame calling after him.

Goujon removed his headphones, and by moving to another seat and donning another set, followed Luke into the kitchen, where he shook hands with the two gendarmes, who confessed to being puzzled; floorboards lifted, plant pots overturned, nothing taken.

'You've no idea what they might have been after, monsieur?'

'None.'

'Can you think of anyone who might bear you or Madame Morrel a grudge?'

Luke considered. 'My bank manager?'

They laughed, shook hands again, and Luke showed the policemen out. As they got in their car, he asked,

'How did they get in?'

'Back window, monsieur, professional job. If fingerprints turn up anything we'll let you know.'

A salute and they were gone.

He crossed the exposed yard, seething with rage: Nathalie Sainte-Claire! Goujon! his wrecked home! and now Isabelle – We're getting rid of those damn goats! – He could have reminded her that she never turned her nose up at the yogurt and cheese or the modest revenue the goats provided, but after nearly forty years with someone you know when not to fight.

He entered the goathouse, animals barely stirring as he passed through, all deceptively undisturbed, but for the carnage of slashed sacks and spilled grain discovered by his hurricane lamp. He found Simone asleep, her kid dead nearby. Crouching down, he turned the furry fully-formed kid to see what sex it was. Bad enough losing the offspring of a champion milker, but a female too. Simone was looking at him now. She seemed peaceful, no obvious sign of another one inside her alive or dead. Her look seemed to say, See what happens, *mon vieux*, when you neglect us.

He looked around until his lamp found the afterbirth glistening in the straw like a jellyfish. He looked at the dead kid. He could have wrapped it in a refuse sack and put it in the trashcan, but it felt important, especially tonight, to bury her properly, and not to wait till morning. Lifting her cold weight in his arms, he took up the lamp and carried her across the road to bury her beside the dog in the wild garden at the back of the cottage.

The ground was winter-hard on top, rocky underneath. He worked off his rage with pickaxe and shovel, and as he worked he found himself missing Laroche, his support at this time, his madcap humour.

He was finishing shovelling when he heard footsteps on the track. He looked round, someone was coming round the cottage wrapped in a coat and scarf. He climbed out of the hole, picked up the animal and laid it in the ground, folding its limbs to fit. When he stood up, Isabelle handed him a hot whisky. They stood for a moment in silence. While he sipped he glanced at her, she looked more bemused than frightened. He put his arm around her and they walked back through the garden and down the track. Back in the house he gave her the photographs to study while he played the tape forward to the crucial point.

'Don't I get to hear the ducks?' she quipped.

'Fuck the ducks.'

Isabelle stretched out on the lacerated couch. 'You're sure this one is Maurice de Montfort?'

'I think so. Shit, since this morning I know so.'

'And the other, you've no idea?'

Luke hesitated, and before he could reply, car doors were heard to open and shut, and a row began with one man accusing the other of making a bloody mess of things. His first thought was to listen closely in the hope of concluding that it was definitely not Goujon. But the nasal supercilious voice was – if *not* his – remarkably similar. Then he found a comfortable position for his back on the floor and listened in the hope of hearing the tape differently this time, discovering some innocent interpretation. But such sentiments as 'it couldn't be better, especially if she dies' and 'our little package has already more than achieved its purpose', left little room for doubt in the context of the quarrel. He had only to look at Isabelle's face, resolutely relaxed at first, almost green now. Bad enough hearing about the conspirators, but actually hearing their voices in your own living room . . .

When she heard the names Batisse and Lusardi, she looked across at Luke to confirm they really were referring to well-known government ministers. She didn't know who Crozier was and didn't feel like asking.

The tape ended, Luke poured two more glasses of wine and went to the front window, parted the curtains an inch and peered out. For once he wished he could flick a switch and illuminate the yard to see if anyone was out there.

Isabelle lay back staring at the ceiling.

'You told me a bit about what happened when you went back to the estate with the commissaire . . .'

From Luke an ironic laugh, 'The nest gone, the bench where they talked vanished and Maurice de Montfort all smiles, telling me with his eyes, You and I both know the score, so be a good fellow and go home and close your door and forget all about it.'

'Forget about it! He must be joking. I'm damned if we're going to be intimidated, we're going to expose those bastards.'

He nodded unconvincingly; she gazed at him.

'You think the police are involved, don't you?' she said quietly.

'What makes you say that?'

Tears sprang to her eyes. '*Chéri* . . .' reaching out to him.

'What?' he came and sat with her.

'If something happened to you . . .'

'I feel the same.'

After a moment she said, 'You've had time to think. What do we do?'

'If I don't hear from the GP very soon, I'll go to the embassy.'

Goujon clapped his headphones tighter. Seldom excited by anything, he felt his pulse accelerate. Since the American had drifted into English again, he had to concentrate all the harder and wait for a pause in which rapidly to play back the tape and hear once more, *'If I don't hear from the GP very soon . . .'*

'Chéri . . .' Madame breaking the silence, *'have you seen the time?'*

'What time is it?'

'Twenty past two . . . it'll soon be tomorrow . . . chéri?'

'What?'

'Let's fuck.'

'Now?'

'Rechristen the carpet, the couch, I hate this place now, you should see the bedroom, my clothes strewn all over, and your room. We've been violated, they're everywhere, they've invaded us, our minds, our pores . . . let's get them out, let's fuck everywhere, on the floor, on the stairs, in the larder — everywhere!'

'Honey, I'm not sure I've the energy to do justice to your splendid proposal.'

'Merde! Let's try.'

'Why don't we fuck here and let our spirits do it everywhere else?'

Goujon shook his head wearily and poured himself another coffee.

13

When the radio-alarm clock woke her just before 7 a. m.
Kasha lay for a time with a headache, recalling how last
night's innocent dinner date with 'Michel Kerlesquin' had
turned into a nightmare.

Bad enough realising that the man whose hand she'd
read in the candlelit restaurant wasn't who he claimed to
be; unbearable to discover who he really was, and that
he'd set her up to make another attempt on the life of the
de Montforts. She could still recall the feel of his gun in her
hand as she waved it at him – the man whose bomb had
critically injured Nathalie, drinking coffee in her apartment! And to think she'd been drawn to him; her cheeks
burned. His gun lay a few feet away in a drawer, at least
she'd surely saved the life of the duke and his son.

Or had she? Was Revallier really only after their plans?

Even now she didn't know what to believe.

I'm a good liar as it happens; but I find it hard to lie to you.

There were three ways to get at the truth, she reflected as
she sat up: test Revallier's claim that he could be reached
through a priest in Montparnasse; track down the American bird-watcher to see if he really made that tape; and
confront the de Montforts directly.

She was pulling on her dressing gown, wondering
whether she could muster the courage to tackle the de
Montforts before they left for work, when the radio
announced Nathalie's death. She gasped, clapped a hand
over her mouth.

'*. . . and in close conjunction with my colleague, Doctor*

Sérard, tests were carried out independently, confirming that the patient, having deteriorated into a deeper coma, had suffered irreversable brain damage and was pronounced dead at eight o'clock this evening . . .'

Kasha sat on the edge of the bed and wept bitterly. When the tears stopped, she slid to the floor and sank into a cataleptic trance, staring into space, beyond hate or sorrow, and might have stayed there, cocooned in shock, had not something in the continuing news bulletin penetrated her mind.

' . . . and in a brief statement last night, Interior Minister Gaston Batisse promised that all necessary resources would be made available to the police in the hunt for those he called Doctor Sainte-Claire's callous killers . . .'

Kasha forced herself to get dressed, washed her face and put on some make-up. She was trembling, but she wasn't worried anymore about confronting the de Montforts. 'I want the truth!' she bellowed as she went weeping through to the living room and stepped out on to the balcony. 'The truth!' she shouted at the street. In the half-light of another freezing dawn, she checked her watch – 7.23, and looked along the street, bracing herself against the cold until a Mercedes and escort came into sight.

Hurrying indoors, she left the apartment. The moment she shut the door her phone rang, but ignoring it she ran down the corridor to the lift. Before she could press the call button, she saw the indicator panel above the door lighting its way up from the ground to the first, second, third floor, where, as she'd feared, it stopped. *Shit!*

She started down the stairs two at a time. The lift was old and slow, but it had a head start and by the time she reached the lobby, the de Montforts were crossing the courtyard with their mail, and the servile smile reserved for the duke was still on the concierge's face as Kasha dashed past her.

'*Bonjour, mademoiselle*, is there anything I can –'

Kasha kept going, closing the gap, '*Monsieur le duc?*'

Edouard and Maurice turned, Edouard's vigorous off-to-work expression softening.

'I'm sorry to interrupt you, gentlemen . . .' catching her breath, 'I wanted to ask you whether you'd recovered from your ordeal?'

'But of course, mademoiselle,' Edouard brushing it aside as nothing, 'our thoughts are naturally with Monsieur Sainte-Claire. I'm sure you've heard . . .'

'Yes . . .' a quiver in Kasha's voice. Hearing it in person, and from the duke, seemed to confirm it with crushing certainty, 'it's such a terrible shock.'

'We're also shocked,' said Maurice.

'I'm sorry we haven't had an opportunity of thanking you properly,' said Edouard, 'for your consideration and assistance the other morning.'

'It was nothing.'

'And now if you'll excuse us, mademoiselle.'

'I won't detain you, gentlemen, except to say that my paper in London is keen to do a major feature on the nuclear industry to coincide with the launch of your plans, and I was wondering –'

'Plans?' smiled a puzzled Edouard.

Kasha resisted the urge to point out the briefcase lurking beneath Maurice's coat.

'Sir, I'd like to do an interview before the weekend.'

Edouard hesitated, his eyes finding Kasha's anew, private desires and professional priorities in conflict. 'I regret I'm far too busy at present.'

'With the plans?'

'With an internal report –'

'Perhaps you could manage half an hour today? I would cancel all my appointments.'

'Very good of you, I'm sure, but it's out of the question.'

'Gentlemen, it's a golden opportunity –'

'For us?' quipped Maurice, 'or you?'

'to put your side of the story.'

'Our side,' Maurice politely reminded her, 'is being put quite well nowadays.'

A little smile and bow from Edouard and they turned away.

'I don't care for lop-sided journalism, gentlemen. Why should the Greens have a double-page spread to themselves?'

Willing the bait to tempt them, she was disappointed when they marched on with scarcely a backward glance, 'Thank you, mademoiselle, another time perhaps.'

Madame Klonowska was bearing down on her, and the security guards were enjoying the diversion as Kasha pursued the de Montforts to the street door to play her last card.

'Gentlemen, a man giving his name as Revallier telephoned my office last night . . .'

The lie stopped them in their tracks.

' . . . making dreadful allegations against you concerning Friday's bomb, and threatening to make hard evidence public.'

Edouard quietly, 'You spoke to him?'

'Ah no!' managing a note of indignation, 'but I am anxious that you should have every opportunity to refute his allegations. I mustn't delay you further, I'll present myself at the château at whatever time is convenient for you.' As Edouard gazed at her, Kasha found a smile, a feminine vane to her arrow. 'I'll telephone to arrange a time. *Bonne journée, messieurs!*'

While the de Montforts went on their way without another word, Kasha paused to look the security men in the eye. Surprised, they respectfully bade her good morning.

'You have no business interfering with the duke like that,' said Madame Klonowska, dropping all pretences.

Kasha leaned away, 'I'm, sure you wouldn't want those charges to go unchallenged, madame?'

'No one would listen to terrorists only for reporters and interfering foreigners.'

'In a democracy, madame –'

'Democracy!' she spat, 'always the same excuse. But here in France we know how to respect our heroes!'

Kasha collected her mail and returned to her apartment, pausing to listen at Nathalie's door, in case Robert was there. But all she heard was her own phone ringing further along the corridor, and she hurried on. Opening her door, she ran in and lifted the receiver in time to hear Alain say, 'I've caught you in the shower again!'

'I was downstairs challenging the de Montforts to an interview.'

'And will they?'

'I didn't give them much choice.'

'That's the spirit!' Pause. 'I suppose . . .' faltering, 'you heard about . . .'

'Yes, on the radio at seven.'

'Kasha, I'm so sorry . . .' a hopeless silence. 'I really thought, we all really thought . . . How are you feeling?'

'I'm . . .' too choked to speak.

'It doesn't sink in, does it?'

'Can we meet?'

'Of course. I'll cancel everything.'

'No, this evening.'

'I should be free around five. Call me.'

'Fine. *À toute à l'heure.*'

'Oh Kasha, how did it go last night?'

'Last night?'

'Your saviour was taking you to dinner.'

'It was . . . interesting, I'll tell you later. Oh Alain?'

'Yes?'

'Did you call five minutes ago?

'No, I'm just up.'

Strange, she mused, dialling a London number, who else would phone at 7.30? Praying he'd answer, she pictured her editor in his penthouse overlooking the river at Putney, downing a cold coffee and dashing out the door.

'Yes!' Hugh's familiar foul temper.

'*Bonjour! Comment ça va?*'

'What? Kasha!' a short laugh. 'Make my day, tell me you're coming to London and need a bed for the weekend.'

'Close! Actually I need a double-page spread for the weekend.'

'Are you out of your tiny mind? Isn't a twenty-four-page special report enough?'

'Forget the tunnel. Two interviews, the Godfather of the nuclear industry versus Jean-Jacques Revallier!'

'Who?'

'Leader of The Guardians of the Planet.'

'Of the what?'

'Hugh! Every cop in Christendom –'

'The Green car-bomber.'

'The very same, well?'

'You're a wee bit late.'

'Hugh, it isn't often I come at you like this –'

'You do, Kasha, all the time, and the weekend is chock-a-block. Mind you, what's his name – Revallier . . .?'

'No one has ever *really* interviewed de Montfort, and no one has *ever* interviewed Revallier, or even knows where he is.'

'And I suppose you do?'

'Two pages! Don't let me down.' She put down the phone and held her head: *Nathalie*, she murmured, tears squeezing through closed eyes.

Now to try to find Revallier! she resolved, consulting a wallmap of Paris in her office for the best route to the church in Montparnasse. If the priest failed to respond to her request to speak to a higher authority, it would be hard to avoid the conclusion that Revallier *was* the bomber.

In the bathroom she threw off her clothes, stepped under the shower and was giving her aching body to its heat when the phone went. Wishing she'd rememberd to switch on the answering machine, she was going to let it ring, when she had the strange feeling it might conceivably . . .

Clutching a towel she ran through.

'Mademoiselle Sharma?' a woman's voice, 'you still want to speak to the highest authority?'

'Yes.'

'Café Modern, rue St-Antoine, Bastille-end in twenty minutes; park in Guéménée round the corner. Got that?'

'Café Modern, rue St-Antoine, park in Guéménée, but I can't do it in twenty minutes.'

'Twenty minutes! And mademoiselle . . . if anything should happen to him . . .' Click.

Kasha gazed at the receiver buzzing in her hand and cradled it. The caller's voice hovered, an implicit threat too understated to leave Kasha in any doubt as to its intent.

Composing herself, she thought about what she needed to take and then rushed to get out as fast as possible.

In the lobby Madame Klonowska peered up from her hoovering to see Kasha hurry by in jeans, jumper and an open coat, hair dripping as she went, and wearing silver sandals.

Her route was straightforward, a run of eastbound boulevards from Haussman to St-Martin, through the whirlpool of Place de la République and south to Bastille, its naked torchbearer of Liberty illuminated in the gloom above the thundering square. Dogged by traffic, twenty-four minutes had elapsed by the time she reached rue St-Antoine, a broad old-world street running into the ancient district of Le Marais. With little prospect of finding a parking space anywhere in the area, let alone in the street quoted over the phone, she began to worry that Revallier would be gone by the time she found the café.

On the right a small square appeared, and through a screen of trees a promenade of shops with a CAFÉ-BAR-TABAC on the corner. Yanking down her window she read its faded sign – MODERN. According to her map, next on the right was Guéménée, a dead-end street, and she tensed as she turned into it. As expected every space was tightly taken, and she was thinking of double-parking when an old corrugated van pulled out of its space with such impeccable timing that she was in there and parked and running down the street before she had a chance to wonder at the coincidence.

Faltering on the corner, she glanced along the promenade and entered the café. A few men stood at the bar, some tables were occupied, some were free, but no Revallier. She stood for a moment bewildered, attracting unfriendly glances, picked an empty table and sat down to recover herself. A waiter looked across, she ordered a lemon tea. She took out a pocket mirror and grimaced at herself. She looked awful, but was damned if she was going to make the slightest effort for a man who might still turn out to be Nathalie's killer. *Nathalie dead*? She covered her eyes.

A window table came free. She moved to claim it and scanned the little square with its wretched trees and solitary statue, lighted shop-fronts on the main road and the grim outline of a byzantine temple. It was nearly nine o'clock, but it was one of those dark Paris mornings when the sky seemed to have fallen to earth, cars and shops were lit up and every tenth figure approaching through the gloom looked like the man she was waiting for.

In the country, Luke woke from a deep sleep. He was in Isabelle's bed, it was ten o'clock, he couldn't hear any major protest across the yard, so he guessed someone had seen to the goats.

Lying with his hands behind his head he marvelled at his exhaustion. Since Sunday's pre-dawn escapade he'd slept little, and last night, after burying Simone's kid and playing Isabelle the tape, they'd made love into the early hours, not a sexual triumph, more a council of war.

Isabelle came in bearing a tray and put it before him: eggs, toast, fruit, cheese, juice and bubbling coffee. He regarded her sternly, she had on her sober grey departmental-meeting suit.

'You're not?' he growled.

'I am,' she sat on the bed out of range.

'Cancel.'

Shaking her head. 'I've a meeting at eleven and seminars to follow, *The Picture of Dorian Gray* at three,' a wouldn't-you-know! smile, '*The Heart is a Lonely Hunter* at four. I'm damned if I'm going to let those swine intimidate me. I'm more worried about you.'

'Me?'

'Yes you, *idiot*!'

'I'm going to call the embassy. It's going to be all right.'

'Ring me,' she rose to leave, 'I'm late.'

At the door she turned and blew him a kiss, and was gone. He heard her drive away, worked through some of his breakfast and got up. Putting on a bathrobe he stepped on to the landing and found a note taped to the loft ladder: *DON'T! We'll tackle it later. Now turn round and go take a bath. You need it!*

Leaving the note in place, he switched on the loft lights and made the grim climb, pausing half-in and half-out to look around and take in the astonishing scene. Over the last few years he'd made this sprawling chamber his own world, a retreat where he could work and read in solitude and roll out a bed beneath the stars in the skylight. Everything had gradually found its home, every reference book, file and thumbtack. Now it looked as if a party of poltergeists had thrown forty-nine fits.

Walking around the room he could only smile . . . filing cabinets spilled on the floor, his wardrobe ransacked, rugs kicked away, floorboards ripped up. As for his cassette library, all the display boxes had been emptied and his two-hundred-plus tapes – classical, choral, African, blues, research interviews, recordings of bird song, his grand-children at play, all taken. Gone.

His manuscript, thank God, was untouched. But then he caught sight of something on the floor which made him wince. The photograph he treasured most lay with its frame broken in pieces. He bent and shook off the bits of glass and stood up. The black-and-white picture was unharmed. It showed a fresh-faced eighteen-year-old French girl sitting across a table from a young heavily strapped American paratrooper, smiling at each other. The night before, he'd fallen out of the skies, a pathfinder of the 82nd Airborne. Wounded on the way down and blown off course, he covered several kilometres before finding the rest of his unit drowned or lost. She found him in the morning under a hedge, and had no idea, as they stared at each other, that she was looking at her future husband.

Beating a weary retreat, he went down and ran a bath and lowered his aching back into the water; he lay for a time in a stupor, topping up the hot at intervals. Finally he hauled himself out, put on his bathrobe and went down to make his call from the kitchen.

When the receptionist answered in the US Embassy in Paris, he asked to speak to the most senior available official on an extremely urgent matter. The receptionist's pleasant 'one moment, sir,' sounded promising, until he found himself sparring with a second or third secretary, new to Europe and anxious not to rock the boat.

'If I may say so, sir, I really do think this sounds like one for the French police.'

'I'm trying to tell you I've already been. Now if you don't mind, I'd like to talk to one of your superiors.'

'Just a moment, please sir.'

The Security Officer in the Administrative Section heard out Luke's terse résumé.

'What sort of crime are we talking about, Mr Morrel?'

'How does politically motivated murder grab you?'

A sceptical pause. 'Sounds like a matter for the –'

'The French authorities? They were involved.'

'Involved? in what way?'

'They did it.'

'I see.'

'I doubt it, and if you don't put me through to someone at the top –'

'Just hold on a minute, sir, I'll see what I can do.'

Luke screwed up his eyes and waited until another voice came on, higher pitched, friendly.

'Mr Morrel? how can I help you?'

'And you are?'

'Lehrman's the name, Hale Lehrman.'

'Thank you for your name, Mr Lehrman, but where do you come on the greasy pole?'

'I'm a legal attaché. You've witnessed some sort of crime.'

'No. I'm in possession of criminal evidence, and before you tell me to go to the police, let me tell you we're talking about foul play with government ministers and the Secret Service involved. The police know I have this evidence because I've been to them. My house has been turned over and I fear for my family. Must I go on, or do I get to see a heavyweight at the embassy?'

'I'd be glad to see you . . . let's say ten o'clock tomorrow morning.'

'Are you kidding? I'm coming down right this minute.'

'No problem, sir. Let me just have a look. I'll see you at four o'clock this afternoon.'

With time to spare, Luke dressed, put on his old jacket and beret and crossed the yard to the goathouse. Isabelle's handiwork was evident, fresh straw was down, and spilled oats, maize and barley swept up and re-sacked. Knowing how little she enjoyed working in here, he felt momentarily crushed. Calling the animals to him one by one for examination and a tête-à-tête, he predicted that eight or nine of them would be dropping kids any day now, and hoped to God this crisis would be over by then.

Crossing the road, he walked up the track to the cottage and let himself in, and was relieved to find no sign of intruders. They'd overlooked the cottage or didn't realise it was his. Finding the tap frozen, he filled a pan from receding snow in the back garden and put it on to boil. As he lit the fire in the grate, he tried to imagine the place finished, Sylvia and the kids coming for the summer, nieces and nephews arriving from the States. But the vision dimmed and his eye fell on the door of Laroche's VW, which had fallen off when he roared away on Sunday, and now stood propped against the wall. His anger with Laroche for tipping off the GP returned, and he fell to wondering about the nature of Laroche's involvement with them, and about his limp and scars, his hit-and-run accident.

A few minutes later, as he swung a lump hammer at the remaining section of dividing wall, he heard a car turning off the road and coming up the track. Smooth and quiet, the engine seemed strangely familiar, so when he took a penknife to the nearest polythene window and peered out, he was relieved to see nothing worse than a standard police car.

The police driver got out and opened the back door. A familiar figure emerged, trim and inscrutable. One hand loosely in his pocket, he came unhurriedly towards the door, and knocked. Luke looked at the poles holding up the ceiling and enjoyed a brief fantasy of bringing the house down on Goujon's head. Pocketing the knife, he opened the door.

Wearing a modest smile, Goujon stepped inside like a prospective buyer. Lifting his shiny shoes over the carpet of woodshavings, he looked about appreciatively.

'I was just making coffee. Would you – ?'

'No thank you, monsieur.'

Goujon continued to look about with interest, his eyes roaming purposefully. Pale light came through the windows, flames flickered in the grate, otherwise indoors was dimmer than out and almost as cold. Gravitating to the fireplace, Goujon stooped to extract a smouldering twig and lit a cigarette.

'As a boy I loved a good fire . . .' carefully replacing the twig, he stood again, his tone nostalgic, 'there was no shortage of dead wood in the forest.'

'You're not a Frenchman by birth, commissaire?'

Goujon clicked his tongue to correct the misapprehension. 'Corsican.'

'A beautiful place, I'm told.'

'Ah, the very air . . .' sniffing as if to rekindle the memory, 'the heat pressing down in the evening like incense.'

His voice echoed through the cottage, a smoker's rasping voice, the voice of the Volvo driver?

'I'm sure you must have such memories of America, monsieur?'

'Ponderosa pine, the air after a thunder-shower, cactus blossom on the desert breeze . . . you never lose it.'

'You should have stayed,' Goujon stood with his back to the fire smoking leisurely, 'We both should have stayed, don't you think?'

Luke met his gaze.

'We're exiles, you and I, monsieur. Exiles can easily find themselves fugitives. It only takes one mistake.'

'What sort of mistake?'

'A lie one wishes one hadn't told.'

'What are you saying?'

Goujon's smile introduced a chill, sharper than winter, into the room.

'What makes you think I lied, commissaire?'

For reply, Goujon, smiling pleasantly, tapped his nose.

Luke surprised, 'A detective relying on intuition?'

'And fact. Your property was entered yesterday.'

'You know something about that?'

'The gendarmerie tell me intruders were looking for something specific. If I'm in possession of the sole copy, why would anyone want to do that?'

Goujon dropped his finished cigarette on the floor and stepped on it. 'Where is it, monsieur?'

Luke didn't reply at once. He let his thoughts follow his gaze about the room, lighting absently on objects that caught his eye: the broken pickaxe handle on the table; the sledgehammer by the door; the planks and poles holding up the ceiling . . .

'I came to you with evidence of a grave crime. You assured me you were going to act,' looking directly at Goujon, 'but you're not going to, are you?'

The hand in Goujon's pocket moved, Luke tensed. All that emerged were lighter and cigarettes. Goujon lit up again and sucked deeply. 'I've a dark feeling, monsieur, that you've been in communication with a certain terrorist organisation . . .'

Luke returned his gaze unflinchingly.

' . . . which is why, with regret, I am obliged to arrest you.'

Luke recoiled inwardly, Goujon's words – *obligé de vous arrêter* rang in his head. His mind raced, anticipating Isabelle's terror. He smiled, 'There I was thinking you'd only be interested in the big boys – Batisse, Lusardi, even the President – I'm honoured!'

Goujon laughed lightly and gestured towards the door.

Luke's gaze wandered again, rash thoughts running amok. Goujon's attention also strayed, eyes scanning the room, still hunting.

'I want to call Paris, leave a message for my wife.'

'By all means, but you *could* save yourself a lot of trouble . . .'

His voice trailed off, leaving the offer hanging in the icy air. All Luke had to do was forget his little trespass last Sunday, forget Nathalie Sainte-Claire and who killed her,

215

and whistle a happy tune every time the media ranted about Revallier and company. All he had to do to go free was to surrender the tape and pictures.

He lifted his gaze to meet Goujon's. 'I'd like to change first, if you've no objection.'

As they emerged, they were observed from the road by a young man poking in the engine of his car. Father Boury had got a message to Revallier late in the night, and Ricardo Cruciano had come from Paris to collect the vital tape and pictures.

But approaching the American's place on the right, Ricardo had spotted the police car up a track on the left, and instead of turning into the yard he'd driven past and pulled over simulating engine trouble.

He recognised both men at once, the towering Morrel and, to his dismay, the unmistakable profile of Commissaire Goujon. Averting his gaze, he concentrated on some imaginary fault in the wiring. If stopped by the police, his papers identified him this time as theology student Paolo Vanzetti, Paolo in honour of soccer star Paolo Rossi, Vanzetti after the anarchist condemned to death in America in the twenties. Maps and guidebooks would confirm that he was on a tour of France visiting religious sites and was heading for nearby abbey ruins. His 1955 Alfa Romeo carried Roman number plates and a certificate of membership of the fictional Vintage Automobile Club of Italy. Normally he felt secure with this cover, but the sight of the elegant detective sent a shiver through him. Goujon was said to see through anyone, his beakish nose more sensitive than the most relentless lie detector. Usually stimulated by danger, Ricardo felt like a rabbit hiding from a hawk.

The police car started up, came down the track and, instead of driving off, crossed the road into the American's compound and bounced over the rutted yard to the main house. Morrel went inside, Goujon got out and looked around.

What was it between those two, wondered Ricardo, coercion or collaboration? As the detective wandered among the wood piles to the garage, Ricardo thought about the machine-pistol in the Alfa. GP policy severely restricted the use of firearms, but wouldn't Revallier and Janine make a glorious exception for Goujon? Since Friday's bomb had branded them murderers anyway, he could imagine Revallier saying, What! you let that swine go?

The American reappeared dressed for town. Ricardo closed the bonnet, climbed behind the wheel and felt for the gun strapped beneath his seat. The police car was already in motion, and to carry out the deed Ricardo would have had to move fast to start the Alfa and give chase. But as his fingers found the ignition, he stopped, knowing full well that in reality Revallier would be livid if he did it, and that he couldn't carry through a cold-blooded killing anyway.

The police car bumped on to the road, he watched it speed away. No tape, no pictures, no Goujon.

Kasha had ordered more tea and had almost given up hope of seeing Revallier when she noticed someone on the pavement trying to catch her eye, a woman about her own age wearing jeans, loose jacket and dark glasses. With a faint jerk of the head, she beckoned.

Leaving money on the table, Kasha picked up her bag and coat and went after her. The woman walked quickly, pausing at the end of the promenade to look over her shoulder. And was gone. When Kasha reached the corner, she was already on the far side of the street, glancing back, leading Kasha deeper into the ancient Marais. With a rush of nerves she knew who it was she was following.

Roads grew quieter, traffic lighter, Janine Vallence was

standing by a van when Kasha turned the corner, the same battered van which had earlier liberated its parking space for her. Janine gestured to her to get in the back. While Kasha obeyed and found a hard seat, Janine closed the doors and got in front beside the driver. As they pulled away, Kasha recognised the driver as her mugger, the man who went for her bag on Monday morning, dragging her to the pavement.

The van worked its way round Place de la Bastille and rattled along the boulevard towards the river.

'How do you feel about being branded for Friday's bomb?'

A snort of derision from Janine, 'We've been accused of many things, you get used to it.'

'Branded as murdering terrorists? Doesn't it hurt . . . if it isn't true?'

'Look, Mademoiselle Sharma,' looking sharply round, 'by the end of today another forty thousand children will have died needlessly and enough rainforest to cover this city destroyed . . . *every day!* If people are too stupid to open their eyes and see the world is dying and *do* something, what does it matter what they call us? What does anything matter?'

Tahar looked sideways at Janine. She'd changed recently, she was always so bright and optimistic.

'Of course it matters,' he said.

She slapped him on the arm, hard. Startled, he looked at her, and saw she was smiling.

They turned off into docklands and drove for a time in silence before pulling up on a quiet stretch of waterway guarded by rusting hulks and cranes.

'Take these,' Janine passed Kasha a pair of wraparound dark glasses. By the time she put them on and found she couldn't see anything, the back doors were open and Tahar was helping her into the road. He led her like a blind woman along the quay and then stopped, gently restraining her.

'We're going down a narrow gangplank on to a boat. I must ask you not to report anything about where this meeting took place.'

As he guided her aboard what was actually a barge, he added, 'I must also apologise for the other morning. I don't make a habit of it, I assure you.'

'It showed.'

She felt rather than saw him smile as he manoeuvred her along a strip of deck and down a few steep steps into a warm cabin. He took his hands away and left.

Someone else spoke, 'You may take off the glasses.' An all too familiar voice.

She removed the glasses and glanced at him, and looked at him again, boldly, dreading to find in his face something that would betray him as the bomber.

'Have you come to interview me or to bury me?'

She didn't reply. He returned her gaze with almost expressionless calm, and motioned her to take a seat.

She sat down. He looked different, no longer modish Michel Kerlesquin. He stood by a porthole in an open-necked shirt and leather jacket, unshaven, his eyes darkly shadowed and bright, and the bandage on his hand getting grubby.

Although she too looked different, younger and more ordinary in jeans and dufflecoat and her hair all over the place, seeing her again sent shivers through him.

The cabin, lined with polished wood, was cramped and dimly lit.

'Coffee?' he gestured towards a narrow galley from where the smell of coffee came.

'No thank you.'

'I'm sorry about your friend . . . particularly as you thought she was making a recovery.'

She looked at him, plumbing the depths of his face. 'I need to know . . . for sure.'

'Know what?'

'That it wasn't you.'

'You read my hands,' spreading them in supplication, 'are these the hands of a killer?' Immediately he remembered his fingers at Claude Lusardi's throat and knew that they were.

219

'Maybe I'm not very good at palmistry.'

She saw a muscle twitch in his jaw, and his eyes film over with anger. 'Get out. I have nothing to say to you.' Turning his back, he stared out over the river. 'Go put your questions to the de Montforts.'

'I am. I'm going to the château this evening.'

He turned slowly, searching her face.

'He granted you an interview?'

'He declined . . until I said you had contacted my office making grave allegations against him and his son regarding the bomb. I offered them an opportunity to reply.'

'He went for that?'

'He hesitated, and I said I'd phone to confirm a time.'

'You don't take no for an answer, do you?'

'Do *you*?'

'Be careful of Edouard de Montfort.'

'Why?'

'Aside from hunting, his favourite pastime is seducing young women and spitting them out.'

Did she detect a note of personal bitterness?

'And he doesn't give a shit for your interview. If he sees you, it's to find out how much I know. He's afraid I may know about the American's tape and pictures, which incidentally will be delivered here any minute.'

She welcomed the news, but didn't show it. Businesslike, she took out a compact tape recorder, placed it on a chair and opened a notepad on her knee.

'I want to begin with your childhood,' switching on the machine, 'where were you born, monsieur?'

'Who cares,' switching off the machine, 'where or when I was born?'

If Kasha was surprised or disappointed, her expression betrayed nothing.

'Instead of covering this story,' he said, 'I invite you to step into it.' She gazed at him evenly. 'We've warned the editor of *Le Monde* to expect a parcel containing a tape and photos incriminating those responsible for the rue de Liège bomb, as well as the de Montforts' secret plans for the nuclear industry. I want you to deliver it.'

'How do you propose to get hold of the plans?'

'That's not your concern.'

'If anyone were to be killed or seriously injured –'

'When we launch an operation, it's done with the utmost care.'

Kasha considered a moment. 'Why no interview?'

'What for? who gives a shit?'

'It's your chance to put your view.'

'What view?'

'Whatever makes you go to such extremes.'

'We *all* share the same cosmic view of the world, only most people have gone blind, and those who can still see can't bear to.'

'Some would call you arrogant, monsieur.'

'Because my eyes are open?'

'Because you judge others to be blind.'

'They're *made* to be. How else can modern industrial society function, except by preparing its young for a life of blindness, blind faith in economic growth, blind consumerism. While half the world is on its knees, the other half is engaged in frantic activity producing things it doesn't need. We're programmed to consume and consume and remain blind and stupid to the damage it's doing to ourselves and to an exhausted planet.'

'A cynical view of society, don't you think?'

'Look at how we're educated. Do schools turn out people capable of thinking for themselves, or dull eager consumers lacking skills and confidence, their initiative stifled? In modern society we put the hearts of our young to sleep, disconnect their minds and feed them dreams of shopping malls. If schools were meant to liberate the scientist, artist and thinker, in a few generations politicians would be blown away in gales of laughter and the young would rescue the world.'

'If education is the way to save the world, why are you a saboteur and not an educationalist?'

'Education takes time, we don't have time.'

'You call yourselves guardians of the planet, but do you imagine for a minute that your kidnapping stunts and attacks on industrial plants can defend the environment?'

'No.'

Surprised, 'No?'

'We were strong once, sister brigades springing up in Europe, the United States, Japan, but the state proved stronger.'

She cocked a doubting eyebrow, 'A successful lawyer turning outlaw overnight because of his political philosophy? What really sparked it?'

As he turned to look out over the river, she quietly started the tape again. It was some moments before he spoke.

'I loved the sea as a boy, I saw it blighted when the *Amoco Cadiz* broke up off Finistère, a tide of oil rolling ashore, three hundred kilometres of Breton coast reeking like a petrol station, creatures wallowing in dark glue. The detergents we used made it worse, students who demonstrated were battered by riot police . . .'

Turning from the porthole, he paced lightly back and forth, 'I saw my Brittany change violently, woodlands bulldozed, walled fields brimming with life replaced by dead tracts, centuries of drainage systems and moisture-retaining capacity wiped out, animals reared on conveyor belts, communities swept away to feed the cities: the terrorism of progress. And then came sixty-eight.' He paused to look at her, 'You remember sixty-eight?'

A smile, 'I was twelve.'

'The youth of the world caught fire in sixty-eight, nowhere more so than in France, where students and

professors demanded reform, an end to the old order.'
Pacing again . . . 'Naïvely I thought we'd be listened to,
that's what governments were for. Instead they did what
no one had ever done before, sent riot police into the
university. Rather than allow demonstrators to leave
peacefully, they beat and arrested us. Paris erupted, France
erupted, hundreds of thousands of students and workers
clashing day and night with the CRS. De Gaulle refused to
speak with us, he was more interested in his state visit to
fascist Ceaucescu's Romania. Even when factories, banks
and airports closed and the whole country ground to a halt,
his response was to turn to the military for reassurance . . .'

Revallier paused, gazed at the ground and smiled.

'I couldn't believe it. De Gaulle, France's champion
during the war, the man who'd said *The flame of resistance
must never be extinguished!* determined to crush us. Why
had men like my father fought in the resistance? To replace
the Nazis' Third Reich with de Gaulle's Fifth Republic? To
substitute foreign repression with our own?'

'Too exhausted to fight on, we fell back as the CRS
recaptured Paris. The rebellion was over, freedom stifled.'

He fell silent.

'You became a lawyer, why?'

'I trained to be.'

'*Blindly* pursuing your career?'

He glanced at her and his voice became sharper, 'Time
and again as a lawyer, I found myself defending people
whose crime was having the nerve to resist the government. When it encountered objectors to atomic power
stations, the government didn't bother with the niceties of
enquiries. It sent in paratroops like thunderbolts of official
will . . .'

'Isn't that how you met Janine Vallence?'

'At Plogoff she was a protest leader – difficult to defend.'

'Why?'

Smiling at the memory. 'Serious assault charge. Can you imagine! prosecuting a young woman for beating up a *para!* Have you ever seen a French paratrooper?'

'A disillusioned young man,' she observed coolly.

Her tone displeased him. 'More than disillusionment, mademoiselle. My own country – *Liberté-Egalité-Fraternité* – had become a police state. Slowly, painfully I understood. The state exists not to look after its people, but to control them, in its own interests, and people the world over have more to fear from their own governments than from almost anyone else.'

She took care not to glance at the tape machine, trusting it was doing its job. A boat chugged by, rocking the barge.

'So you and Janine Vallence formed the GP – why?'

'It followed naturally,' he said, as if it were self-evident.

She was shaking her head, 'I don't believe you.'

'What don't you believe?'

'You've cited powerful influences, but it takes a flame to start a fire. There's something you're not telling, something personal.'

He looked at her, and not for the first time felt naked before her. She gazed at him with the quiet patience of one who won't be denied. With a gesture of impatience he looked at his watch to show he hadn't time. Kasha, unimpressed, persisted.

'What happened, monsieur?'

After a long silence, he leaned back against the table and fixed Kasha with a look which seemed to say, All right, but only because it's you.

'During the war,' he began haltingly, 'after they bombed Rennes, my grandmother Germaine, a young widow, took refuge on the island of Brèche on the north coast of Brittany and became a *hébergeuse* who sheltered downed airmen and escaped prisoners of war – until she was caught by the Gestapo and put to death . . . Her daughter, my mother Irma, a mere teenager, was left to bring up the family . . .' he spoke softly, mechanically, his voice filling the room. 'She took up with a local fisherman and resistance fighter Jérôme Revallier. Early in forty-four, while helping a batch of Allied airmen escape to a British ship, his unit was ambushed by the Milice –'

'The Milice?'

'French security police who collaborated energetically with the Nazis. The unit had been betrayed by one of its own members . . . Edouard de Montfort, double agent.'

'De Montfort?'

Revallier saw Kasha's astonishment clouded with doubt.

'Edouard was a dashing young aristocrat, faithful to the family tradition of anti-communism, anti-semitism, anti-anyone who might upset the prevailing order. His father, Valentin, the then duke, was naturally a Pétainist –'

'A Pétainist?'

'Favouring close co-operation with the Germans, and regarding the Maquis, the resistance, as terrorists.'

'Edouard's father knew he was a double agent?'

'He was proud of him.'

Kasha remembered Edouard de Montfort at her door, red roses and cognac in hand, catching sight of her reindeer earrings: *Dis donc, if I'd known, I'd have come as Santa Claus!*

'It's a grave charge. Why would the de Montforts collaborate to such a degree?'

'They weren't unique. Occupied populations divide into three: those who resist, the majority who keep their heads down, and those who drop their pants.'

'What were the de Montforts doing in Brittany?'

'They had a home there, spent much of the war sailing and entertaining business clients, notably Germans. My mother, just eighteen . . .' his voice trailed off.

'Your mother?'

'pregnant with my sister –'

'By Jérôme?'

Nodding, 'was taken on by the de Montforts as a domestic.'

'Without knowing Edouard had betrayed Jérôme's unit?'

'No.'

'But Jérôme escaped?'

'Apparently. I grew up on tales of his heroism. From time to time he'd visit my mother under cover of darkness, and one moonless night spawned me . . .'

'So Edouard de Montfort betrayed your father's unit, but your father survived.'

He looked away, talking faster.

'Shortly after the war he was lost in a fishing boat off Cap Fréhel. My mother married Henri Molène, a much older man, and took us to live with him in Roscoff, where he worked as a marine biologist.'

'And where you were born?' Revallier nodded. 'Your mother had left the de Montfort's employ?' another nod, 'without ever discovering their treachery?'

'Right. Then in seventy-two –'

'Seventy-two? We're jumping more than twenty years.'

'She was committed to an asylum, where she remained until a few years ago.' Head bowed, he gazed at the floor.

'She died?' Kasha guessed.

He came over and switched off the tape. A glance at her told her he'd known all along it was on. What he had to say now was for her only.

'After my mother was committed,' he drew himself up, 'I was going through her papers when I found letters she'd written . . . to Edouard, copies painstakingly written out of letters he never answered. I didn't want to believe what was in them. I went to see Marie-Thérèse –'

'Your sister?'

'She'd known all along, mother had confided in her, they'd kept it from me. Yes, mother had been obsessed with Edouard, and he apparently was very taken with her,

226

a headstrong girl and a beauty. But she was a domestic, and he returned to Paris to marry and began his dazzling climb through the ranks of the atomic energy industry. But I felt Marie-Thérèse was still keeping something from me. So I went to Île de Brèche for the first time, a beautiful place, warm people . . . until I started asking questions, then they closed like flowers . . .

'They were frightened, thirty years after the war. Only one man would talk, Victor Soro, in his seventies, half blind, formerly the de Montforts' gardener. He told me more of what I didn't want to hear, and he told me where Jérôme was buried. The way he said it . . .' Revallier faltered.

'You went to see Jérôme's grave,' Kasha prompted.

'It was winter, I had to scrape headstones to read the names . . . and then I found it – *Jérôme Revallier, killed in the service of France, 1913–1944.*'

Kasha caught her breath. Silence from Revallier, fixed on a moment he must have relived a thousand times. A smile came to his face, he turned and met her gaze.

'I was born in forty-eight. Some feat, don't you think, siring a son from the grave?'

He ran a hand over his scalp, as though trying to erase the memory.

'Jérôme did father your sister?'

'Yes.'

'But he wasn't lost at sea.'

'No.'

'He didn't survive the ambush?'

'No.'

'So, aged about twenty-four, you discover that your father, far from being a hero of the resistance . . .' she faltered. 'I'm sorry.'

'I hated him.'

'Edouard?'

'Jérôme . . . for not being my father. Why couldn't he

have survived the ambush and married my mother? Then I realised I wouldn't have been me. I *am* Edouard's flesh and blood . . .' He stared out at the sky, 'I'm born of a man who sided with the Nazis and who betrayed my mother's lover, my sister's father, a man who still trades on the medals he won in the resistance, and who is respected the world over as an elder statesman of atomic power.' He shook his head and smiled as if he still couldn't believe it.

'Has he ever met you?'

'He almost did last night, only some over-conscientious journalist stopped me.'

She matched his sardonic smile.

'He knows of your existence?'

'My mother wrote to him often enough.'

'But does he know *who* you are?'

'I think he knew who he was trying to kill.'

'What?'

He motioned her to start recording again.

'I tried to bring a case against him in seventy-six, to prosecute Edouard de Montfort for the murder of seven French men and women at Pointe de la Tour on 17 February 1944. But my chief witness barely survived a hit-and-run 'accident', and my offices were fire-bombed.'

'What evidence did you have?'

'I thought I had the gardener, Victor Soro. He'd seen enough, including an occasional dinner guest spirited into the de Montfort's house – local Milice chief, Pierre-Marie Medec. Soro's wife Anne had also seen letters not replaced in the safe, and once a document with the official seal of Les Chevaliers de la Croix d'Or, an extremist Catholic organisation which provided former Milice men and Nazis with shelter and escape routes. But I couldn't get the Soros to testify.'

'Were they threatened?'

'Not exactly, but I understand that advice from Edouard

can be as persuasive as a pistol. But one man, apart from de Montfort, did survive the ambush –'

'Your hit-and-run witness.'

'It took two years and a private eye to find him, a man we shall simply call Jean-Baptiste, who was seventeen at the time of the ambush. Suspicious of Edouard, he altered his allotted position and, instead of dying on the cliffs, saw the Milice spring their trap, directed by de Montfort.'

'Did he never try to expose Edouard?'

'Edouard put it about that Jean-Baptiste was the traitor. He became a hunted animal.'

'How can you be sure de Montfort wasn't telling the truth?'

'No Jew whose family has been exterminated by the Nazis works for the Milice. After the war he kept trying to persuade people of Edouard's guilt, until he got tired of being beaten up, changed his name and disappeared.'

Footsteps on deck.

Revallier stepped aside and slid a hand inside his jacket.

'Only me!' came a young man's voice.

'Excuse me,' Revallier climbed above.

Kasha heard them murmuring at the top of the steps. Revallier returned agitated. 'No tape, no pictures, no proof. The American's hand in glove with our friend Goujon, a collaborator!' Turning to Kasha he spread his hands as much to say, I'm sorry, what can I do?

Frowning, 'Who's –'

'Commissaire Goujon's leading the hunt for us. It seems he now has the originals *and* the copies.' Gazing away, 'All that leaves is the secret file, which *may* refer to the bomb.'

Their eyes met.

'Will you do it?'

'Deliver the file to *Le Monde*?'

He nodded. She considered. 'As long as –'

'No one's going to get hurt.'

'I have your word?'

A flicker of hesitation. 'You have my word.'

'Then in my capacity as a journalist, a neutral . . .'

He smiled, she rose to leave.

'Tonight then,' he said, 'wait for a call, and have an overnight bag packed.'

She raised an eyebrow.

'You're staying with us.'

She packed her tape recorder away, nodded a farewell and started up the steps.

'Mademoiselle,' he came to the foot of the steps, she turned. 'If you see him tonight, take care. If he knew what I've told you and believed you could do him harm . . .'

His eyes warned her.

As the police car sped towards Paris, its languid blue light clearing traffic in its path, Luke and Commissaire Goujon conversed not as arrested man and cop, more like travellers thrown together, discussing goat-breeding, Corsican separatists and literature.

'I like your countryman Henry James – what a masterpiece, *Washington Square!*'

Luke nodded grudgingly.

'You don't care for it?' said a wounded Goujon, 'who then is your inspiration?'

'He's a bit fussy for me, I'm more at home with Hemingway.'

Undaunted, Goujon sang *Washington*'s praises, and as he listened, Luke had the feeling that either Goujon had a very odd view of the book or had never read it.

In Paris they went not to Goujon's island office, but to an address in the shadow of the Interior Ministry. Until now Luke had remained calm, but getting out of the police car he caught the glances of passersby, and even in his suit and best coat experienced a cold draught of guilt. He felt like a criminal as Goujon escorted him through the entrance of an anonymous building into a labyrinth of passages, and finally into a brightly lit room.

'Help yourself to coffee, monsieur, I won't be long.'

'I'll make those calls if I may.'

'By all means.'

Goujon closed the door, Luke was in a white windowless room. Pouring himself a coffee, he took out a notebook, put on his glasses and tried to dial his lawyer René Fauroux. He couldn't get a line out. There was a second telephone, but it was obviously internal, and he persevered with the first.

Removing his coat, he sat down, pondering his situation. The room hurt his eyes, a clock ticked on a bare wall. He tried the phone again in vain. Perhaps someone could show him how to get a line. Out in the passage he looked right and left down a long bleak corridor. Unseen typewriters tapped, figures appeared and disappeared and, as he stood there, a strange sound reached him, muffled shouts and whining, like a man beating a dog. As he listened, the sound came again, making his flesh crawl. He could have shut himself in the room, but chose to take a walk, vaguely tracking the sound down empty corridors, until suddenly a door opened and Goujon came out.

'What are you doing here, monsieur?'

This was a different Goujon, artless, cold.

'I was wondering that myself. I'm also wondering what's going on in there?'

Goujon brusquely motioned Luke back the way he'd come. They returned in silence to the white room.

'Sit down, monsieur,' said Goujon, taking a seat behind the table.

Remaining on his feet, Luke jerked a thumb towards the passage. 'What was going on in that room?'

Goujon lit a cigarette, exhaled through his nostrils and replied evenly, '*Une chambre des aveux spontanés.*'

Voluntary confessions room, Luke translated and found

a grim smile, 'I suppose some forms of terror can always be justified.'

'Don't make it more difficult for yourself, monsieur. Do I have to remind you that you are under arrest?'

'I think you do. It doesn't sink in.'

'You shouldn't have lied to me.' Goujon's expression conveyed how simple things could have been. 'On top of which you've been in communication with Les Gardiens de la Planète,' holding Luke's gaze, 'have you not?'

Luke had no reply.

'You didn't seek them out, they abducted you, I realise that, but why did you keep it from me?'

Finding his voice, 'They didn't kill Doctor Sainte-Claire.'

'Does that absolve them of their other crimes?'

'I want to see the right people nailed.'

From Goujon a conciliatory smile, 'You've been a little foolish, monsieur.'

'I could get a whole lot more foolish. When are you going to arrest someone?' He cringed at the mocking echo of his question and went on, 'On the estate yesterday morning, I recognised Maurice de Montfort as one of the men on the tape.'

Goujon nodded. 'I think you may be right.'

'And the other man, the driver . . .'

'The other man?' prompted Goujon.

'Bore a remarkable resemblance to you.'

Goujon smiled, as much as to say, Intriguing thought.

The two men regarded each other in silence.

'I couldn't get a line,' Luke nodded towards the phone.

Goujon treated him to a surprised look, and not for the first time he had the feeling that Goujon was deliberately allowing him glimpses of the Volvo driver behind the impeccable façade of Commissaire Goujon.

'Anyway you don't need a lawyer. It gives me no pleasure to detain you, we can settle this in a few minutes. Tell me about the other night.'

Luke remained silent for a time. Finally, 'After the ornithological meeting, I was jumped in the street, bundled into a van and driven to some haunt –'

'What kind of van?' Luke shrugged. 'How long did it take?'

'Hard to tell when you're scared out of your wits and blindfolded.'

Goujon fired rapid questions, going over certain points in unremitting detail, trying to prise from Luke's unconscious memory particulars of the terrorists' appearance, intentions, morale. Luke answered fully, if less than truthfully.

'You recall no clues as to the location of the hideout? busy road, sounds of neighbours, a sense of being near water?'

Luke shook his head.

Goujon stood up. 'You're sure they never mentioned contacting you?'

'No.'

Goujon unlocked a cupboard packed with recording equipment and pressed a button. A strangely familiar voice filled the room – *'Where did they take you?'* Even on an imperfect recording, Luke couldn't fail to recognise Isabelle.

'Some hideout on a canal or river.' Or himself.

Goujon stopped the tape and looked over his shoulder. 'You *saw* water, or something suggested it?'

Luke gaped, unwilling to draw the obvious conclusion.

Forwarding the tape, Goujon stopped it at a given point. *'Chéri?'*

'What?'

'If something happened to you . . .'

'I feel the same.'

A pause on the tape. Luke's anger rising.

'You've had time to think, what do we do?'

'If I don't hear from the GP very soon, I'll go to the embassy.'

He stared at Goujon, mesmerised by the trap he'd fallen into.

'You left me no choice, monsieur,' said Goujon relocking the cupboard and pocketing the key.

Luke trembled with rage. Taking his home apart and stealing his tapes was bad enough, but this, planting electronic devices and listening to him and Isabelle – *Jesus!* making love! recording exchanges of the most intimate kind. Clenching his teeth, he struggled to master himself.

Goujon had the door open, 'Let me show you something, monsieur.'

Luke went after him into the passage, and as they retraced the steps taken earlier a human cry rent the air. Turning a corner, they gravitated towards its dying echo. The sound led them to an unmarked door, Goujon marched in, holding the door for Luke. He faltered and followed.

Low, wide and windowless, the room stank of sweat and aftershave. A yellow smog of cigarette smoke unrolled to reveal a badly beaten man bound to a chair, three or four men in shirtsleeves standing about, drawing themselves up at the sight of the commissaire.

'I was looking for you earlier,' said Goujon.

The interrogator stubbed out his cigarette.

'I was making a phone call, checking the prisoner's lies.'

'No progress, I hear.'

'We'll get there.'

'You've been getting there since Monday.'

Luke was trying to get a better look at the prisoner, pulse racing as he began to put a face to the bruised profile.

Goujon was taking the interrogator aside, addressing him out of earshot, 'Who left a cigarette butt behind when he carried out yesterday's search? Who's the arsehole who smokes Dunhill?'

'Choirmaster' Nitze, a man with a reputation for being able to make almost any suspect sing, blanched, furious, indignant.

'Another mistake like that,' warned Goujon, 'and I'll have you scrubbing lavatories on the quai des Orfèvres.'

'Jesus Christ!'

The outburst of English made all look round in time to see Luke bearing down on them. Unsure of his intentions, two men stepped into his path. Barging them aside, he reached the prisoner, but was immediately set upon.

'Leave him!' Goujon's voice arrested them.

Luke stretched out a hand. Through inflamed eyes Laroche peered fixedly ahead, offering no response to Luke's touch. He was handcuffed to the arms of a chair, shirt open, black-haired chest running with sweat. He was breathing badly, his ear clotted with blood, tobacco pouch spilled at his feet. Luke rounded on everyone.

'This has got to stop . . . people are going to hear about this . . .'

Nitze and his men looked at Goujon as if to say, Who is this jerk? Goujon looked on impassive.

Luke was down on one knee retrieving the tobacco and rolling a shaky cigarette.

'I hope you're proud of yourselves, four fit young men beating up a tied-down man of sixty. Don't you know who this man is?'

'A Yid,' murmured one of them to muffled laughter, 'and a queer.'

Luke got up, stuffed the pouch into Laroche's pocket, eased a rolled cigarette between his swollen lips and lit it for him. Then he faced Laroche's tormentors again.

'This man was fighting for France before you bastards were even born. Do you make a habit of torturing heroes?'

'He's a fucking terrorist,' said Nitze.

'No monsieur,' said Luke, stepping up to the man and looking into his eyes, 'you're the fucking terrorists and I'm going to put a stop to you.'

'Enough!' said Goujon. 'Have the prisoner cleaned up, treated and fed. Let him rest until further notice.'

Nitze's jaw fell, his men exchanged disbelieving glances.

'*Alors, monsieur*,' Goujon beckoned Luke, 'let's go.'

Luke turned at the door, drew Nitze's gaze and aimed a finger at him, 'Hurt that man any more and I swear to God . . .'

Nitze laughed, his men took up the chorus and, with their scorn ringing in his ears, Luke followed Goujon back to the white room.

'You've got to stop that, commissaire.'

'I have.'

'And let him go.'

'Release a man who knows the GP's hideouts?'

'How do you know he knows?'

Without reply, Goujon made a rapid internal phone call. 'I'm ready,' was all he said, replaced the receiver and sat down. Moments later two burly figures filled the doorway. Luke looked at Goujon for explanation, Goujon smiled regretfully.

'There's a little matter of a phone call to my lawyer.'

'Give me the number.'

Luke read it out, Goujon jotted it down, lit a cigarette and waited for Luke to be gone. Luke picked up his coat, folded it over his arm.

'I solve a crime for you, you lock me up. Ironic, *n'est-ce pas, commissaire?*'

He left, escorted by the two uniformed men. Alone, Goujon screwed up the sheet of paper and dropped it in the empty bin.

They walked Luke past the voluntary confessions room – quiet now – down more bleak passages until they stopped before a steel door with spy slot. A bunch of keys jangled, the door was opened. Luke looked in on a barren little cell.

He stepped inside, the door clanged shut.

14

After leaving Revallier, Kasha was driven back to her car. On the way she questioned Tahar from the back of the van.

'May I ask you, monsieur, are you a Moslem?' He agreed that he was. 'Do you have any difficulty reconciling your religion with membership of the GP?'

'To be a Christian, a Moslem, a Hindu and *not* to be an ecologist strikes me as contradictory.'

'And the GP's violent methods, Allah approves?'

'I'm not always sure, mademoiselle.'

It was getting on for noon. She drove across town to her London paper's office and began telephoning European atomic energy headquarters. Between calls she studied archive material relating to the de Montforts, hoping that Revallier was right in believing the duke would be anxious to see her, if only to learn how much Revallier knew.

If he refused she'd be bitterly disappointed. There were questions – about the bomb, about his past – which she could scarcely wait to put to him. If however he agreed to an interview this evening, she'd be left with one tricky problem, the dinner party, friends invited for eight and she hadn't done a scrap of shopping.

As the afternoon wore on and she was about to try the duke again, her desk phone went. Without introduction, a barely polite personal assistant told her to present herself at Château-de-Claireau at six sharp, and on no account was she to bring a photographer.

Six sharp! It was already after three. Her heart raced. If she didn't go home to change, there might just be time to track down the American on the way to the château. According to the map he lived five or six kilometres away. But what to do about the dinner party? Since she'd left it too late to cancel, she decided to phone her favourite restaurant and throw herself on the mercy of the *patron*.

'*Ah, Mademoiselle Sharma!*' Monsieur Duval sounded pleased.

'I've a problem only you can solve.'

'*Ah bon!*' even more pleased.

'Fourteen people coming to me for dinner, I've an important interview, no time to shop or cook, in short monsieur, is there any chance you could fix me up?'

'You'd want it delivered?'

'Could you?'

'When would this be for?'

'Tonight, around nine.'

'Tonight? you're not serious!'

'Please don't say no, monsieur.'

Pause, sigh. 'How could I say no to you, mademoiselle? what had you in mind?'

'Whatever you suggest.'

'One moment, please.' Monsieur Duval went away and returned. '*Pamplemousse en salade et poisson fumé* to start?'

'Fine.'

'*Terrine de lapin* or *boeuf bourguignon?*'

'The beef I think.'

'*Crème de marrons* to finish.'

'Wonderful. And plenty of your best house wine.'

'And a little something without meat for mademoiselle.'

'Most kind, monsieur. About the bill –'

'I'll start collecting clients' bills from the floor, as many as you need in order to claim.' He took down the address.

'You're an angel, monsieur.' As she hung up, she suddenly remembered there would be twelve guests, not fourteen. Nathalie and Robert would be missing.

Fighting back tears, she rushed around to the dry

cleaners, collected a fresh set of clothes, changed in the office and set out as quickly as possible, battling through Paris into the suburbs. With the car straining and shaking on the autoroute south of the city, she made good time until she had to forge west into open countryside. As the fog came down she began to get lost in a web of lanes and villages around Chevreuse.

At 5.20 she rolled down her window in the village of St-Sulpice-en-Maréchaux and asked where Monsieur Morrel lived. Who? The American. Ah, Monsieur Morrel!

A few minutes later her headlights picked out a sign: La Vieille Forge, and she pulled off the road into a wide yard. She tried the main house, no one answered. Lights and voices drew her to a long shed. The smell of animals struck her as she stepped inside. There seemed to be little horned goats everywhere, then in a pool of light two men and a woman, and a goat in labour, propped up with a bale of straw under her belly.

'She's never had trouble before,' the woman was saying.

'Could be one of those years,' the older man replied, putting on rubber gloves, 'everyone's having trouble.'

The other man was far too young, so she took the first to be the American. 'Bonsoir, madame, messieurs . . .'

Isabelle looked round and started in fright.

'I'm sorry to startle you, madame, I was looking for Monsieur Morrel.' As she spoke she glanced hopefully at the man, but the vet returned her gaze blankly.

'What do you want with him?' asked Isabelle harshly.

'My name is Kasha Sharma, I'm a journalist.'

Isabelle excused herself, stepped out of the stall and took a few steps with the stranger.

'I believe he recorded some rare ducks, madame.'

'Is that what you've come about, rare ducks?'

'I believe he also inadvertently recorded something else.'

'Where have you heard this?'

'Word gets out.'

Isabelle glowered, ready to throw her out, trying to decide whether press coverage might help Luke or make his situation worse.

'Your husband, I'm told, taped an incriminating conversation.'

'What's it to you, some juicy little story for your paper?'

'I want to know who killed my friend Nathalie Sainte-Claire.'

Isabelle's expression changed.

'She was my neighbour. I'm on my way to interview the de Montforts. First I wanted to check the rumour that they may not be telling the truth.'

'You're dead right they're not . . .' tears welled in Isabelle's eyes, 'they've arrested my husband. I've just come back, they wouldn't even let me see him, and what really scares me is I'm sure the police are involved.'

Kasha touched her arm. 'I've only a few minutes, but I can come back.'

Kasha's hand felt less a journalist's ploy, more a gesture of empathy from one woman to another.

'Please do what you can.'

'May I hear the tape?'

A helpless shrug, 'I don't know what he's done with it.'

'Then quickly tell me the gist of what he recorded.'

Isabelle gave her a concise résumé.

'Give your number,' said Kasha, 'I'll call you.'

'I'm going to the American Embassy first thing.'

'I'll get you later.'

They exchanged numbers, Kasha squeezed the older woman's hand and left.

Had they spoken in the house instead of the goat shed, their conversation would have been monitored. Even so, Kasha aroused deep suspicions when she was stopped almost immediately at an improvised roadblock. Blinded by lights, she spun to a halt on the snowy road and was rushed by gun-toting gendarmes, one of them shouting at her, flinging open her door and ordering her out with her hands up.

She sat immobilised, rigid with terror.

'Out!' barked the officer.

Fighting the urge to obey, she forced herself to stay put.

'Kindly stop pointing guns at me and then we'll see.'

The officer hesitated.

'I'm not accustomed to being treated this way in France. You should be ashamed of yourselves.'

The men murmured among themselves.

'Your papers please, madame.'

Kasha handed over her British driving licence, and while he examined it she closed her door and rolled down the window.

'What were you doing in that house, madame?'

'Asking directions, I want to get back to Paris. I'm over from London and I thought I'd take a drive.'

'Where are you staying?'

She gave Alain's name and address.

'Occupation?'

'Fashion designer,' she replied.

'You know your way now, madame?'

'Yes, thank you.'

'My apologies,' he said, and waved her on.

Shaking uncontrollably, she drove on, her terror gradually subsiding, her resolve hardening. On her way to the Morrels she had found herself doubting Revallier again. Face to face he was very persuasive, but with each passing hour the memory of his aura faded, undermining her certainty, making her cling to compelling details of his story: his mother's stack of unanswered letters to Edouard de Montfort, the astounding dates on Jérôme Revallier's headstone. Meeting Isabelle Morrel had restored her conviction that Revallier was telling the truth.

It was getting late, 5.55 when she pulled over to consult

her map. As she pressed on, the fog came and went, breaking in waves over the road, reminding her how Friday's murderous fog had enticed Nathalie into the street fifteen minutes early. With a nauseous spasm, she remembered that she was on her way to see the men whose conspiracy had in all probability killed her.

As her headlights probed lonely lanes and ditches, she began to wonder whether she was going to spend the night looking for the château, when around a bend a nebulous glow announced the floodlit gates of an estate. Gendarmes stood out in the glare. She drew up and rolled down her window.

'My name's Sharma, I've an appointment at Château-de-Claireau, am I in the right place?'

The gendarme leaned on the car and spoke into a two-way radio. Kasha flicked on a light to see the time, 6.10. The duke might refuse to see her. The gendarme finished speaking, slapped the roof of her car and waved her on. With a sinking feeling she drove through the gates. Lit like a runway, the road rushed through undulating vineyards, until the lights of the château shone weakly in the fog. Turning through a deep arch, she bounced the car into a lantern-lit forecourt. Slipping into Nathalie's silver sandals she applied a few touches of make-up, grabbed her coat and bag, and climbed into the stillness.

Georges Bolivar was at the top of the stairs to receive her. Whatever his accomplishments as principal bodyguard, Kasha felt his unease with women as he went through her bag and passed her quickly to a lesser bow-tied bodyguard, who took her coat and escorted her through the house, past a grand dining room where staff were setting twenty or more places at a long table, and through an immense salon until finally he paused in a doorway to announce, '*Mesdames et messieurs, Mademoiselle Sharma!*'

Dreading the sight of a crowd, Kasha was relieved to see only the two de Montforts and their wives.

'Ah, there she is!' The duke rose, coming to receive her with a generous public smile, covering a gaze of admiration meant only for her.

Revallier's father! was her first thought, immediately discerning a resemblance between the two men in Edouard's vigorous hair – in his case white and distinguished – his sureness of movement and, most of all, his compelling eyes.

Taking her by the elbow, he led her over to join the assembled company on a terrace beside the glamorous indoor swimming-pool. 'I don't think you've met my wife . . .'

The duchess, a thin ravaged woman, smiled hollowly through a deep suntan. 'I doubt it, there's so little reason to come to Paris nowadays,' she said, looking curiously at Kasha.

'You know my son . . .' Maurice rose and half smiled, 'and my son's wife, Cornelia, the Countess von Hammelburg . . .'

The pale, conventionally beautiful young woman remained seated and erect, 'I'm so very pleased to see you again, mademoiselle.'

Dispensing smiles, Kasha accepted a seat and a glass of champagne, and adjusted to the attentions being directed towards her, particularly Maurice's suspicion and Edouard's desire. Edouard sat back with the satisfied air of a lord in his own home. As Kasha met his shameless gaze, she wondered could he read her thoughts.

'You're late, mademoiselle.'

'The fog delayed me, I apologise. This is a wonderful place.'

'Was! My son initiates improvements at an alarming rate: roads, lights, helicopter pads, swimming-pools!'

Maurice came to life, smoothly asserting himself.

'I'm simply trying to drag this poor benighted house into the twentieth century. My father's a hopeless romantic, wants the estate as it used to be, rustic, draughty and liberally sprinkled with manure – a true ecologist!'

Enjoying the laughter, Maurice sat back and lit a cigarette with the expansive gesture of a man well pleased with himself. Yet his confidence rang false, thought Kasha, a man seeking to strike the right pose.

'The original owner,' exclaimed the young countess, 'held the title Master of the Wolfhounds to the King!' Kasha succeeded in looking surprised. 'Did you know that as late as 1595 there were wolves in the streets of Paris?'

'There still are,' said Edouard drily.

'What do you mean there still are?' objected Geneviève de Montfort.

'Not that kind, my dear,' said Edouard, quick to refill her glass.

'As far as I'm concerned,' Geneviève lifted the glass to her lips, 'the improvements can't come soon enough. *You* must find it terribly cold, mademoiselle, where are you from?'

'Rajasthan, madame la duchesse.'

'Where?'

'In India.'

'India?' The duchess looked mildly surprised, as if she wouldn't have expected one so poised and educated to come from India.

With her hands folded over her belly, the young countess smiled at Kasha as though tentatively welcoming a new friend. Kasha returned her smile, silently congratulating her on her pregnancy.

'Thank you so much,' said Cornelia, 'for all that you did on Friday morning. I'd have fainted dead away, I'm so upset about Doctor Sainte-Claire.'

Kasha nodded sympathetically, and saw that Cornelia wasn't conscious of the unease she had introduced by mentioning Nathalie.

'It's only out of personal gratitude,' observed Maurice with his strained air of authority, 'that we've agreed to a journalist coming here at all.'

'I'm honoured,' said Kasha.

A servant arrived to refill glasses; underwater lights in the pool played on the domed ceiling.

'When are you due, madame la comtesse?' Kasha asked Cornelia quietly.

'My son will be born in March, and do please call me Cornelia.'

A grateful smile, 'A son? You sound very sure.'

'I was checked at nine weeks, a new sampling test.'

'Silly child,' said the duchess, 'she could have miscarried, but would she listen?'

Edouard reached over to pat Cornelia's hand. 'Ah, but she's done it, my little angel.'

Cornelia basked in his approval, and Kasha, recalling Revallier's story, believed she saw how it was in this family: fathers begetting and controlling sons to maintain a strong blood line. Instead, the line was growing progressively feebler. Suave Maurice, for all his aggression and success, oozed weakness. He would have committed himself to Friday's mad bombing to impress his father, just as Edouard impressed *his* father by infiltrating the Maquis. Looking at Cornelia, she saw a plucky young woman whose mother-love might break the de Montfort mould by producing a strong son.

'I've a few things to do,' said the duchess, rising unsteadily.

'I hope I'm not disrupting anything,' said Kasha.

'I wish you would, I'm not sure I can stand another evening of men who imagine that nuclear waste is a suitable topic of dinner conversation. And good luck, mademoiselle,' she added over her shoulder, 'if you squeeze anything out of my husband, you'll be the first.'

Watching her depart, Kasha reflected that this was the woman Edouard married after the war, a more suitable match than the young pregnant domestic he deserted in Brittany. She glanced at Edouard, only to find he was watching her.

'Come, mademoiselle,' he said rising, 'let me show you the engine room.'

245

'Why doesn't Mademoiselle Sharma stay for dinner?' suggested Cornelia, 'do stay! it would be such fun.'

'Good idea,' said Edouard, humouring his daughter-in-law.

'I might learn too many secrets,' said Kasha.

Edouard chuckled, motioned Kasha to bring her drink and with a hand on her arm guided her through the chandeliered hall to a sweeping staircase. Her flesh trembled at his touch as they climbed.

'Would the reception tonight be related to the unveiling of your plans this week?'

Another chuckle, 'What plans?'

'And would your guests include representatives of the European Atomic Energy Commission?'

'What do you know of the CEEA?'

'Rivals in nuclear power – France, Britain, Germany, Belgium, Italy – pulling together to find solutions to radioactive waste disposal and other tiresome problems . . . like the Greens.'

'You've been doing your homework, mademoiselle.'

At the top of the stairs they proceeded around a gallery overlooking the hall.

'This evening's entertainment will help sweeten tomorrow's drastic solution I suppose.'

Once again the duke chortled, distinctly strained this time, she thought. Was she going too far?

'Do I detect a certain lack of enthusiasm for the nuclear industry, mademoiselle?'

'My view is coloured by the industry's record both in Britain and in India.'

'Oh?'

'Especially in Rajasthan, where those living downwind and downriver of atomic facilities have been producing deformed babies born with extra fingers or without genitals.'

'Certain parties are quick to blame the industry,' he

said lightly, 'it's a pity they haven't the evidence to back it up.'

They came to a concealed entrance, heavy curtains parting to give access to a darkened circular passage, a turret linking two sections of the château. Edouard flicked a switch and spotlights struck the far curve of the chamber, illuminating a door without handle or keyhole. Moving briskly forward, he appeared to open it by passing his signet ring over an electronic eye in the doorjamb.

'No need for keys,' observed Kasha.

'Solid gold security!'

With a gallant gesture, he invited her to enter a vast windowless room fitted out like a modern office. The low ceiling, the lack of windows and the great centre-stage model of Europe featuring all its nuclear power plants gave the impression of a war room from which Edouard de Montfort conducted his campaigns.

'How do you like my little domain?'

He stood back, poised to light a slender cigar, demanding her approval. Feeling trapped, she looked about with a detached air, focusing with apparent interest on a wall-chart of the heavens, criss-crossed with the passage of spacecraft.

'That was a scheme we entertained briefly with the Americans, the disposal of nuclear waste in space. Beautiful idea, pity about the cost.'

'You don't feel any unease about leaving behind radio-active waste for future generations to live with?'

'To live with?' Edouard sucked lustily on his cigar, 'nobody *lives* with it, it's expertly stored, well away from human habitation.'

'I understood the experts couldn't agree on a safe way of storing the waste?'

'My dear mademoiselle, no standards of safety to which we could aspire would ever satisfy the Greens. While I'm trying to raise our standard of living – and that of the Third

World – the Greens would like nothing better than to take us back to horses and candlelight!'

'I thought their argument was that with insulation and recycling we wouldn't need half the energy you're producing, and that the energy required could be produced by other means?'

'Wind and waves!' laughed Edouard, 'chiefly wind!'

'You see no possibilities in alternative sources?'

A tolerant shrug, 'I dare say a windmill on the estate could heat my bath water, but these technologies are still at a primitive stage of development.'

'Could that be because atomic energy receives the lion's share of research and development funding?'

He laughed again, scarcely able to disguise his distaste for a woman who combined beauty with political wit.

'I'm sure you're far too bright to believe any of that. The ecologists are dark-age fantasists, I have to wrestle with economic realities. You don't agree?'

'I only ask the questions, sir.'

'And you do that quite well, mademoiselle,' he said, raising a glass in tribute and gazing at her over the rim as he drank.

It was clear from his look what he would rather have been doing than answering her questions, she mused as she sipped from her glass.

'May we talk about your plans?'

'Would you like to see them?'

He caught her blink with surprise and smiled. Then moving smartly to a desktop personal computer, he whisked a template from his jacket, fitted it into place over the keyboard and, allowing Kasha to approach, tapped out with slow deliberation a simple sequence. Before she had time to wonder at his openness, the wallchart of the heavens, as though by suggestion, parted from the middle and opened like windows, revealing a wallsafe. Another simple sequence and the safe swung open.

'This, mademoiselle,' he announced, striding across to lift out a briefcase, 'is going to see us handsomely into the twenty-first century, a simple blueprint for prosperity and progress.'

Removing the tape recorder from her bag, she set it down on the nearest surface. 'May I begin to record?'

'Later.'

Later? Her expression begged to remind him that there was no later.

'I can't ask you to join us for reasons you've surmised, but if you'd care to take dinner in one of the guest suites, the party will break up early, after which I fly to Paris. You might care to join me?'

She regarded him blankly, trying to hide her discomfort, predicting what he might have in mind for her in the late-night intimacy of his apartment . . . in exchange for an interview?

'In the meantime,' he went on pleasantly, 'there are a few things I'd like to ask *you*. Please . . .' inviting Kasha to sit.

Just when she thought she'd captured the initiative he'd wrong-footed her and now, as she carefully took a seat, she sensed traps everywhere. Why had he so obligingly shown her how to gain entry to the room and the safe? Was he hoping she'd take the bait and come later looking for the secret file, so he could catch her red-handed?

'So Monsieur Revallier called your office. What did he have to say?'

'Why are you so interested, monsieur le duc?'

That she answered his question with an impudent one of her own displeased him, but in recognition of her nerve, or to mask his irritation, he found a patient smile.

'France believes in nuclear power, and I am privileged to be its principal representative. A slur on me is a slur on the industry.'

'Do you think anyone will listen to Revallier after Friday?'

'I expect you're right, but I owe it to my industry and to

France to keep myself informed of what the other side is up to.'

Nodding solemnly, Kasha held her tongue.

'You're teasing me, mademoiselle, what did he say?'

'He apparently said many things . . . among them that you and senior figures in government and the Secret Service conspired to discredit The Guardians of the Planet by simulating Friday's assassination attempt.'

Edouard flinched almost imperceptibly. 'I don't quite follow.'

'The bomb, Revallier said, was officially sanctioned and made to look like the work of the GP.'

Edouard laughed heartily, and Maurice de Montfort appeared just then, drink in hand, in the doorway.

'Who in their right mind would believe such rubbish?' said Maurice.

'Some undoubtedly will,' adjudged Edouard, 'what can one do? In a free country the press has the right to report the most malicious stories.'

'We give subversives publicity at our peril,' said Maurice, 'and I'm sure Mademoiselle Sharma wouldn't want to do so at our expense.'

'Nonsense,' said Edouard, without taking his eye off Kasha, 'Mademoiselle Sharma must do her job as she sees fit. What else did he have to say?'

'That you were a double agent during the war.'

'That's outrageous!' protested Maurice.

'Go on,' said Edouard.

'That your father was pro-Nazi, and that you worked with the Milice against the resistance.'

'My father was a decorated fighter in the Maquis,' said Maurice, 'how dare that guttersnipe –'

'Calm yourself,' snapped Edouard, 'are we going to allow the ravings of a terrorist to upset us?' Re-lighting his slim cigar, he rolled it between his teeth and resumed, 'This is most entertaining, mademoiselle, what else am I credited with?'

'Betraying your unit on the night of February the seventeenth 1944, and co-ordinating an ambush in which seven men and women of the Maquis perished.'

'I won't hear any more of this!' said Maurice incensed.

Edouard laughing, '*Imbécile!* it's all part of the game, the fellow's cornered, who wouldn't fight like a rat in his shoes?'

'He claims he tried to bring a case against you, until an attempt on his life and on the life of the only surviving witness.'

'I confess I did, years ago, hear rumours to that effect. If they're true, I can only think that loyal supporters of mine, sickened by zionist and ecologist-inspired smear campaigns, must have lost patience and taken the law into their own hands.'

'You deny all his charges, monsieur le duc?'

With a snort and a wave of the hand, Edouard indicated the suggestion was beneath contempt.

'What do you really think of him?'

'Who, Revallier?' Kasha's question seemed to catch Edouard off balance. Recovering instantly, 'What is the purpose of your question?'

'I'm interested.'

'What do *you* think of him?' Edouard turned the tables, 'I should like to know.'

'I feel nothing but revulsion,' she held his gaze, 'for anyone who can coldly and calculatingly put a bomb in a car and detonate it in a public place.'

'Quite.'

'As a journalist who has covered impersonal wars but never witnessed a conflict as intimate as this one appears to be, I can't help wondering what you think of him?'

Maurice shook his head and looked at the time.

'Our guests will be arriving any moment.'

Strangely hushed, Edouard looked down as if troubled

251

by the question. 'He's . . . tenacious, I'll say that, and I suppose believes in what he's doing.'

Maurice regarded his father oddly, never having seen him giving serious consideration to a journalist's questions.

Emboldened, Kasha probed deeper. 'What if your son, monsieur, instead of being in public relations, was leader of The Guardians of the Planet?'

While Maurice turned away with a gesture of impatience and lit a cigarette, Edouard went very still. Kasha held her breath, she'd found her mark.

Slowly raising his eyes, he focused on her.

Hands folded on crossed knees, she returned his gaze unswervingly. He too maintained an impassive façade, betrayed only by the glazed intensity of his eyes. She felt him boring through her, trying to peel away her innocence. Her heart beat wildly, but she was satisfied. She had the truth.

'I suppose,' he said picking his words with care, 'one would have to be grateful one had produced a man to be reckoned with.'

Still weathering his gaze, Kasha was rescued by the phone ringing. Edouard answered it. 'We'll be right down.' Replacing the receiver, he sought her out again.

'I'll have someone show you to your suite, mademoiselle. Feel free to shower and relax. A meal will be sent up to you.'

'You're most kind, sir, but I've a dinner party of my own this evening.'

'Ah.'

'Perhaps you could spare a little time tomorrow evening for a recorded interview?'

'Why don't you call me?' he said benignly.

Minutes later she was being escorted through the house by a brisk coldly polite Edouard.

'Will you say goodbye to madame la duchesse for me, and to the countess?'

'Of course.'

In the entrance hall, before they could complete their farewells, a guest handing over his coat bellowed, 'Evening, de Montfort!' in bald English.

Kasha turned and blanched inwardly – Randolph Morgan! accompanied by a younger man she didn't recognise.

'You promised us a helicopter!' complained the newspaper tycoon cheerfully, proud of his disdain for foreign languages.

'I control many things,' replied Edouard in his best English, 'but the fog . . .' he smiled and shook his head.

'You surprise me,' said Morgan coming over with his companion, 'with just about everyone else in your pocket, I can't think how God escapes you! Ah! Miss Sharma, *enchanté!*'

Kasha coolly returned his smile, and felt the hard gaze of Morgan's arrogant-looking companion. Kasha looked him in the eye, 'I don't believe we've met?'

'My associate, Peter Lunn,' supplied Morgan, 'this is Miss Kasha Sharma, last of the incorruptible correspondents!'

Her cheeks burned, 'Yes, I am still rather attached to the truth.'

Morgan tut-tutted, 'You really should try to disabuse yourself of pretty illusions about news and truth, and, talking of pretty illusions,' he glanced reprovingly at Edouard, 'I didn't expect to meet anyone from the press here this evening.'

Edouard laughed drily, 'Don't worry, gentlemen, Miss Sharma was just leaving.'

'Aren't *you* from the press, Mr Morgan?' Kasha asked cheekily.

'He *is* the press,' Lunn reminded her.

Edouard helped her on with her coat and lifted her fingers to his lips. 'Keep in touch, mademoiselle,' his blue-green eyes bored into her, a mysterious appeal, a clear warning, 'I'm sure we can come to some arrangement.'

With a serene parting smile and every outward appearance of calm, she fled. But before she could draw breath, she recognised two of the guests coming up the steps in close conversation, Interior Minister Gaston Batisse and Defence Minister Charles Delaye. They passed her without a glance. Too busy covering their tracks, she supposed, trying to catch what they were saying.

The forecourt was filling up with limousines, and she had to move quickly to squeeze her car through the mêlée and avoid being trapped. She passed more limousines as she crossed the estate. When finally she drove through the gates and turned on to the open road, she rolled down her window and breathed in the icy freedom of the night.

Back in the château, Edouard de Montfort excused himself and went to his study to make a phone call to Paris.

On receiving the call at his table in Ristorante il Delfino on the Île de la Cité, Commissaire Goujon explained that it wasn't an ideal place to talk.

'You don't need to talk, commissaire, only to listen.'

Goujon put down his wine and listened, mentally distancing himself from the smooth, coldly charming voice of a man he greatly admired, a man whose society and respect he craved.

' . . . and if I may permit myself a piece of friendly advice,' de Montfort concluded, 'keep close tabs on that journalist and deal decisively with the American, or risk incurring the merciless wrath of some very influential men.'

A weighty pause while Goujon absorbed the warning. 'Yourself included, monsieur le duc?'

'The last thing I wish, my dear commissaire, is to see you destroyed. Enjoy your meal. Goodnight.'

The phone went click in Goujon's ear. He replaced the receiver and glanced round the half-empty restaurant, deflecting one or two curious pairs of eyes with his gaze. Then with a bitter sigh he took up his wine and lit a cigarette. He was trembling, seized by childhood feelings of inferiority. Gritting his teeth, he called his office and spoke in a low whisper,

'Bloque, put a tap on all the de Montforts' telephones.'

'On what grounds, chief?'

'National security.'

Delayed by traffic and a petrol stop, Kasha reached rue de Liège at nine o'clock and walked into more trouble.

'It's outrageous,' said Madame Klonowska, 'especially so soon after what happened on Friday.'

Still high on emotion after her encounters with Revallier and the de Montforts, Kasha scarcely knew what the concierge was going on about.

'You might have told us you were having a party, mademoiselle,' explained the security guards, 'all these strangers turning up.'

Kasha, distracted, found a penitent smile.

'It's just that I assumed men of your calibre could tell the difference between my friends and the average urban terrorist.'

One of the guards raised a doubtful eyebrow.

'No? Perhaps you're right, monsieur.'

When she reached her apartment, Nina Simone was playing and everyone had arrived. *There she is!* great commotion, *we've taken over!*

Alain tried to welcome her, 'Are you okay?'

'Fine, I just have to make a phone call.'

'Kasha . . .' he gently detained her, whispering, 'there doesn't seem to be any food or drink.'

It hadn't arrived. '*Merde*,' she said, breaking into an optimistic smile, 'we'll all just have to go out to dinner.'

He looked at her amazed. Waving at everyone, she slipped through to the office to call her editor in London . . . and got the answering machine. After Hugh's rambling message, she spoke,

'Kasha, Paris, Wednesday 9 p. m. Thanks for being out, you're a great help. I'm only close to establishing police and government involvement in last week's terrorist bomb, and, in the course of my investigations, guess who I ran into at the Duke de Montfort's château? Our good friend Randolph Morgan, who was not overjoyed to see me, plus some sidekick called Peter Lunn. Ever heard of him? Keep my two pages warm for Saturday. *Dors bien!*'

The doorbell rang as she re-emerged, Monsieur Duval in person, entering with a bow and a bottle of champagne, '*A votre service, mademoiselle!*'

Kasha kissed him on both cheeks, Alain organised a posse to the street to collect the food and wine from Duval's van and as Kasha introduced the restaurant owner to the rest of her friends her eye fell on Rod, whom she hadn't seen since London, a dishevelled, ruggedly handsome Englishman who'd been trying to get her to bed since the day they'd met.

Sitting with Chilean exile Arturo in a corner, Rod was even now smiling at her with those eloquent eyes which told her how good it would be. Her reply, as ever, would be something like, Rod, I'm not that liberated. She admired him as a war correspondent who combined the courage to get in close to the action with the knack of writing sharp unclichéd copy, who had never lost his compassion and wasn't afraid to question the assumptions behind the wars. He was, in many ways, the journalist she would have wanted to be.

She pulled him aside at the first opportunity.

'Christ!' he rejoiced, 'is this how women make passes in Rajasthan?'

'Rod, this is serious.'

'Marriage?'

'Nothing so dangerous, just a little dalliance with the

GP, investigating their claim that the authorities planted Friday's bomb.'

'How do you propose doing that?'

'Talking to all sides involved.'

'You're wasting your time, you won't get near the GP.'

Her expression said, Don't be so sure!

'Come on, Kasha, nobody's ever got near them.'

'Listen to me, I'm in the home of the French atomic energy supremo today and I run into Randolph Morgan –'

'Morgan?' mildly intrigued.

'And a cagey hanger-on called Peter Lunn, who made my hackles rise. First of all, what's Morgan doing dining with the nuclear industry?'

'Learning to glow in the dark?'

'Seriously, slob!'

Rod shrugged, 'The French nukes need favourable publicity in the UK, for some reason.'

'Okay, and who's Lunn?'

'British government aide, one of the reds-under-the-beds brigade, pals in the CIA –'

'What would he be doing here?'

'Lunn's speciality is discrediting opponents of the British government.'

'How?'

'Smear campaigns, circulating private intelligence briefings to editors, undermining opposition parties, discrediting subversive elements like . . .' assuming a suitably sinister face, 'church leaders, radical rock stars, Oxfam – anyone who criticises the government.'

'But what's he doing *here*?'

'These guys club together the world over.'

'Pro-nuclear, anti-Green.'

Rod's snappy grin said, You've got it!

Kasha nodded thoughtfully, 'Thanks.'

'Hey,' gently squeezing her arm, 'don't mess with any of these people, keep your distance.'

'Listen to him! I suppose you research your despatches from the safety of the hotel bar.'

He grinned, and that look came over him again. 'What are you doing later?'

'I don't know, probaby having supper with Jean-Jacques Revallier.'

'Seriously.'

'Rod, I like you, enormously. I respect you. But I don't love you and you don't love me.'

'We would, believe me, between the sheets.'

She smiled, kissed him on the nose, 'I'm not like you, I can't love in snatches.'

Alain came shambling over to refill their drinks.

'Still no luck, Rod?'

From the Englishman a regretful sigh. While the rivals poked fun at each other, Kasha's attention wandered, seeking Nathalie's ghost among the guests, listening for her laughter.

The phone went shortly before ten. Kasha had barely started her food. She took the call in her office, closing the door. A familiar woman's voice set her pulse racing. She named a petrol station, a street in the eighteenth *arrondissement*, a time, 10.30, and told Kasha what to do when she got there.

'Wear flat shoes and practical clothing, but bring a smart outfit.' Click.

Trembling, she consulted her road atlas. She had an overnight bag packed, and added the first smart clothes that came to hand. Then she pulled on jeans and gym shoes, made her excuses to dumbstruck friends and left with a worried Alain on her heels.

She thought she'd reassured him, but within minutes of reaching her car and pulling out into the street, she saw his Saab in her mirror . . . and someone in there with him. It wasn't hard to guess who. What she didn't notice was the car which had tucked in behind the Saab.

Putting her foot down she headed north through Clichy, joined the periphery highway at Porte-de-St-Ouen and was swept east in a torrent of traffic, escaping at Porte-de-la-Chapelle with the Saab hard on her tail. Knowing she was close to her destination, worrying that Alain might follow her into the petrol station and ruin everything, she pulled over at the first opportunity, and the Saab drew in behind. Kasha got out and met Alain and Rod halfway, both shivering in shirtsleeves and looking assertive and sheepish at once.

'Kasha . . .' Alain groping for words and speaking in English, 'What are you doing here? It's dark, this is a bad district, you don't know the city so well . . .'

Arms folded, she regarded him evenly.

'You don't know what you're getting into,' Rod took over, 'the Greens-versus-the-government scene is getting very nasty. Get in too close to either side and . . .' he shook his head meaningfully.

'Have you two finished?' They wavered under her gaze. To Alain, 'Did I follow you round Bhopal to see you were okay?' To Rod, 'Do I hold your hand in El Salvador and Lebanon?'

'This is different,' argued Rod, 'I'm not questioning your professional judgement –'

'Aren't you?'

'But this is a bloody guerrilla war –'

'And I'm the one who's covering it.'

'Okay, but let me at least come with you.'

'Rod, thank you – and fuck off.'

Frozen to the spot they gazed at her. Rod started to say something more, but Alain read her face and restrained him.

'Come on,' he said, and they turned back towards the Saab.

'Follow me,' she called after them, 'and you'll lose me, I promise.'

They knew what she meant. They got into their car, U-turned and drove off.

She looked about, the bleak streets and broken lighting, and her breath billowing in her face. In the car she checked her road atlas and drove on until she found the street she wanted. There it was, in the shadow of factories and shabby apartment blocks, a busy petrol station. Almost ten minutes late she pulled in and drew up well away from the bustling pumps. She got out, hitched up the bonnet, and as instructed, walked over to the forecourt shop and bought a can of oil. She returned to her car and someone fell into step beside her, a young man in garage overalls and peaked cap.

'I'll take that,' said Ricardo, relieving her of the can and inviting her to look into the engine with him.

'You realise you're being followed?' he said, pouring the oil.

'What! I told them to get lost. They know nothing, they're just anxious.'

'Black Peugeot?'

'Red Saab.'

'Police,' he said routinely, and then gave her precise directions how to get to a particular street off boulevard de la Chapelle, to park halfway down opposite Le Griffon and then what to do. She nodded, he could see how nervous she was, and how self-controlled. Closing the bonnet, he walked off with the empty can.

A rapid scan of the street and she saw the Peugeot some way off in the darkness lurking between lamp-posts. Taking deep breaths she drove off, noting the way the Peugeot glided off the kerb, kept its distance. She drove carefully, taking her time as instructed. Moments later she saw a motorbike coming up fast in her mirror, a rider in black overtaking the Peugeot, and then as it passed her, slowing to catch her eye through the open visor, letting her know it was him again.

The bike surged ahead, dissolving into the dark. Minutes later, straining to read names, she turned down a long narrow street and saw the Peugeot in her mirror do the same. At the sight of so many tightly parked cars she began to worry. Halfway down the street she spotted the café, Le Griffon, lit up on its own, and no parking space. Slowing down, she was wondering whether to try to double park when she saw an old corrugated van pull out in her path, vacating its space exactly as it had done the day before on her way to another café. Taking its place, she eyed the approaching Peugeot. As it cruised by, she felt its occupants' eyes on her, and further down the street they pulled up.

Grabbing her overnight bag she got out, locked the car, crossed the street and entered the café, walking straight through without looking at anyone, down a dim passage reeking of toilets and out into a back yard, where the young man was waiting to lead her quickly into a dark lane, lifting her bag on to the bike and a helmet over her head. Mounting behind him she encircled his waist and they rode away.

When at first she couldn't see, she felt a rush of panic. The visor of her helmet had been darkened; she was hurtling blind through the freezing night, weaving through unseen traffic, keeling over at corners. Sudden surges of speed snatched her breath away, abrupt loss of momentum made her tense, until gradually she got used to it, calmed herself and, clinging round the young man's waist, surrendered to the power of the machine.

A few more corners and spurts of speed and the rider slowed, stuttering over cobbles. She could feel his tension rising – he pulled up, steadied the bike, and she found the road with her foot, sensed him scanning the view for danger. He drove on, almost unseating her, and turned into an enclosed space, the dying throbs of the engine reverberating through a building. A heavy door slid shut, the place smelled of motor oil, grease and car wax. She was helped up a set of creaking stairs to a warmer room where people were talking quietly. She recognised Revallier's voice, but was guided into another room and heard no more.

Ricardo helped her off with the helmet, and she found herself in a spacious kitchen at the back of the building. Ricardo pulled up a chair for her to the open oven. Shivering from the ride, she drew in close and warmed herself.

'There's coffee in the pot, food and wine on the table.'

As he went to leave, she said, 'Electric?'

He turned, she was indicating the oven. 'Nuclear generated?'

'Of course!' he drew himself up, straightening an imaginary tie, 'clean, cheap and efficient!'

Left alone, Kasha looked out of the window to see where she was, only to find walls and roofs obscuring the view. She sat down again and took out her notebook. Revallier and Edouard de Montfort had both reneged on promised interviews. Undaunted, she would go ahead with a feature contrasting the ecologist guerrilla leader and the atomic energy mogul, all they stood for and all they accused each other of, including the rue de Liège bomb and de Montfort's dubious war record, excluding the son-father link.

Intermittent laughter and argument came from the next room, but she kept her concentration, barely lifting her head for forty minutes. Then came a knock, the door opened.

Kasha finished her sentence and looked up. Revallier entered, closing the door. Their eyes met, he studied her for some moments.

'Did you see him?'

'Yes.'

'And?'

'Same as you, no interview.'

262

'More interested in what I knew about the bomb.'

'Yes.'

'What did you tell him?'

'All that you've accused him of, double agent working with the Milice, responsible in forty-four for the murder of seven members of the Maquis, a subsequent attempt to assassinate you and your witness, and direct involvement in Friday's bomb.'

'He denied it?'

'All of it.'

'You believed him?'

'No.'

His eyes filled with gratitude. 'Did you hear anything of the witness?'

'No.'

'He operates under two names, Jean-Baptiste Laroche and Lucien Grossman.'

She shook her head. He looked troubled.

'What is it?'

'We've been calling him, from public boxes. Yesterday he answered, anxious to talk to us, but not something he could discuss over the phone. My Algerian comrade was about to tell him where to meet when he realised it wasn't Laroche he was speaking to, and hung up. They've got him.'

Kasha filled the silence, 'I'm sorry.' Then, 'But I looked up the American on the way, and I met his wife. He's been arrested too, not the collaborator you took him for.' Revallier looked up. 'She's very worried, thinks the police were involved in the bomb.'

'And the tape and pictures?'

'She doesn't know what he's done with them.'

He frowned, 'They're all there is to prove it wasn't us.'

He took her into the next room, where Janine Vallence reclined in a stuffed armchair, cigarette in one hand, glass of wine in the other, welcoming Kasha with a cautious smile. The other two, Ricardo Cruciano and Tahar Ben Amar, were standing at a table, poring over a map. Revallier took her to the table, where she saw that the map was more of a crude scale model, pieces of coloured cardboard for buildings, pavements and traffic islands, patches of green for public gardens, a strip of blue for the river, white for the bridge, with lanes and traffic flows painted on.

'Forty years on, it's Edouard de Montfort's turn to be ambushed,' Revallier told her, 'here in Place de la Concorde, which he will cross in the morning on his way to CEEA headquarters south of the river.'

'How do you like the little spot we picked?' said Ricardo, 'forty years ago our predecessors in the resistance flung themselves across this square at German tanks, while swastikas flapped their last from Hôtel de la Marine . . .' pointing a scholarly finger, 'and Hôtel Crillon.'

'And where the guillotine stood,' added Kasha to general surprise, 'Marie-Antoinette and Louis XVI losing their heads on these same cobbles.'

'We'd hoped never to have to put this plan into action,' explained Revallier, 'we'd put our faith in Monday's operation, but you foiled us.'

Kasha felt their eyes on her, and her cheeks flushed. Then recalling how ruthlessly they'd used her, she presented a bold smile, 'I hope you're not waiting for an apology.'

'It's for us to apologise,' said Tahar, 'not you, mademoiselle.'

'I still say,' Janine called across, 'this plan was always the best.'

'More exciting,' conceded Ricardo.

'And twice as dangerous,' Tahar reminded them, 'a massive open space, one of the biggest squares in Europe. If anything goes wrong, escape will be difficult.'

'That's one reason why we need you,' Revallier said.

It took Kasha a moment to realise he meant her.

'As our witness if it goes wrong.'

'You don't sound very confident.'

'Old age,' quipped Janine, 'don't listen to him, it'll go like clockwork, they'll be half asleep, convinced we've neither the nerve nor the resources left to contemplate another operation.'

'We also need you,' Revallier went on, 'for practical purposes. The de Montforts should leave rue de Liège at 7.30 a. m. . . .' Introducing a familiar gold cufflink, he used it to trace the progress of the car down rue Royale and into Place de la Concorde, 'reaching the square seven to ten minutes later, where we apprehend them about halfway across, relieving Maurice de Montfort of the nuclear file. You'll be waiting in the Métro station here . . .' Tahar placed a bracelet over the spot, 'to receive the file at about 7.45 and will bring it to our meeting point below Pont d'Austerlitz. You'll sail with us while we get out of Paris and study the file. Then we drop you off and you deliver the file to the editor-in-chief of *Le Monde*, who will be warned to expect you.'

Kasha's face betrayed misgivings.

'What's the matter?'

'I thought he handcuffed the briefcase to his wrist.'

'Don't worry,' Janine laughed, 'we're not going to present you with a severed arm.'

'I'd never do that,' said Ricardo, 'to a fellow vegetarian.'

Kasha smiled briefly. 'What about the police escort?'

'That's not your problem,' said Janine.

'It is, if I'm delivering the file.'

'The gentleman who's going to eliminate them,' Revallier assured her, 'will not even be armed.'

Kasha folded her arms, 'One unarmed man stopping a police escort without bloodshed?'

'*Merde, Jacques!*' complained Janine, lighting another cigarette, her tone plainly saying, What have you landed us with?

'If we fuck things up and kill somebody,' she went on, 'you can always damn us to hell in your paper.'

'I certainly will.'

'Mademoiselle,' said Tahar, 'you're quite right to express reservations, but trust works both ways. We allow you here among us, you see our faces, hear our names, we're in your hands, you're in ours, our pledge stands, no firearms unless under attack from armed police.'

Kasha held her peace, outwardly composed, inwardly in turmoil, scarcely able to believe where she was.

'With Laroche captured,' Revallier resumed, 'given that he has a rough idea where we're based, we need to be doubly vigilant, escape kits ready, two on the roof and two off all night. Anything else?'

'I'll take my turn on the roof,' said Kasha.

Revallier shook his head, Kasha lowered her eyes.

'Weather forecast!' remembered Ricardo.

'Fog to start,' supplied Tahar, 'then clear, cold and sunny.'

'Fog,' Revallier smiled, 'would be perfect.'

The briefing broke up, and Janine went to lie down for two hours. A shivering Father Igor Boury came down from the roof and took to his camp-bed for the night, to be replaced among the chimneys by Tahar and Ricardo.

The sight of short stubby weapons and their uniformly ugly clips of ammunition shook Kasha. She felt a dreamer's sharpened sense of consciousness, only this was real, and she was wide awake and part of it. Lingering at the table with Revallier, going over her role in more detail, she became increasingly anxious, wondering how she would cope during the night or in the morning if she had one of her panic attacks – the legacy of Bhopal, a surfeit of accumulated horrors.

'I'm sorry,' she said, 'can you repeat that?'

His hand on her shoulder startled her.

'It's carefully planned, it'll be all right.'

'Police have been shot by your people, members of the public caught in the crossfire.'

'No one has ever been killed by anyone in this unit. We're not about to spoil our record, especially on our last operation.'

'Your last?' She looked at him surprised. 'And then?'

For a moment she thought he was going to tell her.

'Let's get through this one first.'

It was almost 1 a. m. Waiting on the couch was a pile of bedding which Revallier began to unfold.

'Please,' she dissuaded him, preferring to make her own bed.

'I'll be lying down if you need anything,' he said and started to leave. But he didn't go.

Pillow in arms, she looked around and met his gaze, which seemed to say, You're here, as if it was only just sinking in.

She lay awake in the dark, suppressing twinges of panic, a wedge of light coming from the kitchen, slight movements now and then from the roof. Somewhere a far-off siren wailed. She got up and looked out between the curtains. A canal, street lights and patches of snow, apartment blocks on the far side, a few lighted windows reflecting in the still water. She knew their secret now: water. After operations in Paris they escaped by river, avoiding road-blocks. Their hideout, using the cover of some sort of garage downstairs, lay on a canal.

Lying down again, she felt the stirrings of an attack, flurries of panic threatening to possess her, telling her she'd freeze once the action started tomorrow. A feeling of impending doom oppressed her. Friday had been horrific, tomorrow could be another nightmare. Her breathing deteriorated, she broke out in a cold sweat, she had to do something.

Throwing off her covers, she jumped up and walked up and down in her coat, mastering her breathing, telling herself she was no moral or physical coward, reminding herself that the worst thing about these attacks was the *fear* that she would succumb and go under. Wrapping herself in a blanket, she sat in an armchair, switched on a lamp and took up her article again. To her dismay, as she read it through, it made no impact, it was wordy, flaccid. Even if it got past Hugh in London, it would be treated here with derision by all concerned.

Taking deep breaths, she walked around the room again, and looking once more out of the window over the canal she suddenly experienced a feeling of elation, the sense of a rare moment to be seized. Refusing to believe she could have lost her skill and nerve, she forced herself to re-read what she'd written, and gradually conceded it wasn't as bad as she had feared. Like tuning in to a lost frequency, she began to hear some power in her piece: *Duke Edouard de Montfort, patriot, elder statesman of industry, standard-bearer of modern France. Or traitor and collaborator, ruthless industrial godfather capable of assassinating political enemies and stage-managing a conspiracy of inverted state terrorism against the Greens . . .*

As she read, the name Nathalie Sainte-Claire leapt off the page, triggering a rush of adrenalin. Brain and pencil struggled to co-ordinate for a few minutes, but she persisted and settled into a familiar rhythm. She didn't stop writing and revising until well into the early hours, when she drew a line across the page, rubbed her eyes and looked up.

Beginning with the news of Nathalie's death, it had been a terrible and astonishing day. She'd got the truth out of both Revallier and Edouard de Montfort, and written a feature on them. Tomorrow, with luck, she'd cap the piece with an inside report on the ambush, reveal the coveted secrets of the European nuclear industries, and fax the lot to London for the weekend.

Returning to the couch, she lay listening to the silence,

until she fell into a fitful sleep peopled with the whispered comings and goings of her hosts.

One a. m.: In his stale, icy echoing cell, Luke was lying flat on his back beneath a blanket, staring at the dim ceiling, his mind awhirl with thoughts of lonely frightened Isabelle and helpless Laroche when he heard a growing commotion, cell doors banging, men cursing and shouting. He stopped and listened as, one after another, detainees were taken out and marched away, hands on heads.

His door flew open. *Out!* bellowed a guard. Relieved to see a face and to be going somewhere, he allowed himself to be brusquely escorted by armed men down a flight of stairs and through a maze of subterranean corridors to join the other evacuees in a crowded holding cell. The benches around three walls were already occupied and a dozen more men stood about. No one spoke, Luke looked about and saw men of different shades and moulds, from desperate looking characters to the bewildered, the indifferent and the deeply withdrawn. Some smoked, others cursed them, the room was already airless, tempers boiled over, two innocuous-looking men squared up, others tried to restrain them and Luke stepped in, dividing them with his broad shoulders.

'This space is too small, we all need to stay very calm.'

'Who the hell are you?' challenged a voice.

Luke turned, drawn to the voice, and the throng of men parted to let him through. The little man who'd spoken sat in a corner, his face daubed in sticking plasters.

'Welcome, old chap,' said Laroche in his wretched English.

As Luke stood gazing at him, the cell door opened and names were called out. One by one men departed, Luke expecting at any moment to hear 'Morrel' or 'Laroche' until apart from Laroche and himself there was only one man left, sitting in the opposite corner reading a book. The door was locked, footfalls faded. Silence.

Luke sat down beside Laroche. The little man's ghastly face broke into a grin. '*Tu vois, mon vieux*, how easy it is.'

'How easy what is?'

'To finish . . .' he broke off in a fit of coughing, recovered, wheezing, 'to finish up in the French President's soup!'

Luke laid a hand on Laroche's shoulder, 'Forgive me.'

The man in the far corner tried to engage them in conversation, but each time he opened his mouth, Laroche told him to shut it. The man returned to his book. 'I can smell you from here!' shouted Laroche, drawing closer to Luke. 'He's a stoolpigeon,' he murmured in Luke's ear, 'we'll have to whisper. In fact . . .'

He stood abruptly and, breathing heavily, found his balance and prowled the cell, hunting with swollen eyes for listening devices. He strained and searched and found none and still wasn't satisfied. 'Time is precious,' he said, returning to Luke.

Sitting forward with his short thigh against Luke's, he turned his tobacco pouch inside out to capture the last remaining shreds. Then he rolled himself a scrawny cigarette, lit it with his last match and threw the box away.

'My name,' he whispered, 'is Grossman.'

'What?' Luke leaned closer, beard to beard.

'Lucien Grossman, from Mons in Belgium. My father a baker, mother a seamstress – Jews.'

'You serious?'

Laroche's weary skew-eyed look told him he was.

'You're not Jean-Baptiste Laroche? You're Lucien Grossman?'

Laroche nodded, breathed his cigarette.

Luke speechless. He looked sideways at his friend, a man who had always been a mystery, never more than now.

'May 1940, Germans invaded, fled to France, a plague of refugees. Father set up in bomb-shattered Rouen, we thought we'd be safe, but were betrayed by neighbours. Father, mother, mother's mother, my sisters Rosa and Hanna all taken to death camps, Belsen or Buchenwald, never learned for sure. I escaped to the forest, joined an underworld of resisters, communists, misfits . . .'

He heard a noise, glanced up, and ran on with his whispered story, 'In forty-three I joined the resistance, a Maquis unit operating on the Brittany coast between Tréguier and Saint-Brieuc. *He* was in the unit . . .'

'Who?' Luke glanced over at the stoolpigeon, pretending to read his book.

'Who do you think? Edouard de Montfort, the current duke, then a charismatic young "patriot", sniffed me out quick enough – a Jew. With the chill of his charming smile, he let me know. One night early in forty-four, we were covering the escape of a bunch of Allied airmen from a beach near Pointe de la Tour: Canadians, Australians, Poles, hidden by locals across Brittany, dangerous work. Once captured, we Maquisards were shot or decapitated, never treated as POWs –'

'More like terrorists.'

'Exactly. Like they're treating the ecologists today.' He threw Luke a sidelong look to drum home the point. 'The Gestapo didn't need to hunt us, the pro-Nazi Milice – the French political police – did it for them –' he turned and spat viciously at the wall, causing a little explosion of dust.

'No moon that night, ideal conditions. The British corvette appeared off shore, the airmen were rushed down the beach, boats were raced to the water and then –' he stopped abruptly, gazed at the floor, 'I saw my comrades slaughtered like rabbits, all but Edouard de Montfort, who chatted to the Milice before walking away. As the exposed look-out I should have been the first to die, but smelling a rat, I'd climbed to a higher bluff and saw the ambush unfold before making my escape.'

'What happened to you?'

'De Montfort put it about that *I* was the traitor. You saved me –'

'Me?'

'While you lot landed on the next peninsula, in the confusion I joined another Maquis unit, helping Patton's Third Army liberate Brittany. Edouard, blowing with the wind, also joined a unit, going on to win the Médaille de la Résistance, can you believe it? I tried after the war to denounce him –' a short laugh, 'a lousy Jew against a de Montfort. When the mob was baying for the blood of Nazi war criminals, who was this arsehole pointing to the crimes of French traitors? What was I but a flea in Edouard's armpit? Over the years, job to job, town to town, I monitored his meteoric rise, resolving one day, when the time was ripe . . .'

His sardonic smile faded. His words burned in Luke's ear.

'I moved to his area to do it, bought a rifle, practised in the woods, broke into his estate, time and again, waiting for the moment. When it came, Edouard and Maurice were stripping off at the bench for a swim –'

'The log bench? The one that had disappeared?'

'The same. I tracked Edouard from across the river, not quite the dashing young hound of forty-four who'd betrayed Jérôme, Gabrielle and the rest of my unit, a mature man with luxurious waist and grey on his chest. As he waded into the water, his skull in my sights, I prayed God for accuracy and squeezed the trigger . . . almost to the point of firing. I've been squeezing ever since.' He smiled pityingly at himself, as if observing a disturbed patient forever repeating the same obsessive gesture.

'Why didn't you shoot?'

'Dread of capture, execution, I wanted to live!' he hissed,

clenching a fist. 'Why should I die for him as well? Miserable coward!' he cursed himself.

'That's one thing you're not.'

'That would have been it,' a gasp on the dregs of his cigarette, 'only one day a car drew up, a young man stood in the driveway, soberly dressed, regarding me intently . . .' his voice fell to an almost inaudible whisper and Luke pressed closer, breathing in Laroche's sour odour, and in an adjoining cell Goujon listened intently through headphones, cursing because he couldn't hear what the prisoners were saying. 'He'd come to kill me, I was convinced. I invited him in, he introduced himself as Jean-Jacques Revallier. He was a lawyer, specialising in thankless cases: paupers, immigrants, anarchists, often defending those no one else would, frequently waiving charges. He'd been looking for me for two years, he too had unfinished business with Edouard de Montfort. We fell in together, I had no choice. One look in his eyes and you knew this was a man who would stop at nothing –'

'What kind of unfinished business?'

'As deeply personal as mine,' Laroche replied sharply. 'We spent years gathering evidence, uphill work, no surviving witnesses to the ambush but me. Only one man knew for certain that Edouard was a double agent, local Milice chief Pierre-Marie Medec, but he was spirited away in forty-five by Les Chevaliers de la Croix d'Or' – Knights of the Gold Cross, Luke translated for himself, 'an extremist church organisation which hid fascists and furnished them with new identities. We got close enough to Medec to attract death threats, but never found him. Our last hope were the locals on Île de Brèche where the de Montforts spent the war sailing and fishing, but they were too scared to testify . . .'

'Were you surprised?'

'No. Nor was I surprised when one evening, after keeping an appointment with Revallier, a car travelling at speed along rue Sainte-Antoine performed a remarkable manoeuvre to mount the pavement and flatten me. Only prompt emergency treatment and spite on my part saved me.'

'Your hit-and-run accident?'

Laroche found a grin, he'd kept the truth from everyone all these years. 'The same evening, by curious coincidence, Revallier's offices were fire-bombed. He would have cooked but for roof-top acrobatics.'

He paused, his face gaunt, eyes hollow, an old man looking over his shoulder at his life.

'The authorities,' ventured Luke, 'must have suspected.'

'The authorities!' turning his head once more, Laroche spat violently, setting in motion a dusty slug's trail down the wall. He fell quiet, drawing in on himself.

Luke called him back, 'Weren't you tempted to give up?'

A laugh. 'Yes! but Revallier . . .' breaking off for another coughing fit, 'once he sets his mind on something, nothing short of a bullet will stop him.'

He leaned against the wall exhausted, the disappearing butt of his last cigarette slipping through his fingers to the floor. Luke sat forward deep in thought. Hearing Laroche – Grossman – shivering, he sat back and put his arm around his shoulders. There they sat in silence, Laroche's head on Luke's chest, the stoolpigeon slowly turning the pages of his book.

Guards arrived suddenly to separate them. Before they knew what was happening, they were being marched off in opposite directions.

'Take care, *mon vieux*!' Laroche cried out.

'You take care!' Luke's words echoed foolishly down the long deserted corridors.

Across the city night, above the garage on the canal, Kasha drifted in and out of sleep, each time amazed to find where she was. On the roof Revallier leaned against a chimney

274

and thought of her below as he scanned the murky streets, imagined her warm brown body between the sheets, the taste of her lips, the odour of her skin. Tearing her from his mind, he concentrated on the coming dawn.

Tomorrow, dear Edouard, we strike back.

• • • 15 • • •

Rue de Liège, sometime after seven, Edouard at his desk, breakfast spread before him, the dense leather-backed file open at the appendix. Clotilde enters, clucks her tongue in disapproval.

'You haven't touched your breakfast.'

'Leave me the coffee.'

'Have a little bread and cheese at least, you're losing weight.'

He reached suddenly for her hand, he hadn't touched her in a long time, and she started. He cherished her gnarled hand in both of his. 'Ah, Clotilde,' he sighed.

Tears came to her eyes, he looked up and saw that she knew. Somehow she knew, her expression conveying understanding and profound disappointment. She would never desert him.

After she'd withdrawn with the tray he went to the window and looked out. The street was shrouded in fog – again! Friday had been thick with it and he didn't need reminding what had happened. The image of Madame Sainte-Claire lying at his feet in a pool of blood had shadowed him ever since, and all he could do was beat back the memory. It served no purpose dwelling on it. Instead he looked again at his watch: 7.30, where the hell was Bolivar?

Pacing to and fro with his service revolver chafing

against his ribs, he heard the swish of brakes and looked out to see his Mercedes and police escort in the street below. Minutes later, he and Maurice, carrying the briefcase chained to his wrist, collected their mail from Madame Klonowska in the lobby and proceeded to the street.

Georges Bolivar spread his hands. 'The fog, monsieur le duc –'

'Learn to anticipate!'

Shutting the duke and his son in the back, Bolivar glowered at the street, nodded to the Secret Service men in the car behind and climbed behind the wheel of the Mercedes. Seven minutes late and the duke in ill humour. It was, he feared, going to be a bad day. He was right. No sooner had he thrust into gear and pulled away when a screech of brakes from behind and the sound of impact made him look in his mirror, curse and apply his own brakes. The escort had hit a cyclist.

'Stay where you are,' snapped Edouard at his son and driver as he climbed out and walked back to see a young priest lying in the road, his bicycle entangled in the police car's bumper, his glasses broken, clutching his leg.

'Idiots!' Edouard rounded on the Secret Service men.

Passersby gathered in shock, Madame Klonowska scurried away to call an ambulance. Edouard was in a high rage, tempered by decorum. Satisfied that the priest was alive, he turned away, unwilling to delay any longer. But as he regained the Mercedes, one of the Secret Service men came after him, remonstrating. Edouard swore at him, but despite his reputation for dismissing security precautions with contempt, he allowed the security man to climb aboard beside Bolivar, just what Janine Vallence – encased in a white helmet and watching from a distance astride a motorbike – was hoping wouldn't happen.

Revving her bike, she took off after the Mercedes, easily overhauling it in the traffic down rue d'Amsterdam.

In Café Marly on rue de Rivoli, just off Place de la Concorde, three labourers were making heavy work of a light breakfast. They sat in silence, watching the time, alone in their thoughts.

'It'll be strange,' Ricardo said at last, 'Janine somewhere in France, you two scattered across the globe. Will we ever see each other again?'

'One day,' Revallier assured him, 'when they've forgotten about us.'

'A reunion?' Ricardo lit up at the thought, 'you could all come to Florence. Imagine! walking in the hills together, I know all the mountain tracks connecting the small towns. Or we could descend on Tahar in El Madheur, or track you down in Quebec, or meet up here if we dare . . . or else in heaven!'

They laughed with him and lapsed into silence.

And looked at their watches. Where was Janine? what could have delayed her? had something gone wrong?

'What will you do at home?' said Revallier.

'Fuck everything that moves,' replied Ricardo.

'Good. And you?'

They looked at Tahar, he was searching for an answer.

'He wants six kids,' Ricardo answered for him, 'he's going to take his young lady home to mamma and get cracking, right?'

Tahar had spoken once or twice of a soft-eyed young woman called Leila who had agreed to return with him one day to Algeria.

With Ricardo's arm draped round his shoulder, Tahar smiled, 'That's exactly what I intend to do.'

But it was plain to Revallier, looking into his face, that Tahar wasn't anticipating seeing his home again. Reaching across the table, Revallier took hold of his hand. Their eyes met, Revallier's saying, I'm counting on you, Tahar's replying, You don't need to remind me.

'What's happened to her?' said Ricardo.

'Don't worry,' said Revallier, 'she's coming.'

The two-way radio bleeped in Revallier's tool bag.

'What did I tell you!' He listened to Janine's brief message and rose, 'heavy traffic,' he whispered, 'about eight or nine minutes, and – you'll be delighted to hear – an extra cowboy in front.'

'Terrific!' said Ricardo.

As they paid and left, Revallier caught Kasha's eye across the room, his faint smile wishing her luck. When he'd left, she added another rapid line to her article: Last to leave, Revallier took his time, for all the world a foreman setting off for a building site. She left money on the table and followed.

Wearing tight woollen hats, Revallier and Tahar walked rapidly to the north-east corner of Place de la Concorde, which looked eerie in the fog, robbed of its panoramic vastness. In the centre of the square lay the long broad island they had to reach, obscured now, save for the blur of lights and the great obelisk piercing the gloom.

Hearing the familiar grind of the old Citroën van, they glanced round to see Ricardo grinning inanely as he pulled up at red lights just inside the square. With his baseball cap, bleached hair and matching moustache tacked on with spirit gum, his sisters could have passed him by without recognising him.

The lights remained red, competing tides of traffic swept in and out of the square. High on nerves, he checked his watch, *Sbrighati! sbrighati! Come on!* The lights changed, he rammed the gears, pumped the pedals and lurched into the maelstrom. Fending off turbos, motorbikes and buses, he rattled across the north face of the square and charged south for the river. He'd made numerous dry-runs in the past, but now, as the eight-lane bridge materialised before his eyes, his task looked awesome: to stem the flow of traffic going south over the bridge, and bring the square to a halt.

Beneath the obelisk on the central island, Revallier was monitoring Ricardo's progress when Tahar nudged him. Looking round and following Tahar's northward gaze, he picked out Janine's white helmet floating in the distance. So soon? He looked at his watch. De Montfort must be coming like a bullet. His pulse raced. Any minute now he would meet him for the first time.

Arriving at speed, Janine decelerated enough to hold up two gloved fingers, before sweeping on for another circuit of the square.

While Tahar watched for danger, Revallier crouched with his radio and called up Ricardo as he approached the bridge. 'Two minutes, Professor, *go!*'

Two minutes? *Cazzo!* cursed Ricardo, flinging the van at the bridge and rattling up the long slope in the fast lane. As he reached the brow he tugged on a line of taut rope, springing open the rear doors and releasing an avalanche of traffic cones. With motorists swerving to avoid them, he jack-knifed the van across two of the four lanes leaving the square, provoking a cacophony of brakes and klaxons. Leaping into the back of the van, he kicked the rest of the traffic cones into the road, tossed a pair of smoke grenades over his shoulder and jumped. As thunderclaps shook the van and smoke gushed from open windows, Ricardo kicked and carried cones into a ragged line across all four southbound lanes.

Cowed and confused, the nearest motorists abandoned vehicles and withdrew to a safe distance, while on the northbound side of the bridge, traffic faltered, edged clear and crawled on towards the square. A glance told Ricardo that the effect of plugging the bridge was working its way back through the square, traffic continuing to pour in from all directions, struggling to get out again.

Walking calmly back into the smoke, he vaulted into the van, kicked over a row of petrol cans and left them pumping into the road. Then he jogged clear and hurled a grenade through the windscreen. *'Ciao*, old friend!' he cried, as the van exploded, setting the road on fire.

The seizure was sudden, Place de la Concorde circulating normally one moment, reduced to a state of convulsion the next, and rapidly succumbing to total arrest, sixty thousand square metres of fuming steel.

By the time the third explosion echoed along the river, the Mercedes was hemmed in on all sides.

'What's going on?' demanded Edouard.

Bolivar could see flames flickering in the fog. 'A vehicle on fire on the bridge, sir.'

'Try another route, the Champs Elysées.'

Bolivar peered out despairingly, he was almost level with the obelisk, no turning back, nothing moving, klaxons trumpeting their fury, motorists getting out to stand and gaze.

Edouard losing patience, 'Do something!'

Lurking astride her motorbike, Janine saw Bolivar open his door and get out with an air of purpose, the Secret Service man doing the same on his side. She began to creep forward, steering the machine between cars. As she closed on the Mercedes, she caught glimpses of Tahar and Revallier moving in from different directions.

Bolivar and his colleague came together in front of the car to confer. A hopeless task, but for de Montfort's benefit they pointed energetically, and were still waving their arms when Tahar – masked and pointing a gun – stepped calmly from behind a vehicle and ordered them to freeze.

Janine arrived from behind, leaping off her bike and shouting at the two men to lie face down on the ground, hands behind their backs so she could handcuff them.

In the same moment, Revallier flung open Bolivar's door and ducked into the Mercedes. Up till now all had gone to plan, and disarming the de Montforts should have been straightforward, but Edouard reacted more quickly than predicted, and he and Revallier found themselves pointing revolvers at each other, staring into each other's eyes.

'Shoot . . .' invited Revallier.

Brandishing a gun, Tahar arrived to break the spell and disarm the duke.

With vital seconds lost, Revallier leaned across and tore the coat from Maurice's lap, baring the briefcase handcuffed to his wrist. Seizing Maurice by the arm, he dragged wrist and briefcase towards him, setting off the piercing alarm.

'Steady!' shouted Revallier, swinging a battery-operated chainsaw into play and bringing it to bear on the handle.

Maurice stiffened, tried to keep his hand clear as the chainsaw howled and sank its teeth into the handle. Out-screaming the alarm, the saw chewed through the handle and left Maurice handcuffed to nothing. Seizing the shrieking briefcase, Revallier pinned it to the front seat and attacked the seam. The blades tore into the case, spewing leather, then struck steel and sparks flew, teeth snapped off, the jaws locked and came again. Maurice looked on in horror, Edouard impassively, and while Revallier wondered which would give first, the case or the saw, the case split apart like a coconut and the alarm ceased.

Distant sirens filled the silence. Revallier extracted the leather file marked DOSSIER (XX), thrust it into his tool-bag and backed out of the driver's door – '*Merci messieurs et adieu!*'

The car phone was ringing. Tahar tore out the cord and fled. But to their dismay they found Janine still astride her bike, unwilling to abandon them.

'Go!' hissed Revallier.

Smiling through her visor, she roared off, slaloming between cars on her way to link up with Ricardo on the bridge.

It was 7.54, nearly three and a half minutes since launching the attack. Watched by stunned onlookers, Revallier and Tahar picked their way between vehicles towards the Métro station in the north-east corner of the square. As Tahar tore off his balaclava, one bold motorist spread himself – with the confidence of army training – across their path. Switching direction, they vaulted car bumpers, leaving him stranded.

The square throbbed with engines, klaxons and police whistles, and with sixty metres to go, they faltered at the sound of shots from the direction of the bridge . . . then more shots and screams as people ran for cover. Revallier and Tahar tried to see what was happening, but smoke from the bridge was swelling the fog, and now Tahar was warning of a more immediate danger from the north. CRS troops were fanning out as they cleared a way across the square on foot.

A van driver and a motorist were conferring excitedly in the road. Revallier and Tahar exchanged glances and climbed, Tahar first, into the van's cab on the blind side, just as the black-leather tide burst upon them brandishing submachine-guns. '*Oh, pardon!*' Revallier drew in the door to let an animated CRS trooper sprint by.

Slipping out of the van, they should have hurried the final metres to the Métro, but Tahar found himself walking alone. Over his shoulder he saw Revallier lingering by the van, looking towards the bridge for a glimpse of Janine's helmet. Sirens wailed, and Tahar, spotting the 'army man' who had tried to stop them, hunting among the cars, hastened back to Revallier's side and whispered to him sharply.

A throng of people packed the entrance to the Métro, and as Tahar and Revallier merged with them, a second wave of CRS arrived, more dangerous than the first, confused, pushing and pointing. Bracing themselves for the shout to stop, Tahar and Revallier pressed through the crowd and descended the Métro steps.

The broad ticket hall pulsed with the swell of arriving commuters unaware of the turmoil above. Searching the white walls ahead, Revallier spotted her. Conventionally dressed in a mauve suit and coat, and with her hair up, Kasha had the air of a well-heeled tourist, craning her neck, outwardly composed.

The automatic machines snapped up and returned their tickets. They followed Kasha along the passage and into a huddle to transfer the file to her overnight bag. A brief farewell of the eyes and they separated, Revallier and Tahar following signs for 'Directions Vincennes', Kasha for 'Mairie d'Issy'.

Weak with nerves, she marshalled her legs briskly through the labyrinth of passages to the platform. Her eyes sought the clock. Revallier had said, you'll be on a train by five to eight.

A train rushed smoothly into the station, the minute hand flicked on to eight o'clock. The crowd surged forward, her ticket said First Class, she aimed for the cream-coloured carriage in the centre of the train and lifted the handle. The doors sprang violently apart. She picked a window seat, heart pounding. The doors closed, a bell rang, the train departed. She sighed and looked around at the empty faces of her fellow passengers, travelling blearily to work, unaware that one among them was carrying state secrets in the bag on her lap.

Only now, rocked by the rhythm of the train, did she pause to wonder how violent the theft had been, how grave a crime she was involved in. And only now did she notice the cold eye of the passenger opposite, an over-dressed, heavily made-up woman looking her up and down, grading her from her shoes to her gold nose stud. Eyes wide, Kasha stared back until the woman looked disdainfully away.

Moving to a remote seat, she set to work. Around the file went a layer of perforated padding. Then with gift foil she began to turn it into an expensive present, complete with ribbon, bow and signed tag.

When the train came in, Tahar and Revallier chose the tail-end carriage, crowded like the rest. Wedged in a corner, they willed the train to depart.

It waited. For what? An armed search party now and it would all be over. If they weren't immediately identified, they wouldn't survive a search. The papers they carried didn't match their outward appearance, but went with the smart dress they wore beneath their baggy overalls: Tahar, Moroccan embassy official Muldi Hafid, and Revallier fashion designer Michel Kerlesquin. They were also acutely conscious of the collection of revolvers in Revallier's bag, waiting to be dumped.

The heat was oppressive, passengers growing restless, no one apparently aware of what had happened in the square above. At last the hooter sounded, doors rushed together, catches clicking into place. Revallier and Tahar held their breath, the bell *pinged* for departure and the train surged out of the station.

Discreetly as possible, they began shedding their overalls. It took two stops to achieve the transformation; they emerged in business suits, using windows as mirrors to straighten ties and hair. With passengers getting on and off, or remaining closed in their personal world, no one seemed to take much notice, except for one man, who had been watching all along.

At Châtelet, Revallier stepped off the train, rammed the toolbag containing overalls, two-way radio and guns into a bin and re-boarded. They didn't need to consult a wallmap to know they had four stops behind them and four to go. Nor did they need to confer about the man watching them.

One little bastard, thought Revallier, catching his eye. The young man flinched and became intently interested in his newspaper.

Alighting at Sèvres Babylone to change lines, Kasha was surprised by the density of the crowds, passages and intersections at a virtual standstill. After some minutes of shuffling forward, she saw over the heads of the crowd police carrying out checks and body searches, flanked by heavily armed CRS troops.

Breaking into a cold sweat, she excused herself as she squeezed through the crush to a Métro map and found an alternative route via Montparnasse. But as soon as she retraced her steps she found the other passages just as crowded, all leading to more security checks. The word must be out, the file stolen, the GP on the Métro. Her heart thumped, her breath came thin and fast. The passages were hot and airless, she saw herself passing out and wondered if that might not be the best solution.

Disciplining her breathing, battling to compose herself, she crept forward with the crowd and fell into conversation with the elderly woman alongside her, who wondered what the world was coming to.

The dwindling crowds separated into single-sex queues. Watching while she chatted, she saw that only selected persons were actually being stopped and searched. Her spirits rallied, the queue whittled away, and she let her elderly companion go first.

The policewoman took one look at the old woman and waved her through. At the last moment, as Kasha stepped up and met the expressionless gaze of the officer, her nerves vanished. Calm and dignified, she assumed an air of respectability and was shocked when the policewoman flung out an arm and demanded to search her bags.

While the officer unzipped and searched Kasha's overnight case, a colleague took her Printemps department store bag, removed the exquisitely wrapped parcel, felt its weight and showed it to the first officer. Kasha paled.

'What's this, madame?'

'A gift.'

Probing with her fingers, 'What sort of gift?'

'A jacket for my husband.'

Kasha prayed, the officer looked into her face as she felt around the edges of the parcel, handed it back with a curt '*Merci, madame*,' and waved her through.

Reclaiming her bags, she glided past the CRS guards and proceeded on trembling legs towards a crowded platform.

With one stop to go to their destination, the train pulled into Bastille. The doors opened, passengers alighted, but strangely, no one boarded. Revallier leaned out and saw what he'd most feared: a deserted platform, CRS gunmen planted at intervals, the nearest not twenty metres away. With a look, Revallier communicated the danger to Tahar.

The train was still, the platform quiet.

Revallier looked out again, in time to see two gendarmes and two plain-clothes cops boarding the train at the far end. Did they really intend to search the whole train?

Revallier and Tahar exchanged glances. Their chances of surviving a search would normally have been quite good, but the young man who was observing them appeared to be drawing courage from the imminent arrival of the search party. Revallier now took a closer look at the hero whose furtive eyes watched them as he feigned absorption in his newspaper and who now took his time to look down when Revallier caught his eye. Late twenties, Revallier guessed, a lack-lustre individual wearing a nondescript coat and suit, and on his way to some dreary job, a little man with big dreams and no hope of realising them, thinking maybe he could be somebody by pointing a finger when the moment arrived.

While the searchers worked their way through the train, Tahar concentrated on playing the role of affronted diplomat, and Revallier, feeling for his false glasses, discovered something appalling in his pocket. Seeing the look in his eyes, Tahar's heart sank. Tahar leaned closer and Revallier spread his pocket, revealing the butt of a carelessly over-looked gun. He stared at Tahar, silently asking forgiveness. Both men looked away, wrestling with stratagems. The automatic, if discovered, would be hard to explain; seizing hostages would be foolhardy, and shooting their way out with one wretched weapon ridiculous.

The watcher, sensing their anxiety, looked repeatedly to see if the searchers were coming.

Still grasping at solutions, Revallier was contemplating the desperate course of headlong flight down the tunnel into the labyrinths beneath the Métro when Tahar moved closer and whispered, 'Time to plant an onion.'

Looking Tahar in the eye, Revallier nodded almost imperceptibly, silently stressing that time was running out, the search party was in the next carriage.

While passengers craned their necks and turned to talk to total strangers, Revallier straightened his glasses and shouldered lightly through the throng murmuring, '*Pardon, monsieur, madame . . .*' until he stood beside the young man.

Softly, '*Monsieur . . .?*'

The hero looked up from his paper in alarm.

'You know me?' said Revallier.

'I don't believe so.'

'Curious, you've been looking at me . . .' sounds of police entering the carriage, demanding papers, 'as if you knew me.'

Defiantly confident, 'You're mistaken, monsieur.'

Relaxed and smiling, 'Am I?' Touching the young man's arm, drawing him round a fraction to give Tahar a better angle, 'are you quite sure?'

The young man glanced over his shoulder, 'I assure you, monsieur . . .' beads of fear and resolve glistened on his face.

Tahar was done, the hero seemed to feel something, his hand stirring unconsciously.

'My mistake, monsieur.' A little bow and Revallier withdrew.

Now, Revallier prayed, *find it now!*

The young man was feeling the outside of his pocket. With a puzzled look, he could feel something hard in there and began slowly to draw forth . . . he gasped, holding the gun away as though he had a serpent by the throat.

Screams, people shrinking back, isolating the young man and his gun.

Cops froze, the young man started shouting, waving the gun, pointing it in Revallier's direction, causing hysteria. Cops drew firearms, passengers dived for cover, and Revallier barged through the stampede, seized the hero's wrist and kneed him in the groin. A ghastly groan, the young man crumpling at his feet. CRS troops bounded aboard, the officer in charge of the search pointed dramatically at the body writhing on the floor, who was dragged off the train moaning incoherently.

Revallier held out the offending weapon on the open plate of his hand. The officer composed himself to receive it.

'My apologies, officer, pure instinct.'

Commuters recovered, a spellbound audience.

Grudgingly, 'You did well, monsieur, and you'll be called as a witness,' said the officer producing pen and paper.

'Here, let me save you . . .' Revallier offering his business card.

The officer ordered his men to check the remaining passengers. As they did so, Revallier's eyes darted in search of Tahar. Finally, the officer nodded courteously, took his men off the train and gave the signal, but turned abruptly, eager for another look at Revallier.

Revallier turned his head away, the train exhaled noisily, the hooter sounded, doors closed and the cop was still staring after Revallier as the train gathered speed and rushed into the tunnel. If the officer was as suspicious as he seemed, thought Revallier, he could have a firing squad waiting at the next stop.

When he couldn't find Tahar, he tried the next carriage. There he was at the far end, standing erect reading *Le Figaro*, as though grateful the inconvenience was over.

They alighted at Gare de Lyon. Tense and alert they joined the dense flow of commuters leaving the station. No checks, no strutting CRS, only police at strategic points with too many people to watch.

Tahar struck up a converstaion with a tall dignified Senegalese woman and strolled through with her. Revallier followed, brisk and businesslike. Reaching the street, they walked separately to the river, Revallier amazed by his brief and violent encounter with his father, a first meeting where after all these years Edouard never spoke and all Revallier had to say to him, was, 'Shoot!'

The sun had broken through, helicopters throbbed in the haze down river. Crossing Pont d'Austerlitz, which lay a dozen bridges east of Pont de la Concorde, they caught sight of the barge at its moorings on the south bank, waiting to ferry them out of the city to their rural base. Drawing near, they grew nervous, both of them thinking about the shots they had heard in Place de la Concorde. There was no sign of either Janine or Ricardo among the crew moving about on the barge or on the quayside.

But nearer still, Tahar spotted Janine's motorbike strapped to the roof of the barge. Looking over his shoulder, he signalled the good news to Revallier.

In spite of his protestations that he was fit to drive, Georges Bolivar, relieved of his handcuffs, was ordered to go to hospital in the first ambulance to penetrate the square.

He didn't want to go, but the duke's grim expression

discouraged further argument, and plainly told him he would never drive for him again. Back in the fog of rue de Liège Bolivar had predicted a bad day. It was only 8.20, and already it was a nightmare.

As helicopters blustered over the stricken square, vehicles started to move again. Dismissing offers of a police driver, Edouard de Montfort took the wheel of the Mercedes, and following diversions steered the limousine out of Place de la Concorde with Maurice ashen-faced in the back. Flanked by police outriders, he crossed Pont Alexandre III, picked up speed along the south bank and passed the Eiffel Tower, with the red sun caught in its steel web, before sweeping left into boulevard de Grenelle. Moments later the outriders broke away, the Mercedes turned through the gates of European atomic energy headquarters, a fantastic constellation of glass domes rising out of Old Paris, and plunged into the underground carpark, where Edouard managed a smooth halt and drew breath.

In the back Maurice reached between his legs and pulled out a concealed drawer, from which he lifted a briefcase. It had been Commissaire Goujon's eccentric idea to switch identical cases at the outset and conclusion of every journey.

In the great committee room, the twenty-two-man committee from several countries spoke in hushed tones around an immense polished table. Through up-curving walls of tinted glass they could see across the giant's bowling green of Champs de Mars to the river, where swarms of angry helicopters were spreading the hunt away from Place de la Concorde.

The mood in the room was heavy. Edouard de Montfort had radioed through to say he'd be delayed because Revallier and his gang had sawn through his son's briefcase and barely left him his arm. Those who knew the full contents of the dossier had good cause to worry. Unless it was recovered quickly, careers would tumble like skittles. If prayers were as visible as cigarette smoke, the room would have been thick with it.

'*Il arrive!*'

Hush. The distinctive de Montfort tread along the passage, like a headmaster bent on disciplining an unruly class.

The duke filled the doorway, Maurice at his shoulder, surveying the sea of anxious faces, until someone found the nerve to speak up and offer profound commiserations.

'*Monsieur le duc, nous sommes désolés . . .*'

Attention was drawn to the *two* briefcases Maurice carried.

A flicker of hope.

'Twins, gentlemen!' beamed Maurice. Lifting the briefcase mutilated by Revallier, he held it aloft like a battle trophy.

'The Fake!'

Dropping one arm, he hoisted the other, flourishing an immaculate briefcase, 'and the genuine article!'

A moment's stunned silence.

Then the assembly rose as one, their tumult shaking the rafters, eminent men of science, industry and government beating the table with their fists.

'They're finished, well and truly finished!'

'I'd give a month's salary to see Revallier's face!'

A stooping official was whispering in Edouard's ear, and celebrations were such that Edouard slipped away in a cloud of cigar smoke and took the call in an ante-room, closing the door behind him. 'Yes, commissaire?'

Sitting in a police car in Place de la Concorde, Goujon took a deep pull on his cigarette, 'I hear you had a little tête-à-tête with Monsieur Revallier?'

'And three accomplices.'

'*Three*? The Arab, a motorcyclist . . .'

'And a chainsaw.'

'But I understand my little scheme, which you considered "an over-reaction bordering on the hysterical", worked?'

'Indeed.'

'Nothing lost.'

'No, my dear commissaire, nothing lost, and Revallier's reputation sinking further.'

'It might have sunk altogether,' Goujon's tone took a sharp turn, 'had you contacted me sooner. I could have had him. As it is he's flown.'

'Well, we foiled him,' said Edouard brightly, 'thanks to you. I'm more concerned with – *the other business.*'

'Leave that to me. Good-day, sir.'

Goujon got out and stood in the cordoned-off square, seething.

Kasha hurried along the quayside, it was nearly 9.15, they would think she'd been caught or had run off with the file.

Catching sight of a bottle-green barge, she lengthened her stride until she saw *Le Dragon de Rougeau* painted on the prow. The crew were evidently looking out for her. They weren't members of the GP, Revallier had explained, only clandestine supporters, men and women of varying age and background, eco-farming semi-communally outside Paris.

As soon as Kasha stepped aboard, they drew in the gangplank, eased the barge off the wharf and weighed into the current for the five-hour journey up river.

Descending to the dim cabin, she was struck by the charged atmosphere. Anticipating their relief, or perhaps irritation that she was late, she was met instead by a strange silence. Janine Vallence was lying down, Revallier stood at a porthole gazing out, the Algerian was bent over his maps, and as the young Italian rose to meet her, she saw, even in the bad light, that he'd been crying.

'You got through all right,' he said, 'that's great.'

She'd imagined them crowding around her for the file, but no one mentioned it or so much as glanced in the direction of her Printemps bag. It was as if they'd forgotten, now that the operation was successfully completed, what its purpose had been.

Then she saw why.

Janine Vallence was lying very still on her back, eyes closed, hands arranged on her stomach.

Kasha put down her bags and went over to see for herself. The co-founder of Les Gardiens de la Planète looked deathly pale but untroubled, her mouth slightly curled in the faintest of smiles. Only now did Kasha see the stains on her clothing, the dull gleam of blood on the floor.

'What happened?'

'She was shot leaving the square,' Tahar spoke up, 'she hung around watching over us, she should have been long gone.'

'Stupid bitch,' sobbed Ricardo.

'By the time she took off, they were sealing the square . . .' dropping his eyes, Tahar spoke almost to himself, 'I thought I'd done enough by tearing out the car phone, they must have been carrying radios and alerted the police.'

'She came like the wind,' said Ricardo, 'they were cordoning off the bridge, she burst through, they fired, I thought they'd missed because she kept going. When she reached me I could see she was in trouble . . . I drove with her hanging on for life.'

'You couldn't have got her to a hospital?'

'She made out it wasn't bad!' he shouted, 'and later when I knew she was lying and begged her let me take her to a hospital, she held a gun to my head . . .' as he spoke he was holding his fingers to his head, and then broke off with his face in his hands.

The barge found its course, the east side of the city crept

by. Kasha looked at Revallier, motionless at the porthole, but didn't dare approach him.

'What about some strong tea or coffee?' she suggested.

Tahar rose to fill a kettle.

'Let me,' said Kasha.

Tahar declined with a smile. In the galley he lit the gas and switched on a wireless: ' . . . *and which has seriously disrupted the centre of Paris, is thought to have been carried out by surviving members of The Guardians of the Planet. But Commissaire Philippe Goujon was quick to discount suggestions that classified documents belonging to the European Atomic Energy Commission were seized from the car, insisting . . .'*

'Liar!' Ricardo shook his fist at the wireless.

'Turn it off!' snapped Revallier.

Everyone froze, a helicopter hovered overhead, whipping up the river. The cabin shook, everyone remained still, Kasha caught Revallier's eye and swallowed hard as he stared at her as though he'd never laid eyes on her, or worse, as if the whole thing was her fault.

No sooner had the helicopter sheered off along the river than a new sound took its place, a river launch closing in at speed and rearing up alongside. Tahar looked out on the starboard side.

'Brigade Fluviale,' he said flatly. The river police.

To Kasha's surprise, no one reacted.

'What shall I do with . . .?' she asked, gathering up the Printemps bag in her arms.

'It's okay,' said Tahar, urging her to sit down.

Unfolding a blanket, they spread it over Janine's body.

Shouts were heard, police coming aboard, stamping feet. Kasha sat and watched incredulously as Revallier and his men stood about waiting their fate.

A pair of shiny boots appeared, a genial voice from the top step, 'Anybody home?'

Without waiting for a reply he came down, a stocky figure in a crisp uniform, grey-haired and sly-eyed.

'*Messieurs, 'dames, bonjour!*' The joys of spring.

Adjusting to the bad light he looked about. He evidently knew everyone, caught sight of Kasha, seemed momentarily disconcerted and turned to Revallier, 'Quite a day! the virtually extinct GP strike again under our very noses . . . and mysteriously melt away.'

'Remarkable,' agreed Revallier.

Something in Revallier's manner affected the officer, his expression more discerning as he looked about. His eye came to rest on the body with its feet sticking out.

Kasha lowered her eyes, sank her nails into her palms.

After a time she looked up. The officer had removed his cap and was standing quietly as though paying his respects. Then he put his cap back on, looked round, met Kasha's eye, and lowered his gaze to the Printemps bag by her side.

'Okay, chief!' a cry from above.

'Coming,' the officer replied.

'A drink before you go, capitaine?' invited Revallier.

The officer looked at him. 'Perhaps not today.'

A quick salute and he was gone. An uproar of engines and the launch powered away. Kasha was shaking her head.

'If you're recording that,' Tahar addressed her, 'please say that Janine was overlooked during a vigorous search, otherwise our friend the capitaine will be finished.'

Tahar made sweet dark tea for everyone, and then requested the file. Kasha handed over the carrier bag. With a searching look at Revallier, who remained at the porthole with his back turned, Tahar sat down and pulled out the parcel. Untying the ribbon, he stripped off the red and gold foil and the layer of tissue, and was peeling back the plastic padding when he stopped abruptly.

'Jacques, for God's sake! . . . this *is* what she died for.'

Revallier looked slowly round, eyes clouded with shock.

'Today Janine pulled the short straw,' said Tahar firmly,

'tomorrow it could be any of us, we know the risks, it's our job . . . she doesn't want to see us like this . . .' his voice wavered, 'We've got the file! She would have wanted us to celebrate, drink a toast to our glorious coup.'

'All right!' exploded Revallier. He turned, glowering. Then quietly to Ricardo, 'See what we have.'

Ricardo stooped to a low cupboard and came up with half a bottle of cognac and four dusty glasses, and slopped cognac in each.

'No,' said Kasha, refusing a glass, 'I shouldn't be included. If it wasn't for me stopping you the other night . . .' she met Revallier's hard gaze, 'today's operation would not have been necessary and Janine –'

Revallier snatched the glass from Ricardo and pressed it into Kasha's hand.

'To the file!' he raised his glass, 'we've got them, as Laroche would have said, by the balls.'

He tossed back his cognac, the others followed suit, all but Kasha, who stood transfixed.

'Drink,' said Revallier.

She looked at him. His eyes were commanding her, beseeching her. She tossed back her drink in one.

Revallier sat down with the file. Ripping off the rest of the padding he laid bare the smooth leather cover simply marked DOSSIER (XX). He paused, his enemies' secrets in his hands, his father's mighty industry.

'Avert your eyes, peasants . . . double-X stands for highly classified.'

Hush descended as he opened the cover. They leaned over to read the title page.

THE FUTURE OF ATOMIC ENERGY: *A co-ordinated European Initiative*.

Turning the page, he was astonished to discover a sunken chamber, surrounded by the trimmed edges of hundreds of packed pages, giving the illusion of a thick document. Inside the deep false chamber lay what looked like a scholarly pamphlet or trade magazine. On lifting it out he found himself holding a glossy brochure for one of Paris's most exclusive funeral services.

They gazed at the trick dossier, dumb with shock.

A slip of paper fell out and Ricardo picked it off the floor. *With compliments, Philippe Goujon, Commissaire Principal.* Revallier looked up and smiled grimly.

'The bastard's getting personal.'

· · · 16 · · ·

LA VIEILLE FORGE: Isabelle was going out of her mind. She'd been on the phone since eight o'clock, the nearest she'd come to Commissaire Goujon was his deputy Commissaire Bloque.

'When *can* I see him?'

'I've no doubt he will be permitted visitors in due course.'

'What's to prevent me seeing him this morning?'

'It isn't for me –'

'May I remind you my husband has committed no crime, you've no business holding him, no right to stop me seeing him.'

'I will speak to Commissaire Goujon.'

'And you will kindly ring me straight back.' He promised he would.

That was half an hour ago, it was now 11.30. She called again, neither Goujon nor Bloque was available. She tried the embassy once more, they were still looking into it and promised to call back.

She knew she ought to keep busy, clean up the house – still not recovered from the raid – mark her students' assignments, anything. But all she could do was hover near the phone, making herself ill with cigarettes.

The phone went, she jumped.

'Hale Lehrman here. Good news, Mrs Morrel, I'm seeing your husband this afternoon.'

'You're sure they'll let you see him?'

'Yes indeed, took a bit of doing, but that's what we're here for.'

'Will you find out when I can see him?'

'I sure will, and I'll get back to you soon as I've seen him.' His voice descended to signal the end of the call.

'Mr Lehrman?'

'Yes?'

'Get him out of there, please. He went in good faith to report a crime and now they're holding *him* because . . .' she faltered.

'Why do you suppose they're holding him, Mrs Morrel?'

'Because – I told you, he found out too much.'

'Don't worry, we'll get him out.'

Relief washed over her, the embassy would throw its protective cloak around him, make clear its displeasure at this treatment of one of its citizens. They'd release Luke pending further investigations.

Or would they? What if Lehrman failed, who would she turn to? She'd tried Laroche's number but he didn't answer, she'd called the Asian journalist who'd promised to get in touch and had left a message on her answering machine.

She remembered Etienne, the youth who first discovered the Marbled Teal on the estate, unwittingly triggering a terrible chain of events. She ought to see if he wanted any lunch, but couldn't bring herself to leave the telephone. Taking it off the hook, she hurried into the yard.

'Etienne?' she called.

After a moment, '*Oui, madame?*' the youth's voice carried from the goathouse.

While she waited for him, her gaze fell on Luke's jeep

sheltering in the makeshift garage. Her heart missed a beat. The jeep stood for Luke as nothing else did, a tangible expression of his persona, Luke made metal. If something happened to him, it would stand in the silent yard sounding his echo.

Goujon returned to his office in grim mood. The de Montforts, concerned only with themselves, had failed to alert him in time, Revallier had escaped – again!

'Double-check that every hospital and clinic is being searched for Janine Vallence.'

Bloque lifted the phone and dialled.

'And make sure all units have the registration of the motorbike.'

Bloque was shaking his head.

'Don't tell me no one got the number?'

'The bike wasn't carrying plates.'

Goujon rolled his eyes.

Retiring together to a room down the corridor, they dimmed the lights and studied aerial photographs of the city projected on to a screen, red circles superimposed denoting sightings of fleeing GP members which had been coming in all morning, some wild, some usefully forming themselves into patterns of flight.

On the north side, rare sightings were underground, Revallier and his Shadow spied riding the Métro first as labourers, then as *hommes d'affaires*. The gunman arrested just after eight turned out under interrogation to be neither deranged nor one of the GP, merely a conscientious citizen on whose person the terrorists had planted a gun. Even under pressure the Arab had the presence of mind not to leave fingerprints.

Sitting back, Goujon lit a cigarette and listened to Bloque's rapid commentary. While sightings of Revallier and his Shadow dried up around Bastille, the careering motorcyclist and his wounded pillion passenger had weaved a snaking back-street pattern through the Seventh, Sixth and Fifth *arrondissements* on the opposite side of the Seine, 'clearly intending to link up with Revallier,' said Bloque.

'Both parties going east,' observed Goujon, 'and hugging the river. Get on to the river police, tell them to double-check.'

Returning to his office, Goujon stood in the sun-filled window, trying to worm his way into Revallier's mind. How would he react to the shock of discovering that his brilliant operation in Place de la Concorde had actually been a humiliating failure? No nuclear file, and his partner wounded or dead. He tried to visualise a dwindling band of desperadoes going to ground in some dim-lit waterside hideout with their dying comrade. Dozens of Revallier look-alikes had been picked up at road-blocks, but no call had come through proclaiming the genuine article.

'Chief?'

Goujon was too absorbed in the river to notice Bloque in the doorway of their adjoining offices. Revallier might be licking his wounds, but was it possible he was already in possession of the American's tape and pictures . . .?

'About my wife . . .?' Bloque spoke up, 'You'll recall you agreed to a few days' leave.'

In the sparkling depths of the Seine, Goujon saw not the reflection of the ancient housefronts opposite, but Revallier making last-ditch mischief with the birdman's tape.

'I'd like to take two or three days.'

'Two or three days?'

'It's forty-eight hours since my son was born, I haven't seen him yet.'

Goujon turned to his deputy, a tall spare man in his thirties who'd been attached to him in the Marseille police force for the last three years. An uncomplicated honourable man, he wasn't party to the truth about the rue de Liège bomb.

Or was he?

'Of course you must see your son. You have a name for him?'

'My wife has chosen a name, yes.'

Bloque wasn't the most communicative of men, but Goujon would have expected him to be more forthcoming. There was something odd about him the last few days. Looking at him now, with the awkward slope of the shoulders and that closed expression, Goujon had an idea what was troubling him.

'There's a train this evening at seven . . . if that's all right, sir?'

'It's not all right. You'll have all the leave you like when this is over.'

'He'll have gone to earth,' argued Bloque, 'I doubt we'll hear from him in months, if ever.'

Goujon smiled, 'Have you learned nothing about our Monsieur Revallier these last twelve months?'

They regarded each other uneasily, until Bloque was rescued by one of the telephones on his desk, obliging him to withdraw and answer it. 'No, we're not available, tell her I'll call her later.'

Goujon thought he had put him in his place, but Bloque was back, carrying a padded envelope guiltily by his side.

'The American's wife?'

'Yes,' said Bloque, quickly adding, 'these tapes came this morning, calls to and from the de Montfort residences.'

'Anything interesting?'

'Yes.'

Ah – thought Goujon – now we have it.

Goujon clicked his fingers and Bloque came forward with the envelope. Inside Goujon found two tapes, one marked Château-de-Claireau, the other rue de Liège, and two sheets listing calls.

'You've listened to these?'

'Yes.'

'Did you ask me first?'

'I've never had to, you've never kept anything from me.'

Goujon cast an eye over the lists, and found the crucial call: '11.45 p.m., outgoing, Duke de Montfort to Interior Minister Batisse?'

Bloque nodded.

'Let's hear it then.'

Bloque took the tape to the console of sound equipment, fitted it and found the place. Sitting at his desk, Goujon swivelled to face the window, stretched his feet on the ledge, lit a cigarette and closed his eyes.

'*Allo?*' the deep resonant voice of the Minister's wife.

'*Giselle, how are you?*'

'*Edouard . . .*' a startled whisper.

'*Forgive me calling this late . . .*'

'*Better late than never, when am I going to see you?*'

'*I need to speak to Gaston.*'

'*Ah . . .*' disappointed, '*then I'd better get him for you.*'

Goujon cocked open an eye, 'What do you know, Bloque, the old bull screwing the minister's wife!'

Bloque nodded cautiously.

Goujon chuckled, 'Poor Bloque, so much disillusion.'

'*Edouard! to what do I owe this pleasure?*'

'*I thought you might like to know The Nose has bungled.*'

Goujon slowly opened his eyes.

'*What do you mean, bungled?*'

'*The word is out, a journalist has been asking questions.*'

'*Not about –*'

'*Yes.*'

'*How on earth?*'

'*An overheard conversation.*'

'*What happened to the assurances of absolute discretion?*'

'*You can't get more discreet than the wilds of my estate, one doesn't expect an amateur ornithologist crawling around with a tape recorder at six on a Sunday morning.*'

'Tape recorder!'

'Exactly, mon vieux. The Nose has the fellow under lock and key, but a priceless reproduction of the tape may have strayed.'

'Good God.'

'You better tell the others to keep on their toes, because should any reproductions fall into the wrong hands . . .' de Montfort left consequences to the imagination.

'We can't just sit around waiting for that.'

'No.'

Thoughtful pause. 'Do you suppose . . .' Batisse speculating tentatively, 'it could be arranged that our friend The Nose . . .' rising conspiratorial tone, 'acted alone?'

'Why not? There's a world of difference between fair and foul means of discrediting the GP . . .'

'Naturally . . .' Batisse calmer now, 'we were never in favour of foul.'

'Precisely.'

'I'll speak to the others, keep me closely informed. Good night.'

Bloque looked at Goujon, he'd never seen him go pale before. Shades of self-confidence and superiority were Goujon's colours.

Ash fell from Goujon's cigarette; slowly he lifted the dying butt to his lips. A man who scarcely knew the meaning of fear, he felt a curious gnawing in his belly, as though maggots were at work.

He stubbed out his cigarette and spoke in a remote, detached voice, 'Put a tap on Batisse's phone.'

'We need Batisse's permission,' Bloque reminded him, 'to tap phones.'

Goujon's laughter rang out. 'You want to call him up?'

Bloque stood his ground, 'The others we might conceivably get away with, but Batisse –'

'Has entrusted me with the power to tap any telephone.'

'But in whose name shall I tap Batisse's?'

'His own, fool. His wife's having an affair.'

While Bloque withdrew to issue orders, Goujon gazed out at Pont Neuf, through which the Seine had been flowing for four hundred years, where Molière once watched Tabarin's troupe of actors, where Louis XV's police-lieutenants arrested 'gallant ladies' and shipped them off to Louisiana, and where now, in Goujon's imagination, the top men in France were closing ranks and preparing to hurl him into the current.

Bloque returned, standing stiffly, waiting for his attention.

'What is it?' Goujon looked up at last.

'They didn't do it, did they?'

Goujon met his gaze, sensing trouble from an unexpected source, faithful Bloque.

'The GP didn't plant that bomb, did they?'

Goujon poured himself a coffee and lit another cigarette.

'The whole thing,' persisted Bloque, 'switching chauffeurs, the escape from the car, the call, the *fake* call from Revallier, all the work of . . .'

'Of whom, do you suppose?'

'I thought the American was a crank, but it looks as if he uncovered . . .'

'What did he uncover?'

'A government-backed operation carried out by Crozier's men . . .' By his expression, Bloque begged to be rescued from this misapprehension, 'Why?'

'Use your head.'

'I am, sir, that's just the point.'

'And what is your conclusion?'

'The GP needed to be *completely* smashed, their *myth* had to be destroyed.'

'Very good,' Goujon raised his coffee in a gesture of congratulation and took a sip.

'They had to be discredited.'

'Excellent.'

'Dishonestly discredited.'

'Welcome to the world.'

Bloque shaking, 'Is this how we catch criminals nowadays?'

'Criminals? The GP aren't criminals, they're not even terrorists, they're much more dangerous.' Bloque frowned, baffled. 'Society needs criminals, I've told you often enough, it can use terrorists too, but these people . . .' pointing at the display of photographs and impressions on the far wall, 'are a particularly virulent strain threatening the very fabric of society.'

Bloque shaking his head, more in disenchantment than dissent. 'You've always said it's not our job to think politically.'

'The GP are the exception.'

'I don't believe you . . . sir.'

'Oh?'

'You don't give a damn about the GP or the threat they pose, you just couldn't catch Revallier fast enough, he and Vallence had become living legends and your great reputation was in danger, or else . . .' nodding with growing assurance, 'they put pressure on you to agree to something drastic.'

Bloque stood rooted.

'Not bad,' said Goujon, 'for a budding detective.' The smile faded, 'only I'd have thought you knew by now I don't bend under pressure.'

'The conspiracy, sir, who thought of it?'

'De Montfort thought it was time for something . . .' a wave of the hand, 'unorthodox. He sent his son, Maurice, as emissary, to put his plan to men he could trust in the government. Most were a little coy at first, turned their noses up . . .' smiling at the memory, 'but they soon came like dogs to raw meat.'

'And where do you come in, commissaire?'

'I merely had to make the right noises, assure them that as the investigating officer, I would take the outrage at face value, the work of Revallier. Better to hunt down a fallen angel, a pariah, than a living legend. It also amused me to put temptation in their way, to see what jackals these fine men are underneath, what cowards. Now that they might get caught, they threaten to leave me to swing for them.'

'Even the duke, who seemed such an admirer.'

'The duke,' a grudging smile, 'is a survivor.'

Bloque stood head bowed.

'I've always admired you, sir, but this . . .'

Goujon was surprised to feel the sting of Bloque's tone.

'Stop making an ass of yourself,' he snapped, draining his coffee, 'there's no room for sentimentality in this line of work.'

'I don't feel sentimental about the rue de Liège bomb – but what's her name, that doctor? not blown up by the GP as everyone believes . . . but by us.'

Goujon was on his feet, 'That's just the kind of emotional rubbish I'm talking about. Do you beat your breast every time some innocent dies in a car chase, or intercepts a stray bullet in a siege?'

'With respect, sir, that's entirely different.'

'Nonsense! She was unfortunate enough to walk into an operation mounted against the GP, an unusual operation I grant you, but in principle no different from a dawn raid.'

Bloque took a few moments to speak.

'I think it would be best if I took that leave.'

Goujon cleared his throat, 'Suit yourself.'

Bloque retired to his office, gathered his things and hesitated at the door. 'Perhaps you should find someone to replace me.'

First de Montfort, mused Goujon, now my own disciple.

'You pick your moments, Christian.'

'I can't help that, chief.'

'If my gamble comes off, and the American leads me to Revallier, watch them return like dogs to their own vomit. It would be a pity to miss it.'

Bloque was gone.

Alone, Goujon sat down and lit a cigarette to clear his thoughts. If de Montfort wanted to play dirty, that was fine by him. First of all he would instruct his men in the basement telecommunications laboratory at Hôtel des Invalides to send over tapes not daily, or even twice daily, but on the hour around the clock. Automatically he looked to Bloque to make the arrangements – only Bloque had gone. He'd overestimated him; he manifestly had neither the stomach nor the vision to make a really good detective.

He'd also seriously *under*estimated him, he realised: his courage, his integrity. As he dialled the lab, he thought about a replacement, knowing full well that no one could take Bloque's place.

No sooner had he made the call than one of Bloque's phones rang. He went through to answer it. It was from one of his mobile surveillance units reporting that the Indian journalist still hadn't returned home, nor had she collected her car from the eighteenth *arrondissement*.

'Remind me what time you prodigies lost her.'

'Eleven o'clock last night, sir.'

'She went into a café and vanished, if I recall.'

'Out back, yes sir. By the time we realised –'

'Keep me informed.'

Two more phones were ringing, he answered one: another sighting, this time in the travel bureau of Galeries Lafayette, Montparnasse, an impossibility even for Revallier to be on both sides of the river at once. The other call informed him that Monsieur Lehrman from the American Embassy was downstairs.

Before driving the diplomat to visit Morrel in gaol, he checked once more the location of Mademoiselle Sharma's late-night escapade. Could someone have warned her she was being followed, and picked her up at the back of the café, with the panache one would normally have associated with . . .?

He juggled the tantalising thought that perhaps Mademoiselle Sharma might be the one who would lead him to Revallier.

• • • 17 • • •

Luke had been locked up for nearly twenty-four hours. But for deliveries of meals and an eye peering at intervals through the spy slot, no one came near . . . until he started pounding on the door, demanding to speak to his wife, his lawyer. Each time the sergeant appeared, he promised to forward Luke's requests. Still he waited.

The concrete cell was a shock to a warm-blooded human being. Three metres long by less than two wide, it was fitted with a bed and toilet, the bed a slab of concrete and a thin stale mattress, the toilet a hole in a tiled recess which flushed every fifteen minutes day and night. A luke-warm pipe provided heating, he wore a musty blanket over his coat like a cloak. There were no windows, only an air vent over the door, and a bare electric bulb shining through a transparent screen in the ceiling. Nothing to do but think, fret and doze. The night had seemed endless, and now the day crawled interminably.

He lay on the bed, hands behind his head, trying to concentrate on the plot of his novel. In what little space was not taken by the bed, he paced like a caged animal, worrying about Isabelle, feeling lousy about Laroche and his grim story – he couldn't get used to thinking of him as Lucien Grossman. If he hadn't gone to the police, Laroche would never have been taken and tortured.

Footsteps approaching, slowing, ceasing at his door. The spy slot was drawn back, an eye introduced itself, the massive door was unlocked.

'Vous avez un visiteur, monsieur.'

Isabelle, thank God!

Then he realised the sergeant had said *un visiteur*, masculine, and in walked a spruce gentleman wearing an optimistic smile.

'Mr Morrel . . .' offering his hand, 'Hale Lehrman!'

Seeing the wretched cell, he grimaced.

'This is terrible, Mr Morrel, we've got to get you out of here.'

'I haven't seen my lawyer or spoken to my wife.'

Lehrman shook his head sympathetically.

'It's reciprocal, we don't violate their citizens rights, they don't violate ours.'

With an open-handed gesture, Luke invited the legal attaché to take a seat, the only seat, the bed.

'No thanks, I'm fine. Listen . . .' frowning thoughtfully, 'try not to be too down-hearted, Commissaire Goujon seems pretty reasonable, I doubt he wants to hold you here longer than he needs to.'

'What does he need to hold me for, Mr Lehrman?'

The prisoner's soft tone was disquieting, and in a room along the passage, Commissaire Goujon pressed his headphones tighter to his ears to hear.

'I'd say he'd be willing to release you . . .' pause, *'if you could be just a little bit more co-operative.'*

'How much more co-operative can you get?'

'If you could give him some kind of guarantee that you're going to leave the authorities here to do whatever they have to without –'

'Do me a favour, Mr Lehrman, check out a car for me, a white Volvo, registration 177PG2A. The owner is one of the men behind last Friday's car bomb.'

Goujon yawned, lit a cigarette and took a deep pull.

A regretful sigh from the attaché, *'We can't do that, sir, we don't have the facilities.'*

'You've got the connections, you can do it.'

'Even if we could . . . listen, Mr Morrel, between you and me, don't get involved . . . We don't get involved, it leads to all kinds of complications, we're guests here, you and us, it's not our business.'

'A woman's been blown up, and I have the bombers on tape.'

'I understand —'

'You don't understand. This was no terrorist outrage, we're talking about a bombing officially sponsored by senior members of the French government, maybe by the President himself.'

'If what you say is true —'

'You're damn right it's true. Get me out of here and I'll bring you the tape and pictures.'

'To be perfectly frank, Mr Morrel, I don't think anybody wants to see them. I believe we can get you out of here, but only if you forget this whole business.'

'Forget it! A woman's dead, for Chrissake, I'd have to live with knowing who did it.'

A faltering pause, the attaché momentarily lost for words.

'It's not for me, Mr Morrel, to tell you what to do —'

'You don't want to know, do you?'

'We don't, we can't get involved in the private tragedies —'

'Private!'

'Of French citizens. We got our hands full dealing with . . . people like you, stuck in gaol. Try and see it from the wider perspective, Mr Morrel, it's not in the interests of the US and her European friends to fall out over isolated incidents —'

'Don't insult the US by equating US government interests with those of ordinary Americans who would demand you act on my evidence.'

'With respect, sir, ordinary Americans are the government, we merely represent their interests, interests which are not served, and nor, to be perfectly frank, are the interests of the bomb victim served —'

'The interests of the bomb victim!'

The American ablaze, an ominous silence. Goujon sat

up, ready to intervene. It wouldn't look good, an American attaché . . .

'*Get out, you goddam dummy, before I give Goujon serious cause to hold me . . .*' Lehrman calling anxiously for the door to be opened, '*Get out of here, before I flush you down the pan!*'

Suppressing a smile, Goujon hurried out in time to meet Mr Lehrman rearranging himself in the passage.

'How did you get on?' said Goujon in his best English.

'Fine, fine, he's just a bit excited, that's all.'

'Not entirely co-operative?'

'I'm sure we can work something out.'

Goujon ordered a car for him and accompanied him to the street.

'As a gesture of appreciation,' Goujon touched the attaché's arm as he showed him out, 'I'm going to risk the wrath of my superiors.'

Lehrman surprised, 'You're going to release him?'

'Shall we say you persuaded me.'

'I'd appreciate that.'

The official car drew up, they shook hands, Goujon holding Lehrman's in his grip. 'If you should hear from him, if he brings you any so-called evidence of alleged crimes . . .'

'I'll get straight on to you, commissaire.'

An exchange of grateful smiles and they parted.

Luke sat with his head in his hands. No release, no progress on the tape, no Isabelle, no lawyer, no way of knowing how long they were going to hold him, days? years?

The embassy would only get him out if he forgot about *the whole business*. If he did that he'd be free, free to carry his secret knowledge for the rest of his life. There would never come a day when he didn't look up from his typewriter or milking stool and remember . . .

Voices startled him, keys in the lock. The door swung open, the sergeant stepped aside for someone arriving along the passage with clipped unhurried steps.

Goujon paused to contemplate the prisoner. The merest nod invited Luke to join him.

Luke rose tentatively, looked for his coat, and found he was wearing it. Goujon led the way in silence through the building to the street.

'You must have made quite an impression, monsieur. You're free to go.'

Luke's ears and eyes filled with the bustle of the street.

'I want to see Laroche.'

'He's gone.'

'What do you mean, he's gone?'

'Moved to Fresnes prison, the infirmary.'

'I want to see him.'

'You'll be able to visit him next week.'

'What will happen to him?'

'He'll go on trial.'

'For what?'

'Membership of the GP.'

'A supporter maybe, never a member. What's happening to this country? Your eyes are green and you're a subversive?'

'May I offer you a car?'

'No.'

He saw a taxi and ran to hail it. As it U-turned and pulled up to the kerb, Goujon opened the door as he would for a departing guest.

'*Au revoir, monsieur.*'

'*Adieu, commissaire.*'

Goujon watched the taxi go; an unmarked car slid off the kerb and took off in casual pursuit. Dusk had fallen in sharp relief over the rooftops, Goujon sniffed the air, felt a tremor of anticipation.

· · · 18 · · ·

Leaving the raging city behind, *Le Dragon de Rougeau* laboured against the current to reach its moorings thirty-five kilometres south-east of Paris.

The plan was for Kasha to disembark at Choisy-le-Roi, ten kilometres out of Paris, making her way back to the city by train to deliver the file to *Le Monde*. With the captured file revealed to be a hoax, she was going to return to Paris anyway, fax her story to London and then contact Isabelle Morrel as promised. But as she was getting ready to get off, Revallier, who hadn't spoken for an hour, asked her not to leave.

'What about Isabelle Morrel?'

'Knowing Goujon, she'll be bugged and tapped. Go there and they'll seize you and this time they won't let you go.'

'I'm a journalist, they can't hold me.'

From Revallier an ironic laugh.

'I still have to fax this story to London.'

'Fuck your story.'

'*Your* story, probably your only chance of publicly telling the truth.'

'She's right,' said Ricardo. He had more to say, but a look from Revallier quelled him.

'Today was catastrophic,' said Kasha, 'but you can hit back through the media. Imagine the furore when the article comes out in London: French ministers, industrialists and police implicated in car bomb atrocity. I'll kick up such a stink . . .'

'Stay,' he said simply.

His eyes rested on her.

The journey seemed never-ending. Police helicopters twice hovered to identify 'the Dragon'. No doubt they then checked with the river police, who reported that the barge had already been boarded.

Ricardo stroked Janine's hair, wept from time to time, swore obscenely in Italian and finally busied himself preparing a hot meal in the cramped galley.

Revallier sat with Janine, resting his head on her blanket. After a time he sat up, gazing at her death mask as though conferring.

'You only have half a story anyway,' he broke the silence and looked at Kasha, 'tomorrow night you'll have the full story.'

Ears pricked up, Ricardo peered in, Tahar, stretched out on a bunk, opened a speculative eye. Catching the air of expectancy, Kasha was alone in not knowing what Revallier was getting at. He addressed her.

'Remember Michel Kerlesquin?'

'Dimly.'

'You willing to give him another chance?'

The name sent a shiver through her, how could she forget the other night in her apartment, her rage and terror as she pointed a gun at a man she'd just had dinner with.

'Does Monsieur Kerlesquin want to use me again?'

'Yes.'

'For another go at the file?'

'According to our less than perfect intelligence,' he spoke in a careless tone, as if the matter was of no consequence, 'today was a preliminary hearing of the plans. The de Montforts are expected to go away and make final adjustments, in order to unveil the file at a private function in Lille on Monday.'

Lille. Monday. Kasha couldn't conceal her surprise. On

Monday, the British Prime Minister and the French President were to meet at a summit in Lille, formally to agree to the construction of a Channel tunnel.

'They'll bring the file back to rue de Liège tonight, to work on it over the weekend. Normally they don't leave for the country until Saturday morning. There's a chance that tomorrow evening they will have it with them in town . . .'

'One floor below me,' Kasha concluded, 'again.'

He looked at her, a relaxed look which said, It's up to you.

A deep intake of breath, 'My reservations, my conditions would be the same as before.'

At Plessis-Chênet, where the Seine cascades without warning, the barge went through a lock, took a sweeping bend and came to rest in sheltered waters beneath a wooded bank. The sun was descending into wintry forest; a small crowd waited in the fading light. No smiles, no welcome – they must have had advanced warning, Kasha thought, they seemed prepared for the body.

Though lightly built, Janine was heavy in death, and Revallier concentrated to deliver her with slow dignity as if bearing his own child. In silence they lowered the tailboard of a trailer and helped him lift her up and lay her on a pallet of straw. Before proceeding, Tahar took one of the young farmers aside and questioned him. Apart from road-blocks on all routes into nearby Melun, no police had been near.

Except for the young woman who drove the tractor, everyone walked, Revallier close enough to have touched the body, Tahar and Ricardo at his shoulder, Kasha among the rest strung out behind. They proceeded at a measured pace along the edge of a wood, until they came to a road carrying light traffic through the countryside. Covering the body, they crossed the road, and once clear on the far side, resumed their procession as far as a fork in the lane. One way wound towards distant buildings scattered around a windmill like a village around a church; the farm commune, Kasha guessed. But they didn't make for the farm, they took the rougher track leading away through a scrap of woodland, where Janine's body was jolted by the ride over the hard rutted ground.

Kasha drew alongside Tahar, 'Where are we going?' she whispered.

'A little farther.'

'Not to the commune?'

'We don't want to put them in danger, so our base is a kilometre away. It's safer for us too, away from the prying eyes of the children.'

'Do the police know you have a rural base?'

'Since Goujon's arrival, they've begun to take the possibility seriously.'

'How do you know?'

'Lately there have been sweeps through the countryside around Paris by the Gendarmerie Mobile.'

Known as Les Joncs, or The Rushes, the GP's rural base consisted of a cottage and outbuildings clustered around a pond and screened by trees. Closer, Kasha could smell wood burning, saw smoke curling from chimneys, and ducks standing still on the bright surface of the pond. So this was where Revallier spent much of his time, she reflected, recalling how curious she had been about his outdoor complexion.

At first glance the cottage had an abandoned look, its closed shutters hanging crookedly, the roof missing tiles and mossed over. The door was unlocked. Bearing the body, Revallier stooped inside and, turning her sideways, carried her upstairs and laid her out on her bed. Two older women also entered the house, inviting Kasha to join them.

A log fire burned, drawing her to its flames. In its glow, and in the soft light of tasselled shades, the cottage took on an unexpected snugness. While the women heated basins of water and gathered towels, Kasha took in the human touches of Janine's home: empty bottles and unwashed cups, a clotheshorse hung with shirts and underwear, two, three vases of recent flowers, wrapping paper and ribbon in the wastepaper basket, birthday cards on the mantelpiece, a hair dryer, magazines and make-up on a sofa stuffed with bright cushions.

Upstairs Revallier rooted in the wardrobe and laid out the garments Janine had specified: plain black dress, red scarf and favourite jewellery. When the women came up he said, 'I want her to look great.'

He turned to Kasha, 'You have a camera?'

'Yes.'

'I want the world to see her at her best.' He turned to go.

'I have to call London,' she reminded him.

'Hold the story till Saturday. Once it's out, you won't be able to take two steps without being arrested, and I'm going to need you . . .' fixing her with a clear hard gaze, 'for more than reporting.'

She returned his gaze unflinchingly. 'What about Monsieur Morrel's tape and pictures?'

'I'm working on it.'

'You haven't lost hope of –'

'No.'

'Also . . .' following him down the stairs, 'I need to know more about Janine.'

'Later. It's going to be a long night.' He turned at the front door, 'They've always preferred the version of *me* as founder-leader. She was the real founder, often the real leader.'

'You were lovers?'

'Yes.' Icy air entered as he stood there in the open door.

She wouldn't let go: 'Did you never want to marry?'

'No.'

'No desire for children?'

'I wanted children,' he confessed, 'she didn't.'

317

'It wouldn't have been practical, would it?'

'That wasn't the point,' he said, and looked at her, wondering if she understood what he was saying. 'We had a child . . .' Kasha's eyes widened, 'a little boy, a *little* boy!' he laughed, 'obviously it was little!' The smile left his face, 'here, in this house.'

Gently, 'And?'

'A childless couple took him,' motioning in the direction of the commune.

'Does he know you're his father?'

'No,' he laughed again, covering his feelings. Then quietly, before turning and walking across to his quarters, 'He has a good life.'

After saying mass at eight o'clock that evening, Father Igor Boury went out to telephone for the third time. Although he intended to sound innocuous and give nothing tangible away, he knew that each time he called he increased the risk of getting caught. If the Morrels' phone was tapped, the police would trace the call and catch him, if they were quick enough and he wasn't. To be safe he found a different kiosk each time, and covered his clerical collar with a scarf.

His limp was not affected, he'd bruised his knee throwing himself under the wheels of the police car in rue de Liège that morning. At the hospital he'd resisted the urge to ask questions. Only when he got home did he see on the lunch-time news the mayhem in Place de la Concorde, blue lights whirring, swarms of CRS, and from the air a sensational view, the blue Mercedes stranded near the obelisk, just where Revallier had said it would be. Then the blow fell. Nothing of substance stolen, one terrorist hit by gunfire, probably Janine Vallence, possibly dead.

The first time he got through he described himself as a friend, wondering had Madame Morrel any news of her husband. She'd hesitated an agonisingly long time, fearful of his anonymous voice, and the term *friend*, the very approach of an enemy. A good friend, he stressed, in the same line of business, all the time watching the boulevard for danger. Finally she must have guessed roughly who he was, and said her husband was still being detained. He thanked her and foolishly, as he later realised, said he'd call back.

In the afternoon it was announced on the radio that the police had released without charge an unnamed American questioned in connection with terrorist activities in the city. Igor went straight out again. From a booth in Montparnasse station, he tried to reach Revallier and, if she was still alive, Janine. No one answered at The Rushes. He tried the Morrels again. Also no answer.

Now, just after nine in the evening, having rushed the mass and delivered a sermon on God knows what, he hurried from the church and pedalled painfully in the opposite direction this time, pausing to look about before picking an open-air booth in Place du 18 Juin 1940. Leaning the bike against the booth, he dialled the number. It rang and rang, and he was ready, with some relief, to give up, when he sensed someone watching. A glance over his shoulder and there was a man, not five strides away, hands in coat pockets, regarding him expressionlessly.

Suddenly the phone was answered by an anxious Madame Morrel, 'Yes?'

Lost for words he faltered. Then, 'Your husband, madame, I heard the news, is he there?'

'You called earlier.'

'Yes.'

'One moment.'

The one moment stretched interminably, Igor watching the approaches, trying to remain calm when even now the police could be tracing the call to this booth. He glanced at his watch to see how long it was since he'd dialled, but he hadn't noticed what time he'd called. He couldn't wait much longer, he knew he must hang up and was about to when to his dismay a gruff voice came on, 'Yes, who's that?'

'Remember the other night, monsieur,' he whispered hoarsely into the mouthpiece, 'we met at mine, you needed to talk . . .?'

'I remember. You still interested in . . . the merchandise?'

'Very much so . . .' Both men groping in the dark, 'Perhaps,' he resumed quickly, 'you could send someone, avoid complications, as soon as possible?'

'Okay, soon as I can.'

'Merci, monsieur.' Igor replaced the receiver, felt the man close in from behind, turned to face him and caught his breath as the man brushed past him, jingled some coins and lifted the receiver.

Weak with relief, Igor wheeled his bike into the road, mounted shakily and was pulling away when there was a howl of brakes, a car screeching to a halt. Pedalling blindly, he heard doors fly open and men bursting out shouting 'FREEZE!' Braced for the worst, he struck the kerb, stumbled to a stop and lifted his hands in surrender as he looked around . . . and saw the petrified man in the call booth surrounded by armed police bawling at him.

Passersby froze, traffic slowed, Igor spirited himself away on his bike, took the first corner he came to and rode like the devil.

• • • 19 • • •

Over dinner along the quays that night, Goujon cursed Bloque in his absence. He sensed the hunt reaching its climax, and without his deputy he would be stretched to respond with his customary speed.

Angry but undaunted, he decided it was time to pack a suitcase and move into his office for what he believed to be the final forty-eight hours – well within his twelve-month deadline.

At 10.30 p. m. he left the restaurant and drove his car across the river to his hotel on the right bank, where Luke had followed him two nights earlier. As he mounted the hotel steps, a police motorbike drew up, siren wailing. Running up the steps, the rider saluted and handed him a padded envelope. Goujon thanked him and went inside.

At the reception he returned the manager's greeting and collected his messages.

'And congratulations, commissaire! Quite a coup this morning, I saw it on TV.' Goujon fluttered a modest hand. 'I'd say he's finished now, wouldn't you?'

Revallier finished? Goujon's parting smile said, I wouldn't count on it. Crossing the lobby he nodded affably to a familiar resident reading the paper and read through his messages: URGENT – *call Duke de Montfort.* URGENT – *call Interior Minister Batisse.* URGENT – *call CL.* For a moment he was puzzled, CL? But then of course! Claude Lusardi, also named on the American's cassette.

He took the lift to the third floor, where a modest suite overlooking the street and the old church had been his home for the past twelve months. Removing his jacket and tie, he lit a cigarette and opened the padded envelope, extracting a collection of tapes.

Edouard and Maurice de Montfort had evidently been busy on the phone, as had Maurice's young German wife, but he began by slotting into his portable machine a tape marked *MORREL, La Vieille Forge, 15 Jan. 21.00-22.00.* Ignoring for the moment Madame Morrel's twenty-minute conversation with her son in Philadelphia, and other family calls, he zeroed in on a call received at 21.13 hours from a public booth in Place du 18 Juin 1940 – the caller who got away.

'Remember the other night, monsieur,' hoarse whispering, 'we met at mine, you needed to talk . . .?'

Met at mine, reflected Goujon, where did Morrel go the other night, and which other night? Bloque would have run it up on the computer in a thrice. Ah! but it was coming to him, didn't the American pay a mysterious visit to a church in Montparnasse?

Releasing PAUSE, 'I remember. You still interested in . . . the merchandise?'

'Very much so . . . Perhaps you could send someone, avoid complications, as soon as possible?'

'Okay, soon as I can.'

Good, thought Goujon, just as he'd anticipated. The moment he released Morrel, they homed in on him like wasps to jam. He lifted the phone and dialled.

'Ici Commissaire Goujon, give me Colonel Prustin-Vollon.'

In the time it took to wriggle out of his shirt, he was through to the taciturn commander.

'Bonsoir, commissaire.'

'Bonsoir, mon colonel, the Morrels haven't stirred?'

'No.'

'No sign of the Asian journalist?'

'No.'

'Or the GP?'

'None.'

'Don't let your men be fooled, colonel. If the GP show up they won't be wearing Save the Whale sweatshirts.'

'I realise that.'

'Let them through and take them on their way out, so as to maximise the chances–'

'Of catching them with a particular cassette and photographs, I know.'

'I'm sure I don't need to remind you of the grave national interests involved.'

Goujon wished him a successful night and hung up.

Although the paramilitary forces of the rural Gendarmerie Mobile were under Ministry of Defence control, Goujon had been granted full rein, and the fields and lanes around The Old Forge were ringed by troops supported by helicopters. Would Revallier chance his luck to break in, or was the American mad enough to try to break out? Or might Mademoiselle Sharma oblige him and be the first to flutter into his trap?

Switching incoming calls to the answering machine, Goujon went into the bathroom and was no sooner stripped when the phone went. Moments later it went again. News of him releasing the American was triggering a grand panic among his illustrious superiors. Smiling to himself, he stepped under the shower.

The Old Forge, 11 p. m.: 'Aha, another one!' cried Isabelle triumphantly, high up on a step ladder. Running her hand along the top of the pelmet once again, she checked there were no more offenders and came down with her catch in her fist.

Luke received the tiny electronic device into his palm.

'They look like goddam Colorado beetles, don't throw them in the potatoes.'

They spoke in English all evening, communicating in the kind of cryptic shorthand long-standing couples are so good at, teasing their eavesdroppers and laying the occasional hopeless smokescreen.

'Why do they harass you, honey, when you gave them your only copies?'

They put on coats, unbolted the front door and walked slowly arm in arm across the silent yard. Holding a lantern aloft, they toured the goathouse. No new life and none lost.

'I know this is going to sound terrible,' said Isabelle calmly, 'but what we're doing isn't going to change anything. If those bastards do get exposed, and prosecuted, there are plenty more waiting to take their place.

And as for Nathalie Sainte-Claire, we can't bring her back. She's dead, but you're alive and free again.'

'Are you ready to live with it if we give in to them?'

'I'm not ready to see you sacrificed.'

Hooking up the lantern, they put their arms around each other and stood holding on in the silence.

The Rushes, midnight: The night still and overcast, Ricardo crouching in the look-out post perched like a crow's-nest on top of the barn, vainly scouring the lanes and hedges through binoculars. In his lap he cradled an antiquated submachine-gun, and looped around his wrist was the end of a length of twine, which ran along the roof, down the side of the barn and in through an air vent of the lean-to in which Revallier had his quarters.

Revallier and Tahar sat around a table, backs to a fire, the tail end of Ricardo's twine tied round the neck of a chianti bottle on the table. A yank on the twine and they'd know a raid was on. Bicycles waited by the back door, and with them a slim chance of reaching the barge through the woods.

The lean-to was high and narrow, with space for a combined kitchen, living room and office, complete with charts, maps and filing cabinets improvised from wine crates. A hay loft reached by ladder served as Revallier's bedroom and library.

Two more dated submachine-guns lay on the table where Revallier and Tahar pored over maps of Paris. They spoke in hushed tones, as though afraid that shadows might be listening, planning the following evening's final operation.

Over in the cottage Kasha sat curled on the sofa, constantly aware of the body upstairs. Despite heat coming from the open fire, she couldn't get warm. She worked in mittens in the subdued light, her article growing longer and longer; what had begun as a profile of de Montfort and

Revallier was turning into the last days of the GP. After the bustle of Paris, the silence around the cottage was startling – every little sound made her look up from her work.

Around nine o'clock she had finally got through to Hugh at home in London, who as foreign editor began by telling her forcefully in his Scots brogue that two pages were out of the question. Tell Richard the front page will do fine, she joked. Once dug in, Hugh was impervious to frontal assault, so she nonchalantly listed the information she had on the car bomb. He went very quiet, a sign that he was listening instead of reacting.

She switched tack; 'Hugh, you wouldn't believe how cold it is here. We've had nothing but sleet or snow since –'

'Kasha, are you saying the chauffeur – Bolivar? – running in the cemetery last Friday, was jumped by the Secret Service, who then put a bomb in the duke's car, who then gets into it knowing it's about to go off?'

'That's exactly what I'm saying. I'm sending you the story anyway, in instalments . . .

As it grew late, Tahar and Revallier were drawing up lists of contacts who might still be willing to perform some small service – a door left unlocked; a vehicle delivered at a certain time and place – when the bottle on the table with the twine around its neck *moved*.

They froze, the twine falling from the air vent had grown taut and was tugging gently on the bottle, as if Ricardo was trying to tell them that something was out there and it might be a raid. As they got to their feet, the twine gave a sudden jerk, tipping the bottle over, Revallier springing to catch it halfway to the floor.

Seizing weapons, they scrambled, Tahar through the kitchen to the back door, Revallier up the ladder to the loft. Hearts pounding they each prised open a door, Tahar to scan the fields at the back, Revallier to lift himself through the trap-door to the roof. Expecting to encounter Ricardo signalling frantically, he was surprised to be met by total quiet.

No sight or sound of Ricardo.

Safety-catch released, weapon poised, he crawled over the icy roof, until he heard the faint purr of someone snoring.

Peering into the crow's-nest, he found Ricardo slumped forward fast asleep, the twine around his wrist.

Soon after midnight, Commissaire Goujon left his hotel and drove back across the river to Île de la Cité. He drove fast along quai des Orfèvres, listening to tapes of phone calls as he went, and swung through the arch of number thirty-six to park in the almost deserted courtyard.

Taking the lift to the third floor, he carried his suitcase and fresh suit down the long silent corridor, half-expecting Jean-Jacques Revallier to slide out of a darkened doorway and slit his throat. Safely reaching his office, he unfolded a camp-bed, slung his case on it, hung up his suit and went to Bloque's computer to try to find which church the American had visited the other night, and whether Bloque had a man watching it. Struggling to make the computer work for him, he was roundly cursing Bloque when a phone rang, making him start. At twenty past midnight, it had to be something important.

Lifting the receiver, he instantly recognised Nitze's self-satisfied voice, announcing that the Jew was ready to sing at last. However sceptical of Nitze's bragging, Goujon couldn't help his blood racing.

'I hope you're not wasting my time.'

'You like arias, commissaire, let me provide!'

Goujon hurried down to the courtyard. Snow was falling, trying to gain a hold on his car. Slapping a whirring blue beacon on the roof, he swept on to the quays, left the island and drove north and west across the city. If Laroche was really ready to sing, the hunt could be over by morning. All Goujon needed to know were Revallier's hide-outs. He would unleash his men in the dead hour before dawn, and it would be over in minutes. The precise outcome immaterial; dead or alive, Revallier would have been deprived of the consolation of sympathy or martyrdom by the rue de Liège bomb. Terrorist shot dead, end of story.

Except for the American's tape and pictures.

Speeding along rue de Rivoli, he crossed Place de la Concorde, with the memory of the morning's successful ruse bringing a smile to his lips. He drove faster, he knew the route well, his relentless pursuit of the GP having delivered a copious supply of suspects to the interrogation centre.

At this time of night the place was quiet; his steps echoed down long deserted corridors. Past the white office and around the corner he heard raucous laughter, men relaxing after a good night's work. Without knocking, he walked in. The stench hit him like a wall, the prisoner had vacated his bowels.

Still strapped down, Laroche sat slumped in his chair, his flies gaping, the tiny electrodes which had done their work tangled at his feet.

Through the nicotine haze, Goujon saw Nitze sitting with his feet on a chair, holding court, his sweaty shirt-sleeved men gathered around, smoking and drinking. Proud of his professional standing, Nitze resented the celebrity from Marseille and feigned not to have noticed him.

Goujon waited. Nitze's men grew uneasy.

'Ah, commissaire, there you are!' Still with his feet up, Nitze raised a beer in invitation, 'Won't you have a drink with us?'

'What have you got for me?'

'Busch or Heineken, that's it I'm afraid.'

Goujon fixed him with a hollow gaze. 'I'm talking about the prisoner.'

Nitze's smile gave way to mock solemnity.

'He's broken, commissaire, he's all yours.'

'You mean he's told you nothing?'

'I refuse . . .' the voice, barely audible, came from Laroche, 'to talk to a common torturer.'

'Pompous little fucking Jew,' laughed Nitze.

'But gutsy,' conceded one of his men unexpectedly.

Goujon stepped closer to the prisoner, taking care not to soil his shoes. 'You'll talk to me, monsieur?'

'Only you.'

'Get him cleaned up and bring him to me in five minutes.'

Goujon left, and paced the white office. Five minutes went by, ten. Finally a handcuffed Laroche arrived, half supported, half dragged by two men, followed by Nitze wearing an obscure smile.

'I'll see him alone,' said Goujon.

Nitze made no move to leave.

'Alone,' repeated Goujon.

With no attempt to hide his anger, Nitze withdrew with his men.

Goujon studied the prisoner. Lighting himself a cigarette, he offered one. Laroche, hands shackled behind his back, nodded. Goujon squeezed a Gauloise between the prisoner's shaking lips and lit it. 'You have something to tell me, monsieur?'

Had the prisoner heard?

'Monsieur, I haven't all night.'

'What . . .?' Laroche gripped the cigarette in his teeth, 'do I get?'

'You?' Goujon could only laugh.

'You don't get Revallier . . .' Laroche squinted at Goujon, 'for nothing.'

Goujon eyed him distastefully, he hadn't time to haggle. A patient smile. 'What can I do for you, monsieur?'

'Immunity.'

'From prosecution? Granted.'

'Liberty.'

'Soon as you tell me where Monsieur Revallier hides, and we confirm it, you walk free.'

Laroche broke into a fit of coughing. Goujon stepped on the prisoner's fallen cigarette.

'Anything else, monsieur?'

'Dignity.'

Goujon cocked a questioning eye, Laroche rattled his handcuffs. Striding to the door, Goujon wasn't surprised to find Nitze and his cronies nearby.

'Free the gentleman's hands.'

Nitze arrived unhurriedly. With a contemptuous glance at the prisoner, he transferred his cigarette to his lips and unlocked Laroche's wrists.

'And security,' wheezed Laroche.

'What kind of security?'

Laroche raised a hand, rubbing thumb and forefinger together. Goujon glanced at Nitze.

'Didn't you offer inducements?'

'Didn't need to.'

Goujon turned again to the prisoner, 'Name your price, monsieur, and get on with it.'

'Million francs . . . ticket to Paradise.'

While Goujon turned away reflectively and lit a cigarette, Nitze was unable to stifle a smile.

Laroche, shaking uncontrollably, waited patiently.

'All right,' said Goujon, 'I'll fix you up abroad with a million francs.'

Laroche's bruised expression sought assurances.

'You have my word, monsieur, before this witness.'

Laroche glanced at his witness, a man who'd personally put an electronic current through his genitals. He sighed, resigned. It was the best he could do.

'Where is he?' whispered Goujon encouragingly.

Eyes drooping, Laroche wagged his head in conflict with himself. Then he licked his parched lips, trying to speak.

'Get him a beer.'

Nitze went to the door. 'A beer, quick!'

The men arrived, one came forward, uncapped a bottle and closed the prisoner's fist around it. Letting his head fall back, Laroche drained half the bottle before breaking off for another coughing fit.

Goujon perched on the edge of the table and stubbed out his cigarette.

'Okay, let's have it.'

Laroche leaned forward, one hand over his eyes, the other making a tight fist . . . as if the one was trying to shield him from what the other was about to do.

'Cigarette,' he murmured.

Goujon caught Nitze's eye, Nitze produced a Dunhill and slid it between the prisoner's fingers and lit it.

The moment had arrived.

'You want to know,' rasped Laroche with a deep pull on his cigarette, 'where to find him? All right . . .'

With a mournful sigh, as if remembering good times, he paused to gaze at his own clenched fist, and began to open it like a flower . . .

'My friend Revallier is hiding in a fairytale wood under a toadstool.' Elevating his hand, he peered down into his palm to find him, *'Voilà!'* he chimed and, lifting his hand higher, offered his audience Revallier on a plate.

For a trancelike moment, everyone stared at the prisoner's empty hand. Then glances darted Goujon's way.

Dark with rage, Goujon turned slowly and fixed Nitze with a withering gaze. The interrogator contemplated his feet.

Goujon unrelenting, 'Call that an aria, capitaine?'

The prisoner hit the floor.

For a moment no one moved. Then Goujon got down and saw that Laroche was unconscious.

'Get him an ambulance, guard him, keep the press away and no more interrogations without my sayso.'

Goujon went out into the night. Snow was settling in the streets as he drove away.

At 2 a. m., at his post on the roof of the barn, Tahar was trying to stay awake. From time to time he followed the lights of a helicopter tracking across the sky. Otherwise all was quiet, not a murmur, flurries of snow deepening the silence.

In the loft below, Kasha was trying to sleep. Despite heaps of blankets she couldn't get warm. And her mind was in turmoil. How had she allowed herself to get into this? Tagging along with the GP was one thing, Rod would be green with envy. But she'd overstepped her professional role by carrying what she thought was the genuine file from Concorde to the barge, and she was stretching it recklessly by agreeing to co-operate in tomorrow night's operation against the de Montforts.

Why had she agreed? for Nathalie's sake, for justice? Were there other reasons she didn't want to admit?

As she lay staring into rafters lit by embers of the fire below, she felt her breathing deteriorate, the familiar twists of panic starting in her belly. She had to do something, she sat up suddenly, dragging her blankets with her.

The only sensible course was to tell him:

Look, I'm sorry, I want your plan to succeed, but I can only report it, I mustn't get involved, I can't let you use my apartment. Tell Monsieur Kerlesquin that Mademoiselle Sharma regrets very much, but it's off . . .

She could just see his contemptuous expression.

So you're prepared to let de Montfort get away with Nathalie Sainte-Claire's murder?

Leave Nathalie out of it.

And his other crimes?

You're confusing the issue. I'm a journalist . . . not Janine's replacement.

The panic began to abate, she lay down again. It didn't help that he had given her his bed. Not only the first correspondent to meet him and accompany him on operations, but sleeping in his bed with his odour faintly on the sheets. Nor did it help seeing him reeling from Janine's death and reduced to an army of three. Without her co-operation, they might have to abandon all hope of capturing the real file. How was she going to tell him?

Over in the cottage Ricardo slept on a mattress by the fire. He'd been ashamed, caught asleep at his post, at a time like this; relieved and even more ashamed when Revallier, instead of reproaching him, swore affectionately at him in Italian.

Upstairs in the bedroom where Janine lay, Revallier sat on a chair by the window, submachine-gun on his lap. If time passed, he didn't notice it. Shock, which had lifted earlier to admit waves of pain, had settled again like stupefying fog. He stared into space. Outside the window snow was falling, deepening his trance. Now and again he looked over at the bed, her dim outline in the darkness. Years ago they spent entire days in that bed making love. It was easier to pretend she was asleep.

But if she were sleeping, she wouldn't be lying serene on her back in a thin dress, bare feet and no covers.

After a time he got up and found a blanket. Slinging the gun over the bedpost, he lay down beside her. Spreading the blanket over them both, he lay down facing her, the back of his hand against her cold cheek.

20

THE OLD FORGE: One week on from the rue de Liège car bomb, another Friday dawned bright with overnight snow, dark with leaden skies. In his old jacket, scarf and beret, Luke paused on the doorstep, surveying the yard.

He'd been up twice in the night, imagining he heard prowlers. Armed with a piece of lead piping, he'd gone down in his bathrobe to check doors and windows and look outside. Now, as he did a circuit of the house in the uncertain light, he saw nothing suspicious, and went across to milk the goats.

An hour later he left a full churn by the side of the road for collection, carried a steaming pail to the house, and was kicking snow off his boots when something about the strip of flower-bed beneath the house wall made him deposit the pail and go over and look. Bending down he looked closer. There *were* footprints, almost covered by snow, the faintest impressions, as though ghosts had been in the night.

Crouching and moving forward, he followed what appeared to be two sets of prints going right around the house and congregating under certain windows. But to no effect, it seemed . . . until he noticed something odd in the top corner of the kitchen window.

Fetching the step-ladder, he went up and removed a gadget no bigger than a beetle from the frosted pane. Humping the ladder round the house, he collected a handful. Indoors, with his glasses on, he confirmed them to be listening devices and pinhead cameras, enabling their sponsors to spy and hear. Clenching his fist around them, he willed the day to come when he would produce these exhibits, along with the tape and photos, in a court of law.

Going upstairs to show Isabelle, he found her sobbing at the dressing table, reaching out to him. Pocketing his dubious treasure, he was going to her when the doorbell rang. They both started.

Luke went to the window. A young man with a bicycle looked up. 'It's Etienne.' He went down and opened the door.

'Come in.'

The youth gripped his handlebars and shook his head.

'My parents don't want me to see you any more, monsieur.'

'What's the matter, am I contagious?'

'I slipped out, I wanted to tell you.'

They walked across the yard together to the road.

'What's it about?' Luke asked gently.

Etienne grimaced, it made him uncomfortable to have to reveal that all the village was talking.

'What are they saying?'

Etienne lowered his eyes, 'That you and Monsieur Laroche are with the GP.'

Luke scratched his beard. Etienne looked up, relieved to have been spared a storm of denials . . . dismayed not to be receiving any. His eyes innocently asked, Is it true, monsieur?

'No, Etienne, it's balls.'

The boy looked away, 'Why, everyone is asking, were you arrested?'

Luke considered for a moment whether to tell him everything – or nothing.

'For trespass,' said Luke, 'Duke de Montfort did not take kindly to my cutting his wire and making myself at home on his river.'

'And Monsieur Laroche?'

'My guide, he gave me a foot-up. Which reminds me,' pointing an admonishing finger, 'you tell that bighead Bajolet and the rest that they still owe me that heap of money on the table. Marbled Teal they *were*, and I've film and tape to prove it!'

Etienne grinned.

'One more thing . . .' slipping an arm about the youth's thin shoulders, 'the place is going to be empty this weekend, we're taking a break. I'd appreciate it if you'd look in on the goats and milk them.' Luke's appealing expression said, Am I asking too much?

'No problem, monsieur.'

Conjuring a couple of crisp new notes, Luke stuffed them in the boy's top pocket. As Etienne turned to go, he paused to say,

'I was stopped by the police on my way home yesterday.'

'Wanting to know if you were carrying anything for me?'

'They made me take my clothes off in a mobile hut.'

'I'm sorry,' Luke smiled apologetically. 'I suppose you had a fit?'

The boy, who was prone to epileptic seizures, smiled sheepishly.

Luke watched him cycle away, returning his wave as he went out of sight. How often would they search him? he wondered. Would it be right risking the tape and pictures with him? Clearly not. Or should he approach Thomas who collected the milk for the co-operative, or Monsieur Blémant, the postman, who mysteriously hadn't been seen for a couple of days? Isabelle was keen to carry them herself.

A wolf-whistle made him turn; Isabelle in the open doorway, smiling coquettishly, as if all was well and nothing had happened.

Eleven a.m.: Cutting a suitably sombre figure in black coat and tie, Commissaire Goujon was flown to Chaville, close to

Versailles, where at the gates of the cemetery his car was rushed by reporters shouting questions. Without troubling to turn his head to look at them, he rolled down his window to say he'd simply come to pay his respects, and drove through.

He'd timed it well, the service was over, a black thread of mourners trailing from the church. He spotted the impeccable de Montforts and Ministers Batisse and Lusardi, and waited patiently for a glimpse of the one person he'd come to speak to, looking for her darker skin in the white crowd, trying to see which car she would board. Then he signalled his driver to tag on behind the cars winding through the bitter winter cemetery to the graveside. So convinced he was that she would still show up, that as the coffin was lowered into the ground and the priest finished and still she didn't appear, he persuaded himself she was merely late. Then all at once he realised she wasn't coming, and felt pricklings in his scalp reawakening a hunch that somehow she had made contact with Revallier and was perhaps at this very moment reporting another funeral, that of Janine Vallence. She'd obviously set her sights on the story of the rue de Liège bomb and would shortly release her findings like grapeshot through the media.

Standing in the biting cold with dead leaves blowing over his shoes, he had time to wonder where Revallier was. There had been no further useful sightings, and forensic tests arising from the Place de la Concorde ambush had not yet yielded any clues. He'd simply vanished. Following his gut feeling that Vallence was dead, Goujon had ordered every cemetery within a twenty-kilometre radius of the city to be put under surveillance. With luck, careless in grief and believing himself to be safe in some obscure graveyard, Revallier would be caught before the weekend was out.

Standing apart from the crowd, he watched first Batisse

and then Lusardi, both wearing masks of official sympathy, gravely shake hands with members of the family, and then up stepped the de Montforts, the duke white-haired and splendid in black, the duchess thin and pale as the surrounding snow, and waiting their turn a strained looking Maurice de Montfort, who might almost have been perspiring, and the stately young countess, hands demurely folded. Goujon moved in closer to overhear Geneviève de Montfort lecturing the deceased's mother on the healing qualities of time and to observe Edouard tenderly patting Robert Sainte-Claire's hand, almost as if he were trying to reassure himself, instead of the widower weeping behind his dark glasses. As he watched, he experienced a delicious fantasy of shouldering lightly through the throng to arrest the lot – Batisse, Lusardi, the duke and his son.

Instead he watched them return to their cars and leave without unseemly haste, and followed them out of the gates, where he motioned his driver to pull over. When the mourners had concluded their graveside sorrowing and departed, Goujon tailed them to the reception at the grand town house of the deceased's parents. Double-parked, he waited, just in case a taxi were to arrive bearing Mademoiselle Sharma. But she didn't come, and, as he told the driver to take him back to his helicopter, his thoughts returned once more to Laroche's punchline: *My friend Revallier is hiding in a fairytale wood under a toadstool.* Spellbinding nonsense . . . or a riddle waiting to be unravelled?

By now Janine should have been buried. Half an hour late, Father Igor still hadn't arrived.

Janine lay downstairs in an open coffin hastily knocked up on the farm from strips of wood and odd handles, and bedecked with bright ribbon and posies of primrose.

Tahar worried. Ricardo should by now have collected

Igor from the train station. Where were they? If arrested, Igor, unlike Laroche, would spill everything before they even asked for it. Not out of suspect loyalty, but horror of pain. Though Igor didn't know the precise location of The Rushes, it wouldn't take Goujon long to work it out.

Revallier, who seemed not to hear the throb of distant helicopters, contemplated Janine. She looked not peaceful, but absent. Snowdrops in her hair were already fading.

'Jacques . . .?'

Revallier met Tahar's gaze. 'Ten minutes,' said Revallier.

Tahar raised an eyebrow. Every minute they delayed could be their last.

'Okay,' said Revallier, 'five.'

Kasha sat by the fire studying the newspapers she'd requested: *GP AMBUSH ENDS IN FIASCO*, proclaimed *L'Aurore*, *VALLENCE BELIEVED DEAD*, while *Libération*, under *DEATH OF A LEGEND*, bemoaned the fact that were it not for last week's horrendous bomb, Janine Vallence might have joined the exclusive society of French heroines.

'Could you manage a few prayers?' Revallier asked.

Tahar's smile said he'd think of something.

Going outside, they looked once more in the direction of the road. Then they returned indoors and moved purposefully to close the coffin, faltering at the last moment – the lid poised to blot out Janine's light for ever. Their eyes met, they took a breath and set the lid in place, hammering home the nails.

Borne on the shoulders of Tahar and Revallier, and Fabrice and Françoise, the 'parents' of Janine's child, the coffin was carried around the pond and through a broken gate into the tiny hedged field at the back. A tractor had squeezed in earlier to dig the grave, throwing heaps of frozen earth on the fresh snow. The coffin was set down by the graveside, and a small crowd gathered.

Just then, as Tahar was steeling himself to offer up a

prayer, shouts came from a look-out: vehicle approaching! People scattered, white sheets were flung over the coffin, Tahar and Revallier drew weapons from under their coats and took cover.

A motorbike appeared, labouring up the track against the snow. Relief swept the field, mourners returned, the riders came on as far as the terrain permitted. Clambering off the pillion, a shivering Igor spread his hands in apology. 'I had to take precautions . . .' pulling from his woven shoulderbag a bunch of long-stemmed lemon-yellow roses, 'I missed my train.'

The poor man, Tahar saw, was a hive of nerves.

'You're sure you weren't followed?'

Igor shook his head. Ricardo leaned his motorbike against the gatepost and, taking Igor's arm, led him to the graveside, where he recovered himself and smiled bleakly at everyone.

In a long military coat and scarf, Igor spoke up in a flu-ridden voice, *'Seigneur Jésus-Christ*, grant our sister Janine peaceful rest . . .'

While Igor spoke, Kasha watched Revallier, the emotions jostling in his face. When and how was she going to tell him that she couldn't help him tonight?

'If I ascend into heaven, you are there, if I make my bed in the grave, you are there also . . .'

As Igor apologised and broke off to blow into a handkerchief, Tahar was monitoring the arrival of a helicopter over the distant wood, hovering for a closer look at the scattered farm.

'If I spread my wings towards the morning, or dwell in the uttermost parts of the sea, even there your hand shall lead me . . .'

After exploring the far-flung stretches of the farm, the helicopter turned lazily and began to drift across country towards the little group in the field. Ricardo and Tahar exchanged glances, Tahar caught Igor's eye, and Igor glanced nervously over his shoulder at the slowly enlarging aircraft.

All eyes now trained on Revallier, who would surely abandon the funeral for everyone's sake. But refusing even to look round, Revallier unfolded a tricolour and carefully spread it, with Tahar's help, over the coffin, smoothing down the edges. From his pocket he took Janine's maroon beret and placed it on top.

'We have entrusted our sister Janine to God's merciful keeping,' Igor hastily intoned, 'now we commit her body to the ground . . .'

While the coffin was lowered on ropes into the grave, Igor removed from his pocket a phial of holy water, and tried with frozen fingers to open it. With the helicopter combing the terrain ever nearer, Tahar politely relieved Igor of the phial, uncorked it for him and handed it back.

'As the deer longs for running brooks, so longs my soul for thee O God . . .' While Igor blessed the spot with holy water, Ricardo silently distributed the roses, one for each person to toss into the grave. The helicopter blustered nearer, shaking the sycamores.

The sensation of the limp odourless rose in her hand was suddenly too much for Kasha. The other funeral, which she had pushed to the back of her mind, swept to the fore, the tears welled up and brimmed over. The roses also reminded her of Edouard de Montfort, the night he arrived with a bouquet and his alluring smile, and she found herself crying too because of him. How cruel appearances could be, and how close she had come to liking him.

Risking Revallier's wrath, Tahar bent his lips to Igor's ear, 'Finish off, father, or you'll be burying all of us.'

Igor glanced around and then turned with an appealing look to Revallier, who grimly returned his gaze: Carry on.

'Death, where is thy victory . . .' shouted Igor over the increasing din of the closing aircraft, 'be steadfast, beloved brethren, immovable, knowing that in the Lord your labour is not in vain . . .'

At last Revallier gave the signal, white sheets were flung down and spread with stones to cover the grave. The helicopter stood white against the slate-grey sky, the police pilots dimly outlined. Mourners ran in all directions, flinging themselves under hedges. Only Fabrice and Françoise remained with their barking dog in the open, waving to the pilots as the machine passed over The Rushes and clattered away towards the river.

Buoyed by their narrow escape, everyone gathered animatedly in Janine's house for drink and food.

Tahar stayed close to Igor, who was circulating cheerfully. Tahar wasn't taken in. 'It's all right,' he assured him, 'It's almost over.'

Igor looked crestfallen, he'd thought he was putting on a good show. 'I'll be honest,' he whispered, 'I wasn't cut out for this.'

'You can relax from now on . . . unless, by some chance, Monsieur Morrel does get through to you.'

Igor nodded gamely.

While some of Janine's favourite music filled the cottage, Revallier took Kasha aside. Oh God, she thought, knowing the moment had come, wishing there was some way to lighten the blow.

'You've seen the sketches of Tahar and Ricardo...' he began.

Artists' impressions, duplicated in all the papers, had an unnerving resemblance to his men, closer than any efforts had come before.

'I can't risk either of them in the final stage of tonight's operation. Can you drive a fast car?'

Kasha regarded him blankly.

'It's a very old, very powerful machine, but handles beautifully.'

'Look, about tonight,' she said firmly, 'the *first* stage of the operation . . .'

Their eyes locked, his gaze soft and penetrating, 'You're not going to –?'

'No, of course not,' she said hastily, 'I just wanted to be sure . . .'

'What?'

'You're not going to do anything to your father?'

'Kill my own father?' he threw back his head and laughed, and was quiet again, looking at her anew with soulful questioning eyes, as if recalling buried feelings. Touching her wine glass with his, 'To a spectacular success tonight!'

On the brief flight from the funeral to Paris, Goujon called up the commanders of his forces in and around the city, but there was still no sign of the GP or Kasha Sharma, and little to report from the American's place except that Monsieur and Madame Morrel had discovered most of the electronic bugs.

Sweeping in low over Jardin des Plantes, he crossed the river and landed on the heli-pad at Port Henri IV. A car was waiting, but before boarding he looked along the waterfront to the floating headquarters of the Brigade Fluviale, the river police, and its covey of bobbing boats.

Walking briskly down, he presented himself in the main office. His unannounced arrival brought instant hush. Capitaine Arnaut seemed to pale as he looked up from his desk.

'Just passing, capitaine.'

Rising, 'Delighted, commissaire, how can I help you?'

'Any news of the GP?'

'I'm afraid I haven't any.'

Goujon stood before a wallmap of the city, taking in the buff-coloured built-up areas, pale green parks and the brilliant Seine splitting the city in a continuous arc, immune to road-blocks. 'Yesterday's ambush isn't the first GP operation to take place close to the river.'

'We boarded everything that moved, commissaire.'

'Houseboats?'

'Those too.'

Goujon turned to face him, a burly grey-haired man with dubious eyes. As Goujon left, he privately resolved to look into the officer's record. You never knew, he could be lazy, a boozer . . . or worse.

Returning to quai des Orfèvres, he found headquarters back to normal after its eerie quietness during the night. The third-floor corridor, where he'd imagined Revallier lurking in a doorway, was abuzz with typewriters and telephones, people acknowledging him as he passed.

Approaching his office, he was surprised to hear a familiar voice. Entering lightly, he found someone on the phone in the adjoining office. He stopped and peered in. Only yesterday his deputy had abandoned him. Bloque was back. Or seemed to be. He didn't look up when Goujon appeared. Even when he finished his call, he turned away to tap some new data into the computer.

Resisting the urge to celebrate, Goujon took off his coat, lit a cigarette and stood in the window looking out over the river.

'Just as I thought,' Bloque called through, 'it was bothering me all the way down on the train.'

Goujon turned slowly. 'When did you get back?'

'This afternoon.' Goujon's cold welcome alarmed him. 'You're probably wondering, sir . . .' he began, rising to stand in the dividing doorway.

'It was the thought of those bastards knifing you in the back.'

'I never thought I'd hear you refer to such eminent men as bastards.'

For a moment Bloque was deceived by Goujon's stern expression.

'But where does that leave your delicate conscience, my dear Bloque?'

'I've had time to think. I confess I'm still shocked. We

shouldn't need to resort to . . .' Unnerved by Goujon's gaze, he dropped his chin. And rallied, 'I suppose if the woman hadn't left early for work, it all would have been all right. It *was* accidental.'

'So you want to come back?'

'If I may.'

A quick laugh, 'I'm sure we can find some use for you. What was it that bothered you on the train?'

'The American visited a church the other night. The man knocked down by the police escort yesterday morning was a priest. Since the accident benefited the terrorists, I wondered about a connection. It turns out the injured priest – a Father Igor Boury – runs the church the American visited.'

'They also spoke on the phone last night.'

Bloque raised an intrigued eyebrow.

'I take it,' said Goujon, 'we have men watching the priest?'

'I've just seen to it.'

* * * **21** * * *

It was all over so quickly, he reflected, locking the cottage, sliding the key under a stone. Since acting as her lawyer all those years ago, he'd lived with her and fought alongside her, and now he'd buried her. In a telephone call to a press agency in Paris, he'd identified himself as Jean-Jacques Revallier and had simply stated that Janine Vallence was dead, and had been buried at noon on 15 January.

He walked through the wood with the others to the river, Kasha and Tahar talking together in hushed tones ahead, a silent Ricardo taking up the rear. When they reached the barge, it was being loaded with a token cargo of milk, cheese and vegetables. The swift current would reduce the run to Paris by up to an hour.

As the *Dragon de Rougeau* got underway, Revallier stood on deck, hands behind his back, the icy air on his face. Snow blanketing the countryside to left and right gave off a steady illusion of daylight well into dusk. Then suddenly the sky came down and it was dark. Tonight, he vowed silently, if all goes to plan, I'll meet my father face to face.

Perched on the edge of his desk, Goujon pondered the announcement of Janine Vallence's death and funeral, which could only have passed off undetected in the depths of the countryside.

A phone rang, Bloque answered, signalling with a look to Goujon that here was the information he was waiting for. As he listened, Bloque took rapid notes, thanked the caller and hung up.

'As you suspected, chief, your river police captain is one of the clean-up-the-cops brigade.'

Bloque lowered his eyes. He himself could so easily have followed the example of those like Capitaine Arnaut who was campaigning through his police trade union to purge the police of fascist elements, and to persuade the government to set up a parliamentary commission to investigate 'irregularities', such as the 1980 synagogue bombing and the scandal of so many policemen belonging to neo-Nazi organisations.

'He's a leading activist,' added Bloque, 'he's been making repeated complaints about an official cover-up.'

Goujon nodded gratifyingly, and ten minutes later was airborne again, enjoying an aerial view of Place de la Concorde, before ordering his pilot to fly very slowly east along the Seine. Despite gloomy skies, visibility was good and he could see first his hotel and then his office on the island as he followed the direction in which the GP had fled the previous morning.

As the light faded and he looked down, it was striking how much more eloquent the living city was than the map, the boulevards choked with traffic, the smooth river flowing uninterrupted. The Seine was slow but sure, the river police all that stood between Revallier and his toadstool wood.

Still further east, past snow-swept railyards and high-rise suburbs, Goujon hovered above the point where the Marne joins the Seine, presenting an escaping boat with a choice of rivers.

Before sweeping the Seine once more and returning to base, he called up Bloque to order round-the-clock patrols of both rivers. Unlike those in the press and government who'd written off Revallier, the question occupying Goujon as he peered down wasn't whether or not the GP leader was a spent force, but where and when he would strike next.

In the early evening, with snow beginning to fall and the urban landscape pressing in from right and left, a hush fell over the barge. Tower blocks loomed, headlights streamed out of the city and a shout from the young skipper above warned of something up ahead.

Revallier and Tahar went above to look. In the distance, an unseen helicopter flung its searchlight through the iron web of the viaduct at Austerlitz. It was too risky to proceed; Revallier requested the skipper to go alongside at the first opportunity.

Sliding beneath the bridge carrying the city's periphery boulevard, the barge docked just long enough for Revallier's party to seize hold of a slimy ladder fixed to the sheer riverbank and climb to the deserted quay.

'Mademoiselle,' Revallier gallantly addressed Kasha, 'Monsieur Kerlesquin will be delighted to call by around nine.'

Kasha gave a gracious little bow of assent. They'd barely

spoken during the journey, and now, in the bleak shadows of the docks, the gulf between them felt wider than ever, and Revallier wished there was some way to bridge it before they separated.

Wearing a discreet *duppatta* around her head and chin, Kasha took the first taxi that came along and headed for her office in town to fax part one of her feature to London. The others, all smartly dressed, dispersed to find separate taxis, planning to meet up at base.

Paying off his cab well short of destination, Revallier arrived first. Instead of going directly, he made his approach from the far side of the canal, scanning for danger as he walked. The night was still, light snow was falling, but he had a good enough view of the dilapidated tree-lined street across the water.

Base consisted of extensive ground-floor garages with office and living quarters above. No bold sign drew attention to the business, only G. PASQUIER in weathered lettering over the garage doors. Advertisements were placed in trade journals, clients were also attracted by recommendation, for Guy Pasquier enjoyed a high reputation, even though he didn't exist. Pasquier, the maiden name of Janine's mother, was the fictional owner of a firm run by Tahar and Ricardo and employing four more specialist part-time mechanics, who were ignorant of the fact that they were working for the GP. Automobile enthusiasts who bought and sold rare models, or had them restored or repaired at Guy Pasquier, were similarly unaware that the considerable sums they handed over went mostly into the coffers of Les Gardiens de la Planète.

As he was warned to expect, a light had been left on in the living room Tahar and Ricardo shared over the garage. Otherwise there was no sign, at a distance, of occupation. He crossed the bridge and turned along the near side of the canal. The street was quiet, a car slithered towards him over shiny packed ice. He watched it pass and carried on.

A few doors short of G. PASQUIER, a shabby hotel advertised rooms at forty francs a night. Two men were talking on the front steps. Instead of walking on to reach the garage, Revallier brushed past the men and entered the hotel. A narrow passage opened into a dim reception area crowded with men watching television, the flicker of the screen on their faces. The old man behind the desk looked up at Revallier's approach, returning, through a veil of cigarette smoke, his almost imperceptible greeting.

Revallier climbed the stairs to the top of the building, proceeded down a dank corridor and sidled up to the window at the end to peer out over snow-smooth tiles to the staggered roofs of the GP's Paris headquarters.

Detecting no signs of danger, he climbed out of the window on to the fire balcony, closed the window behind him and descended a short ladder. Moving with the confidence of practice, he crossed a succession of slippery roofs to reach a bank of chimneys and a concealed skylight. Lying flat, he drew a revolver and peered down into the apartment. Softly opening a catch, he lifted the skylight and listened. Then easing himself down the ladder, he stood rooted in the unlit hall.

Revolver drawn, he pushed open the living room door and followed it in. All was just as they had left it to carry out the Place de la Concorde ambush the day before. He checked the bedrooms and then the kitchen, where Kasha's chair was still drawn up to the oven. He looked into the office and, switching on lights in advance, went downstairs to the garage, which echoed with the silent presence of half a dozen classy old cars. The garage smelt of grease and chrome and an obscure sense of sanctuary, a place where they'd openly toiled and successfully remained hidden for five years, the base the police had never found.

Satisfied, he ran upstairs and switched on the blue lamp in the hall, the all-clear signal. Then with a rush of nerves he stood over the telephone and checked his watch: just after eight, the de Montforts should be in rue de Liège by now.

Though he'd never used it, his father's number was engraved on his mind. Steadying his breathing, he concentrated on raising the pitch of his voice and slightly altering the accent, a little less Brittany, a little more Marseille. He lifted the receiver and dialled.

The phone was answered at once, 'Yes?'

Revallier stiffened. 'Bonsoir, monsieur le duc, Commissaire Bloque here, I hope I'm not disturbing you–'

'You are, commissaire, what now?'

Revallier had thought a great deal about this call. He knew next to nothing about Goujon's deputy Christian Bloque, except that it was unlikely Edouard de Montfort knew much about him either, permitting certain licence to improvise. The Bloque he invented was poker-faced and dogged, polite but unintimidated by powerful men.

'Concerning security arrangements for the dossier, sir, obviously they need to be changed–'

'For heaven's sake, I've only one more journey to make with it.'

'That's precisely our concern.'

'Revallier's hardly likely to strike again tomorrow.'

'We would strongly advise against complacency.'

'Your commissaire's getting jumpy.'

'Under the circumstances, sir . . .'

'All right, all right, what did you have in mind?'

'I'll call by in an hour, if I may?'

'Here? Out of the question. We're working on the dossier tonight.'

'With respect, sir, you wouldn't have a dossier to work on were it not for–'

'Then give it to me over the phone.'

'That wouldn't be wise, it will take all of three minutes, will nine o'clock suit?'

A world-weary sigh. 'Ten o'clock, commissaire, and three minutes it will be.' Click.

He remained head bowed for some moments, until the sound of a car aroused him. He turned to the window, parted the curtain. A taxi was drawing up, just the cabbie, no passenger. The driver got out, nervously lit a cigarette and stood in the road with flakes of snow settling on his head and shoulders.

Revallier went down and slid open the wide garage door on silent rollers. A last drag and the cabbie dropped his cigarette and came forward haltingly. Revallier motioned him to enter. A long-standing, unswerving supporter of the GP, he followed Revallier into the garage.

Shaking hands with him, Revallier met his unhappy gaze.

'How's your good wife?'

'Well, thank you, monsieur.'

'And the children?'

'Also well.'

'There she is,' said Revallier nodding towards the venerable 1938 Citroën. 'The maps and papers are in the glove compartment.'

The cabbie looked uneasy, working up to something, hands restless in his pockets.

'Monsieur, I need to know . . . that it wasn't you.'

'You have my word.'

The man shifted, ran a hand through his hair. 'They all say you did it, monsieur.'

'I just told you, you have my word. If that's not good enough –'

The cabbie met Revallier's calm gaze and nodded. 'Okay'.

'Good. There's cash in an envelope for expenses and emergencies. Otherwise buy something for the kids.'

'*Merci, monsieur*. What about the weather?'

For reply Revallier prodded one of the Citroën's snow tyres with a foot.

They exchanged car keys.

'The ticket?' Revallier reminded him.

'Ah!' The other man took from his wallet a rail ticket, Paris-Melun, single.

Revallier took out his own wallet to pay.

'*Ah non, monsieur.*' The cabbie declined to accept the money. Moments later the Citroën nosed out of the garage, turned into the street and drove off along the canal.

Watching its tail lights melt into the darkness, Revallier saw two men approaching from opposite ends of the street, collars up against the cold. He was about to step back into shadow when he smiled to himself for failing to recognise first Tahar and then Ricardo. As he watched them coming, he felt a glow of warmth for these two men with whom he'd been through so much. It was nearly over, and suddenly he felt a terrible weight of loneliness well up inside him.

Admitting them, he slid the door closed and tossed Ricardo the taxi's keys. Ricardo grinned and ran upstairs to dye his bleached hair black. Tahar followed Revallier up to the living room. 'You called him?'

'Yes.'

'It went all right?'

Revallier was fingering the ashtray beside the phone. In it lay the mangled remains of two cigarettes Janine had smoked two nights ago.

'Yes, it went fine.'

'Let me come with you tonight, you're in no fit state.'

Shaking his head, 'No Algerian will be safe on the streets tonight, and I need you here.'

Their eyes met. If all went to plan, Tahar would be bound for Algeria in the morning, Revallier en route for Canada via Ireland. In all probability they would never see each other again. A moment's hesitation and they came together and embraced, holding each other tenderly.

* * *

Leaving her office, Kasha did not attempt to retrieve her car, but took a taxi straight home. Part one of her piece had arrived safely in London, but Hugh had proved elusive, perhaps avoiding her.

Warned by Revallier to anticipate police surveillance, she scanned the street as the taxi turned into rue de Liège. At eight-thirty on a snowy winter's evening the street was busy with traffic, pedestrians making their way home from the Métro and motorists jostling for meters, but Kasha saw nothing suspicious. The taxi left her outside her door, she went in quickly and ran down the passage past Madame Klonowska's *loge*.

As she started to cross the courtyard, she shivered at the sight of the security guards, afraid that this time, because of the questions she'd put to the duke and the way she gave the police the slip that night, they would actually search her and find Revallier's accessories hidden in her bag.

'*Bonsoir, messieurs,*' she smiled.

With no attempt to step across and stop her, they returned her greeting with unsmiling courtesy. She'd been absent nearly forty-eight hours, leaving abruptly on Wednesday night in the middle of her own party. This in itself would not account for their coolness, and she feared for Revallier, who would be arriving shortly.

Feigning an air of distraction, she crossed the courtyard to the lobby and the lift, and with a sigh of relief rode to the top floor and hurried along the corridor, pausing to listen at Nathalie's door. She rang, and rang again. No one answered. She hadn't spoken to Robert, had failed to attend the funeral or send a card. It must seem she didn't care, yet her decision to help Revallier tonight was motivated in part by her outrage at Nathalie's death. Tonight Nathalie's family were grieving for a loved one murdered by terrorists; tomorrow, with luck, they would learn the truth.

Wondering but not caring in what state she'd find her apartment, she was surprised to walk into a tidy home, everything washed and stacked, flowers from Alain and a note: *Some party without you! Rod and I too glum even to get drunk.*

On the answering machine was a message from Rod – *For Christ's sake call me!* – who was leaving for London Friday evening, this evening. Kasha checked her watch, he'd gone! And two from Alain, trying not to sound worried. She'd tried in vain to reach him from the office, and didn't dare to use the phone now.

Expecting Revallier in twenty minutes, she stripped off, took a quick shower and rushed into the bedroom to choose a set of clothes to fit Revallier's recommendation: Western and non-conspicuous, smart but loose enough to move in. Applying a few light touches of make-up, she wondered what had happened to Revallier and went cautiously into the darkened office to look out.

They're probably watching you, he'd warned, *you could be tapped and bugged already.*

Coming at the window from the side, she peered out, wondering if she might spot the men who'd followed her the other night. But she could see nothing suspicious and looked at her watch. He'd said nine o'clock, it was 9.15.

Packing a fresh overnight bag, she ran around looking for personal things to take which she wouldn't want found when – as seemed certain – they searched her apartment, and could think of nothing but her diaries and a drawerful of letters, which she stuffed in a handbag. She checked the time again, 9.30, where was he? She made a tisane, and saw how her hand trembled each time she took a sip. What the hell are you doing? she asked herself. Couldn't she report a story without getting swept away by it? Catching herself in the mirror, she was surprised how intact she looked.

Taking her tea into the darkened office she peered out of

the window once more. At first she saw nothing unusual, but after a time she began to distinguish the outline of a figure deep in a doorway across the street.

A taxi drew up, a man got out, glancing up at the building. It was him, *Michel*! As he picked his way between parked cars to the entrance, the figure emerged from the doorway.

The intercom buzzed, Kasha ran to it.

'Hello, it's Michel–'

'There's a man behind you!' she cried, pressing the button to open the street door.

A pause. Then Revallier whispering, 'I think he's more interested in you than me, mademoiselle.'

Bracing for the shout to freeze, Revallier safely entered the building, closing the door behind him. Wearing an immaculate suit and false glasses, and carrying a coat, briefcase and two bunches of flowers, he made his way quickly down the hall hoping to avoid the concierge. But no sooner had he passed her *loge* than her voice arrested him.

'*Monsieur*?' she rasped, shuffling forward like the sly-eyed keeper of a citadel.

Revallier turned, smiling, '*Bonsoir, madame*.'

'What do you want, monsieur?' she intoned, chewing on her evening meal.

'Mademoiselle Sharma's expecting me. These . . .' indicating a delicate bouquet, 'are for her, and these . . .' gallantly presenting the long-stemmed chrysanthemums, 'are for you.'

Madame Klonowska eyed the flowers warily, and wouldn't take them until Revallier put down his case and gently closed her fingers round them.

'I'm late as usual,' he excused himself.

She glanced at him, afraid of being mocked.

He picked up his case and pressed on. The guards were waiting for him. With relief he recognised them as the same men who'd searched him the other night. This didn't prevent them regarding him with interest as he approached, running a metal detector over him, rummaging through his case and scrutinising his papers again. Observing the men, he drew courage. They weren't really interested in *him*, their antagonism, he sensed, sprang more from coarse male reaction to a potent rival, even from resentment of his apparent liaison with Mademoiselle Sharma – or disgust.

'*Merci, monsieur,*' said one with exaggerated tedium as he returned Revallier's papers.

With a civil nod, he continued on his way, taking the lift to the top and hurrying to the end of the corridor, where he found Kasha's door open. He knocked and went in – and halted. She was perched on the arm of a chair pointing the revolver at him.

Slowly he closed the door behind him. She went to speak but he put a finger to his lips, reminding her of electronic ears which might be listening.

She spoke clearly and carefully.

'So nice to see you again, Michel.'

'And you.'

The weapon, the one she'd confiscated the other night, was still pointed at him.

'Been working hard?' he said.

'Oh, much as usual.'

'Not too tedious, I hope?'

'Utterly.'

Depositing his coat and case on a chair, he tried to present her with the flowers.

'For me? You shouldn't have,' she said firmly, levelling the gun at his chest.

He spread his hands, silently demanding to know what had got into her.

'We won't be needing this tonight, I hope?' she said pointedly.

'We'll take it just in case.'

Trusting she'd made her point, she lowered the gun. He didn't immediately reclaim it. Still clutching the flowers, he went into the darkened office and looked out of the window. She was at his side, whispering in his ear, 'He was in the doorway of the dry cleaners across the street.'

Her breath on his skin sent a shiver through him. He looked at her, her scent in his nostrils, her face closer to his than ever. She tried to move away, he caught her wrist. She stared him out, a warning look. With his free hand he produced the bouquet of freesias. Continuing to outstare him over the tips of blossom, she accepted the flowers and went through to the kitchen calling airily, 'I hope I've a vase worthy of these.'

He looked again out of the window. After a time he saw the man leave his doorway, approach an unmarked Peugeot and lean down to confer with the driver. He studied the men briefly and came away from the window.

'There we are!' Kasha emerged from the kitchen with freesias spilling from a jug, to find Revallier reading Alain's note beneath the flowers on the table. Their eyes met, Revallier's deep and brazen and seeming to throw a challenge to her, Kasha's clear and calm and replying without answer. Then with the faintest of smiles playing on her lips, she gave Revallier's freesias pride of place on the mantelpiece.

He looked at his watch, she looked at hers: 9.50. De Montfort had said ten o'clock.

'We've plenty of time,' he said aloud, pointing meaningfully at the radio-cassette player on the sideboard.

'Fine,' she said, pressing PLAY, 'will you have something to drink?'

'Whatever you're having.'

With a rock tape playing to frustrate possible bugs, Revallier gathered up the revolver, and the accessories Kasha had smuggled in, distributing them on his person.

Finally he put on his coat. 9.57: very quietly she opened the front door for him, he stepped into the corridor and turned to her. Her face was pale, her eyes steady, he brought his hand to her face, she trembled at the unexpected sensation of his fingers caressing her cheek, his eyes in hers.

'Monsieur,' she murmured, removing his hand.

He held her gaze a moment longer and was gone. She went inside and softly closed the door, her face burning from his touch. In theory both she, and the secret dossier, would be on a train leaving Gare de Lyon in forty-five minutes' time.

Revallier made his way down the corridor, past the lift to the stairs, and went quietly down to the third floor, pausing on the last step to listen. All was quiet, he stepped out into the corridor and walked quickly to the duke's door. Donning his false glasses, he switched the revolver to his coat pocket, tucked the briefcase under his arm and rang the bell. Expecting Edouard to peer through the spy-slot, he turned his back and waited. Even after so many years of pursuing his father, the last few seconds seemed interminable.

Then the sound of someone coming to the door and beginning to draw the bolts. 'Who is it?' a woman called.

He hadn't expected the maid to be there at this hour.

'Commissaire Bloque, I've a ten o'clock appointment.'

More bolts and chains and the door gave to reveal Clotilde stepping back to admit him with a faint smile, her grey neatly-bunned hair matching her skirt, her face drawn with tiredness.

'*Bonsoir, madame,*' a deft little bow.

'Come in, commissaire,' she smiled, surprised by the detective's tentative charm, 'may I take your coat?'

'It's scarcely worth it, thank you, madame. I'm only granted three minutes.'

'*Holà!*' she laughed, 'how can anyone possibly talk sense into monsieur le duc in three minutes?'

While arthritic Clotilde led him through the apartment, he rapidly surveyed the lay-out, which regrettably did not echo Kasha's and seemed much larger. On the right they passed an extensive dining room, on the left a sumptuous salon. Passing the closed doors of several bedrooms, Clotilde paused at a sharp turn in the hallway and pointed to a room at the end of a passage, 'He's in his study, commissaire,' a conspiratorial smile, 'good luck!'

But before he could proceed, she suddenly said, 'How did you get in?'

'I beg your pardon?'

'The street door, Commissaire.'

'Someone happened to be coming out.'

'Ah.' A twinge of suspicion?

'Forgive me, Madame, I should have rung the bell anyway.'

An indifferent shrug and she withdrew.

He waited for her to retrace her steps before following the drift of cigar smoke along the passage. The door of the study was ajar, no sound came from within, and only glimpses of polished floor and Persian rug. He knocked.

'*Entrez.*'

Revallier entered, quietly closing the door behind him.

Edouard sat at his desk, poring over the spotlit dossier. He worked in shirtsleeves, his jacket and tie on the back of the chair. A cigar smoked in an ashtray, he had a glass of cognac close at hand – and a revolver. Heavy curtains behind him blotted out the city. A wall safe, exposed by the removal of an oil painting, lay wide open.

'So!' exclaimed Edouard, putting down his pen finally and looking up, 'what's it to be this time, Mirage jets?'

Taking up his cigar, he regarded his silent visitor. So this was Bloque, the-man-behind-the-Nose. No one at Police Judiciare was good enough, Goujon had to bring his own dog from Marseille, a flashy-looking one at that. And wasn't there something strangely familiar about him?

'So you're the indefatigable Bloque, I don't believe we've met.'

'We met yesterday,' Revallier stepped into the light, 'we should have met long ago, in court.'

Revallier removed his false glasses, Edouard leaned forward, peered at the impostor, and paled.

The two men stared at each other.

Edouard sat still, colour returning to his face, trying to comprehend how security could have been breached. He wasn't one to be easily alarmed, but the stark reality of Jean-Jacques Revallier in the room with retribution in his eyes was somewhat unexpected. Hands outspread before him, eyes fixed on Revallier, his thoughts strayed to the sleeping revolver on the desk.

'Don't even think of it,' said Revallier.

But Edouard reacted instantly to snap up the gun . . . and froze before he could reach it.

Revallier was pointing a revolver at him. Edouard sat back disconcerted, then brightened.

'What am I thinking!' a flippant laugh, 'you people hold life precious, you would never commit murder.'

From Revallier a frown of mock incomprehension.

'Wouldn't I? What about Friday's 'little package'?' Stepping forward, he picked up Edouard's gun, broke it open, spilled the bullets over the desk and dropped the gun in the wastepaper basket. Then slowly he raised his pistol and aimed it with a straight arm at Edouard's chest. 'By blowing up your neighbour and trailing her blood to my door, haven't you already made me a murderer?'

'That was an accident, monsieur, this is cold blood.'

'No, sir, this is personal . . .' a loud click, Revallier cocked the gun ready to fire, 'and goes back forty years to before I was born.'

'Think, monsieur,' advised Edouard, 'don't make your situation hopeless.'

'It already is.'

'They'll put you away for ever.'

'They will anyway.'

Edouard gazed at him, 'What on earth have you to gain from this?'

'Nothing.'

Edouard looked away, took stock, changed tack.

'Very well,' spreading his hands in invitation, 'do it!'

Smiling broadly, he reached for his cognac and raised it with a flourish, 'To the next life!'

Before he could take a sip, Revallier rounded the desk and dashed the glass from his hand. Or so he imagined. Instead he stood trembling with elation and fear, picturing the glass crashing to the floor, an outraged Edouard rising to defend himself, and he seizing Edouard by his shirt, flinging him back into his chair and pressing the gun to his temple – *Bastard! you bloody contemptible bastard!*

But he said nothing, did nothing, and as Edouard wetted his throat and re-lit his cigar, Revallier could only lower the gun and gaze at him, dismayed with himself for feeling no blinding rage, no hatred, no urge to kill or punish, no burning interest even in the dossier lying open on the desk. Pocketing the gun, he turned to the telephone. 'If you'll excuse me,' he said; and, pulling a glove over his right hand, lifted the receiver and tapped out a number.

Across the snow-blown night, a phone was immediately answered in a room overlooking the canal. 'It's me,' Tahar confirmed.

'Any time,' said Revallier, 'and warn him there are two men and a pale Peugeot.'

Reassured by Revallier's calm tone, Tahar dialled a call-booth in Gare St-Lazare. Ricardo picked up. A brief exchange and he was on his way out of the station. There was ample time, but he hurried in case anything occurred to delay him and put Revallier in danger. The cab might fail to start and, despite his newly dyed hair, the cops watching the station might stop him.

Downtown on quai des Orfèvres, another courier dismounted in the courtyard of number thirty-six just as one was leaving on his return journey.

Emerging on the third floor, the arriving courier, conscious that his job depended on it, hurried to the end of the corridor, knocked on Commissaire Bloque's open door, silently deposited a padded envelope on his desk and hastened away again. Since Bloque had scarcely opened its predecessor, he didn't reach immediately for the latest delivery.

In the adjoining office Commissaire Goujon was just back from the washroom, refreshed by a shave and change of shirt.

'What would you say to some supper?'

Bloque looked up, 'I'm not sure it would be wise to take a break at this point.'

'Delivered here, *imbécile!*' Goujon laughed.

'Ah well, in that case.'

Goujon lifted the phone and spoke to the proprietor of Ristorante il Delfino along the quay, wondering would he be so kind and send up a working dinner for two. Goujon listened with interest to the menu and called through to Bloque,

'*Sardines fraiches grillées, entrecôte Pizzaïola.*'

'Excellent.'

'That'll do, monsieur,' Goujon relayed, 'and perhaps a glimpse of your superlative cheese platter.'

'Wine, commissaire?'

'I'm sure France wouldn't begrudge us a bottle of your best red.'

Goujon lit a cigarette and stood in the window looking out at the slanting snow. Bloque put on another tape.

Having briefly examined the dossier and stuffed it in his briefcase, Revallier asked Edouard to oblige him by moving away from his desk to one of the Louis XV chairs in the open. Edouard shrugged, as much as to say it was all the same to him, rose nonchalantly, went over to the chair, but then turned impatiently.

'What more do you want, monsieur?'

'I want you to sit down,' a dull-eyed deferential nod, 'if you please.'

From Edouard an indulgent smile as he sat down, crossed his legs and neatly tapped his cigar over the nearest ashtray.

Turning his attention to the open safe, Revallier found it crammed with bundles of letters bound by coloured ribbon, and tall boldly labelled files. Keeping Edouard in view in the corner of an eye, he pulled forth packets of letters like bricks from a wall until he found it – an almost invisible black security box in the depths of the safe. He dug it out, the size of a small suitcase, and carried it to the desk.

'What do you want with that, monsieur?'

Revallier glanced up and met Edouard's eye. A chink in the duke's armour, he thought, freeing one of two tiny keys taped to the box, inserting it in the lock, turning it and lifting the lid.

'What's in there is none of your business!'

On the scratched face of the box, which must have seen the insides of many safes in its time, were painted the initials TdeM, VdeM and EdeM, white on black: Théodore de Montfort, Revallier's great-grandfather, Valentin, his grandfather, and Edouard. Next to be painted on would undoubtedly be Maurice. Ignoring Edouard's protests, Revallier rummaged among letters and papers until he found what he was after, one, two letters dated 1943 and 1944 and stamped with the wax seal of Les Chevaliers de la Croix d'Or, assuring Valentin and all his family, including Edouard, deliverance and shelter in the event of their activities being uncovered.

Edouard was on his feet, 'Put that away at once!'

Now it was Edouard who was nervous, Revallier calm.

'Sit down,' he said, lethally quiet, transferring his hand to the pocket which held his gun.

Edouard still came towards him, intent on snatching back the letters and reclaiming the box, 'We both know you're not going to use that gun, so let's put a stop to this –' before he could complete the sentence with 'charade', Revallier's hand caught him on the side of the head. Momentarily stunned, Edouard felt himself bundled back to the chair.

Just then a voice from the passage arrested Revallier.

'Monsieur, would you or the commissaire like anything before I turn in?'

Edouard shook himself alert, sensing a source of rescue. Revallier reacted quickly, holding up the two damning letters to Edouard, 'Laroche,' he offered in a low voice, 'in exchange for these.'

Edouard non-plussed, 'What?'

'Monsieur le duc!' cried Clotilde, 'may I get you anything?'

'Laroche–Grossman,' breathed Revallier, 'have him freed, and these . . .' waving the letters, 'remain undisclosed.'

Edouard stared at him. Clotilde could be heard grumbling, *'Ils sont sourds, ou quoi?'* as she came down the passage, and Revallier, shaking his head regretfully, drew his pistol and moved purposefully towards the door.

'Non, merci!' called Edouard, 'we're splendid.'

'Alors, bonne nuit, messieurs.'

'Bonne nuit.'

They heard Clotilde withdraw, on her way out of the apartment to her room in the servants' quarters at the top of the building. Revallier put away his gun, folded the letters and slipped them inside his coat.

'You just said –' flared Edouard.

'Relax, monsieur, you have my word. Provided I hear over the radio tomorrow morning that Grossman is free, the world need never know about those seven good Frenchmen and women you had slaughtered that night in forty-four. War hero! Industrial Messiah of France!' jeered Revallier, shaking again with fear and loathing, 'how have you lived with it all these years?'

Holding his head where Revallier had struck him, Edouard defiantly returned his gaze.

'Don't worry,' Revallier resumed savagely, 'I won't betray you, I won't tell how you tried to kill the only surviving witness as well as me—*me!*' he almost said *me, your son!* but couldn't bring himself to. Instead, slapping the breast pocket containing the letters, 'You think I'd want to acknowledge you publicly with these? Bad enough my father head of the nuclear industry, but a Nazi to boot.'

Edouard lifted his cigar from the ashtray, re-lit it with resolutely calm fingers and, leaning forward in his chair, stared down at the brilliant rug.

'You're mistaken, monsieur,' he said wearily, 'we weren't Nazis, we despised them, their vulgar brutality and moronic doctrine, but Germany represented – as it seemed then – the future. France's interests lay in partnership with her, and the Resistance was threatening that future. It was a choice between a prosperous, powerful pro-German France, or a France in chains and under Nazi rule.' Raising his smoke-wreathed eyes to meet Revallier's, '*We* were the guardians of France, we were the true patriots, we *are* the true patriots. *You* monsieur are a brave, honourable, admirable fool.'

Closing his eyes, he rubbed them, suddenly a worn old man.

Revallier looked at him as if for the first time, the manicured nails and heavy wedding ring, the shining head of hair, the broad shoulders drooping, and he experienced a surge of twisting emotions, the urge to vilify

Edouard, to embrace his knees and beg forgiveness, to throttle him. A glance at the clock sobered him.

'I never tried to have you killed, monsieur,' Edouard opened his wide weary eyes, 'my orders were quite specific. *That* I could not have endured.'

'And Grossman? flung two metres in the air by a wayward car?'

Edouard shrugged indifferently. That was life.

'You destroyed my mother,' Revallier said softly, 'you had her lover Jérôme killed and seduced Irma when she was at her most vulnerable. You used her, abused her and tossed her away when you were finished with her–'

'No, monsieur!' fire from Edouard at last, on his feet again glowering at Revallier, then pacing back and forth across the fireplace puffing clouds of smoke. 'Your mother and I were very happy, for a time, in that dreamworld lovers inhabit. We were young, it was wartime, she was lonely.' He stopped abruptly, fixed Revallier with a fervent look, 'Think what you will, monsieur, but you were not casually conceived in some sordid little liaison with a domestic. There were others, notably my future wife, but Irma–'

He broke off, remembering Revallier's mother perhaps for the first time in years, 'Irma was a dazzling young woman, uninhibited, wilful and far too intense, but she was *life*, with all its terror and beauty and I was very taken with her.'

'Is that why you had to destroy her?'

A withering look from Edouard, and then he drew himself up and assumed a superior air. 'I had my position to consider, my responsibilities, my destiny. Irma was, if you like, my temptation, my Eve. I had to choose, the choice was painful, but clear. She always knew there was no future, she tried to cling, I released her as gently as I could and sent a very considerable sum of severance money when I learned she was with child.'

Revallier's blood ran cold.

'No, monsieur,' reasoned Edouard, 'she destroyed herself, she broke up on the rocks of her own dreams. Don't expect me to carry the blame for your mother.'

'But you had Lucien Grossman carry the blame for your treachery in forty-four, and now you've arranged for me and my organisation to answer for your latest crime.'

Edouard composed a wistful smile.

'Life is a game of choices, monsieur, hard choices which are hard to live with, which is why most people are merely spectators, and only the brave are players, and, in our case monsieur, you and I have chosen opposing sides. Why don't you sit down?' he said brightly, 'have a drink with me, talk this through seriously?'

His spontaneous smile said, Well, what about it?

Seduced for an instant, Revallier smiled at the thought, even as he shook his head and motioned Edouard to sit down again.

'You're consistent, sir, I'll give you that,' said Revallier, 'choosing duty before love, before life. You're too afraid to live, so you exploit and destroy, use and discard. Afraid of loving Eve, you destroy her, afraid of wild Eden, you destroy it too. You've chosen death, monsieur, while some of us would gladly settle for life.'

'The arrogance of you people!' said Edouard without rancour, 'don't you realise that life *is* destruction, decay and regeneration? You're the ones afraid of evolutionary progress and life, and in your panic you want to yoke us and drag us all back to the middle ages!'

'Regeneration?' Revallier losing his temper, 'how can there be regeneration after you've laid waste to everything in your path? '*We*,' jabbing himself in the chest, 'are the true devotees of technology, the disciples of progress, calling for development on a human scale, rationally and intelligently planned, to aid life not destroy it. You are the terrorists of consumption, and what you call progress is really a progression, a remorseless and blindly stupid progression towards the annihilation of us all. You know all this, but you've made your miserable choice, and those of us who are fighting for the world must be silenced. And so you plant a bomb to discredit us . . .' his voice fell, became a menacing sigh, 'and the bomb kills your neighbour, but what's that to you? just another piece to be sacrificed for the game.'

'No,' murmured Edouard, 'no,' and he looked away and dragged a heavy hand slowly over his face, down to rest over his mouth, as if he dared not say any more.

Revallier saw the clock and winced inwardly. Time was turning against him and he moved quickly to handcuff Edouard's wrists to the gilded arms of his chair, and his ankles to the gilded legs. 'I regret this,' he said, gagging Edouard with a silk scarf and tying it tightly behind his head, 'I'll alert the police as soon as I'm clear.'

Halfway across the room, he turned and met Edouard's vacant gaze . . .

With his feet up on the window sill, Commissaire Goujon sat behind his desk, smoking thoughtfully as he looked out across the Seine.

On the other side of the windowpane, snow was settling on the ledge. Across the river, the Latin Quarter was revving up for another long Friday night. He saw none of this, he was occupied in trying to worm his way into the minds of Revallier, Sharma and Morrel.

In the adjoining office, as one unrevealing tape came to an end, Commissaire Bloque sifted through drifts of paperwork to find the padded envelope which had arrived fifteen minutes earlier. Breaking open the seal, he extracted the latest set of tapes from rue de Liège, calls made or received between eight and nine that evening.

Checking the list, he saw that Mademoiselle Sharma had made no calls but had received several. Before listening to them, he cast an eye down the Duke de Montfort's list and was astonished to discover his own name at the top: 20.03, *Commissaire Bloque to Duc de Montfort, duration 59 seconds.* He shook his head good-humouredly, how could they have made such a mistake?

Putting on the tape, he went over to the percolator to pour himself another coffee, and was stirring it and lifting it to his lips when he realised what it was he was hearing.

'Chief!'

Rewinding the tape, he upped the volume.

'Bonsoir, monsieur le duc, Commissaire Bloque here, I hope I'm not disturbing you?'

'You are, commissaire, what now?'

A puzzled look came over Goujon. Swivelling his chair, he faced his deputy.

'For heaven's sake, I've only one more journey to make with it.'

As the tape relayed the argument, Goujon grew livid. What the hell was Bloque up to?

'That's not me, chief, I never made any call!'

'I'll call by in an hour, if I may?'

'Here? Out of the question . . .' Goujon and Bloque held their breath, *'give it to me over the phone.'*

'That wouldn't be wise, it will take all of three minutes, will nine o'clock suit?'

Deep sigh from de Montfort; Bloque and Goujon looked at their watches.

'Ten o'clock, commissaire, and three minutes it will be.'

Goujon was on his feet, 'It's ten-twenty, we might be lucky, despatch nearest units, seal rue de Liège.'

Grabbing his coat, he ran.

Wearing her overcoat and carrying her overnight bag, Kasha was listening on the stairs between floors when she heard a door close and someone approaching along the corridor, and seconds later was relieved to encounter a calm businesslike Revallier carrying a bulkier looking briefcase.

In the lift she waited for him to speak, his silence and pallor ominous.

'You got the dossier?'

'Yes.'

'Are you all right?'

'Fine,' he said emphatically.

'So how did it go?' she asked tentatively.

'A bit tense,' he smiled, 'for a first meeting.'

'You didn't have to resort–'

'You're obsessed with violence, mademoiselle.'

'With non-violence, monsieur,' she corrected him.

Walking easily, they crossed the courtyard, conscious of the guards smoking in the shadows, of their eyes following them. They kept walking, Kasha chattering inanely, trying to give the impression of a carefree couple heading off for the weekend. Passing Madame Klonowska's quarters, they hurried into the snow-swept night, picked their way between parked cars and, as they ducked into the back of a waiting taxi, Ricardo accelerated smoothly away in an effort to beat the lights at the end of the street.

Almost taken by surprise, the men watching the building reacted quickly, bursting from their parking space to give chase.

As Ricardo tried to rush the lights, they turned red.

'*Merde!*'

'Go!' said Revallier.

Plunging his foot down, Ricardo launched the cab at the junction, inviting a howl of klaxons as he veered right into rue d'Amsterdam and led the rush for the city centre.

To stay with the cab, the Peugeot mounted the pavement and lurched into the traffic flow, provoking even deeper outrage and screeching brakes, and attracting the attention of police units arriving to seal rue de Liège.

In his mirror Ricardo saw the Peugeot jostling to break

free of traffic, and further back the whirring blue lights of police cars in hot pursuit.

The eruption of sirens made Revallier and Kasha look round in alarm.

'It's okay,' said Ricardo, 'they think we're the Peugeot.'

Rushing towards Place de Budapest, the lights turned red.

'Go!' said Revallier, and Ricardo careered through the junction. Approaching Place du Havre, the lights, as if answering personally to Goujon, turned red again, causing a surge of traffic from left and right as Revallier cried '*Allez! allez!*' and Ricardo slammed his foot down and hurtled through the dwindling gap.

At boulevard Haussman luck changed the lights to green, taking the cab smoothly on to Madeleine, round the great temple and down towards the open vista of Place de la Concorde, touching off in all their minds the thought that maybe fate had arranged an ironic end for them in the great square.

With the lights of the square whirling by, Kasha looked at her watch, 10.33; the train left at 10.45 – twelve minutes.

Despite traffic and falling snow, Goujon's driver managed high speeds to reach rue de Liège. The street was cordoned off, marksmen lurking in doorways, the rear of the building covered.

Goujon rang the concierge's bell. Madame Klonowska came fearfully at the mention of police and was ordered to shut herself in her *loge*. Flanked by plain-clothed cops, Goujon crossed the courtyard and came face to face with the armed guards, who apologised as soon as they recognised him.

'Is he still up there?'

They regarded him blankly.

'The man posing as Commissaire Bloque?'

Still blank.

'Have the de Montforts received no visitors?'

'None, commissaire.'

'No stranger's been here this evening?'

The guards briefly consulted, and shook their heads.

'Has *anyone* been?'

'Madame Snoek in Apartment Four received a visit from her daughter.'

'And Mademoiselle Sharma,' remembered the other, 'received a visitor an hour ago.'

'Male?' wondered Goujon.

'Yes.'

'Not by any chance bearing a passing resemblance to Jean-Jacques Revallier?'

The guards exchanged looks.

'They're still upstairs, I take it?'

'No, commissaire, they left a few minutes ago.'

Goujon scarcely had time to react when his mobile phone bleeped, Bloque on the line. The men covering the building had just chased Sharma and a male companion in a taxi as far as Place de la Madeleine and lost them.

'Lost them!'

'Forced off the road by our own men taking them for the suspects.'

Goujon swore obscenely, 'Have you got the cab's details?'

'Yes, with conflicting number plates front and back.'

'Circulate them anyway.'

'I already have, chief.'

'Seal the city!'

The cab raced east along the river, a fast run interrupted by occasional red lights which Ricardo did his best to skip.

In the back Kasha and Revallier watched the time, 10.43, two minutes to go as Ricardo swung the cab into boulevard Diderot and rushed across the forecourt of Gare de Lyon. Opening her door as they slewed to a halt, Kasha jumped out with her bag and the briefcase and ran.

With a scarf tied tightly over her head, she half-walked, half-ran through the station, maintaining the dignified urgency of a respectable traveller anxious not to miss her train. From the corner of an eye, she spied the military caps and submachine-guns of loitering CRS troops, but their postures spoke of cold and boredom and she attracted no special attention as she passed through and presented her ticket at the barrier, and calmly boarded the train.

She found an empty block of seats and looked out, heart pounding. A whistle went, she held her breath, the train began to move. She subsided with a deep sigh.

Driving away from the station, Ricardo raced back towards the river, only to be thwarted again by traffic lights. He cursed and slowed to a halt. A crescendo of sirens rose over the city. Hemmed in at the red light at the foot of the boulevard, grateful for the close company of other taxis, Revallier and Ricardo compared watches. Revallier's train was due to leave soon after eleven; twenty minutes, plenty of time, too much time.

'Look!'

As the lights changed and they pulled away, Revallier followed Ricardo's gaze to the far side of the boulevard where a taxi of the same make as theirs had been pulled up, passengers being frisked, the driver interrogated. Revallier fingered the gun in his pocket, Ricardo drove faster.

Crossing the river on Pont d'Austerlitz, they were overtaking a fast-moving coach, a second identical one and a third, when Ricardo suddenly realised what it was they were overtaking.

'Don't look!' he warned.

Revallier looked – a CRS convoy! armed men in every window, on their way to saturate Gare d'Austerlitz. Ricardo forced his speed higher, Revallier gazed benignly ahead, Ricardo overhauled the leading coach and slewed the cab left in a screeching turn on to Port d'Austerlitz.

Driving flat out along the quays, they left the lights of central Paris behind and turned off at last into the bleakest corner of the thirteenth *arrondissement*, where a labyrinth of deserted streets and darkened warehouses led them into a barren plain of railyards and sidings.

Pulling off the road, Ricardo parked the cab among a row of abandoned container lorries, cut the engine and lights and turned to grin at Revallier. In the dim snow-light, gazing out across the railway tracks, Revallier looked old and haggard . . . and strangely absent.

Sirens murmured distantly. Otherwise all was quiet.

'The bastards are sweating tonight,' ventured Ricardo.

'How did they react so fast?' Revallier wondered, patting Ricardo's knee in congratulation as he climbed out.

Ricardo got out and joined him on the edge of the wilderness. Snow was falling more heavily now, covering the tracks, spreading a white tablecloth over the whole area.

'You better not go far with that cab,' said Revallier distractedly, 'dump it and hire another. We'll talk later.'

Ricardo didn't want to leave. He would never see Revallier again. He felt sick. He touched Revallier's sleeve.

'I'm going now.'

Revallier looked at him, almost as if he'd never seen him before. Tears sprang to Ricardo's eyes.

Revallier roused himself, 'Come here you fool.'

Seizing Ricardo by the lapels, he enveloped him in a close embrace. Their faces burned where they joined, and caught the snow on their exposed cheeks.

'Go!' pushing Ricardo gently away, 'Tahar will be getting worried.'

Ricardo ran back to the cab. Reversing on to the road, he rolled down his window for a last look at the lone figure standing in the darkness.

22

While his daughter-in-law Cornelia sat and held his man-acled hand, and his son Maurice smoked and paced feverishly, a strangely withdrawn Edouard de Montfort answered Commissaire Goujon's questions in a monotone and waited patiently to be rescued from his handcuffs.

'At least you're alive, papa,' said Cornelia helplessly, 'he could have killed you.'

'Once more, monsieur le duc,' urged Goujon, consulting a note book, 'all he said on the phone was, "I'm ready; look out for the Peugeot."?'

'*C'est incroyable*!' complained Maurice, pointing an admonishing finger at Goujon, 'you assured me my father was safe.'

Ignoring Maurice, Goujon was trying to coax some further response from Edouard when Bloque came through again on the phone to report that Revallier's brief call on the duke's phone had been traced to an address in the tenth. Goujon's pulse galloped. Waving Maurice away angrily, he spoke clearly and softly to Bloque.

'Move forces quickly and quietly into position, no lights, no sirens.'

Chimes from the Chapel of St-Joseph echoed along the canal, announcing 11 p.m. Tahar moved quietly about the flat, making final preparations.

In the office he filed away forms relating to the sale of the business, in the bedroom he continued packing a suitcase and bagging up what he couldn't carry. In the kitchen he chopped onions, tomatoes and peppers for a stir-fry *chakchouka*. He was too anxious about the evening's operation to be hungry, but Ricardo would return famished and light up at the smell of a hot meal.

Tahar would have liked to play some music to soothe his nerves, but he needed the silence, and frequently tip-toed to windows at the front and back to look out. Earlier there had been a worrying storm of sirens across the city, and he'd listened in softly to the news, but without hearing any mention of Revallier or rue de Liège.

Now all was quiet again, and he lit a candle and lifted down from the shelf an unfinished game of chess which Ricardo confidently imagined he was winning. Ricardo's chess reflected his life: impetuous moves and reckless sorties, sometimes brilliant, sometimes disastrous.

Reaching into the back of a cupboard, he found a dusty bottle of Cuvée du Président, a wine for special occasions. Tomorrow they would part, making their separate ways south, Ricardo, alias Paolo Vanzetti, driving home through Switzerland, Tahar hoping to be smuggled over to Cherchell on the Algerian coast by supporters in Montpellier.

Uncorking the bottle and leaving it to breathe, he thought of Fatma, his mother, and his younger brother and sister, Ahmed and Salima, whom he hadn't seen in seven years and who didn't know he was coming home. How they would scold him! If only you'd warned us, they'd complain, we would have laid on such a welcome! If he got there safely, he would send for Leila.

A little draught from somewhere ruffled the candle flame, jogging him back to the present. He got up and went through to the darkened front room and peered around the curtains. Snow falling against the dark backdrop of the canal was carpeting the street, smoothing over the tracks of Revallier's and Ricardo's borrowed taxi, making him wish it would stop, all at once afraid of seeing their tracks erased.

The quays seemed deserted, but he still felt uneasy. Pulling on a white anorak, he pocketed a gun and, climbing the ladder to the loft, eased himself through the skylight on to the roof. Snow made the tiles slippery, but they'd practised the rooftop escape in all weathers. From the observation post among the chimneys, he scanned the view. Barely a soul either side of the canal, someone walking a dog, someone trying to start a car. No movement that he could see in the street below, until it met the boulevard at the far end, where the overhead Metro line was carrying a late train blinking between roofs and out of sight.

Silence again.

He was inclined to breathe a sigh of relief, but knew better. Inching low over soft tiles to reach the back of the building, he crouched close to the edge and listened. Apart from his own breath, all was quiet enough to have imagined the sound of the snow landing on his head and hands, and he was about to return below when he heard a fragment of glass disintegrate under the heel of a boot in the alley below. His heart hammered, he dared not look over the edge for fear of being seen, but had to assume the worst. Even as he prayed that he was wrong, that some vagrant had rolled over on to a broken bottle, he heard the faintest murmur of voices, the almost soundless conferring of coherent men.

Without hesitation he began belly-crawling away. The escape route, provided no one heard or spotted him, would carry him over the rooftops, across the timber yard and out on to the boulevard, where his chances . . .

Suddenly he remembered.

From afar Ricardo would see the blue lamp – the all-clear signal – in the hall below, and believe it was safe to drive up to the garage. Tahar squinted into the hopeless night. To take flight now was to put Ricardo in grave danger. Not to would lose precious time. His fear urged him to scurry away over the rooftops, but he couldn't.

He crawled back the way he'd come, carefully lifted the skylight, eased himself into the loft and slid down the ladder into the hall to switch out the blue lamp and switch on the red. He stood rooted, listening to the silence beating through the flat.

Then he started down the stairs as far as the landing, where from a certain position one could look out and focus on a discreet security mirror perched outside the garage entrance. Steeling himself to look, he saw nothing at first, only a restricted view of the deserted street as far as the hotel. But moments later, straining his eyes, he saw what he'd feared, shapes and shadows along the wall coming to life, growing limbs, firearms and camouflaged faces as they drifted closer and became one with the wall again.

Allah Ikūn fee ăouni, he murmured, God help me.

Moving quietly, hoping there might still be time, he ran back upstairs to the hall and climbed into the loft, dragging the ladder up after him. But as soon as he surfaced into the night, he saw, between the chimney pots, the ghostly outline of commandos dropping from the hotel window on to the neighbouring roof.

It was all over.

Shrinking back through the skylight, he considered the humble arsenal in the loft, a box of grenades and a few outdated machine-pistols, enough for a brief and bloody display, taking one or two state minions with him into the next life.

But he experienced no decisive nod from Allah. On the contrary, a terrible serenity came over him, as though Allah had contrived to slip him some potent tranquilliser. Descending the ladder, he made his way to the bedroom and began to undress. Naked, he pulled on a fresh *gandoura*, the long white smock he wore for bed, and went into the kitchen, switched out the light and sat down at the table.

But for the eerie red haze emanating from the hall, and the candle burning beside him, the flat was in darkness.

Resting his pistol on the table, he reached for the wine and poured four glasses – for himself, Ricardo, Revallier and Janine. In a drawer he found a half-smoked packet of Algerian cigarettes and lit one in the candle flame. Hoping that fate and the Secret Service could spare him a few more minutes, he took a couple of puffs of his cigarette and some sips of the strong wine and composed his thoughts. He would have liked the chance of another thirty-four years, but the choice wasn't his. Life had been a great gift, and never had it tasted better.

Picking up the gun, he broke it open and emptied the bullets on to the table, where they rolled, caught the candle flame and fell still. Replacing the weapon close at hand, he envisaged how it would be. The iron bars on all rear-facing windows would make spectacular entry through the kitchen window a miracle. They'd come in, at any moment, from the front.

He waited.

Shivering in his cotton *gandoura*, he closed his eyes and prayed that Ricardo and Revallier would survive and escape the country, that the American would find the will and a way to spirit his tape and pictures to Igor, and that Kasha Sharma would, as promised–

The night erupted, windows shattering, stun-grenades exploding through the building, pursued by the thunder of boots as swarms of unseen gunmen stormed up from the garage and down from the loft.

Raising in his hand the useless pistol, Tahar looked up in time to see a figure fill the doorway and fire.

23

Goujon was furious when he arrived minutes later. He'd given no orders for an assault.

There was a gunman on the roof, the commanding officer explained. Goujon told him to anticipate disciplinary charges and ordered him to remove his men from the building and to take up discreet positions in case other members of the gang appeared.

He went inside alone. Most of the lights were on and he found a garage full of fine old automobiles, some damaged in the attack. So this was their cover, he reflected. Casting his eye over a fifties Alfa Romeo, he recalled where he'd seen it before, in the road outside the American's place. Preoccupied with Monsieur Morrel and his tape, he hadn't given the Alfa and its young driver more than a rudimentary glance – a serious error.

Silence, smoke and cordite filtered through the building as he went upstairs and wandered from room to room, making mental notes as he went. Arriving in the kitchen, he found a man they'd been hunting for five years lying on the floor on his back, his white garment garishly bloodied, and splashed with wine. What use was a dead man?

To judge by the number of stems of broken wine glasses, three more people were expected: Revallier, the Alfa driver and, if he wasn't mistaken, Mademoiselle Sharma. Plus their stolen trophy, the dossier.

Repelled by the dead body, he left the kitchen and switched out all the lights except for the red one in the hall, which had been on originally. Then he went to the front room, lit a cigarette and looked out over the canal, uplifted and strangely moved by the double-coup of the GP's Paris base and Revallier's Shadow. With luck, close examination of these premises would yield the clues to the whereabouts of Revallier's toadstool wood. In the meantime, airports, ports and mainline stations were covered, river patrols doubled, rural road-blocks trebled. Every hotel and pension in the city would be visited, and every likely address in Mademoiselle Sharma's carelessly overlooked pocket book raided some time during the night.

It was only a matter of time.

Standing on the edge of the iron wilderness, taking shelter each time a helicopter passed, Revallier welcomed the biting cold, the slanting snow. Like the fog the day before in Place de la Concorde, the snow was something to hide behind, another layer of darkness.

Across the tracks, an indistinct huddle of men was lit by the glow of a roaring brazier, flurries of wind carrying their laughter. Otherwise all was still and silent.

Trying to read his watch, he was calculating that it must almost be time, when the church of Nôtre Dame de la Gare tolled for 11.15. Hands deep in his pockets, he started to cross the tracks. Having no way of knowing down which line the train would come, he picked a spot halfway across. With a long view back towards the station, he stood perfectly still and waited. Huge flakes of snow gathered on his head and shoulders, and his mind wandered. Provided she had caught the train, Kasha should be safe from now on. In theory she would reach The Rushes an hour before him, and then they would be alone together, a compelling thought.

After a time the train appeared, endlessly uncoiling. Feeling out the gloom with its headlamp, it beat a slow creaking tattoo towards him. Lowering his cap over his eyes, he stepped clear of the engine's eye and let the early

wagons crawl by, each one marked PARIS-TOULOUSE-
BARCELONA, and then walked with the train until the
middle order caught up, a score of double-decker car
transporters reaching into the sky like bridges, each one
bearing eight brand new vehicles.

Revallier counted the transporters as they slid by. The
end car on the bottom row of the last unit would not be
locked. Trotting now to keep up, he waited for the last
transporter to draw alongside and grappled with the door
handle of the end car. At first he thought it was locked,
then stiff, then it opened and he clambered in, closing the
door carefully behind him.

Crouching on the virgin seats in front, he peered out at
the slowly receding city.

Delayed by the freezing weather, Kasha's train took more
than an hour to reach the small town of Boussy-St-Antoine
twenty-five kilometres south of the city. She'd envisaged a
small crowd of people in which to lose herself when she
got off, and was surprised to find herself almost alone on
the platform of a very quiet station.

Wrapping her shawl-like *duppatta* over her face and
head so as to leave only the eyes and forehead showing,
she trailed through the ticket barrier.

'Terrible night, madame,' a man cheerfully took her
ticket.

'*Affreux!*' she agreed, '*bonne nuit, monsieur.*'

Passing quickly through the station, she found the
unmistakable car waiting outside, a snow-covered saloon
reminiscent of an era long before she was born.

Not a policeman in sight.

Locating the keys tucked away on top of a rear tyre, she
cleared snow from the windows and let herself in. With
Revallier's briefcase and her own overnight bag covered
by her dufflecoat, she strapped herself in, tested the pedals
with her stockinged feet and tried the ignition. The engine

coughed twice, sparked and settled into a deceptively gentle hum. Handle her with care, they'd told her, she's a devil.

She carried detailed roadmaps, but it was Revallier's sketch-map she taped to the dashboard. The route was straightforward, with luck she'd reach The Rushes in twenty or thirty minutes.

She found gear and flicked a switch. Wrong one. Revallier had talked her through the controls with the help of a diagram, but the real thing was never the same and she tried several switches before the protruding headlights beamed on, feeling their way nervously over the snow as she eased the over-eager car in jerks into the road.

With the Citroën responding to the slightest touch, Kasha recrossed the tracks and found the road through the Forest of Sénart. She wanted to drive faster, but the snow was undermining even her special tyres. Controlling her impatience, she worked the controls with cunning, going with the swell of the slippery road, riding the snow instead of fighting it. The weather and the lateness of the hour seemed to have reduced the traffic, and the farther she drove from the town, the quieter it became, until the night belonged to her.

Pulling up at a crossroads in the forest, she checked her maps, and, feeling the effects of tiredness, rolled down her window to breathe the icy night and check the time. It was two minutes to midnight, and all was silent but for the wind and the soft panting of the engine.

Taking the left-hand road, she steadied the car and accelerated gradually, the road straightening out indefinitely, an arrow splitting two rows of giant poplars. Fifteen kilometres to the farm, her excitement mounting, her mind beginning to grasp the full meaning of what she was doing . . . She drove with the window down and the heat full on, poplars rushing by, white fields fanning out to left and right, welcome snow flakes flying in to melt on her face. *The nearer to base you get,* Revallier had said, *the more confident you'll feel.* He was right, the blood was coursing through her, her mind sharper by the minute, and as she pushed the speed up along the straight flat road she thought of Nathalie and the men who had killed her, and prayed that their guilty bomb plot would be revealed somewhere in the dossier. She thought of public reaction to her articles, the panic in the de Montfort camp. *Nathalie!* she cried silently, *Nathalie!*

Something in the road ahead . . .

She realigned her focus . . .

Way ahead, a red light swinging like a pendulum, a signal to stop.

Her hands froze on the gear stick and wheel, her mind searching desperately for a way out. But the road was straight, with no turns, she was doing eighty or ninety kmph and the red light was rapidly getting larger. Transfixed, she kept going, running through a gauntlet of strategies: slam on the brakes and U-turn? too late; accelerate and hurtle through? too dangerous; or try to bluff her way?

She drew breath and dropped down through the gears. Unhappy at the sudden change, the car unwound noisily as she brought it to a sliding halt, taking in the shapes of several figures off the road in the trees, shouldered firearms dully gleaming.

As a uniformed man approached, his chilled features catching the red glow of the stop light, Kasha remembered the sketchmap, tore it from the dashboard and scrunched it under her thigh.

The squeak of leather boots on snow, the officer stooping and waving a flashlight in Kasha's face.

'*Bonsoir, madame.* I apologise-'

He clammed up mid-sentence.

Shielding her eyes, '*Ho-là-là!* am I that famous?'

'Your papers please, madame?' resumed the officer nervously.

While Kasha rooted in her bag, the officer ran the torchbeam through the interior of the car, over the coat and luggage on the passenger seat and back to concentrate on Kasha's half-hidden face.

She handed over her British passport with an air of confidence. The officer took it and examined it closely by the light of his torch. Depressing the clutch, Kasha gently engaged the gears.

'Will that be all, officer, because it's getting late and I – '

'Switch off your engine and step out for a moment, *s'il vous plaît, madame.*'

His tone frightened her, he plainly knew what he was looking for, and to his amazement appeared to have found it.

Shocked, she rallied, 'If you insist,' she agreed cheerfully, fumbling to unfasten her seatbelt.

But as he reached for the door and started to open it, she released one footpedal and pressed down on the other. The Citroën shrieked, back wheels whirred, tyres seared through snow, propelling the car forward as Kasha slammed the door.

The officer tried to keep up but slipped, figures in the trees came to life in slow motion, the road pulled as in a clinging nightmare, poplars began to rush by, the needle climbed through 40 . . . 50 . . . 60 . . . and the bullets came . . . 70 . . . 80 . . . 90 . . . hammering into the spare tyre case on the back, ricochetting off curved wings and shattering the rear window.

Crouching behind the wheel, braced for the splitting of her skull, she cut her lights and pressed the accelerator to the floor, trusting the white road and the tunnel of trees . . . 100 . . . 110 . . . 120 . . . the bullets wilder now, all but one winging through the trees, the exception coming clean through the car, passing within a foot of her head to punch a hole in the passenger side of the windscreen, and to transform her side into a mosaic of crystals.

The car swerved, and through a patch of clear glass she saw an oncoming car and regained her side of the road just in time as the car blazed its lights and whipped by blaring its horn. Teeth clenched, heart pounding, she opened up her lights again, glancing repeatedly in her mirror as she kept the car steady down the middle of the road. One minute her mirror was reflecting a clear road behind her, the next it was flickering with a chasing blue light.

Somewhere in her terror she remembered the turning she was meant to take leading off to a village. Was it still ahead or could she have missed it?

The straight road kept on and on, the chasing blue light kept coming, a turning materialised on a bend ahead and she knew she had to take it – without seeming to. As it arrived, she peered forward through her windscreen to get a mental picture of it, cut her lights, dropped down through the gears and swung the car sightless into the lane, hoping that the vanishing of her lights would be misinterpreted by her pursuers.

Taking the turn a fraction too early, the Citroën struck an obstacle, mounted the verge and almost keeled over before bumping on to the road, and righting itself. Keeping her speed down and lights off, Kasha zigzagged along the lane, glancing back from time to time to catch glimpses of the relentless blue beacon chasing blindly across the countryside.

Lights back on, she clicked home her safety belt and opened up the throttle, tearing along a hedged-in lane which broke suddenly into open countryside around a village. She believed it was the right village but couldn't be sure, and every time she thought she was approaching it, the road veered away again. Though her wipers were still beating back and forth, visibility through the damaged windscreen was restricted, and moments later she registered a lonely crossroads rushing towards her, but not the danger coming from the side, until the last moment

– a moment of horror cutting her breath, the sudden realisation that the other car wasn't going to stop, that it was too late for her to.

The moment unfolded – the headlights of a white limousine meeting hers like crossed swords in a midnight duel, the majestic bonnet of the Rolls Royce rearing in her lights and providing a glimpse of the driver in a white fedora.

Dropping down a gear, Kasha tugged the wheel and plunged the accelerator in a desperate bid to swerve past the tail of the other car and keep going . . . successfully skimming the Roll's rear wing, she almost prevailed, but the narrowness of the road defeated her. The rising bank loomed, she swung the Citroën's shoulder to cushion the impact: a searing skid, the crunch of the bank, the upward thrust of the car as though lifted out of the sea . . . her mind and body plummeting while she flew with the car and braced herself as it crash-landed, rolled over and settled with its wheels spinning in the air.

In the sudden stillness, she discovered she was unscathed.

On the far side of the crossroads she heard the Rolls struggling to free itself. Anxious for a lift, she grappled with her seatbelt, wrenched open an upside-down door and crawled out in time to see the driver and his female companion glance in Kasha's direction as the Rolls swept away white-on-white into the darkness.

Her jaw fell in amazement, and it took several seconds to realise that she was up to her stockinged ankles in snow. Shaking with shock and cold, she tried to take in her situation: the upside-down car, the dossier, the pursuers who might find her at any minute.

Still shoeless, she scrambled up the bank and scanning the landscape saw no sign of the chasing blue light. Instead, she caught sight of the Rolls reappearing in the distance, its main beams being chopped at intervals by tall trees in an avenue leading to . . . she climbed farther up the bank in time to see the headlights feeling out the perimeter wall of an illuminated mansion.

Running down to the car, she crawled in to rescue her belongings and the dossier, and set off in her boots and coat in the direction of the mansion.

She needed another car.

Revallier's train gathered momentum, dragging its weight through the bleak suburbs of the city, the river on the left, Orly Airport to the right, the march of tower blocks receding.

Twenty kilometres south of the city, the train veered away from the river and picked up speed beneath the N7 to Fontainebleau, where illuminated road-blocks were amassing long tailbacks. As though feeling for the open spaces, the train creaked through the last built-up mass of St-Geneviève-Des-Bois and strained forward, beating a steady rhythm through the countryside.

Snow clung to his clothes in the icy interior of the car and he rubbed his limbs to keep the circulation flowing. Then with his destination getting close, he used a pen-sized flashlight to pick out landmarks on his map as they appeared: the château guarding the little town of Bretigny and the aerodrome off to the left, where a few weeks ago they amazed the authorities by destroying the new *Éclat* nuclear bomber.

As he prepared to jump, he was shocked to see away on the right a squadron of gendarmerie deploying across a white plain, and helicopters drenching the village of Cheptainville with searchlights. Crawling to the other side of the car, he loosened his leg muscles with vigorous flexing, and when the train slowed for the bend before the village of Lardy he opened a door, climbed out on to the rim of the transporter, squinted into the swirling snow and flung himself into the night, bending his knees and rolling into the snow to break his fall. A short walk along the track and he slid down the embankment to the road.

Conscious of the gendarmerie minutes away up the same road, he brushed himself down and broke into a run, and didn't stop until he reached the turning he was looking for. He passed a number of houses, some lit, others in darkness, and set off on a three-kilometre walk down a winding lane, stepping back from headlights when an occasional vehicle passed. The wind had risen, snow was slanting into his eyes and blurring the landscape. He walked at a keen pace until the lights of a village came dimly into sight, and on the far side he found the church, and close by the house dwarfed by snow-bowed maritine pine trees rocking in the wind.

He walked through the open gate and up the curving drive, faltering at the sight of a face at a lighted window. He paused, while the woman pressed her face to the window and saw him. She looked at Revallier for some time before lifting a tentative hand. Revallier answered with a shallow wave, the woman withdrew, closing the curtains, and Revallier proceeded into the open garage, where a smart family saloon waited facing into the night.

The car was unlocked, keys in the ignition. Revallier removed his coat, beat the snow from his cap and climbed behind the wheel. Starting the engine, he drove quietly away.

Midnight: Stimulated by the capture of GP headquarters, Goujon left the forensic scientists to their work and was rushed back along snow-swept boulevards to quai des Orfèvres, through the arch of number thirty-six and into the courtyard. The only cars still there at this hour belonged to Bloque and his team of detectives.

He took the lift to the third floor and strode down the long deserted corridor, his nose twitching to the aroma of cooked food. He could hear Bloque on the phone, appeasing somebody with excruciating politeness. Bloque looked up when he entered, covering the mouthpiece.

'Batisse, a little out of sorts.'

Goujon deposited a bag of groceries on Bloque's desk and took the phone. The Interior Minister was blazing.

'I don't believe this, commissaire, you've let Revallier steal the dossier right from under your nose . . .' Goujon noted the sly insult. 'If he succeeds in smuggling it to the media, can you imagine the fall-out! How on earth did he manage to penetrate all that security?'

'Impersonating my deputy, minister.'

'What! and simply walked in?'

'Since he was impersonating my deputy, he'd hardly come down the chimney.'

Audible pause.

'I only hope,' hinted Batisse, 'for *all* our sakes, that you're fully aware of the seriousness of the situation –'

'Save your breath, minister. I missed Revallier tonight by the skin of his backside, and only the best detective work in France could have brought me that close. I've uncovered GP headquarters and nailed another of his gang; Revallier's running for cover and if you've no objection, I should like to get back on his tail, good night.'

Goujon hung up, swore and lit a cigarette.

'With respect, chief, you'll go too far one of these days.'

'They'll be eating out of my hands,' replied Goujon going through to his office, 'you'll see.'

Bloque's phone went, both men started, eager for news. But Bloque was shaking his head, nothing new.

Goujon lifted the covers off a number of dishes bubbling on electric hotplates and inhaled the glorious vapours.

'Before we dine, my dear Bloque, take a look at the contents of that bag on your desk.'

Expecting purchases to go with their meal, Bloque was unsure what to make of the bottle of wine, jar of preserves and stick of bread, all unconventional fare. The wine and jam, with their naïvely drawn labels, were the product of some small-scale enterprise, and the *baguette* was not the traditional white, but *pain complet*, wholewheat.

'I found them in the guerrillas' kitchen,' Goujon called through, 'look at the logo.'

The logo displayed on the bread wrapper and on both labels portrayed a windmill in silhouette against a rising sun, with *culture biologique* printed underneath – organically grown.

'Find out where they come from.'

'At this time of night?'

'Some of the environmentalists we've rounded up might know. Let Nitze loose on them if you have to, raid whatever organisations you like, but find out. It might just lead us into a toadstool wood.'

Bloque threw him a doubtful look and was about to lift the phone when another one rang on his desk.

'Yes? *Chief*! Where?'

Bloque's controlled voice quivered with excitement.

Goujon came to the door, pulse quickening.

'Registration?' demanded Bloque, scribbling furiously, 'and what was she wearing?'

He finished taking notes and hung up.

'They stopped Mademoiselle Sharma a few minutes ago in a pre-war Citroën on a road near Melun. When they asked her to get out, she took off, and they fired and gave chase.'

'How can they be sure it's her?'

'They've got her passport.'

Goujon cocked an approving eyebrow, 'Show me.'

They met at the wallmaps. 'They fired and hit the car and maybe her, *here*,' stabbing an approximate point on the map with a green flag-pin, 'and then lost her.'

'*Espèce de cons*!' swore Goujon, and turned elegantly on his heel and lit a cigarette with a flourish, 'Two things, three! Circulate details of her car, contact the colonel and have him saturate the area . . .' seizing his coat and heading for the door, 'and have my helicopter waiting by the time I reach the carpark.'

Still dazed from the accident and carrying her overnight bag and Revallier's briefcase, Kasha covered a kilometre in the dark on foot to reach the avenue.

A car was just leaving the mansion, its lights bursting through the gates and weaving down the avenue in a display of bravado. Stepping into soft snow, Kasha hid behind a tree and watched the Turbo spin on to the road and roar away.

After the freezing trek in driving snow along the road, the wind was dying down, the snow falling quietly again, and she could hear strains of music coming from the mansion. Glancing back as she broke cover, she wondered how long it would take for the snow to cover her trail.

She ran along the avenue, pausing at the imposing gates. The driveway and forecourt were crowded with cars, rock music boomed from the house, strobe lights flinging multicoloured pulses out of windows into the trees.

She walked through the gates and quickly spotted the white Rolls, parked askew, the couple still inside, their backs to her. It was a long time since she'd practised any self-defence but in this mood . . .

Salaud! – she mentally rehearsed, approaching the Rolls – *in too much of a bloody hurry to get to your party to stop to see whether I was all right* . . .

At the last moment, as she reached the car, she realised the folly of confronting them and giving herself away. Hoping they wouldn't look round and see her, she was on the point of hurrying on when a final glance told her there was no one in the Rolls, the headrests had deceived her. Looking over her shoulder, she went up to the car. Flakes of snow drifting in through the driver's half open window had formed a collar round the seat. And the keys? she prayed, leaning closer to see.

No such luck.

Braced for an alarm to go off in her face, she tried the door – it yielded with smooth metallic precision. She brushed snow from her coat, threw back her hood and got in. The elegant interior was awash with empty beer cans and chocolate wrappers, an ashtray bulged with cigarette butts.

Digging out her make-up, she switched on the overhead light, angled the driver's mirror, touched up her face and tightened her hair clip. Then she stuffed her overnight bag down the back of the seat and got out, quietly closing the door. Starting towards the house, her eye strayed to the Rolls's number plate: MAX 1.

With the briefcase in one hand, covered by her coat, she hurried along the drive and up the front steps and rang the bell. From where she stood she could see through a wide mullioned window crowds of people enjoying themselves.

The door was opened by a bleary-eyed young woman. With a sing-song '*Salut!*' Kasha brushed past her, making much of getting out of the cold. 'What a night!' she said, wiping her feet on the gilt-edged mat, 'Is Max here yet?'

'Max?' laughed the girl dreamily, 'yes, he's here all right.'

From her tone, Kasha gathered that Max was quite a character. He wasn't hard to find; Kasha spotted him holding court at the foot of a magnificent staircase, the white fedora tilted at a rakish angle on his head. Fresh from some formal function, he wore a white dinner jacket and bow tie. One hand in trouser pocket, the other expressively waving a gold-tipped cigarette, he was entertaining a circle of admirers, ignoring the girl on his arm – the passenger.

Closing in, Kasha saw that he was about her own age and size, a little taller.

'Max?'

He finished his sentence and looked to see who'd interrupted.

'A word.'

Kasha's voice carried authority, her smile charm.

With a grin for his friends which said, I don't even know her, he drained his champagne, handed his girlfriend the glass and went after Kasha.

'I don't believe we've met . . .' he said, suave, confident, slurred.

'Fate brings us together,' she smiled, 'in the shape of a white Rolls Royce.'

'Oh yes?'

Flying in from the north with the blizzard, Goujon looked out at the mansion lit up on the horizon.

Minutes later he was jumping into snow, ducking across a field to a crossroads spinning in blue light. A pre-war Citroën, discovered by a local man driving home, lay on its back like a stricken insect. A sergeant of the gendarmerie saluted crisply at the approach of the great detective, and pointed out the tyre marks of a second vehicle involved in the accident, and footprints belonging to the Citroën's driver.

'They both lead to the Marquis de Trivolet's country residence, commissaire. 'The marquis is away, the brats are letting their hair down. We've surrounded the place.'

'How long ago?'

'Ten minutes.'

'Anyone leave?'

'No, commissaire.'

'Turn the car over, examine it with a toothcomb, list anything you find from maps to hairpins.'

Commandeering a staff car, he was driven at speed along the road to the avenue and up to the gates of the mansion. Helmets and carbines shone beneath the high wall, music and voices came in waves from the house.

She's in there, he told himself, almost certainly with the dossier, conceivably with the American's treasure as well. But doing what? Having injuries treated, calling a cab, charming someone into giving her a lift?

Opting to go in alone, he followed the journalist's footprints through the gates and, with his eye on trees, shrubs and the broken lines of the house, skirted pools of lamplight and walked up to the entrance. He was ready to ring the bell and pose as a taxi-driver responding to a call from a fictional guest, but as he reached the steps, the door opened and a couple emerged, engaged in heated argument.

'*Merci!*' he said, and before they could close the door he mounted the steps and slipped into the house. Taking off his coat, he breezed through a chandeliered hall. To the left a throbbing dancehall, to the right an immense reception room seething with people.

Ignoring the reek of illegal substances, he went quickly into one room, and across the hall into the other, and when he didn't spot his quarry, he tried the adjoining salons, the dining room and kitchens, and finally shouldered his way through the throng on the stairs to reach the first floor, where apart from a few guests huddled in conversation in the gallery, he found no one and ran to the top of the house. Gasping for breath, he tried each bedroom in turn until he encountered a locked door. He listened. Silence. He knocked.

'Who is it?' a startled voice. He knocked insistently until the door was opened and he barged in on a couple still making themselves respectable.

'What do you want, monsieur?' demanded the man.

Goujon looked around, realised the futility of his lone search and marched out again. Radioing the officer of the gendarmerie, he hurried downstairs to open the front door and admit a column of gendarmes.

'What the hell's going on?'

He turned to a furious young woman in a cocktail dress.

'Is this your party, mademoiselle? Police . . .' he waved his identification, 'Stop the music.'

'Go fuck yourself.'

Goujon conjured a smouldering reefer from behind his back. 'We can discuss this in Paris if you prefer. I've enough men and transport to detain the lot of you. Assemble everyone here in the hall.'

The marquis's daughter complied.

Goujon bore down on the guests still lounging on the stairs and scattered them. While his men searched, he addressed the multitude from the stairs.

'Forgive the interruption to your evening, *mesdames et messieurs*, I wouldn't trouble you over some petty felony, this is a case of national importance. Has anyone seen an Indian woman, tall, thirty years of age, possibly injured after a road accident?'

Murmurs from one portion of the crowd encouraged him. Glances were aimed at one distressed and intoxicated young woman being supported by her companions. Goujon broke through the ranks to reach them.

'We were just enjoying ourselves,' one explained in confidential tones, 'when the woman shows up, wants to talk to Max. Two minutes later, he's gone off with her. Hélène's understandably upset . . .'

'You saw them leave?'

'No, but they went out together and his car's gone.'

'Make of car?'

'A white Rolls Royce.'

'Registration?'

'Max-one.'

'When did they leave?'

The companions conferred, 'Fifteen, twenty minutes ago.'

Teeth clenched, Goujon spun on his heels and made for the door.

'I hope she kills him!' Hélène called after him.

Goujon scarcely heard. As he hurried into the night, he was trying to imagine the scenario between Max and Mademoiselle Sharma, when along the drive a gendarme beckoned. Around the side of the house, a huddle of cops parted to allow him through. A young man in a white dinner jacket was sitting up dazed under a bush. Goujon bent down and slapped his face back and forth.

'Wake up, Max!'

With luck and intuitive guesswork, Kasha had fled the mansion in the right direction, her headlights stumbling on a sign for Cesson, a village four or five kilometres from The Rushes.

Concentrating hard, she drove straightbacked, arms extended, eyes devouring the smooth white road rushing beneath her. Like the abandoned Citroën, the Rolls responded to a touch of pedal, a glance of wheel, but unlike the old saloon, these tyres were unexceptional, and hard as she tried to keep the majestic bonnet in line, the car tended to slide drunkenly back and forth across the road.

It didn't help that she was still shaking, yet she'd been cool enough at the time, luring him into the night with a confession that she'd scratched his car trying to free her own. She recalled his puzzlement and irritation when he found no car anywhere near his and no damage, and his shocked disbelief turning to fury when she started kicking the Rolls, provoking his assault. She could still smell his breath as he seized hold of her and shouted into her face, still feel her own terror and exhilaration as she broke his grip with upthrusting arms and silenced him with a knee to the groin and a fist in the stomach. As he doubled up before her, she delivered a clumsy *coup-de-grace* to the back of his neck, and was surprised to see him dissolve at her feet. She needed all her strength to drag him round the side of the house. Then a brief interference with his clothing, a jingle of keys in her hand, and she'd left him to freeze a while beneath a bush.

With the lights of Cesson winking across the fields, her heart leapt, her speed soared. The snowfall was starting to ease, visibility improving, and she was beginning to anticipate Revallier's welcome when a searchlight surfaced suddenly over to the wood to the right.

She hit the brakes, skidded to a halt and switched off her lights. Pressing a button, she lowered her window, admitting the din of an approaching helicopter on the night air. Almost at once a flicker of light drew her attention to the left, where over the low hill came a second helicopter, its beam trembling in the darkness, feeling its way over the surface of the fields towards the road she was on.

Trapped. Another few minutes and she'd be bathed in light from both sides.

Recalling clearings on the edge of the road, she reversed at speed as far as the first opening, reverted to forward gear and slid the Rolls off the road and into the cover of the trees. Jumping out, she dashed back to the road and disrupted her tyre marks as best she could, before running back to the car and driving deeper into cover.

Rows of tall pines reached for the sky, sparsely clothed below, well covered on top. A helicopter whistled closer, its searchlight probing, its rotor blades shaking the canopy of the wood, flinging down snow and splinters of light.

Kasha held still, engine idling.

The helicopter hovered nearer, bending trees, howling through the wood before slowly blustering away.

Releasing the handbrake, she steered the Rolls further into the trees and, with the roar of helicopters fading, she went faster, bouncing over roots, scraping her roof on low branches, peering forward as the wood deepened and darkened. Time and again she rammed unseen obstacles, reversed and tried another route, frequently resorting to manual gears to charge an obstruction. The darkness thickened, she dared not use her lights, and drove blindly forward.

Shapes and outlines gradually returned, it grew pale ahead, the wood petering out.

Breaking out into the open, the Rolls demolished a flimsy fence and sank into a sloping field. Jumping out, she freed the wheels and bumpers of undergrowth dragged from the wood and stood scanning the view. While helicopters still swept the horizon behind her, all was clear ahead, a smooth expanse descending gently towards a distant road, if only she could reach it.

She climbed back into the car. The wheels spun at first, then found their hold on rough hard pasture underneath and the Rolls pressed on, swishing down the slope, the wind rushing in through the window as it gathered momentum.

Suddenly a ragged fence appeared, and beyond it a curiously flat open space. Also strange was the rowing boat stranded in the eerie light, but by now she was committed. Rushing the fence, she ploughed through it, shattering headlights and dragging wood and wire on to the wonderfully even surface of the field. Robbed of their grip, the wheels reacted at once. Realising what was happening, she switched off the engine and resisted the impulse to hit the brake. The wheels sailed on, the car went into a gentle spin and curved gracefully to a halt.

A moment's silence.

Then the slow, sure creaking of ice, like the cautious opening of a giant's door. Silence again. She was sitting in a car on the edge of a lake which was about to open up and swallow her. Not only her, but the dossier in the briefcase, and part two of her article in the overnight bag.

Reaching inch-slow around the back of the seat, she tried to lift the overnight bag and found it was jammed. Feeling for the zip, she opened the bag and delved with her fingers until she located the folder containing the article. As she sat up again, the car shuddered, the creaking spread, moaning dismally from below.

Silence.

She gingerly opened her door, placed one fragile boot on the ice, and then the other. Endeavouring to distribute her weight, she stood up carefully, briefcase in one hand, folder in the other. The lake trembled, she stood waiting, holding herself in.

Resisting the urge to sprint the ten or fifteen metres to the bank, she pushed one foot forward at a time, watching the distance shrinking. About halfway, the ice gave another groan. She stood still, not daring to breathe.

The depths moved beneath the ice, the lake held.

She resumed her delicate walk, the lake protesting at every step, the bank reaching out to her . . . until with one more breathless stride, she hopped on to firm land.

A final moan from the depths echoed over the fields and Kasha turned in time to see the Rolls tip up, hang for a moment as though taking a deep breath, and then nose-dive.

A ruffling of ice and water and it was gone.

Taking care to avoid road-blocks, Revallier criss-crossed the night, approaching base around one in the morning, expecting to find Kasha waiting. But already from a distance he could see the place was in darkness.

Pulling up well short, he left the borrowed car on the track and came at The Rushes through the wood and around the little field where Janine was buried. Pistol drawn, he crept around the back of the barn hoping for a glimpse of the old Citroën inside. No car, no tracks, no footprints. The whole place had an air of doom.

He stalked around the frozen pond and through the side garden of Janine's cottage. Loosening a stone, he found the key, turned it softly in the back door and entered. Cold and silence greeted him. His fingers felt along the wall for the light switch and flicked it on. Nothing happened. He froze, listening to the stillness. Then he tried the nearest lamp, click – nothing. He tried several more lights – still nothing.

He had to telephone Tahar, but first he crossed cautiously to his own quarters, and quietly letting himself in, found no electricity there either. Taking a torch, he climbed through the loft to the roof and scanned the night. The farm, one kilometre away, generated most of its own power and had a few lights burning. Otherwise, apart from the searchlights of distant helicopters and the lights of occasional traffic on the Melun road, the whole area was in darkness.

What could have happened to Kasha? She should have arrived long before him. He waited a few more minutes, willing the familiar perched headlights of the old Citroën to appear. Then he retraced his steps across the way to call Tahar.

Even as he went in, lit a candle and placed it on the floor in a corner, he felt Janine's presence in the house and looked up, half expecting her to appear down the stairs with some wisecrack.

He drew the curtains almost closed and sat where he could see out. Placing the gun on the table, he lifted the receiver. It was an old appliance, slow to react, but as he repeatedly tapped to try and rouse a dialling tone, he realised the line was dead. Power and telephone lines must be down, he had no way of knowing whether Ricardo had returned safely to the garage.

Still in his suit, he lit a fire and crossed over again to his quarters to change into warm clothes and a white anorak. Then he climbed once more to the look-out post. It was almost 1.30 a.m. Kasha had been caught, they'd stopped her at a road-block, instantly recognising her. It was all his fault, he'd put her in terrible danger. He'd thought she'd be safe once clear of the city, but even now she was being interrogated, threatened, abused. When it became unendurable, would she disclose his whereabouts? She might stall them by feeding them false information, but eventually she'd succumb.

Or would she? Looking into her eyes once or twice, he thought he recognised a will as stubborn as his own. He could picture her being taunted and shouted at and worse, and responding with quiet fearful dignity. What cut deeper than losing the dossier was the thought of not seeing her again.

He bowed his head. Janine dead, Kasha arrested, the dossier recaptured, the American unable or unwilling to deliver the tape and pictures. Even Revallier, who scarcely knew the meaning of defeat, was close to giving up.

He opened his eyes and gazed out from his barn-top perch across the night. Time passed, she didn't come, his spirits sank deeper, and he had just decided to go below and see if he could pick up any news on the radio, when he remembered there was no electricity. In the same moment he spotted a figure on the approach road.

The figure was walking, running, walking. Shortly he would reach the top of the lane and in all probability hurry on, whoever he was. Lifting a pair of binoculars to his eyes, Revallier picked out the hooded figure, watched him hesitate at the top of the lane and began to sense, even at this distance with the snow still falling and the darkness, that it wasn't a man. He scrambled to the edge of the roof, switched on a flashlight and waved it in slow circles. The figure appeared not to see it at first, but then started decisively down the lane.

By the time Revallier reached the ground, Kasha was emerging into the open on the far side of the pond. Preventing himself from running, he met her halfway round.

'You all right?'

'I'm afraid you've lost your lovely old car.'

She smiled wanly, but could barely speak for cold.

'Long as you've got the dossier!'

She held up the briefcase, he took her arm, steered her to Janine's door and into the house. Helping her off with her coat, he went upstairs for a warm blanket, and when he came down she had dragged a floor cushion to the fire and was subsiding cross-legged into it. While he spread the blanket over her shoulders, she unravelled her *duppatta* with frozen fingers, baring her head. Her hair was up, but with the hairclip and attendant pins coming loose, it was all ready to fall. 'I'm sorry I'm so late,' she laughed helplessly.

'I should think so! What happened?'

'An accident . . .' she started to tell him, then closed her eyes. 'In a minute,' she said, controlling her breathing, concentrating on calming herself. She felt his hands on her shoulders, silently applauding, telling her to take her time. Standing so close behind her, his blood ran hot, he let go her shoulders and brought his hands to alight on her head. While the touch of her sent pulses rushing from his fingertips to his loins, she went very still, her scalp jumping at the feel of his fingers travelling lightly through her hair and finding her scalp with the sensitivity of a blind man.

'It's coming loose,' he said, 'shall I let it down?'

'Yes,' she said, 'please.'

He drew forth the claws of the clip and one by one the pins, her hair rising like a night-tide and spilling in shades of blue and black over his hands, heavy and silken and smelling dimly of mysterious oils. Fanning her hair over her shoulders, his fingers trailed through it, combing it out very slowly, savouring the feel of each thick curl, before delving to touch the tips of her ears, and to linger with her fleshy lobes in his possession. Doe-still she endured, and took pleasure, neither granting nor refusing her permission, while his fingers shimmered over her neck.

'Are you hungry?'

'I don't know,' she laughed.

'Something hot to drink?'

'Please.'

He left her and went through to the unlit kitchen. Waiting in the dark for the water to boil, he leaned an elbow against the window frame and peered out at white hedgerow and spectral trees through slats in the shutters, the man and the fugitive in him in play at the same time, the man swollen with an almost unbearable desire for the woman in the other room, the fugitive watching the night, acutely alert. Turning to look back into the living room, he saw Kasha silhouetted by the open fire, gently rocking herself as she thawed.

'You all right?'

Another little laugh escaped her, 'It hurts!'

God, I'd warm you, he thought, how I'd warm you.

'That'll teach you to lose my car,' he said instead. Their beloved Citroën, Tahar and Ricardo's baby.

The water came slowly to the boil, he made her a tisane in a tall glass and took it through. Down on one knee, he tried to place it in her hands, but they recoiled from the hot glass and he put the glass down and reached for them.

'It's okay,' she said hastily.

Too late. Her hands were in his and he was looking into her huge solemn eyes. Sideways to the fire, his face was half in darkness, his eyes bright and brazen. They looked at each other without speaking. She felt herself watching him from a great and reassuring distance; at the same time she felt held in his spell, inches from his face, from his slightly parted lips and glinting teeth.

Then he broke her gaze, let go one of her hands and lifted the other to his lips. Anticipating nothing more alarming than a kiss on the hand, she saw he had other ideas, opening his mouth wide to take her raw fingers, all but the thumb, deep into the hot, wet cave of his mouth. A quick intake of breath and she took refuge in closed eyes, and bit her lip against the heat of his mouth and the terrible pleasure. Then he drew out her hand and she expected to have it back, only now he took her frozen fingers and thumb one at a time and closed his mouth around them, sucking the circulation back into them, sucking them and kneading them with tongue and teeth, each one emerging glistening when he'd done with it, before taking the next and the next. Then he started on the other hand.

Outwardly composed, she sat trancelike, her eyelids quivering, her breath coming quicker and the vigorous actions of his slippery tongue sending spasms through her. She wanted to pull away from him, and wanted to let go, wanted to keep him at a field's distance and wanted to drift, slide and fuse with him. He finished sucking her remaining fingers and gave her thumb a concluding nip with his teeth. 'Ouch!' she opened her eyes to find him gazing at her evenly, a grin playing round the corners of his mouth. Then with mock solemnity he planted a kiss on the back of each hand and returned them.

'I'm pleased to see a little respect, monsieur!' she said.

The smile left his face. And hers. He was engaging her again with that awful look which threatened and promised so much. He was coming closer, his gaze falling on her mouth, the full lip-heavy mouth after which he had secretly hungered all week. She held her breath, the space between them shrank, his shadow fell over her face, his breath burned her brow and then his lips landed, closing one of her eyes and leaving the lightest of kisses on one eyelid and then the other, before sliding down the bridge of her nose to brush one flared nostril with a feather-light kiss and then the other, then gliding remorselessly down to find her mouth. Their eyes locked, his mouth hovered over hers, her rushing breath mingling with his. Their lips barely touched, his mouth tentatively nudging hers, leaving a store of dry kisses, just audible, scarcely tangible on her

404

parted lips, lips which allowed him to land but did not answer. He drew back. 'Your tea's getting cold.'

She reached obediently for the glass.

'Tell me what happened,' he said.

'I was stopped,' she began, 'eight or nine kilometres from the station. They knew who they were looking for, they've got my passport, I drove like hell and the car must have been hit quite a few times . . .'

He sat on the floor listening to her, taking her in.

'You weren't hurt?' he interrupted when she recounted the accident with the Rolls.

'No, just astonished, amazed that anyone could drive away like that.' She took a sip of tea, closed her eyes and let out a breath. 'I hope to God I didn't kill him.'

'How could you have, if he drove away?'

'I caught up with him.' A little smile, 'I'd always wondered what it would be like to drive a Rolls.'

He looked at her incredulously. She told him about the mansion, the party, luring Max into the night. *'What!'* she mimicked, *'you've scratched my car? Women!'* She described his drink-sodden fury when she started kicking the car, and his amazement, and hers, when she broke his grip and dropped him like a sack at her feet. Her smiled wavered, 'Could I have killed him?'

'I doubt it.'

'Wouldn't it be ironic, after going on and on about non-violence?'

He laughed at her, suddenly mute with the relief of seeing her again, and reached to stroke her cheek with the back of his hand.

'What happened after you beat up poor old Max?'

She told him about her initially smooth getaway, then the terrifying helicopter hunt, the flat field with the rowing-boat clue she saw too late, and her ice walk to safety.

'You mean in one night you've lost a vintage Citroën *and* a Rolls Royce!'

Their eyes danced, hilarity rising in their throats. He burst into laughter, she into tears. A rush of uncontrollable sobs and she composed herself and wept quietly into her knees. It wasn't every day she was fired on and hunted by police, and this at the end of a traumatic week. His hand rested on her arm.

She blew her nose discreetly and fell silent. He wanted to hold her, kiss the tears from her eyes, wipe her nose and ravish her. With a sigh he rose and peered out of a window, then went outside, snow slanting into his eyes. No one was on watch, he had to take a chance. He came in again, closing the door. She sat straightbacked now, her legs folded beneath her in the lotus position, eyes closed, her face aglow with the light of the fire.

Suddenly – how could he have forgotten?

'The sketch map, what did you do with it?'

She gasped, hand over mouth. He looked at her dismayed, the map left in the Citroën, a gift for Goujon. The thought made him spin round instinctively, listening to the night, and while he stood rooted, casting about for their best move, Kasha was conjuring something from the folds of her blanket, a screwed up bit of paper which she proceeded to unfold, hold up and wave. As he stared at it, the blood returning to his cheeks, her tear-stained face broke into a grin.

A grave smile flickered in his eyes, he started towards her, arms loose by his sides, eyes wide with vengeance and humour. Oh God, she thought, foreseeing how this game could end. He was almost upon her, hands spread to strike. She cringed in mock terror, laughter spilled, he pounced, falling upon her, seizing her wrists, 'You had me worried, mademoiselle.'

'Did I?' all innocence.

'You really enjoyed that, didn't you?'

'Yes!' she laughed, 'and you should have seen your face.'

His mouth seized on her lips, choking her laughter. No

tentative trespass this time, no tender bouquets, but a rapacious kiss which forced her head back to the floor. Grappling with her considerable weight, he lifted her violently back to the cushion and fell upon her again, clasping her head, holding her face, closing her gasping mouth with his. No dry lip-brushing kisses now, a storm of love, a ferocious bruising kiss, sucking the juice out of her. He broke off, they caught their breath, pumping into each other's face, glowering. Still he held her head and face, hurting her cheek with ardent fingers. She held on, gripping his arms, suspended beneath him.

'I love you,' he said fiercely, 'Kasha, I love you.'

She beheld him in horror. 'That's absurd.'

'It's not absurd . . .' he came slowly again, descending for another assault, 'and you know it.'

But before he could pounce, she struck back, grabbing his head, thrusting up her knee and rolling him violently over to fall upon him, her fingers crushing his face, her mouth catching his mouth to inflict a gale of kisses as savage as his.

Two a. m., skies clearing over Paris, Goujon's helicopter coming in over the open space of Jardins des Plantes and the white roofs of the Faculté des Sciences, before dipping across the Seine to touch down in the carpark on quai des Orfèvres.

He walked briskly to number thirty-six, took the lift to the third floor and gravitated down the long corridor towards the aroma of coffee. An unshaven, shirtsleeved Bloque was slumped at his desk, lightly snoring. Electric fires hummed, a coffee pot bubbled in a corner. Tapping Bloque on the shoulder, he went through to his office, lit a cigarette and stood in the window. The city was almost hushed, late traffic moving with care along the icy quays, the lights of the Latin Quarter dancing in the slow dark river.

He sucked sharply on his cigarette and shook his head.

Revallier defied belief. Forty thousand men looking for him and, instead of lying low, he struck twice in thirty-six hours, returning for the prize he missed the first time. As for the journalist . . .

He crossed to the spotlit wallmaps and focused on the area where Mademoiselle Sharma was last seen. Bloque had marked the crash site, the mansion and the initial direction of her stylish flight. Now it was a race to follow her tracks before the snow, gradually fading from the north, covered them over. Revallier was nearby, he was convinced. She was trying to reach him; she may have succeeded.

Uncapping his fountain pen, he was tracing a bold circle on the map when Bloque brought him a coffee.

'They're somewhere in *there*.'

Bloque nodded, impressed by Goujon's confidence.

'Tell the colonel I want a steel girdle thrown around the entire area. Have you traced those organic labels yet?'

'Not yet. We'll have them by morning.'

Goujon grimaced. He wanted them now.

'The Prime Minister phoned, chief . . .'

'Really?' a mild note of derision.

'Congratulating you on tonight's splendid coup, GP headquarters and the Arab.'

Goujon turned to the hot plates which were still trying to keep his supper warm, and speculatively lifted one or two lids.

'What did the PM really want?'

'To call an emergency meeting of the Internal Security Council for 11 a. m. You're to attend.'

'Aha, the panic is spreading,' Goujon chortled, favouring a slice of Gorgonzola.

While Goujon picked and sampled, Bloque stood silent for a few moments. Then, 'Was the Prime Minister involved?'

'Involved?'

'In the rue de Liège bomb?'

Goujon shook his head as he chewed, 'The poor fool's in the dark, but smells a scandal.'

Bloque took courage, and voiced his greatest anxiety.

'What about the President?'

'What *about* the President?'

'Was he . . . involved?'

A thin smile from Goujon. 'Yes.'

Bloque gaped.

'And no. He knew the GP were going to be discredited. He wasn't anxious to know how. What you might call giving the amber light.'

Bloque frowned, willing to be reassured.

'But it's *my* head they want on a plate,' said Goujon, pouring himself a glass of wine.

'They'll soon change their tune, when you bring them Revallier's.'

Goujon slapped his deputy's face affectionately, 'Get some sleep, I want you razor-sharp in the morning.'

They had rolled and writhed, kissing feverishly one minute, with fragile tenderness the next, Revallier so lost in her mouth juices, her gasps and sucking sounds, her forbidden breasts and the wet between her legs, that he barely heard her say No! when he wanted to part her legs and penetrate her, so that she had to find all her strength to turn him on his side, grasp his face, kiss his mouth and say *'Non, Jacques! tu m'entends? non!'*

A dark reproving look crossed his face and he lay back quivering, riding the storm. Her hand found his sex, offering to release him, but he removed her hand, lifted it to his lips and held it against his chest. They lay in silence under the blanket, half-dressed, dishevelled and panting, gazing at the sinking firelight on the ceiling. With Revallier's heart beating against Kasha's hand, Alain crossed her mind with a wave of concern, affection, guilt. 'What about Janine?' she heard herself say.

'What about Janine?'

'This was her home, I still feel her here.'

'If she'd have minded, we'd have felt it. You think she'd want me to spent my last years, or hours, a monk?'

'But you've only just buried her.'

'Don't worry about it,' he said, getting up to root in Janine's jackets and coats hanging on the door until he found a cigarette.

'Must you?' she said.

He turned to look at her. I don't know you at all, he mused, and yet I *know* you well. He had the cigarette between his teeth, a lighter poised to strike. For some it was coffee, booze or nerves which triggered the urge. For him it was usually sex.

'You fight for a healthy environment,' she observed, 'and rot your lungs. Is that sensible?'

He laughed, snapped the cigarette in two and tossed it on the fire. Then he got down beside her and ran a damp finger over one of her magnificent eyebrows. 'Whoever said I was sensible?' he said, bending to kiss her, 'I'm a tower of contradictions.'

Before his lips could reach hers, she held him off and sat up.

'Yes, I'm the sensible one, remember?' She was on her feet, straightening her clothes, 'and it seems to me we've forgotten what we're here for.'

'I'm still asking myself and I'm nearly forty.'

'Here in this cottage, fool!'

Opening the briefcase, she lifted out Edouard de Montfort's file, carried it to the table, sat down and tried the lamp. Still no electricity. He tried the phone; still no line. He sat down with her at the table, looked at her broad strong hands, the hands which tended his self-inflicted wound the other morning, pointed a gun at him more than once, and tonight seized his face in a fit of passion, and tenderly handled his sex, and was now holding his father's secret file, licking her fingers and crisply turning the pages.

'See first if there's any allusion to the car bomb.'

She went back to the Contents. He suppressed a laugh.

'What's up with you?'

'It won't be listed under car bomb, mademoiselle.'

'You surprise me, monsieur.'

He looked at her, she was so drawn and tired she looked almost ugly, and his desire swelled. '*Tiens*,' he pointed out the double-X awarded to the Appendix. She turned quickly to the Appendix and read avidly, her eyes straining in the weak light, tracing the text with a finger like a child, murmuring excitedly, then aloud, ' . . . with every means at their disposal. But in the case of France, the government reserves the right, in the national interest, to counter the scourge of eco-terrorism with special measures –'

Phone taps and raids, thought Revallier, detentions and torture.

' . . . and, where deemed necessary, and under strict controls, progressive and unorthodox methods, involving co-operation at the highest levels between carefully selected members of the government, Secret Service, police and industry, with the specific aim of undermining popular support for the GP . . .'

She looked at him aghast.

'What's wrong?' he said, 'you knew this, didn't you?' he challenged.

'But it's *there*, in writing.'

'No, it's not, it's not enough to convict anyone.'

'It's enough for me.' Her eyes brimmed over, she had in mind the sunny elegant Nathalie she'd loved at first sight, and the comatose body she'd found at the hospital. Revallier laid his hand on hers.

'I need the American's tape to go with it. With this

veiled reference *and* the American's tape,' he reflected, 'we might have enough evidence.'

'*Progressive* and *unorthodox* methods,' Kasha spat the words out, 'in the national interest.'

Revallier got up and stood staring into the fire, wondering had Igor any news of the American, wondering . . .

'An engineering feat to dwarf the pyramids!' Kasha read, returning to the beginning of the dossier.

'Leave it,' said Revallier wearily, 'it's late, we'll go through it tomorrow.'

She looked at him amazed.

'It'll only make my blood boil, why disturb –' his brusque gesture took in the flattened floor cushion, the discarded blanket.

She smiled regretfully. *Ça ne nous mène à rien* – there's nothing for us, she was going to say, but with a pang the words caught in her throat, and she said ruefully, 'Jacques, I think you must be a hopeless dreamer.'

He looked at her, her face half in shadow, and he wanted to say, No, chérie, I'm one of the few who's not dreaming, I'm the brutal realist, the ugly prophet. Instead, as he lit a candle and carried it to the table, he said in a whisper, 'You give me more exquisite pleasure than anyone I've ever known.'

'Don't say that.'

'Why?' he laughed at her expression.

Confused, she looked down, and over the next half hour, with tiredness pulling at her eyes, she tried to extract from the text some of the starker points. 'They're going to build the world's biggest storage repositories in Britain, two kinds, on land and offshore, big enough to take all of Europe's radioactive waste, East and West, as well as Japan and America's. *Great* Britain,' she shook her head, 'the nuclear dump of the world.' She looked over at him, 'Can they get away with this?'

'Of course. They'll rush it through and make it sound

clean, chic and indispensable. Only Britain,' dropping to a baritone, 'was man enough to take it.'

'Yes,' she said, flicking on several pages, 'M de M – Maurice de Montfort's company? – will launch a multi-million pound public relations package to sell the dumps as great national assets, and the British public and neighbouring shores will be persuaded that the dumps will be leak-proof –'

'Even though no fail-safe method for disposal has been discovered,' said Revallier, 'and high-level waste requires monitoring for thousands of years. If the Romans had buried nuclear waste, we'd still be watching it.'

'You knew about this,' she charged.

He stood at her shoulder, admiring the diagrams.

'The Channel Tunnel is going to be used,' she continued, 'to speed the waste from all over Europe to the new sites . . .' she tossed her head, as much as to say, I should have known.

'You see,' he said, 'I even do your research for you.'

'Jesus!' she blurted in English, 'the nuclear authorities in the UK and the government will work together to block any public enquiry.'

'Democracy in action.'

While Kasha scribbled feverishly on her pad, Revallier tried the phone again – dead! – anxious to get through to Tahar and Ricardo.

'A Europe-wide campaign is to be launched to co-ordinate the undermining and discrediting of alternative energy sources . . .'

Revallier frowned approvingly. 'They're taking us seriously at last.'

'Don't pretend you knew all this too.'

'They've always been experts at deception, now they're making an art of it. They could have sold Auschwitz to the Jews.'

'One hundred and forty pages' Kasha resumed, 'dedicated to a co-ordinated European response to the "Green menace"; an eighty-page section on measures to counter opposition to the nuclear industry . . . "official-secret" laws to be used to restrain disenchanted employees, smear campaigns against dissenting scientists to be managed professionally –' she threw him a glance.

His wide-eyed smile said, So what's new?

'Right! did you know they're setting up an international counter-ecologist centre in Paris, so that governments, industries and police the world over can pool data on environmental organisations?'

Revallier raised an intrigued eyebrow.

'Ah!' she noted his admission and inhaled deeply, 'Jesus, this is going to cause a stir.'

'You think so?' he doubted.

'Yes! look at this . . .' rummaging to find the paragraph: 'In the event of a serious leak at an atomic plant becoming public knowledge,' she read angling the file to the candlelight, 'radiation figures for the affected area should be withheld in favour of *average* figures for the whole country, thus reducing public alarm.'

Revallier gave a scornful grunt and turned back to the fire.

'You really think anyone will take any notice?'

'How can you be so stubborn? People will be horrified by all this.'

'Now who's dreaming? People are used to official deception, they feel comfortable with it, demand it! What really worries me,' he came towards her, challenging her for a response, 'is why ordinary people deceive themselves with such blind determination, as though their lives depended on it, pretending that nothing's wrong, that we're not – all of us – destroying the world, poisoning our children. If I had a child,' he gazed helplessly at her, 'I'd want to know that the air it breathes, the water it drinks, the food I feed it is uncontaminated, but nothing is natural any more, we've fouled everything, you can't even trust the rain, you think twice before taking your children to the beach – to the beach, for God's sake. Land, sea and air, our entire life-support system being relentlessly poisoned. This isn't the regrettable price of progress, it's madness. It isn't progress at all, it's suicide. The world is dying, and nobody will admit it!'

She returned his gaze just as helplessly.

'We wouldn't need organisations like the GP,' he stormed, 'if the youth of the world roused themselves and demanded, Give us our world back!'

In the sudden silence he realised he'd been shouting. Ears pricked, he listened to the night. But all he heard was a click from the table, a small tape recorder, adrift in a sea of papers, reaching the end of its cassette. He flashed Kasha a withering look.

She smiled. 'I've got you at last.'

His gaze remained fastened on her. 'Come with me.'

She blinked. 'Come with you where?'

'Canada.'

Her heart hammered.

'Tomorrow afternoon. First Ireland, in a couple of weeks a boat to Quebec.'

'I want to get the dossier to *Le Monde* tomorrow, and fax the rest of my article to London. Then on Monday I have to be in Lille. With what I now know, it's even more important to be at the signing ceremony for the Channel Tunnel, to ask some awkward questions.'

Smiling tenderly, 'You don't understand, oh brave tigress, you're a fugitive, you won't get anywhere near *Le Monde* or Lille. Hitch a ride with me to Ireland. From there, if you won't come to Canada, you don't need a passport to take the dossier to London.'

She looked away. His invitation had stunned her, as had the thought that she was a fugitive.

'Look,' he said, spreading a map over the table, and tracing a route with his finger, eight or nine kilometres to a little web of runways and the symbol of an aeroplane. 'Weather permitting, a small plane will land soon after dark, apparently with mechanical difficulty, taking off shortly after, picking me up as it taxis for take-off. I'm sure there's space for two.'

'Who's the flier?'

'A Swiss millionaire, a sympathiser. It's our only chance.'

'Your only chance. I've got to get to Lille.'

He turned away with a gesture of impatience, and tried a light switch – still no electricity. He tried the phone – still dead. Finally he lifted another log on to the fire and went to leave. At the door he turned. 'I'm going to keep watch for a while. Get some sleep, you'll be warmer here, there's plenty of bedding. *Bonne nuit.*'

He went out, closing the door. It was about three o'clock, the wind had dropped, snow lightly falling. Keep coming! he urged the heavens. Tiredness washed over him, he badly needed sleep. But as he walked across to his quarters, telling himself he had to stay awake, he stopped before his door, and turned his head slowly to catch sight of a hooded figure behind the rushes on the far side of the pond. He froze, one hand sliding into his anorak to find his gun . . . which he'd left behind in the house.

Was the man looking at him? Revallier thought so. Did he know him? He was about to find out, the man was making his way round, hands in pockets, shoulders hunched. Halfway, he pulled back his hood. Ricardo!

Revallier ran and took him by the shoulders.

'What are you doing here?'

'When I got there,' he spoke in a chilled, un-Ricardo monotone, 'I saw the red light from across the canal, burning in the hall . . .'

'The red light,' murmured Revallier.

'I told the cab to keep going, the area was crawling, you could tell. Have you heard anything?'

'No, the lines are down, no phone, no radio.'

Revallier led him indoors and lit a candle, and they sat down at the table where Revallier had worked with Tahar the previous night.

'How did you get here?'

'Made the cab take me into the Eighteenth, bought a clapped out motorbike off a gang on a corner, came cross-country to avoid road-blocks, and ran out of petrol.'

They sat in silence.

After a time, Ricardo spoke, barely above a whisper.

'You think he got away?'

A deathly pause. 'I'm sure of it.'

The man he was firing at didn't look like Revallier, but Goujon knew it was. He also knew he'd hit him repeatedly in the back and legs, yet he kept running. Somewhere a phone was ringing, and Goujon woke with a start. In the adjoining office, Bloque was stumbling from his camp-bed to answer the phone. Initially groggy, he snatched up a pen.

'Any possibility she could have survived?'

Goujon was up, reaching for his trousers.

The caller's reply drew a solemn nod from Bloque.

'Looks as if your Indian lady has met her end, chief,' he called through, 'a watery grave.'

Goujon dressed quickly and was airborne by 5 a. m. for the thirty-five kilometre flight south towards Melun, the pilot's route keeping the snaking river in view for most of the journey. Looking at the map, he noted with satisfaction that the lake which had apparently swallowed up Mademoiselle Sharma was only just outside the bold circle he'd traced when making a stab at Revallier's hiding ground. The hunt was unfolding remorselessly towards its climax.

Snow was swirling as they approached, but the lake-site, with its pulsing lights and gigantic crane, was visible from a distance. They landed close to the lake. Goujon pulled on boots, and while divers with thermal imaging cameras stood by and the crane sank its jaws into the ice, he was shown the eccentric route the car had come, from the wood on the skyline, through several fields and fences and on to the ice before taking the plunge. The water would almost certainly have been too cold for anyone to have survived.

Standing muffled against the cold, watching the crane at work, a mischievous thought brought a smile to his lips: What if de Montfort hadn't taken the precaution of keeping a copy of the nuclear file?

Up came Max's streaming Rolls, hauled through the air at an undignified angle and dumped at Goujon's feet. Not sharing some of his colleague's fascination for female corpses, he approached soberly to receive Kasha Sharma's dripping overnight bag.

'There's no one inside, sir, but the driver's door was open.'

Goujon ordered divers to go down and look for a body. Then he rapidly turned out the overnight bag, leaving a heap of sodden clothes and letters on the snow. No dossier.

'No other box, bag or briefcase?'

'No, sir.'

Despatching two more divers to scour the bottom of the lake for the dossier, Goujon lit a cigarette and looked out across the ice.

'I suppose she must have drowned, sir.'

The twinge of regret in the young policeman's voice struck a chord in Goujon, until something occurred to him more disquieting than the thought of Mademoiselle Sharma's death. She might conceivably have survived – with the dossier.

A promenade across the ice?

As light crept into the sky, Revallier came down from the barn roof and tried the lamp beside his bed. Still nothing.

He jogged Ricardo gently.

'I'm going over to the farm to try and get some news.'

Ricardo shook himself awake and reached for his coat. Revallier climbed down from the loft and went out. The morning was cold and grey. Snow had ceased, the wind had died, a deep silence lay all around.

He skirted the pond and was starting down the track when he heard a shout and looked round. Ricardo was beckoning from the doorway, the *lighted* doorway. He ran back.

Ricardo already had the radio on and he entered in time to hear- '*and is believed to have been, after Janine Vallence, his closest comrade and most senior figure in the GP. For the significance of his loss to Revallier, so soon after the death of Vallence, I turn to specialist-in-terrorism –*'

Revallier reached violently to switch off the radio.

'He might be captured,' protested Ricardo.

Revallier shook his head. Ricardo ran out. Revallier went to the door and saw Ricardo vault a fence and bolt blindly across the field bursting his heart.

Over in the house Kasha woke. The incoherent shouting receded. Pale light was washing through the curtains, a log smouldered in the grate. She got up, lifted her boots from the hearth and pulled them on, grabbed a coat and went cautiously outside. Ducks shuffled on the pond, somewhere a dog barked, otherwise all was quiet. There was no one on the barn roof, no one in the open doorway of Revallier's lighted quarters. Her stomach lurched, something terrible had happened.

She crept along the wall of the house, and breaking cover reached the laurel hedge and came to the broken gate of the little field. There they were, by Janine's grave,

Ricardo face-down in the snow, Revallier sitting on the ground a little apart.

A hollow-eyed Bloque was at his desk when Goujon returned from the lake.

'Have we identified the organic labels yet?' demanded Goujon, picking up the jar of preserves found at GP headquarters and studying the sun-and-windmill logo.

'Not yet, chief. We've been raiding premises and questioning people all night. It shouldn't be long.'

Goujon grunted and was on his way through to his office when the phone rang. Bloque answered, paled, and hung up. 'It's Lusardi . . .' astonished, 'he's on his way up.'

Goujon looked at his watch – a visit from Lusardi at eight in the morning? Hanging up his coat, he changed his shoes and withdrew to his desk. Lighting a cigarette, he heard the Security Minister, who only a week ago had been released by the GP, striding down the corridor.

Lusardi filled the doorway, and entered without knocking.

'What the hell's going on?'

Goujon drew nonchalantly on his cigarette and looked up. Lusardi came forward, thick-set, craggy and hovering menacingly.

'Revallier makes idiots of us, terrorises de Montfort and walks off with the nuclear industry's plans. When is that man going to be caught?'

Goujon did not reply.

'And the tape, commissaire,' dropping his voice, 'I now hear the American kept a copy.'

'Tape?' Goujon feigned a dim recollection, 'ah yes, the one you're mentioned on.'

'Don't fuck with me, Goujon, or I warn you I'll have you out on your arse and back to Marseille before you know what's hit you. Now what are you doing about that tape?'

Bloque cringed at his desk, he had no wish to see his boss humbled. When he managed a furtive glance, he expected to find compliance, shame or rage on Goujon's face, anything but what he saw instead, a look of cool indifference, with only an arched eyebrow to express mild irritation. When Goujon spoke again, his tone was a trifle weary.

'Commissaire Bloque, kindly show this gentleman out.'

With that, he found a file and swivelled to face the window.

Lusardi stood rooted; Bloque gaped. Goujon was a celebrated but humble policeman, Lusardi one of the most powerful and dangerous men in France. Bloque hesitated, then without quite knowing how he was going to show Lusardi out, rose and moved purposefully to perform his duty.

Lusardi ignored his arrival and addressed Goujon.

'All right, commissaire, perhaps I spoke hastily.'

Goujon swivelled slowly around and directed his visitor to take a seat as if nothing had happened. Lusardi sat down, recovering his composure by striking a relaxed pose and lighting a cigarette with a flourish.

'So, commissaire, what can you tell me about the tape?'

'You're right, the American has a copy.'

'And what, may I ask, are the prospects of recovering it?'

'I'm waiting, in case he leads me to Revallier.'

'A risky strategy, wouldn't you say?'

Goujon shook his head judiciously.

'Where is the American?'

'At home.'

'Under surveillance?'

'Most certainly, and discreetly ringed by . . .' looking to Bloque for assistance.

'Two hundred and fifty men, sir. I spoke with Colonel Prustin-Vollon half an hour ago. Monsieur Morrel was milking his goats.'

Lusardi took a thoughtful pull on his cigarette. Goujon had a feeling he knew what was coming, and predicted it would be served up with delicate ambiguity.

'Perhaps the moment has arrived, commissaire . . .' groping for the right words, 'to remove our American friend from the picture.'

A heavy silence permeated the room: Bloque engrossed in his work next door, Lusardi examining his nails, Goujon expressionless.

'We can't allow people to undermine the due process of government with malicious inventions. Wouldn't you agree, commissaire?'

'I'm sure you're right, minister.'

'About this morning's security meeting . . .' Lusardi rising to leave, 'I'm sure you agree the Prime Minister should remain . . . unencumbered by the facts. None of us knows anything. Some deranged American is making absurd allegations, that's all.'

Goujon rose, came round the desk and held the door open.

'So good of you to call.'

Lusardi shot him a dark look and left.

Bloque came through wearing an awed expression, as though expecting to have to help Goujon to a chair. But Goujon was in full control, waiting for Lusardi's steps to fade before placing on his desk a pocket-sized tape recorder and rewinding it to a certain point. Pressing PLAY: *'Perhaps the moment has arrived, commissaire . . . to remove our American friend from the picture.'*

Goujon extracted the tiny cassette and tossed it to an amazed Bloque. 'File it away.'

'Under . . .?'

'Life insurance.'

Opening a drawer, Goujon lifted out a pistol, checked it was loaded and pocketed it.

'I'm off to pay a visit,' he called, putting on his coat.

'Don't forget the meeting at eleven, chief.'
'This shouldn't take long.'

• • • 24 • • •

THE OLD FORGE: Milking his goats that morning, Luke spoke to them in hushed tones, the usual rough endearments, and appealing to them not to give young Etienne a hard time while he was away.

He had the radio on, a little light classical going well with the early morning bustle of the stalls, and was finishing off when the eight o'clock news delivered startling headlines: *Les GP ont encore frappé. Jean-Jacques Revallier is believed to have escaped with secret documents after a serious incident late last night at the home of Duke de Montfort: GP headquarters uncovered, one man shot dead; and terrorist suspect Lucien Grossman released without charge . . .*

Laroche free!

There was barely time to assimilate the news or celebrate Laroche's release when at eight-thirty, two carloads of Isabelle's mostly younger friends arrived in high spirits: *sisters in solidarity! official rescue party!* The prospect of near certain strip searches on their way out frightened them, but there was strength in numbers. Isabelle, who feared for Luke more than for herself, outdid everyone in bravura and hilarity over a lavish breakfast: *Tuck in! express yourselves!* Heaps of fruit and croissants were demolished, and several bottles of wine downed by all but the car drivers. The bastards would be given no further excuse to harass them.

At nine o'clock everyone embraced Luke, loaded up the luggage and left. Or tried to. When it came to her turn, Isabelle wouldn't let go of him.

'I can't leave you,' she said.

'Honey, I'll be with you tonight.'

Isabelle was to collect some work from the Sorbonne and go on to Sylvia's, where Luke would join her later.

'We've been through this over and over,' he said, 'we've been over my plan, we've alerted the press, we're in control.' Rubbing noses with her, 'I'm an American citizen, for Chrissake, they're hardly going to walk in here and shoot me.'

Yes, she reassured herself, that was one thing they wouldn't dare do.

'I, *we* have to do this,' kissing her wet eyes, 'for me, for us, not to mention –'

'Shut up! I know.' She found a smile, 'God, what a vacation we're going to have when this is over!'

Wiping her tears from his face, she kissed him hard on the mouth and ran to her car, where a friend waited behind the wheel. With klaxons blaring and coloured balloons flying from the windows, the cavalcade swept out of the yard on to the road. Luke waved, watching tail-lights dissolve in the mist.

In the silence after the singing and hooting had faded, he crossed the road and walked leisurely up to the track to the cottage. If anyone was watching, he wanted it to appear that he wasn't going anywhere. He let himself in, and then moved quickly to put a match to the made fire and ran upstairs. Stepping carefully over the perilously supported floor to the end window, he parted a tear in the polythene and followed the road with binoculars. It looked as if the convoy had been stopped, he could make out car lights and milling figures in the mist.

Downstairs the fire was roaring, smoke from the chimney broadcasting the desired signal that he was getting down to work. Instead he loosened a stone in the wall and removed a small plastic bag, in it a brown-paper package, stamped and addressed to the nameless priest at the church in Montparnasse, small enough to fit in his pocket. Soon as this goddam thing's mailed, he told himself, we're free!

He went out of the back door and wheeled a barrow of stones through the garden to the wall he was building at the end. Confident he couldn't be seen, he ducked along the wall and out through the back gate, startling a flock of gulls in the meadow and cursing himself.

He hurried on. A run of hedgerows took him around the meadow to the cover of an oak copse sunk in a hollow. From here he could make out the village spire on the misty skyline. It wasn't far, a string of connecting ditches, a road to cross and then the home-run along the river into the village.

He set off along the ditches, crunching through ice and snow, tearing through brambles, frightening himself and a cock pheasant which burst from under his feet in an explosion of noise and colour.

Quiet returned. Hunched and panting he reached the road, the most exposed point on the route. Along the road he could see the tail-lights and fumes of a queue of cars moving up to a road-block. The entire area was evidently under surveillance, and all because he correctly identified an obscure feather in the bistro exactly a week ago this morning.

Ankle-deep in freezing water he waited until he felt sure it was safe to cross. On the far side of the road he slid down a depression and took the path along the river until he reached the bridge on the edge of the village. He'd made good time, encountering no one. His confidence soared.

Then at the first corner he was shocked to look down the main street and see armed police deployed in the square. Doubling back, he cut through the churchyard and re-emerged further down the street, almost opposite the bistro. Not a gendarme in sight, and across the road, and a little way along – the post office, with the mailbox outside.

Scanning up and down the street once more, he was about to cross when he noticed an elderly woman approaching the mailbox, and simultaneously a man materialising from the shadows to intercept her, so that as she drew from her bag a bulky letter, he stepped between her and the box, stooping politely to question her.

With careful backward steps, Luke shrank inside the cluttered entrance of a builders' yard. A rabid-looking dog leapt up, straining on its chain to snap and snarl at him. Moving clear, he looked through the broken fence to see the man, whom he'd never seen in the village before, smile reassuringly while he tested the bulging letter in his hands, with the elderly woman looking on bemused, trying to imagine why her letter could possibly be the subject of such interest. Not satisfied, the man returned the letter but patiently directed the woman towards an unmarked van along the street. No sooner had she moved off muttering to herself, when a car pulled up, a young woman jumping out to mail a wad of letters, only to find her way blocked by the same mild-mannered man.

While the scene was re-enacted, this time with the woman permitted to post her letters, Luke slipped away, retracing his steps through the graveyard and along the river away from the village. Doubling across the road, he made his way back along the same ditches and hedgerows, loosing a rich stream of anglo-saxon obscenities as he stormed home, kicking open the back door of the cottage and collapsing on to a crate against a wall.

Okay, you sons of bitches, he vowed, loosening his collar and getting his breath back, I'll take the jeep, I'll take back lanes and cattle tracks, I'll drive across fields if I have to, and if I hit any roadblocks I'm going right through . . .

The jeep was in the garage, the keys in the house. He got up, marched to the door and was on the point of flinging it open when he heard the approach of a car on the road, and had the presence of mind to check his rage and peer through the lacerated polythene window to make sure it wasn't . . . his heart stopped.

A white Volvo.

For a moment he clung to the hope that he was seeing things, that it wasn't a Volvo, or that it was pure coincidence, but as it turned on to the track there was no mistaking it. He couldn't see who was behind the wheel, he didn't need to. Nor was there any point in praying this was a routine visit. The choice of the Volvo was the clearest possible message.

He was shaking. Isabelle's nightmare had come true, one which he had only dimly contemplated, enough to take one wild precaution, a grotesque idea, the only one he could think of: an abundant supply of rope, cut into lengths. He found them now and threw them on the floor, and with strangely calm, methodical fingers began tying a length of rope to each support pole holding up the ceiling.

The car was arriving up the track, breaking ice, whispering over snow.

Of the three pairs of poles, Luke had secured only the set nearest the fireplace when the car stopped outside. He heard the engine cease, then the metallic *clunk* of the Volvo's door opening and closing, the very sound he had heard on Sunday morning by the river, and in each replay of the tape . . . the tape in his pocket.

He was working as fast as he could on the poles propping up the centre of the ceiling when the knock came. He kept going.

Another rap of knuckles.

'One moment!'

Two sets of poles would have to do. Scuttling backwards, he trailed the ropes across the floor into the shadows beneath the stairs by the back door.

The footsteps of a lightweight man moved away from the door. Luke flung dust sheets over the floor to cover the rope.

A blurred figure tried to peer in through the polythene.

'Coming!'

Grabbing a filthy hand-towel, Luke unbolted the door, leaned his forehead against its cool face, steadied his breathing and opened up. He took two steps back and was innocently wiping his hands as he met Goujon's gaze.

'*Bonjour, monsieur,*' said Goujon hollowly.

'*Commissaire.*'

Luke stepped back to admit him, Goujon entered looking gaunt. He cast an eye over the room and then gravitated to the fire and turned to face Luke.

'I hear my builder's been released,' said Luke, 'I'm grateful.'

He wasn't to know that it was Revallier who had clinched Laroche's freedom, and Goujon didn't trouble to tell him. Instead his hand went to his pocket, felt for something and gripped it. Luke froze, measuring the distance between himself and . . . Goujon pulled out his lighter and cigarettes, lit himself one and took a deep pull. 'The tape, monsieur, where is it?'

Luke came out with a nervous laugh, 'Those ducks will never know the trouble they caused.'

'The tape, monsieur.'

Luke shuddered; those bird-of-prey eyes.

'You're not even ashamed, are you?' said Luke changing his tone.

Goujon drew a gun.

Luke shook his head, 'You can't do it, commissaire, I'm –'

'An American citizen,' Goujon's turn to smile, 'I know.'

'I'm serious, you hurt me and you're in deep shit.'

Goujon's smile withered, not because he believed it, but because he knew Luke didn't believe it either, and was stalling.

'No more pretences, monsieur. To your people in the embassy you're a busybody putting your nose where it doesn't belong. To the authorities here you're a criminal consorting with terrorists and liable to a lengthy term of confinement. You won't recognise your grandchildren when you come out, they won't recognise you. Only one man can save you, and you're looking at him. Your freedom, monsieur, for the tape and pictures.'

Goujon's words reverberated through the cottage, *Only one man can save you, and you're looking at him*. The silence lengthened, heightened, rather disturbed by the crackling of the fire, the flickering shadows on the walls. Luke put his hands in his pockets, he couldn't stop them shaking, he feared Goujon was lying. It wasn't in his voice, or even in his eyes, it was more the aura of deception emanating from him. He'd come for the tape, and to silence the man who'd recorded it.

The gun was still in Goujon's hand, casually, almost regretfully. The most patient man in the world, he continued gazing at Luke, waiting.

Luke nodded philosophically, 'Okay.'

Goujon smiled understandingly, as though in praise of Luke's wisdom.

'Tell me one thing, commissaire. How do men like you and de Montfort sleep at night?'

'Men like de Montfort don't get where they are by tearing their hair out over life's little tragedies. Perhaps that's why he's a great man and you're a goat keeper.'

Luke acknowledged the point with a wry smile.

'And you, commissaire, what do you believe in?'

'Why should I believe in anything?'

Luke speechless.

'I happen to believe in keeping things as simple as possible. The tape, monsieur.'

'You're welcome to it,' snapped Luke in English, 'I'm sick of the goddam thing . . .' turning away, 'over here.'

'Where?'

'Under the floor.' Picking up the first tools that came to hand, he crouched in the shadows beneath the stairs and began loosening an imaginary floorboard, 'I never want to see the goddam thing again.' Hearing Goujon lighting another cigarette, he groped under the dustsheets for the knotted ends of the rope. 'Come on, dammit!' he urged, as though straining with the floorboard, and with a final 'that's it!' gave a mighty pull and kept pulling.

A jarring noise just behind him made Goujon glance around in time to see a support pole strike the floor. With poles tumbling and planks raining down, he reacted quickly, twice firing his pistol as the ceiling sagged and he dived for non-existent cover.

Luke rolled, bullets flew, the ceiling came down in an avalanche of joists and masonry, and Luke, saved by the overhead stairs, burst free through the back door with a mind to run and keep running.

Midway up the garden he halted, staring out into the boundless white landscape. What the fuck am I doing? he blurted aloud. Bolting around the cottage, hoping to God he wouldn't run into Goujon, he reached the Volvo. The keys were in the ignition, he got in, started the engine, executed a rapid reverse U-turn and roared away.

A police car's blue beacon sat invitingly on top of the dashboard, lead and plug dangling. The only visible power supply – the car's cigarette lighter – clearly matched the plug. He thrust the plug into the lighter and the beacon burst into life. Lowering the window as he drove, he reached out and slapped the revolving light on the roof.

The road-block materialised through the mist, and he hunched down and lifted his collar. He was concerned to see as he approached that Isabelle's army was still there, and not all the cars occupied, some of the women still being searched in the mobile hut off the verge.

Seeing the Volvo coming, armed police stepped back. Going at high speed with headlights full on and blue light whirring, he hurtled through, waving a hand to a gendarme's hurried salute.

The controls were unfamiliar, the road treacherous, his sodden boots kept slipping on the pedals, and it was a battle to keep the car on the road as he dashed north-west for Paris.

With the dust still settling, Goujon began the task of freeing himself. At first he'd thought he was dead, but regained consciousness to discover he'd only been out a few minutes. Blood was congealing round a bump on the back of his head, otherwise, apart from minor bruising, he was uninjured. Coughing dust, he began shifting joists and rubble, all the time looking for his gun so he could attract the attention of the police down the road. But he didn't find the gun, and lost vital time extricating himself from the cottage before striding dazedly all the way to the road-block, where a string of cars was pulling away trailing balloons.

Alarming the police with his appearance and ill-humour, he barged into the mobile hut, seized a phone and ordered a search for the Volvo. Then he tried summoning a helicopter for himself, met with stiff resistance to flying in prevailing conditions and had to issue stern warnings of what would happen if a machine failed to appear in precisely five minutes.

Slamming down the phone, he rounded on the attending police sergeant, 'Are your men blind! couldn't they see it wasn't me behind the wheel? I arrived clean-shaven, how could I leave with a beard?'

The apologetic gendarme brushed him down. Then Goujon washed his face and hands, dabbed his head wound and was towelling himself dry when the helicopter landed.

It was 10.45: he should have been on his way to the security meeting in town, when he took off to follow the Paris road, hoping to overhaul the American and his tape, if he hadn't already been stopped. Morrel had a thirty-minute start, and Goujon was trying to calculate where on the map he might have reached when the pilot veered off course, throwing the world sideways. 'What in God's name –?'

'Look, commissaire!'

Through pockets of mist below, Goujon saw the Volvo motionless in open ground just outside the little town of St-Rémy-lès-Chevreuse. The helicopter swooped, subsiding into a field. Goujon jumped out and walked over to his car. It had left the road at speed and was stuck in snow. Footprints led back to the road, and were lost in car tracks. The little town beckoned.

Head pounding from his knock, he hurried back to the helicopter. As he lifted off, he was issuing instructions for police to seal the town, stop all trains, buses and taxis, and to have a car waiting for him wherever he landed.

'Drop me as near as you dare to the railway station,' he ordered the pilot.

As the town shifted in the mist, the pointed roofs and sweeping grounds of a château broke through.

Madame de Chéron was still in her dressing gown when she looked out and saw a helicopter touch down and a police car racing across the lawns to meet it.

Goujon ran across the smooth white expanse to the police car. Rushed away, he reached the station at 11.05. St-Rémy-lès Chevreuse lay at the end of the line from Paris. A train, ready to leave in a few minutes, was already being searched. No sign of a six-foot-three-inch American. The previous train had left at 10.45. With a jolt Goujon realised Morrel could conceivably have caught it. A ticket clerk nodded emphatically, a man fitting the American's description had bought a ticket to Paris, Gare du Nord just before the train departed.

'You're sure he specified Gare du Nord?'

'He said: does the train definitely stop there?'

'Where would the train have reached by now?'

The clerk checked the time and looked up at a timetable. Goujon controlled his impatience.

'Approaching the outskirts of the city, commissaire. It's a fast train with limited stops.'

'Arriving at Gare du Nord?'

'Eleven-thirty.'

It was now almost 11.10. Goujon hurried from the station and was driven, siren wailing, back to the château. Without so much as a wave to the lady of the house and her staff calling from the drive, he ran straining his lungs to rejoin the helicopter and took off. No sooner strapped in than he was calling up Bloque, ordering a full reception for Morrel at Gare du Nord, and a search carried out of every passenger alighting from the train. 'And Bloque, in case by some miracle he eludes us, put *every* letterbox in Paris under round-the-clock surveillance – understood?'

Exceeding maximum speed limits, the pilot made exceptional time, calming a frayed Goujon, whose concern was not so much that he might lose Morrel but that the American might take it into his head to talk someone else into delivering the tape and photos for him.

Sweeping in over the suburbs, with the Eiffel Tower appearing on the left and the Montparnasse Tower on the right, Goujon realised he was going to pip the American by minutes. Still reeling from his head wound and his exertions, he felt a surge of new energy, a flush of grim satisfaction at the thought of Monsieur Morrel stepping lightly from the train into his arms.

The helicopter skimmed the domes and spires of the city. Another glance at his watch, 11.24. Six minutes, provided the train wasn't early.

'*Commissaire,*' the pilot's voice hummed in Goujon's headphones, 'directly ahead.'

Goujon craned his head, the massive façade of Gare du Nord loomed afar in the seething tenth *arrondissement*. A great cordon had been flung around the square, throwing back the traffic on all sides. The helicopter banked, steadied, and lowered itself gingerly down on to the cobbles, blowing a gale along the street. Goujon straightened his tie and climbed out, ducking under the blades to walk briskly into the station.

A burly CRS commander saluted. 'All exits covered, commissaire, it's coming in on number nine, two or three minutes late.'

'Pull your men out of sight, but don't let anyone through until I say.'

'Is he armed?'

Goujon hesitated. Then decidedly, 'Armed and dangerous.'

Their eyes flickered; an unspoken understanding.

Goujon walked to the railhead. The empty tracks on platform nine stretched away into the gloom beyond the station. He turned and checked his watch against the station clock: 11.31.

Platforms to left and right had been cleared to give a clear view of the target. Headlights weakly leading, the 10.45 from St-Rémy-lès-Chevreuse wound its way home, straightening up to roll smoothly into the station.

Goujon lit a cigarette and walked calmly down the platform.

'Do we stop at Port Royal, madame?'

'*Oui, monsieur,*' replied a fellow passenger.

Port Royal was the station nearest to the church, falling two stops short of Gare du Nord, the destination he'd stressed to deceive.

Shortly after 11.20, Luke alighted from the train, made his way quickly out on to boulevard du Montparnasse and hailed a taxi. Assisted by obliging traffic lights, the straight run along the boulevard to the church took a few minutes. Paying off the driver, he stooped to merge with the crowd arriving for eleven-thirty mass and slipped into the church.

Father Igor Boury was in the vestry getting dressed for the service.

'We didn't think you'd come.'

I've got the merchandise, I need to get hold of our mutual friend quickly. They're after me.'

Igor paled. 'I'll follow you down to the crypt.'

Luke went downstairs and was surprised to find the improvised dormitory crowded. In this weather Igor evidently took people in day and night, young couples, homeless men and the wild-eyed fellow in a wheelchair Luke remembered from his last visit, a little more sober this time and playing draughts with an imaginary partner. Pierrot looked up before Luke could escape.

'Ah, you again! Give us a game, this fellow's useless.'

Goujon stood on the deserted platform, unfamiliar nerves gnawing at his stomach, wishing a shout or shot would suddenly announce that the American, by some stroke of fortune, had been found. The train and passengers were still being searched, the station, railyards and surrounding streets. But Monsieur Morrel must have alighted earlier or jumped.

He lit a cigarette and hurled the empty packet on to the tracks. He'd misjudged the bird-watcher. Head pounding, he bought himself an espresso coffee and carried it on to the concourse to call Bloque.

Bloque picked up at once, 'The organic labels, chief . . .'

'What?'

'The produce you found in the GP's headquarters – they come from a farm near Melun –'

'Near where we lost Mademoiselle Sharma.'

'Exactly. I took the liberty of alerting the colonel. He's moving into position to await your orders.'

A surge of adrenalin, 'Tell him to surround the place and keep out of sight. I want to take Revallier myself.'

'If I may ask, chief, where are you? You're meant to be at that meeting, they've called twice.'

'Bloque, listen to me, the American breaks out, takes a

train to Gare du Nord and doesn't show. Where does he go?'

A moment's thought. 'The church in Montparnasse, the priest, remember?'

Eleven-forty, the delayed mass had barely begun when the side door of the church flew open, ejecting a grimy vagabond roaring abuse, wheeled by a livid priest in full vestments.

'You go too far, Pierrot, I'm through with you!'

Leaving the wretch in the hands of a young homeless couple, Father Boury withdrew, closing the door. The vagabond shook his fist at heaven and took a swig of wine, and while the two men watching the church suppressed their laughter, the young couple wheeled him away through the little frozen park, humouring him.

Minutes later, the men on surveillance were surprised by the arrival of police vehicles, not one or two but a swarm in the space of seconds, detectives and marksmen scattering to cordon off the grounds of the church and take up positions all around.

Soon after came the rise and fall of a siren, faint at first, then screaming nearer down the boulevard, a solitary police car flanked by motorcycle outriders. The police car screeched to a halt, out stepped the diminutive figure of Commissaire Goujon, who walked briskly up the path to the steps of the church, where a detective informed him that the priest was saying mass and that the man watching the church suspected that the American was in there too.

'When did he arrive?'

'If it was him, about twenty minutes ago.'

Goujon clicked his fingers, 'Let me have your weapon.'

The priest was leading the congregation in prayer when Goujon entered the dim, candlelit church, accompanied by two detectives. A nod from Goujon, and the detectives took one ambulatory each, peering into confessionals as they went, while Goujon proceeded up the nave, scrutinising kneeling communicants.

Igor stopped in mid-prayer. He knew who these men were, living manifestations of his worst nightmare.

'May I help you, gentlemen?' his tremulous voice lifted to the vaulted ceiling.

'Forgive us, father,' Goujon continuing to scan the rows, 'I believe a dangerous criminal may be among you . . .'

'You will kindly conduct your search after the service is over.'

'A tall, bearded American . . .' eyeing the congregation, prompting a reaction, 'an associate of yours, I understand, father,' turning his gaze on the young priest.

Igor wavered. A sea of faces awaited his response.

'I must insist you remove your men. You will be welcome afterwards.'

With a flick of the wrist, Goujon waved his men away. He himself, far from leaving, continued to the end of the nave and made his way under Igor's nose towards the vestry. Following him with fearful eyes, Igor steadied his voice and resumed the mass.

Gripping the borrowed gun in his pocket, Goujon tried every room he came to, flinging open closets and potential hideyholes. Then he went quickly and quietly down the stairs and found himself in a kitchen, where a young woman, head in sink, hummed to herself as she washed her hair. A curtain was drawn across an entrance, hushed voices coming from the far side. Parting the curtain, he went in.

Reading, sewing, sleeping, a host of homeless people looked up. The crypt, he observed, was a stark uncomplicated chamber with nowhere obvious to hide, save perhaps in the rows of uninviting tombs.

'My name is Commissaire Goujon,' announced the stranger benignly, 'I'm offering a reward for information leading to the arrest of a dangerous man.'

437

Inspecting the tombs and finding them sealed, he described his man and then proceeded down the aisle between the mattresses, trying to draw the averted eyes of his audience. No one spoke, he sensed their unease, sniffed their guilt, and came at last to a bruised defiant character propped against a wall, scratching the exposed stumps of his legs.

'And you, monsieur, the prospect of five thousand francs doesn't appeal?'

'He was a lousy player,' growled the wretch, 'I beat him easily.'

Goujon cocked an eyebrow, 'He was here?'

'How else could I play him, you think I made him up?'

Sensitive to the lies of the sane, Goujon was almost foxed by this lunatic. Turning on his heels, he made his way up through the church and out of the side door into the daylight, intent on interrogating the two men on surveillance duty. He scarcely needed to, since he found himself gazing down at wheelchair tracks in the snow, leading through the little park to a side street. He summoned one of the two men from their car.

'Has *anyone* left the church,' he demanded, 'in the past half hour?'

Yes, he recalled, they'd even made a note of it, 'A couple of punks pushing a cripple.'

'That'll do,' said Luke, and hauled himself painfully out of the chair to find his feet. He'd been sitting on his legs for several minutes, knees covered by a blanket.

Back in the church he'd believed himself safe, until the agitated priest followed him downstairs, saying he'd tried to warn him by phone, it was possible the church was being watched. Not taking any chances, Luke hastily exchanged his jacket for the greatcoat, scarf and hat of the largest resident vagrant, called for boot polish for his face and borrowed Pierrot's battered wheels, promising to return when he could with a new set.

Now, several blocks clear of the church, he pressed money on the young couple, advising them to stay clear of the church for the time being, and 'One more favour,' he asked, 'take this thing off in another direction.'

The girl jumped in the chair. The boy, roaring and hooting, propelled her away. Luke ran.

In his pocket he held the little parcel, in his fist a scrap of paper with Revallier's phone number in Igor's scrawl. Ignoring snowballs hurled by daring children, he crossed Jardin du Luxembourg, and faltered at the edge of boulevard St-Michel, listening to the sounds of sirens across the park. He crossed the road, and with the brim of his hat pulled down bought a pair of pancakes from a street vendor. Stuffing them in his pocket, he found a kiosk and called his daughter.

Isabelle hadn't arrived yet; Sylvia sounded sick with worry.

'Everything's okay,' he reassured her, 'I've one final rendezvous, and tonight we'll all be together.'

Sirens were growing nearer, he had to go.

'Papa, tell me they're not for you.'

'See you later,' he said and hung up.

Postponing the call to Revallier, he hurried on. Sirens reverberated ever louder, and Left Bank crowds, accustomed to police frenzy, stopped in their tracks and looked about uneasily. Luke reached the Métro, stumbled down the stairs and joined the throngs filing through the labyrinth beneath the city.

Around 11 a.m. Revallier was walking alone in the wood, saying his private farewells to France. Unless fate intervened, he would be out of the country by nightfall, never to see his son again – whom he saw occasionally, distantly, painfully, but to whom he never spoke – never to return, unless they pardoned him one day, which wouldn't happen as long as he carried the blame for the rue de Liège bomb.

He came to the edge of the wood and looked back towards The Rushes. At least we buried Janine, he reflected, crushed by the thought of not being able to pay his last respects to Tahar, wondering would they ship his body home to El Madheur. He traced a simple cross in the snow with his boot and looked down and remembered his comrade. Then he thought of another comrade, Jean-Baptiste Laroche, or Lucien Grossman, and wondered in what state they'd released him. He found himself smiling at the irony of Edouard, having tried once to murder the little Jew, obliged to arrange for his freedom. Forgive me, *mon cher Laroche*, for not being there to welcome you; *je t'embrasse fort*.

He thought of his brief encounter with his father, Edouard so genial and superior at first (*So it's you, Commissaire Bloque, I don't believe we've met*), then the drawn grey silent man he had left chained to a chair. He recalled Edouard's strictly rational defence: *We despised the Nazis, but they were the future*, a sensible, sustainable view? or the cold repressive reasoning of a coward? And he remembered Edouard's scorn and grudging respect when he said, *We are the true patriots; you monsieur, are an honourable, admirable fool*. A bruising encounter, filial feelings trampled underfoot.

He turned and walked slowly back the way he'd come, moving silently through the trees, watching the dead lines of the wood move with him, thinking of Edouard and Irma – *Your mother and I were very happy . . . in that dreamworld lovers inhabit*. His thoughts turned to Kasha, and as he approached the cottage he imagined that he and Kasha lived there together: summer, the lanes bursting with song, the cottage awash with blossom, he goes inside and she's at the table typing, immensely pregnant, perspiring

440

in a loose cotton dress. She looks up, a knowing smile. Making love in the heat of the afternoon, a clumsy game with her shape and size, grappling and sliding, convulsed with laughter . . .

He entered the cottage, she was at the table, working hard on her extended article, quoting freely from the dossier and from his taped 'interview'. He closed the door and stood gazing at her bowed head. She wore no make-up, no bangles or earrings, she looked tired, drawn, painfully beautiful. He'd known her less than a week and was more powerfully drawn to her than to any woman he'd ever known. How could he bear to lose her so soon?

She looked up at last, that steady indomitable gaze which held him at bay.

The phone went, Kasha jumped. 'That'll be the farm again.'

Revallier answered it, listened, thanked the caller.

'One last favour,' he said, 'have the dinghy ready early.'

He hung up with a sigh.

'What is it?' she asked.

'A look-out has reported increased police activity in the area. We may have to leave sooner than we thought.'

'We?' she questioned, and relented with a pale smile.

He threw her a searching look and went to the door to wave Ricardo down from the barn.

The phone went again, Revallier picked it up.

'This is Morrel,' said the breathless caller, 'is that . . .?'

Revallier astonished, 'Yes.'

'Still interested?'

'Of course.'

'I'm in Paris –'

'Where?'

'Métro Port d'Orléans. The place is crawling, I'm dressed as a tramp but I can't last long.'

Revallier looked at his watch, swivelled a map, and gave Luke a meeting place and time. Luke hung up almost at once, leaving Revallier slowly, thoughtfully cradling the receiver. He'd been wrong about the American, and now there was a tenuous chance that he might be able to clear his name – and the GP's reputation – after all.

When Ricardo came in and learned that Revallier intended going to get the tape and pictures from Morrel and deliver them with the dossier to *Le Monde*, he flew into a rage.

'Are you out of your mind! You think I want to lose you too? It would be suicidal, you might get in, you'd never get out again –'

'I got out all right yesterday.' snapped Revallier.

'Yesterday was nothing to what it's going to be tonight. I'm small fry, it's you they want. But you've done your bit, Jacques, leave the rest to me and catch that fucking plane.'

'You?'

'Yes, it's a one-man job and I want to do it for Janine and Tahar and for you.'

'He's right,' said Kasha, 'this is your one chance to get out.'

'Listen to you,' Revallier jeered good-humouredly, 'you think you're a veteran of the brigade already.'

'What brigade?' she reminded him gently.

The retort stung, the cruel reminder that only he and Ricardo were left.

'I'm sorry,' said Kasha, 'but Ricardo's right.'

Ricardo ran upstairs.

'Where are you going?' called Revallier.

'I'm sure Janine wouldn't mind!' called Ricardo.

Revallier avoided Kasha's eye. Private motives for not wanting to risk Paris, intimately connected with her, left him shamefully open to persuasion.

Ricardo came down with a pile of Janine's clothes, wigs and make-up. 'What do you think?' he said coquettishly, holding up to his body one dress and then another, 'the red velour, or this little black number?'

'Police . . .' murmured Kasha, gazing past him out of the window.

They all crouched down, Revallier and Ricardo surfacing at the rim of opposite windows. Each shook his head in turn, neither could see anything. They looked at Kasha doubtfully.

'I saw them,' she insisted, 'moving tree to tree, all in white.'

Revallier was about to run upstairs for a better look when soft footfalls made them all freeze, two or more men whispering past the front window . . . a soft knock on the door.

Revallier belly-crawled across the floor and silently drew closed the lower bolt. Another tentative knock. Revallier reached up and secured the other. A final rap of knuckles and someone tried the door, shaking it. Footfalls moved on.

Revallier crept to the front window and peered out. No sign of anyone. The silence lengthened, he signalled to Ricardo to go upstairs and to Kasha to take Ricardo's place at the back window. Finally, none of them with anything to report, he drew his revolver, unbolted the door and went cautiously out. He looked around, all was still.

Using shrubs and rushes around the pond for cover, he crossed to his quarters, entered safely, climbed to the roof and trained his binoculars in the direction of the farm.

At first he saw nothing. But after a time the misty skyline moved, almost a trick of the eye, as a human wave – camouflaged in white – moved forward in unison towards the farm and dissolved into the background. Moments later the wave rolled forward again, once more melting into the landscape. His binoculars didn't stretch to the far side of the commune, but he was convinced the same manoeuvre was being repeated over there, tightening the noose around the farm.

Turning round, he aimed his binoculars across the fields

and woods leading to the river, and saw no sign of the enemy. He scrambled below and recrossed to the house.

'They're surrounding the farm, we must warn them.'

Dragging the telephone to the floor, he lifted the receiver.

'Dead! No accident this time.'

'Time to get out,' said Ricardo.

'And for you to decide,' Revallier turned to Kasha, 'to Lille or Ireland. There's a car in the barn, I'm sure you're welcome to it, but you wouldn't get far.'

She looked at him, her face blank, for a moment incapable of grasping that she really wasn't free to go where she pleased, that she was a hunted person obliged to decide *now* whether or not to take flight – literally – with Revallier. 'All right. But then I'm going on to London with the article.'

Ricardo stuffed Janine's clothes and accessories into a holdall. Revallier seized the dossier and Kasha gathered up her papers and grabbed the briefcase. They slipped out the front door and scuttled round the pond to Revallier's quarters, where he had a slim bag packed. Kasha, having lost her bag in the Rolls, had a holdall ready with a few clothes belonging to Janine and Revallier. While Revallier scanned the fields from the back door, Ricardo and Kasha strapped luggage on to three waiting bicycles.

Then each took a bike and pushed it through the frozen vegetable garden, over the footbridge spanning the stream and into the first field. Once behind the hedgerow, they mounted and rode hard for the wood, where mist shrouding trunks and branches compensated for the thin leafless cover of the trees. The hardened path was obscured by a spread of snow, but Revallier knew the wood, and following his earlier footsteps he led the others swiftly through the trees towards the river.

A bag slipped and fell from Ricardo's bike. They pulled up, caught their breaths and held a brief final conference in the hollow of a holly bush, concluding with Revallier taking from his pocket two tiny packages for Ricardo to give the American. Remounting, they pressed on.

Afraid of finding the river covered by police, they were relieved to set eyes on a deserted quay, *Le Dragon de Rougeau* snug among a huddle of boats and barges in the sheltered dock. Alongside the *Dragon* bobbed the little sailing dinghy Revallier had asked to borrow from the farm. The barge was for Ricardo's journey north to Paris, the dinghy would take Revallier and Kasha a few kilometres south in the direction of the aerodrome.

Time to part. Ricardo turned to Kasha and grinned. 'We were just getting to know each other.'

'*Buona fortuna!*' she wished him, 'I look forward to tomorrow's edition of *Le Monde!*'

Kissing Kasha's hand, 'Take care of yourself, mademoiselle, and keep that scoundrel out of trouble,' he said with a jerk of his head in the direction of Revallier, who was training binoculars into the mist, visualising Ricardo's long lonely journey up the river.

'I shouldn't let you go,' he said.

'Give it a break!' said Ricardo, 'I've obeyed you enough, today you listen to me. You get caught and their victory is complete; escape and they won't know where to put their faces. I don't need you today, you're *excused*! This is *my* mission, my gift to you. Don't you trust me with it?'

'It's not that I don't trust you –'

He seized Revallier by the shoulders, 'Think of the pleasure I'll get walking in the hills at home, a secret smile on my lips, knowing you're free.'

With that he kissed Revallier on both cheeks and turned away. Pushing his bike along the quay to board the barge, he never looked back.

'*Ciao*, professor,' murmured Revallier, eyes watering.

Confident that Revallier and Sharma were encircled in the farm near Melun, Commissaire Goujon delayed in Paris to go after the suspect invalid.

When the wheelchair was finally tracked down, the children playing with it reported only that an able-bodied man and woman had abandoned it, no invalid in sight. The search was rapidly widened to the entire city.

Goujon returned grim-faced to the church, where Father Igor Boury was under guard in his vestry, while every nook and chalice in the church was being searched by police officers.

Goujon stood over the young priest. Despite the air of calm, Father Boury was plainly terrified.

'Bad conscience, father?'

'Yes, commissaire.'

Surprised, 'Really?'

'Bringing down all this upset on my congregation.'

Goujon lit a cigarette and inhaled hard. 'Two pieces of information, father, and you'll be left in peace . . .' Igor swallowed. 'Did the gentleman give you a highly classified tape and photographs, and where did he go?'

Igor spoke up, 'He gave me nothing . . . and I doubt if *he* knew where he was going.'

The detective's gaze sent a shiver through him.

'He came for shelter, commissaire, I never turn anyone away.'

Goujon's fist hit the table, making Igor jump. Goujon placed a pocket-sized tape recorder on the table and pressed PLAY.

'Remember the other night, monsieur, we met at mine, you needed to talk . . .?'

The colour drained from Igor's face.

'I remember. You still interested in . . . the merchandise?'

'Very much so . . . perhaps you could send someone, avoid complications, as soon as possible?'

Goujon found a smile, 'Now father, are you going to talk to me, or must I introduce you to someone who has a way with people?'

Luke rode the Métro, his ferocious appearance and malodorous coat keeping fellow passengers at bay . . . and attracting their attention. At every station he tensed, breathing again when the train pulled away.

Away from the city centre the trains became less crowded, and he found space to himself – time to worry about Isabelle and to wonder whether he'd killed Goujon in the cottage, a thought almost too absurd and appalling to contemplate.

The heat and motion of the train were clouding his mind, he wondered whether he dared come up for air while it was still light. Minutes later, as the train drew into a station, he was jolted by the sight of CRS troops falling upon a vagrant asleep on the platform, and frog-marching him away. Not sure in what part of the city he was, he alighted at a major interchange and located a wallmap which traced the most direct route to stated destinations in tiny coloured lights. He changed lines twice more and surfaced cautiously at quai de la Rapée, an isolated station on the north bank of the river, not far from where he was to meet Revallier at six.

No one appeared to take any notice of him as he emerged from the station and shuffled away to take refuge under a railway arch. The weather had deteriorated, a low grey misty afternoon poised for an early night. It was still only three o'clock and sirens were wailing across the city.

Ordering five more companies of CRS into the city to hunt for the American, Goujon flew out by helicopter, repeating his middle-of-the-night journey to the lake, before touching down on a hillside a few kilometres further on.

As soon as he landed, a heavily armed gendarme in white combat tunic guided him through a narrow ridge of woodland to where Colonel Prustin-Vollon waited at his improvised command post. Although Monsieur Luke Morrel and his tape were still at the back of his mind, the prospect of the imminent capture of Jean-Jacques Revallier set Goujon's pulse racing.

The lean taciturn colonel passed him a pair of field-glasses. It was just after 3 p.m. and the scattered farm appeared surprisingly lively in the pale grey light, people wandering between buildings, children gleefully tobog-ganing, the wheel of a water mill churning in the valley.

'Whenever you're ready, *mon colonel*.'

The softly-spoken colonel gave the order. Moments later Goujon was entering the commune on the back of an assault wave of gendarmerie, alighting amid shouts and shrieks, the shattering of glass and splintering of wood. Parents screamed for their children, children ran in all directions, Goujon bestrode the farm, watching men and women rounded up and herded into the communal hall, but interested only in coming face to face with one particular man.

When Revallier and Sharma were not immediately found, he wasn't seriously worried. Revallier would have had years to prepare for such a critical event, who could tell what hideaways he had devised, perhaps in the wine cellars of some of the older houses. But by four o'clock he was sufficiently concerned to have members of the com-mune isolated and interrogated. Threats to arrest and detain every adult, leaving the children by implication in the hands of the state, prompted the desired response.

Goujon gazed at a map. Either to protect their friends on the farm, or for tactical reasons or both, Revallier and Vallence had secluded themselves in a smallholding a full kilometre south of the commune. He was driven over at once, but the long anticipated pleasure of uncovering the GP's rural base was erased by the shock of knowing that he'd missed Revallier.

The embers were still glowing in the grate, fresh mint tea was cool in the pot, it looked as though the fugitives had been gone several hours. Still dazed by his head wound, Goujon caught himself against the fireplace, nerves gnawing at his belly: the American on the loose in Paris with the tape and pictures, Revallier and Sharma God-knows-where with the dossier.

He lit a cigarette and tried to clear his head, reminding himself that he'd recovered from far more dismal situations before and almost always triumphed. Regaining his composure, he calmly toured the site. There had been no attempt to use the car discovered in the barn, and while he was considering this, footprints and bicycle tracks – three sets, not two – were found leading away towards a belt of woodland in the direction of . . . the river!

He'd been right. Revallier, over the years, had made the waterways his own, and he was waterborne again, either to make his escape, or to deliver the dossier to parties unknown, or both. Persons questioned on the farm had so far professed ignorance as to Revallier's intentions, insisting he always kept them to himself.

While helicopter crews were alerted, Goujon got through to Bloque. Capitaine Arnaut of the river police was to be arrested, every barge and boat stopped and vigorously searched.

Returning to the smallholding, hunting for clues, he found himself once more in the converted lean-to, a makeshift dwelling belonging, if he wasn't mistaken, to Revallier. Standing at Revallier's desk, sifting through private letters and files, he looked up once again to study the map pinned to the wall. If Revallier was aiming for Paris, he could not possibly have got there yet and would be caught. If on the other hand he'd sailed south . . .

Seeking one last inspiration, Goujon found himself gazing at the symbol of an aeroplane, a small aerodrome, not ten kilometres away.

The fleeting light-weight dinghy, with its slack sails and willing motor straining against the current, took nearly two hours to reach the outskirts of Melun, Kasha turning blue in the stern, Revallier throwing nervous glances at his watch.

They approached a remote pier with caution, Kasha covered by a tarpaulin, Revallier casting a fishing line in the water. Over the town, which they knew to be ringed by road-blocks, a team of helicopters hovered, scouring the landscape.

They docked, tied up and crept ashore. Eyes alert for danger, they picked their way by bicycle through the back streets of the town, Kasha with her face covered by a *duppatta*, Revallier wearing his hood up, until at last they broke out into open country to the north. Keeping to minor roads they made methodical progress, picking each other up from time to time when one or the other went over on the ice.

With the blood pumping through her, and a late sun setting the fields alight, Kasha began to feel exhilarated. And remembering Edouard de Montfort's expression, his almost imperceptible flicker of fear when she reported Revallier's accusations concerning the rue de Liège bomb, she experienced a wild surge of hope.

'God, we really could bring them down!' she cried aloud.

He laughed, '*Could*? We will!'

Pedalling alongside each other, breathless with exertion,

they fell to talking, not about her work or his war, but lighter things that came to mind: childhood experiences of cycling in Rajasthan and Brittany, as though on an innocent excursion, with only the occasional serious note.

'Did you never regret starting up the GP?'

'Why would I regret it?'

'Living like this, a perpetual fugitive?'

'Only in weak moments.'

'And you,' he said, 'did you never want to get married?'

'Why would I want to get married?'

'I don't know. Love, companionship?'

'Only in weak moments!'

'Don't you ever think about having children?'

'Sometimes.'

Feeling the heat of his gaze, she glanced at him, answering his look with a wry smile, and looked away again, focusing on the road ahead, trying to imagine what a life with him might be like. 'What will you do in Canada?'

'Set up as an accountant.'

She threw back her head and laughed.

'Your poor clients, is all I can say. But seriously.'

'Once I've changed my name and fiddled a new identity, I might try a serious occupation for a change.'

'After all this idle play.'

'Exactly.'

'What will you do?'

'Who knows? develop another progressive energy centre.'

'How will you live?'

'A small plot; the earth provides.'

'Will *you* marry?'

'Only if she insists.'

'And will she work the land with you?'

A smile, 'I doubt it. She'll go to work and I'll keep her in pumpkins, peppers and oregano.'

'And you'd stay at home with the children?'

'Gladly.'

'After all this . . .' a backward glance to indicate the past, *'excitement*, would Monsieur Revallier, the warrior, really settle for a smallholding?'

'With the right person, yes.'

'And if she loved the city?'

'Then they would live near a railway.'

'And if she could only bear to live *in* the city?'

'Then he would live in the city.'

'He wants her that much?'

'Yes.'

With the flat evening light fading over the plain, darkness closed in. Lapsing into silence, they fell into single file.

Soon after five o'clock, as exhaustion was setting in, a signpost materialised: Aerodrome 1½ kms. A brief rest and they pressed on. They seemed to ride on for a long while before the lights of the airfield appeared through the mist, and they pulled off the road and took shelter in the shell of an unfinished house. Carrying bikes and luggage up a flight of stairs, they spread a map on the concrete floor and studied it by bicycle lamp to try to work out precisely where they were. Through a gaping window the control tower shone weakly in the gloom.

'That's fog,' whispered Kasha, 'what if it can't land?'

He'd been asking himself the same. 'It'll land,' he said firmly.

With mist encroaching on the river, the barge made strong progress towards the city, Ricardo grimly elated at the wheel, watching the bends ahead, wondering at the stillness, the lack of traffic.

Passing through the locks at Le Plessis-Chênet, he found time to dwell on events of the last few days which had taught him that fate had no favourites, singling out Janine and Tahar, whom he had always considered blessed, and throwing them away as if they counted for nothing. For the first time in his twenty-two years, he felt his own fragile mortality.

On the roof of the cabin a small ship's boat was secured. While the barge found its level, Ricardo busied himself easing the little boat down on to the deck. Noticing a man watching him from the bank, he called below to imaginary companions berating them for their laziness. The arm of the lock swung wide, the barge pushed through.

Soon after four o'clock, with the city still more than an hour away, the fog came down and as darkness descended a barge approached coming from Paris, buffeting the waves, sounding its mournful horn. Its skipper, outlined in his cabin, appeared to recognise the *Dragon* and began calling across. Ricardo cupped his hands and replied that he couldn't hear. As the barges crossed, the man was shouting louder, something to do with *Going completely crazy, and arresting everyone to hell*! Ricardo waved in appreciation of the warning. Thank God, he mused, for Captain Arnaut.

But on the next major bend, with the first tower blocks of the city looming eerily, he heard a helicopter ahead, and peered out to see its ghostly shape wrestling with the fog, probing the river with its searchlight.

Ricardo broke into a cold sweat, convinced it was madness to press on.

As six o'clock approached, Revallier and Kasha crept from their shelter and set off on foot carrying their bags. Light traffic passed along the periphery road, otherwise all was quiet, and they crossed over and made their way around the aerodrome's high fence.

Kasha's doubts were growing but she said nothing more. The weather was if anything worse than when they arrived, the aerodrome's lights and buildings muffled in fog, no planes arriving or taking off.

They reached a shallow depression and crouched in the dark under the fence. It was six o'clock. With luck, Revallier reflected, Ricardo would be meeting up with the American about now.

Minutes dragged, 6.05.

'The fog may have delayed him,' said Revallier, 'don't worry, I know him, and if it's humanly possible . . .'

All was still, not a breath of wind, no movement across the airfield: 6.10. For the Place de la Concorde ambush Revallier had prayed for fog. Now it was the last thing he wanted. They sat on their bags in silence, Kasha shivering. Revallier drew closer and put an arm around her. They sat in numbed silence, listening . . . listening . . .

'Listen . . .' he said.

A distant murmur, constant for a time, as if passing in the night but growing into a steady confident drone.

'That's it.'

Wire-cutters in hand, Revallier set to work clipping a gash in the fence. They squeezed through, closed the breach behind them, and began to cross the airfield.

The lights of the plane should have been visible at a distance, but it roared nearer and nearer unseen, passing overhead like an illusion and disappeared, its engine receding over the far side of the aerodrome. Silence descended. Revallier and Kasha looked at each other, standing in the dark in the flat open space, willing the plane to return.

Their prayers were answered, the plane audible again, gradually making its way back for another pass.

Suddenly lights opened up, a phalanx of huge blazing headlights throwing a bright haze over the runway to guide the aircraft. Or so they thought, desperate to believe it, even as the plane passed overhead and faded farther and farther in the direction from which it had come . . . even as the headlights on the ground began to move, beating a path towards them.

Grabbing their bags they started to run back towards the fence, only to see the squat shapes of military vehicles drawing up on the road, the outlines of men and arms dispersing along the fence. Abandoning all but the briefcase, they turned and ran off into the darkness, hoping against hope they hadn't been detected. Searchlights flew after them, flicking to left and right, making them weave as they fled. Then as the thunder of pursuing engines gained on them, a low long building took shape ahead, a dark windowless hut, a last refuge.

Engines drummed nearer, bellowing voices pursued them, warning them to halt. Shots rang out, Revallier lost his footing, Kasha stooped to help him and together they staggered round the side of the hut with bullets screaming by. Kasha reached the door first to find it locked. Together they attacked it with frenzied kicks, and bursting it open fell inside and flung the door shut.

Pitch darkness, not a thing could be seen, only the air of dank space around them. Feeling in the dark, they searched for something to drag against the door, to give the illusion that it was still locked. Or rather Kasha searched, unaware of Revallier's condition as he forced himself blindly around the hut. Nothing met their groping hands, only bare walls. The hut was empty.

Everything had gone quiet, save for Revallier's rasping breath, the sound not of a fit man recovering from exertion but of someone in difficulties.

'You all right?'

Her anxious voice hung in the stillness.

He leaned heavily against the door, and through the broken lock peered out, or tried to. 'I can't see . . . you look.'

'You're hurt!' she cried.

'Look!'

She put her eye to the hole and squinted into the glare of lights, a solid ring of armour encircling the hut, glimpses of helmets and guns.

A hand found hers. 'Come,' he said.

He led her by the hand down the centre of the hut to the end wall, or rather she led him, drawing him down beside her on the floor.

A voice from without shattered the stillness, distorted by a megaphone, ordering Monsieur Revallier and Mademoiselle Sharma to appear with their hands in the air in sixty seconds, or face the consequences.

Silence once more.

'Where are you hit?' she pleaded.

'It's superficial,' he wheezed, 'like the other time, remember?'

'I see. So you arranged this too, all to get past my defences?'

'Impressed?'

'Very. Now for God's sake tell me where you're hit.'

He was twisted on his side, holding himself, but however she strained to see and feel she couldn't discover where he was hurt. 'You have matches?'

'Why would I have matches?!'

He leaned against her, she held his head, pressing her lips to his wet brow, while her free hand explored, following the contorted shape of his body until she found his hand, sunk inside his anorak, drawn to the critical point in his lower back. Her hand covered his, felt the warm sticky sensation of his life-blood. 'Jesus!' she tried to rise, 'this time you're going to hospital.'

'TIME,' boomed a voice. 'IF YOU DON'T COME OUT . . .'

Their interlocking fingers tightened, he opened his eyes, trying to make her out in the dark.

'Coming to Canada?' he whispered.

She felt his breath hot on her face.

'I want you to have my child . . .' he spoke softly, his words caressing her.

She couldn't speak. She stroked his face, kissed his

eyelids. Then she gently disentangled herself and pulled away and, rising unsteadily, went quickly towards the light.

'What are you doing?'

She didn't reply.

'*Careful*!' he shouted, or thought he did. Her shape in the darkness dissolved, and he was lost and at peace. She was his. He knew in his heart she was his.

She opened the door and stood in the glare, shielding her eyes, bracing herself for the volley of screaming bullets. 'He's badly hurt!' she bellowed, taking a bold step forward, 'he needs an ambulance.' No reaction. '*Quick*, for God's sake!'

She sensed a movement straight ahead, heard a commanding voice mention the word ambulance. Then another order was given and all at once figures broke rank and charged forward. Kasha turned on her heels and beat them to the door, bursting in and slamming it in their faces as she stumbled to reach Revallier.

He was slumped on his side, she fell over him.

He didn't budge, made no sound.

Light flooded the hut.

'Get away from him!' bawled an officer.

Throwing herself over Revallier's body, she twisted around and pointed a warning finger.

'Don't you dare come near.'

Defying the weather, Goujon came in by helicopter and strode across to the hut. The officer-in-charge quickly briefed him, presented him with the abandoned luggage containing clothes and personal effects – no documents, files or tapes.

Goujon entered the brightly lit hut, and stood for a moment contemplating the scene at the far end, the journalist sitting on the floor against the wall, Revallier's head in her lap, his blood on her hands and clothes. She

457

was – he repressed a smile – making a pathetic attempt to hide a briefcase behind her back.

He lit a cigarette and came forward.

She was looking at him with great hollow tear-stained eyes, but she didn't interest him. He was savouring a unique moment, the hunting down of Jean-Jacques Revallier. He looked down into the GP leader's distorted face. He'd finally caught up with him.

'The briefcase, please, mademoiselle.'

She didn't move. Her fingers covered Revallier's eyes, as though shielding him from the world.

Goujon stooped, eased the briefcase free and turned his back to open it. He found the dossier at once. He also found, amongst papers and articles belonging to Mademoiselle Sharma, the two wartime letters Edouard de Montfort was so concerned about, and which Goujon had agreed to retrieve, but which he intended to entrust to Bloque's safekeeping for the time being.

'There's an ambulance waiting, mademoiselle. I've no objection to your accompanying the body, before I take you into custody.'

As he turned away, she was praying no one would find the tape she'd made of Revallier talking passionately last night, which she had tucked in her underwear.

Goujon walked through police lines to his helicopter. Climbing aboard, he ordered the pilot to call up Commissaire Bloque, and while he waited to speak to him Goujon permitted himself a peep at the contentious dossier.

Embossed in gold, DOSSIER (XX) gleamed in the lights of the cockpit. *THE FUTURE OF ATOMIC ENERGY: A Co-ordinated European Initiative.* But as soon as he opened the leather cover, he knew something was wrong. Leafing through the title pages, he was met with a sunken chamber surrounded by the neat edges of hundreds of packed pages, giving the illusion of a mighty document. Inside the chamber lay a familiar publication, a glossy brochure for one of Paris's exclusive funeral parlours . . . and a note in pen.

Your funeral, commissaire. JJR

• • • 26 • • •

Rowing in vain against the current, Ricardo steered the little boat as best he could between moored barges to reach the sheer river bank. Seizing an iron rung he scrambled out of the boat and rung by slippery rung climbed to the top, flinging himself flat on the quay.

Down river, the runaway *Dragon*, like a riderless horse, was disappearing into the mist, police launches swarming round it. A volley of warning shots reverberated across the water.

Throwing a bulging refuse sack over his shoulder he hurried among cranes, coalstacks and warehouses to reach the main road into the city. Descending the underpass, he emerged on the far side and walked quickly along the street until he spotted a café on the corner. It looked rough, but it was nearly six o'clock, he had no choice.

He entered, ordered a beer and made his way down a narrow passage to the toilets. Finding no ladies' room, he locked himself in the men's. From the sack he lifted out the smart carrier bag with its precious item, and Janine's holdall, and began to change, putting on a black satin dress, stockings and high clinging boots, earrings, a choker and a wig of cascading red curls.

Footsteps in the passage. A man tried the door, grumbled and went away.

Propping a mirror on the sink, he bent and applied foundation, mascara, eye-shadow and lipstick, concluding with a spray of perfume on both sides of his neck. Finally he stuffed his own clothes and the holdall in the sack, put on a silk scarf and lightweight coat, and left, dumping the sack in a recess in the passage.

When he failed to find a back way out, he retraced his steps through the café, drawing a puzzled frown from the barman and turning every head. He was almost at the door when a man pushed over his chair and stepped across his path.

'How about a dance, Beautiful?'

Yielding to the man's mock-gallant embrace, Ricardo smiled, waltzed a few steps with him and in one deft manoeuvre, deposited him lightly on the floor.

With guffaws of astonishment ringing in his ears, he strolled out on to the waterfront and hailed a passing cab.

Freezing mist rolled off the river, a huddle of men sat round a fire beneath a dripping arch, keeping the cold at bay with drink and song, a grimy battered crew, and among them one who was taller and heavier, a bear of a man and a stranger, but willing to share his bottle of altar wine.

He scarcely listened to his new companions. He knew it was after six and kept watching for Revallier, trusting he was in the right place and wondering what he would do with the tape and pictures if Revallier failed to appear.

Sirens near and far had reached a pitch, prompting jokes from the men.

'Milo, I told you not to rob that bank.'

'No, Fredo, it's you they're after, you never completed a tax return!'

Luke was well aware that present company was not the safest to be in, but this was a secluded spot, they'd insisted he join them and a brief thawing out was welcome, his boots still waterlogged from the morning's dash through ditches to the village, his back giving him hell, and he was relieved to lean against a wall and stretch his feet to the fire.

Rubbing his wood-smoked eyes, he glanced surreptitiously at his watch, 6.15, and this time, when he looked up, he saw, over the heads of the company, a figure appear along the quay and thought it might be . . . but it turned quickly into another vagrant, casting furtive glances over his shoulder as he hobbled up to the fire.

'CRS swine, seizing us like dogs and throwing us in gaol, have they no one else to pick on?'

A relatively young man, he was relating how he'd got away, when one of the men blurted, 'Ssh! looks like visitors.'

Heads turned, men squinting to make out distant figures and lights coming down the quay. The company became nervous but, knowing their aching wine-soaked bodies were ill-tuned for flight, tended to draw closer together for comfort rather than run.

'I could do with a night in the clink,' said one as Luke got to his feet, detached himself from the group and appraised the wall he'd been leaning against.

'Give me a leg up,' he roared, 'it's me they're after.'

There was no compelling reason to believe him, yet his voice carried authority and authentic fear.

Along the quay a van took shape, figures with flashlights walking alongside.

'Quick, for God's sake!'

The men got to their feet, stumbled to his side and shakily hoisted him up and over the wall.

Breaking through the gloom, the CRS fell upon the cringing knot of men and flung them in the back of the caged van. Warming their hands a moment over the fire, they kicked the vagrants' bottles into the Seine and moved on.

Luke remained crouched on the far side of the wall.

When at last he ventured clear, it took time to find his way out of the brick yard and back to the river. He was standing there trying to read his watch when he heard heels clicking along the quay, and saw a striking young woman materialise, swinging a carrier bag and coming towards him as if she knew him. He started to turn away.

'Mr Morrel?' she'd spoken his name – in English. 'He couldn't make it. I have a taxi waiting.'

Luke hesitated, she jerked her head, and he followed.

On their way out of the port, she stopped him to make sure he really had the incriminating tape and photos. Satisfied, she insisted he open one of two little packages Revallier had sent.

'What's this, for Chrissake?' Luke held up to a light what looked like a war medal, bronze with red and black ribbon.

'La Médaille de la Résistance,' the young woman confirmed, 'won posthumously by Revallier's stepfather Jérôme in World War Two. He wants you to have it, a token of his appreciation.'

'That's ridiculous.'

Taking back the medal, Ricardo pinned it to the inside of Luke's torn lapel, 'For services rendered to the GP,' he said grandly, 'to France, to the world!'

Luke shook his head and laughed, both for the absurd gesture and because this pretty girl had given himself away.

'I remember you, trying to convert me to your cause.'

'I'm not doing so badly, wouldn't you say?'

Keeping to the shadows they hurried on to reach the road. The cab driver was kicking his heels, wondering what had become of his fare. When he set eyes on her 'friend', he balked, refusing to take either of them. Throwing up his hands in disgust, he got back in his cab and drove off.

Luke and Ricardo drew back and looked about. As they

hesitated, sirens persisted, whirring blue lights approaching at speed. Seizing Luke's arm, Ricardo steered him across the road and into a side street. They walked fast, seeking a back way into town, the air thick with sirens.

'*Putain!* you smell,' Ricardo complained, releasing him.

'I'm sorry, I must be getting used to it.'

As they walked on, debating how best to proceed, a caged van turned the corner ahead. They faltered, and pressed themselves into a doorway. For a moment it looked as if the slowly approaching van might cruise by, but as it drew level it stopped, doors flew open and men jumped out.

'Get your filthy hands off me!' Ricardo cried shrilly and, pushing Luke away, broke free. Luke cursed him obscenely and bolted the other way.

'Get him!' barked a sergeant.

Straightening his dress and hair, Ricardo ignored the sergeant's lewd gaze, while at the end of the street they were catching up with Luke. Slamming him against a wall, they frisked him, slapped him about and went through his pockets.

'So glad you gentlemen still believe in chivalry,' said Ricardo, but the sergeant was no longer paying any attention. His men were calling to him animatedly, and as he boarded the van to drive down and investigate, Ricardo walked on.

They had to break Kasha's grip to remove Revallier's body. Goujon then ordered something to be brought for Kasha to sit on, but she returned to the blood-stained spot on the floor where Revallier had died.

'A young man fled with you and Revallier, mademoiselle, I want to know who he is and where he is making for with the dossier.'

Kasha remained mute and still, her head tucked into her drawn-up knees.

A knock on the door, an officer presented himself to

deliver the news that the barge belonging to the organic farm had been stopped on the approaches to Paris, only to be found abandoned. A vigorous hunt was underway. Covering his frustration, Goujon nodded judiciously, the officer withdrew, Goujon rounded on the prisoner.

'Aiding and abetting a terrorist organisation and stealing state secrets,' he said, slapping his palm with her passport, 'not to mention the assault last night and unlawfully driving away the gentleman's car . . . you'll be lucky to escape with ten years. I'm the only one who can save you.'

Kasha made no reply. She felt keenly the loss of the body she had been guarding, but in her state of shock she was confused as to who he was, a guerrilla leader called Michel who once took her out to dinner, or that man with the brazen eyes who only last night had declared his love for her.

'Your obstinacy serves no purpose, *ma chère mademoiselle*,' Goujon was saying when he was interrupted by another knock on the door. Different officer, same respectfully lowered tone. As he listened, Goujon's expression lifted like a mask.

'How can we be sure it's him?'

'I don't think there's any doubt, commissaire.'

'Was he carrying anything significant?'

'I believe so, sir.'

Goujon nodded evenly, 'I'm going directly to Paris, take this woman into custody and question her about Revallier's young accomplice.'

'Commissaire . . .?' a plea in Kasha's voice.

He turned at the door, 'Well?'

'I don't want any harm to come either to Monsieur Morrel or to the young man.'

'What are you trying to say?' he strolled back to her.

'I'll tell you what you want, provided —'

'No harm will come to him, you have my absolute word.'

'The young man's name . . .' lifting a fictitious name from her memory, 'is Michel Kerlesquin.'

'Description?'

Picturing Ricardo in Janine's wig and clothing, she looked directly into Goujon's eyes, 'blond, mustachioed and wearing overalls.'

'And he's delivering the dossier to . . .?'

'*Le Canard Enchaîné.*'

Goujon lit a cigarette and held Kasha's gaze. Her tone was convincing, and *Le Canard*, leading satirical journal and thorn in the side of the establishment, was certainly a plausible recipient of the dossier.

Issuing Kasha's description of Revallier's man, and orders for the offices of *Le Canard Enchaîné* to be put under strict surveillance, Goujon defied the fog again and flew to Paris.

Transferring to a fast car, he was rushed to Place du Panthéon, pulling up with a flourish outside the town hall annexe of the fifth *arrondissement*.

Inside, at the end of a row of cells crowded with genuine vagrants, Luke occupied a cell alone, awaiting his fate. His face and body throbbed from the modest beating the CRS had awarded him, but aside from concern for Isabelle he was calm. He'd done his best, he wouldn't have to spend the rest of his life reproaching himself.

Footsteps in the passage ended at his door, the spy-slot was drawn, someone looked in. When the door wasn't opened, he raised his head to meet the faceless gaze of a pair of unblinking eyes. Though he couldn't see to whom they belonged, he experienced a sudden shiver of recognition – the man he'd almost killed earlier in the day in the collapsing cottage: Commissaire Goujon.

Coming away from the cell, Goujon went through to the office where the American's personal effects were waiting.

Emptying the transparent bag on the desk, his eyes censored a pile of worthless paraphernalia and seized upon a slim tantalising parcel. He tore it open and sighed. At last!

'Have you finished breathing down my neck?'

The officers present withdrew, closing the door.

The photographs were in a sealed, sellotaped envelope marked Private and Confidential. He put it aside for the moment, placed his miniature tape recorder on the desk and inserted Morrel's tape. Head pounding, he lit a cigarette and subsided into a chair to listen, and opened the envelope.

The tape connected, hummed for a few moments and then, to Goujon's surprise, it wasn't the trifling sound of rare ducks which emerged but *'Salut, commissaire!'* the distinctive mock solemn voice of Jean-Jacques Revallier, *'vive Les Gardiens de la Planète, vive la France,* fuck you.'

The tape fell silent.

Goujon rose, tore open the envelope, spread the contents across the desk and found himself gazing at a selection of picture postcards of Paris: Moulin Rouge, Sacré-Coeur, Place de la Concorde.

Leaning forward, hands spread on the desk, he stared at the wall. The nerves in his stomach were back, seething like maggots. Only one hope remained: to stop Revallier's young accomplice.

$$\bullet \; \bullet \; \bullet \; 27 \; \bullet \; \bullet \; \bullet$$

While well-concealed police closed in on the offices of *Le Canard Enchaîné* on rue St-Honoré in the first *arrondissement*, Ricardo's taxi was pulling up in boulevard des Italiens in the ninth.

Putting away his make-up, he climbed out, tipped the driver, returned his thanks with a fetching smile and walked round the corner in the direction of the offices of *Le Monde*. He'd phoned from a kiosk to make sure the edito.-in-chief would still be there. He was told the editor was just leaving, who was calling? Please advise Monsieur Mortaigne, Ricardo had said, to expect a visit from a representative of The Guardians of the Planet within the next fifteen minutes.

Approaching the building, threading his way among office workers on their way home, he caught sight of two policemen standing in the cold across the street. Without faltering, he kept walking, lightly swinging his hips, recovering stylishly when he slipped. As he came nearer to the entrance, he felt the heat of the gendarmes' eyes on his legs, curves and cascading hair.

Taking his time, he entered the building and presented himself at the desk, '*Bonsoir*, Monsieur Mortaigne is expecting me.'

'Your name please, mademoiselle?' said the receptionist doubtfully.

'Tell him Jean-Jacques Revallier's envoy has arrived.'

A tremor rippled through the hall, the woman looked up, Ricardo nodded towards the telephone. The receptionist lifted the receiver and pressed a button.

Seconds later Ricardo was shown along a carpeted walk which extended through an imposing entry, all the way to the desk of the editor-in-chief. The editor rose as Ricardo approached. Betraying signs of tension, he looked keenly at Revallier's envoy and motioned her to sit.

Ricardo looked at the editor, appraising the man Revallier had put his faith in, a portly handsome man with dark hair smoothed back off his forehead. Remaining on his feet, Ricardo removed the dossier from its carrier bag and handed it over.

'*Merci, mademoiselle*,' said Monsieur Mortaigne guardedly.

'We feel the people of France and Europe should know,'

said Ricardo, 'what their government-sponsored atomic energy industries are up to. We would ask you to pay particular attention to the Appendix.'

Also remaining standing, the editor opened the dossier and glanced down the contents page, his associates craning to see.

'Given your record of exposing official corruption, monsieur,' Ricardo resumed, 'we also trust you will make the best possible use of these.'

He set down a small package on the desk, addressed to the church in Montparnasse.

Monsieur Mortaigne looked up.

'Please . . .' Ricardo urged him to open it.

The editor carefully untaped the package; out spilled a cassette, a set of photographs and a lengthy typed statement signed by Luke Morrel. Instructing his assistant to put on the tape, the editor spread the photos on his desk: shots of ducks, frozen meadows. . .

Ricardo leaned across to isolate the prints of a white Volvo, 'It belongs to Commissaire Philippe Goujon, whose voice you will hear in conversation with the Duke de Montfort's son, Maurice, glimpsed in this photo, in the wilds of their estate last Sunday at dawn.'

Ricardo accepted the seat and sat still, hands folded, eyes resting on the carpet, while duck-talk filled the room and then gave way to two men engaged in bitter argument.

At first Ricardo was merely conscious of an air of curiosity in the room, attention divided between him and the boss, his surprising appearance and Monsieur Mortaigne's reaction. He was picking up whispers, people beginning to suspect he wasn't a woman. But as the tape progressed, the room became very still.

'*Crozier laughs in my face, he couldn't care less . . . Damn the fog!*'

'*For what time should he have arranged it? Does everyone leave home early when it's foggy?*'

468

The editor sat down, listening intently, legs crossed, pencil to his lips.

'*On the contrary, it couldn't be better, especially if she dies . . . our little package has already more than achieved its purpose.*'

Looks were exchanged, people confirming what they were hearing. When Interior Minister Batisse and Security Minister Lusardi were mentioned, *Le Monde*'s political editor whistled through his teeth.

The tape ended with the Volvo turning round and fading over the meadow. There followed a moment's silence, like the hush immediately after a bomb. Then the room was abuzz with talk, and through the rising tide of excitement Ricardo met the editor's gaze.

'Can you prove this is genuine?'

The room fell still.

'That's your job, monsieur,' Ricardo replied, 'but you might like to know that a British journalist, Kasha Sharma, expected to have the full story in a major London paper today . . .'

Monsieur Mortaigne held up the very paper. Front page:

FRENCH GOVERNMENT AND SECRET SERVICE IMPLICATED IN ANTI-ECOLOGIST BOMB

Repressing a hoot of joy, Ricardo sustained his businesslike exterior. 'You also now have the statement of the man who recorded the tape and took the pictures. He was arrested half an hour ago. You will, I'm sure, look into that. They're also looking for me, so if you'll excuse me, *messieurs, 'dames.*'

A little bow and he turned away.

He got as far as the doorway.

'*Mademoiselle?*'

He turned.

'When did you last see Monsieur Revallier?'

Ricardo hesitated, suspicious. 'Why?'

Suddenly he knew why. He saw it in Monsieur Mortaigne's face, and in the expressions of fellow editors and staff.

'They've caught him . . .' said Ricardo.

The editor nodded, Ricardo stared past him, holding himself upright, even though he wanted to throw back his head and scream. He stood riveted, one more question to ask, but unable to speak. Even as he fought to hide his feelings, the mascara was running.

'Is he dead?'

Another restrained nod. 'Yes.'

'Thank God,' Ricardo murmured.

The building was suddenly unbearably hot and airless, and he gravitated like a man in a nightmare to reach the cool of the night.

A Selected List of Fiction Available from Mandarin

While every effort is made to keep prices low, it is sometimes necessary to increase prices at short notice. Mandarin Paperbacks reserves the right to show new retail prices on covers which may differ from those previously advertised in the text or elsewhere.

The prices shown below were correct at the time of going to press.

☐	7493 1352 8	**The Queen and I**	Sue Townsend	£4.99
☐	7493 0540 1	**The Liar**	Stephen Fry	£4.99
☐	7493 1132 0	**Arrivals and Departures**	Lesley Thomas	£4.99
☐	7493 0381 6	**Loves and Journeys of Revolving Jones**	Leslie Thomas	£4.99
☐	7493 0942 3	**Silence of the Lambs**	Thomas Harris	£4.99
☐	7493 0946 6	**The Godfather**	Mario Puzo	£4.99
☐	7493 1561 X	**Fear of Flying**	Erica Jong	£4.99
☐	7493 1221 1	**The Power of One**	Bryce Courtney	£4.99
☐	7493 0576 2	**Tandia**	Bryce Courtney	£5.99
☐	7493 0563 0	**Kill the Lights**	Simon Williams	£4.99
☐	7493 1319 6	**Air and Angels**	Susan Hill	£4.99
☐	7493 1477 X	**The Name of the Rose**	Umberto Eco	£4.99
☐	7493 0896 6	**The Stand-in**	Deborah Moggach	£4.99
☐	7493 0581 9	**Daddy's Girls**	Zoe Fairbairns	£4.99

All these books are available at your bookshop or newsagent, or can be ordered direct from the address below. Just tick the titles you want and fill in the form below.

Cash Sales Department, PO Box 5, Rushden, Northants NN10 6YX.
Fax: 0933 410321 : Phone 0933 410511.

Please send cheque, payable to 'Reed Book Services Ltd.', or postal order for purchase price quoted and allow the following for postage and packing:

£1.00 for the first book, 50p for the second; **FREE POSTAGE AND PACKING FOR THREE BOOKS OR MORE PER ORDER.**

NAME (Block letters) ....

ADDRESS ....

....

☐ I enclose my remittance for ....

☐ I wish to pay by Access/Visa Card Number

Expiry Date

Signature ....

Please quote our reference: MAND